'It was dawn when the all-clear sounded. Stiff and shivering, they clambered up the steps to the outside world. Rose heard the cries of despair before she got to the top of the steps, and as soon as she came out into the daylight she understood what had prompted them. The world they knew had utterly changed. Where there had been a busy, familiar street with shops and houses, buses and cars and bicycles, there was now a wilderness. Rubble was strewn across the road, broken glass was everywhere and everything was covered in a thick layer of brick dust. When they raised their eyes from this to find its source, the real horror struck them. Where rows of terraced houses had stood there were now huge gaps, like missing teeth, and on each side, still clinging to the walls of the remaining buildings, were the pathetic remnants of the inhabitants' lives – a wall decorated with nursery characters for a child's bedroom, a wardrobe hanging perilously in a corner, its contents scattered, a fireplace and above it a mirror, miraculously unbroken.'

Also by Hilary Green

We'll Meet Again

Never Say Goodbye

THE FOLLIES SERIES

Now is the Hour

They Also Serve

Theatre of War

The Final Act

About the author

Hilary Green is a trained actress and spent many years teaching drama and running a youth theatre company. She has also written scripts for the BBC and won the Kythira prize for a short story. Hilary currently lives in the Wirral and is a full-time writer.

HILARY GREEN

Now is the Hour

HODDER

A CIP catalogue record for this title is available from the British Library

ISBN 9780340898970

Typeset in Plantin Light by Hewer Text UK Ltd, Edinburgh
Printed and bound by Clays Ltd, St Ives plc

Hodder Headline's policy is to use papers that are natural, renewable
and recyclable products and made from wood grown in sustainable
forests. The logging and manufacturing processes are expected to
conform to the environmental regulations of the country of origin.

Hodder & Stoughton Ltd
A division of Hodder Headline
338 Euston Road
London NW1 3BH

This book is dedicated to the memory of my parents,
Doris Lees (née Gladdon), dancer,
and Newton Lees, bass-baritone,
who were both concert party artistes
in the years before The Second World War.

As always, I am indebted to my agent,
Vivien Green, and my editor, Alex Bonham,
for their help and encouragement – also
to my husband David for proof-reading.

HISTORICAL NOTE

The main characters and events in this book are fictional but some of the peripheral ones are drawn from real life. Colonel Basil Brown was a prime mover in the establishment of the army's Central Pool of Artistes, later known as Stars in Battledress. Paul Cole, whose real name was Harold, Ian Garrow and the noble Dr and Mrs Rodocanachi were all members of the escape line for allied personnel which later became known as the O'Leary Line. Their further adventures are related in the next volume in the Follies series. As always, while I have invented actions and dialogue for these people, I hope I have in all cases remained faithful to their essential characters, insofar as I have been able to divine them from existing sources.

Prelude – Kindly Leave the Stage!

Rose Taylor looked around the stage. Almost the entire company of the Fairbourne Follies had assembled, drawn together by fear and the need for mutual support. The theatre had the chill, damp feel that always seemed to seep up from the sea below during the night, not to be banished until the audience came in for the evening performance. The sea was rough today and Rose could feel the waves thudding against the timbers that supported the pier. After the September sunshine outside the single working light above the stage hardly seemed to penetrate the gloom.

Monty Prince, the company's proprietor and comedian, was trying to keep up spirits with a succession of gags. The holiday audiences, out for an enjoyable evening after a day on the beach, loved him, but this morning the wisecracks sounded tired and empty. His wife was sitting a little apart, stiffly upright on a wooden chair. Dolores da Ponte was a daunting spectacle, clad from chin to ankle in black, her once slender figure struggling against the confines of her corset, her hair, which was a little too dark and glossy to be natural, drawn back into a tight bun, scarlet lips clamped round a long cigarette holder, from which a dusting of ash fell on to her ample bosom. To most of the company she was Madame, though everyone knew she had been born simple Dolly Bridges somewhere in the East End of London.

Rose looked round at the other girls of the chorus line. Sally Castle was perched on the edge of the props table, swinging her long legs and painting her nails. Her sister Lucy crouched on the floor with her arm round Pamela Jones, who was crying softly. Near by, Barbara Willis, known to them all as Babe because her fresh face and golden curls made her look like a schoolgirl, stared into space, tense and pale. Down in the orchestra pit Franklyn Bell, the company tenor, who had obviously been drinking in spite of the fact that it was not quite eleven o'clock, was boring the boys in the band with his perpetual complaint about modern crooners, who sang through their noses and could not be heard without a microphone. His partner, Isabel St Clair, was sitting in the stalls, ignoring him. Rose found herself wondering why they stayed together, when they obviously fought on a daily basis. It was easier to think about that, a distraction from what might be about to happen.

'Anybody seen Chantal?' Monty Prince asked.

'Not since last night,' someone said.

'She'll be on the ferry by now, I should think,' Sally said. 'She's got family in France, hasn't she?'

Rose's gaze travelled on from one face to another. These people were like a second family. All summer they had worked together, shared lodgings, weathered the ups and downs in the company's fortunes, lent each other money, put up with the temperaments and petty jealousies inherent in the performer's life. Many of them had been together for two or three summer seasons. Now it struck her that she might be seeing some of them for the last time. There was one face she could not find. Then the pass door to the stage opened and closed and three young men came through. In front was the tall, gangling figure of Guy Merryweather, always ironically known as Merry, their pianist and musical director, his normally lugubrious expression more sombre than ever. Next in was handsome, blond-headed Felix Lamont, alias Mr Mysterioso, the conjuror and magician. And behind him Rose saw at last a dark head of wavy hair that no amount of Brylcreem could tame, and warm brown eyes beneath strongly marked brows met and held her own.

Richard Stevens came across the stage to join her. 'Have you been here long? Nothing's happened, has it?'

'No, not yet. We're still waiting for the prime minister's broadcast.'

'I'm sorry I'm late. We've been packing.'

'Packing? Already? You're sure this is it, then?' Rose felt a cold chill work its way through her guts.

'Not much doubt, I'm afraid.'

'What will you do, if . . . if the worst happens?'

He took her hand and pressed her fingers tightly. 'I'll have to join up. But I must get home first and see my parents. Then I'll probably sign up with the South Lancs – that's my dad's old regiment. The trouble is, if the bombing starts straight away as people seem to predict, there's no knowing what will happen to the trains. Felix has offered to give me a lift up to town immediately after we've heard Mr Chamberlain. That way I can catch the earliest possible train.'

'So you're going straight away? No time for . . . for anything else?' She felt as if the lump in her throat would throttle her.

He looked down into her eyes. 'I'm afraid not. Felix wants to go at once. He's desperate to get to Uxbridge and join the RAF.' He hesitated, then went on. 'Rose, I must talk to you – privately, before I go. Come over here a minute.'

He drew her into the wings where they were out of sight of most of the company. 'You know what I'm going to say, don't you?'

'Please don't,' she said. 'We've been through it all before.'

'But things are different now. I know you asked me to wait, until we were both sure, but I can't go off to fight and leave everything up in the air like this. I know I've no right to ask you to commit yourself, when there's a chance I may not come back. But at least promise me you won't forget me.'

'I'll never forget you,' she said. 'But it would be better if you forgot me.'

'But why?' he demanded. 'Why, Rose?'

'You know why. It wouldn't work, you and me. We're too different. You know this isn't the life for you. This summer's just been a bit of fun for you, but you told me yourself what you really want is to sing in opera. And with your voice and your background you can do it. I know you can. You can't waste all those years training in Italy.'

'But I don't see what that's got to do with you and me,' he said, and Rose could hear the desperation in his voice. 'What difference does it make?'

'Because that's not my world,' she replied, and her own voice was beginning to quiver. 'We come from such different backgrounds. I could never feel at home with the sort of people you'll be mixing with. You didn't want your mum and dad to come and see the show, because you knew they wouldn't approve. What do you think your mother would say if you went and married a cockney chorus girl from Lambeth?'

'That's not the point,' Richard protested. 'I could fall in love with a duchess and she still wouldn't be good enough for my mother. I've told you before, my dad may own the factory but he's just an ordinary working man at heart. It's my mum who's always thought of herself as being from a different class. She's always on at me to "better myself". But it's nothing to do with her. I know I couldn't do better than you. It doesn't matter what she thinks.'

'Yes it does. Families matter. You didn't get on with my mum and sister when they came down here.'

'I tried! I just didn't know what to say to them.'

'And they didn't know what to say to you. That's my point. The gap's too big, Richard, and it would pull us apart sooner or later.'

He stared down at her in silence for a moment, and the pain

in his eyes made her want to cry out and take him in her arms. At length he said, 'There's no point in going round and round over this. The chances of me making a career of any sort are pretty slim, in the present circumstances. Can we just agree to keep in touch? And when this war is over, if I'm still alive, I'll ask you again – and perhaps then you'll believe that I'm serious. Can we do that?'

'Of course we can,' she answered, and the tears she had been fighting back welled up in her eyes. 'But you mustn't talk about dying. You've got so much talent . . . so much to give to the world. You have to stay alive!' *And you have to stay alive for me!* she wanted to add, but she forced the words down.

'Quiet, everyone!' It was Monty's voice. 'The PM's speaking.'

Rose and Richard moved back on to the stage. Monty had brought in a wireless set and plugged it in in the wings. In the silence that followed they all heard the flat, exhausted tones of Mr Chamberlain.

'I am speaking to you from the Cabinet Room at Ten Downing Street. This morning the British ambassador in Berlin handed the German government a final note stating that unless we heard from them by eleven o'clock that they were prepared at once to withdraw their troops from Poland, a state of war would exist between us. I have to tell you that no such undertaking has been received, and that consequently this country is at war with Germany.'

For a moment the silence remained unbroken. Then Pam let out a wail. The sound seemed to release everyone else from some kind of trance and all around Rose people began to hug each other with tears in their eyes. She saw Felix give Merry a brief pat on the arm.

'Cheerio, old chap. Best of luck!'

He turned away and she saw the stricken expression on Merry's face as he looked after him and thought automatically, *Poor Merry!* So desperately in love, and with so little hope.

As the noise subsided the prime minister's voice became audible again. 'Now may God bless you all and may he defend the right. For it is evil things that we shall be fighting against, brute force, bad faith, injustice, oppression and persecution. And against them I am certain that right will prevail.'

Richard gripped Rose's hand. 'I'm sorry, Rose. I'll have to go. But perhaps it's just as well. I don't know if I could stand a lingering goodbye.'

She nodded, swallowed. 'Yes, you're right. This is the best way.'

He touched her cheek with his free hand. 'I'll never forget these last months.'

'Nor will I,' she answered.

He sighed. 'I have a feeling that one day we shall look back on this summer of thirty-nine as a kind of paradise.'

'And Adolf Hitler as the snake in the Garden of Eden?' she said.

'Exactly.' He gave her a tight smile. 'What will you do?'

'Go home to Lambeth, I suppose. The show will have to close if all you chaps are going to join up.'

He frowned. 'I don't like to think of you in London. Can't you find somewhere to stay in the country? After all, your sister's boys have been evacuated, haven't they?'

'Yes, poor little mites. I suppose it's for the best. But I'll have to stay with Mum. She won't leave the shop, I'm sure.'

'Try to persuade her,' Richard said urgently. 'London's going to be a very dangerous place if the Huns start bombing.'

'Don't worry about me. You take care of yourself, please!'

From the wings Felix called, 'Richard, are you coming?'

'Yes! Hang on a moment.'

He leaned down and kissed Rose once on the lips. 'Goodbye, my darling. Look after yourself.'

'And you!'

She watched him cross the stage, which was rapidly emptying. As he reached the wings she called, 'Write to me!'

He came back. 'I almost forgot! I don't have your home address. Here, write it down for me.'

He handed her a used envelope from his pocket and a fountain pen and she hastily scribbled her address.

'Give me yours.'

'Richard! Are you coming or not?' Felix was shouting impatiently from below the stage.

'Coming!' He looked back at her. 'There's no point. I shan't be at home. I'll write from wherever they send me and let you know how to get in touch.'

'Promise!'

'I promise.' He kissed her once more, very briefly, and hurried across the stage. In the wings he paused and looked back and she lifted a hand in farewell. Then he was gone.

Chapter One

Rose turned up her collar and pulled her coat around her, hugging her hands under her armpits. The night air was bitter. She thought that she could not remember a winter as cold as this and wondered for a moment, illogically, if the blackout could have something to do with it. The street was almost deserted and she could hear her own footsteps clicking sharply in the frosty air. They reminded her how much her feet ached. After two performances in the chorus line of *Babes in the Wood* it was not surprising, but that did not make them hurt any less. But in spite of everything, she hummed a song from the show as she walked. She was eager to get home. She had news – good news.

She reached her mother's shoe shop and fumbled her key into the side door that led to the flat above. Upstairs, in the sitting room, there was light and warmth and the table was laid for supper. Her mother and her sister Bet were waiting for her. They always waited up for her to come home after the show, although she'd told them there was no need.

'Oh, thank goodness for a fire!' Rose exclaimed, pulling off her coat. 'It's *freezing* out. Talk about brass monkeys!'

'Now, Rose, language,' her mother reproved her. 'Sit down, you look all in. I'll put the kettle on. I've kept your meal hot for you. I managed to get a nice marrow bone from the butcher so I made some soup.'

'Lovely, Mum.' Rose sat down at the table. 'Just what I need.'

Bet wrinkled her nose in disgust. 'Before the war marrow bone was something we gave to the dog, not something we ate ourselves.'

'There's nothing wrong with good marrow-bone soup, my girl,' her mother said. 'You wait till they bring in meat rationing, like they're promising. You'll be glad to eat it then.'

'Honestly!' Bet wailed. 'What are they trying to do, starve us? Four miserable ounces of butter every week, four ounces of bacon. I can eat that in a day!'

'Yes, and look what it's done to your figure!' Rose could not resist the jibe.

'That's what motherhood does for you,' Bet returned. 'You wait till you've had a couple of kids.'

'Good audience tonight?' her mother asked.

'Packed out. People seem to have made up their minds that the war's not going to stop them enjoying themselves.' Rose took a mouthful of soup and decided that this was the moment to broach the subject uppermost in her mind. 'Actually, I've got some news.'

'What sort of news?' her mother asked.

'I've been offered a new contract.'

'Who by? The panto's closing in a couple of weeks, isn't it?'

'Monty Prince. He was at the show tonight and came round afterwards.'

'But I thought there weren't going to be any summer shows this year,' Bet said. 'Nobody will be going to the seaside for a holiday while the war's on.'

'It's not a summer show. It's something called Entertainments National Services Association.'

Bet giggled. 'Blimey, that's a mouthful.'

Rose laughed in return. 'I know. I told Monty, that'll never catch on! Apparently it's got government backing. I think the idea is to take people's minds off the war.'

'He's not asking you to join up, is he?' her mother said suspiciously.

'No, Mum. It's a civilian outfit, nothing to do with the military.'

'So where would you be performing? Here, in London?'

'Oh no, I don't think so. Monty said we'd probably be touring. But it's a job, that's the main thing. I was beginning to be afraid I wouldn't find anything once the panto closed.'

'Oh no, Rose.'

Rose looked up from her plate. Her mother was frowning. 'What?'

'I don't want you going off again. Not while there's a war on.'

'Oh, don't be daft, Mum,' Rose said, smiling. 'It's not as if I'm going into the army. What harm can come to me?'

'You don't know what might happen. Suppose Hitler starts bombing London like they said he would? We could be bombed out and have to move. Or suppose there's an invasion? If you were at the other end of the country, how would we ever find each other again? We need to stick together at a time like this.'

'But there hasn't been any bombing!' Rose replied, trying to keep the exasperation out of her voice. 'There hasn't been any fighting at all. Everyone's saying it's a phoney war. It might all blow over in a month or two.'

'Well, if it does people will be able to go to the seaside again and the summer shows will start up and you can get a job in one of them.'

'But suppose it doesn't? I have to work, Mum!'

'No, you don't. There's a job for you here, helping out in the shop. I can do with an extra hand, now Fanny Carter's decided to go and live with her sister in the country.'

'But that's not a proper job!' Rose could feel a tide of desperation rising in her throat. 'I have to dance, Mum! You know that.'

'That's all you care about, your blessed dancing!' her mother grumbled. Her face was creased with anxiety and Rose felt a stab of guilt. 'I can't go through it all again, Rose. Not a second time.'

'Go through what again?' Rose demanded.

'What I went through in the first war, waiting every day for a telegram telling me your father had been killed. He came through it, thank God, but he was never the same again, you know that. The gas did for him in the end.'

'But I'm not going anywhere near the fighting,' Rose said. 'You'd have no need to worry.'

'But I would worry. And what about the shop? I can't manage on my own.'

'You've got Bet here.'

Her sister looked up from her knitting. 'Don't look at me! If the boys come home I'll be moving back into my own place. I'm thinking of bringing them back. I don't believe they're happy where they are. You can't rely on me.'

I never could! Rose almost answered, but she swallowed the words. She had always suspected that Bet had married at the age of seventeen in order to get away from the monotony of the shop and that now she was jealous of the freedom her younger sister's career on the stage gave her. Rose looked from her to her mother. Bet's face was sullen and obstinate; her mother looked ready to cry at any moment. She felt trapped.

She pushed her plate away with a sigh. 'Look, nothing's been decided. The show doesn't close for two weeks and anyway Monty's got to sort out the rest of the company and find a place to rehearse. He probably won't be ready to go ahead until next month at the earliest. Let's wait and see what happens, shall we?'

Her mother's face cleared. 'That's a good girl. I knew you'd see it my way. Things will all work out for the best, you'll see.'

Rose dropped her eyes to hide the anger in them. She knew

her mother's fears were genuine, but she felt, too, that she was being blackmailed.

'Oh, by the way . . .' Bet rose and took an envelope from the mantelpiece. 'There's a letter from your fancy man.'

'He's not my fancy man!' Rose protested, the anger she had been struggling to suppress rising to the surface.

'Fancies himself, if you ask me,' Bet replied.

'No he doesn't! Just because he's educated and well spoken you think he's putting on airs.'

'Oh, now, Rose,' her mother put in, 'you've got to admit he's a bit out of your class.'

'What's that got to do with anything?'

'What do you want with someone stuck up, like him?' Bet demanded. 'You should stick to your own kind.'

'Stuck up! You just can't bear anyone who isn't exactly like us. What's wrong with us all? Why are we afraid of people who are cleverer or better off? It's not him that's stuck up! It's us that's stuck down!'

As soon as the words were out of her mouth Rose heard how ridiculous they sounded.

Bet giggled. 'You make us sound like envelopes.'

Rose spluttered into her teacup, torn between laughter and tears of annoyance. 'Oh, you! I can't have a serious conversation with you.'

'Aren't you going to read your letter, then?' her mother asked.

Rose fingered the envelope. 'I'll read it later. You two get off to bed. You've got to be up early for the shop. I'll wash the dishes.'

When they had said goodnight and gone she slit the envelope. This was the fourth letter she had had from Richard since he had rushed off to join up. The first had informed her that he had joined the South Lancashire Fusiliers, and was undergoing basic training; the second that he was going on embarkation leave prior to leaving for some undisclosed destination; and the third that he was 'somewhere in France' but could not tell her more than that.

This letter was no more informative. He was still in the same place, conditions were bad . . . eighty men sleeping on the floor of a disused factory . . . *The MO came round and said there wasn't enough ventilation for that many men so they knocked two blooming great holes in the wall. That let the air in all right – and the wind, and the snow!* Food was monotonous and only relieved by occasional visits to an *estaminet* in the local village where the proprietress did a nice line in egg and chips. Nothing was happening and everyone was bored and fed up. The only bright spot had been a pantomime, which he and his company had staged for Christmas. *The adjutant found us a piano and there were a couple of chaps who could play a bit but they had no idea about arranging music for the assortment of other instruments we put together. How I longed for dear old Merry! (By the way, I had a letter from him last week. His regiment is still in England but, reading between the lines, I think he's pretty fed up with army life.) Anyway, we decided to have a go at* Aladdin, *with me as Abanazer and a young lad with quite a nice light tenor voice and the most amazing legs as the Principal Boy. We had a lot of fun rehearsing and I must say the performance seemed to go down really well. The CO invited some of the local bigwigs but I'm afraid they were totally bemused by the whole thing! The concept of a man dressed up in tights pretending to be a girl pretending to be a man was something beyond their comprehension.*

Rose chuckled to herself over that bit, but the letter left her with a feeling of emptiness. He addressed her as *my darling Rose* and wrote of how much he missed her and longed to be with her, so he hadn't forgotten after a few months apart, as she had been sure he would. She had convinced herself that, for him, this was just a summer romance. It seemed she had been wrong. She missed him far more than she had ever imagined and was beginning to regret what had been simple common sense at the time. But was he writing to the real Rose, or was it some imaginary ideal he had in his head? Distance makes the heart grow fonder, ran the old adage, but was that a basis for a real relationship?

In bed she tried to envisage his face, but she could not see it clearly. It was his smile that she remembered best, the wide, uninhibited grin of pure pleasure in being alive or the tender, dreamy smile when he looked into her eyes and told her he loved her. She remembered the tea dances at the Palace Hotel in Fairbourne, when their two bodies moved together in perfect harmony, and heard in her imagination the sound of his voice when he sang – powerful as a great river, warm as velvet . . .

She woke the next morning to a sense of loss, which she was unable to place at once. Was she grieving for Richard, or for the opportunity of a new job, which had been snatched away from her almost as soon as it was offered? *It's not fair!* she found herself thinking. *It's not fair!* Was she being selfish? She knew her mother had made sacrifices to pay for her dancing lessons. Perhaps she owed it to her to stay at home now the situation was so uncertain. The thought of being cooped up all through the summer in the little flat and the shop below made her almost frantic with frustration. It wasn't staying in London that she minded, or being with her family. Despite their differences they had always been close. It was not being able to dance that would drive her mad. Nothing gave her so much pleasure as dancing. Ever since she could remember it had been as natural to her as breathing. She sometimes felt that the urge to dance had been woven into her muscles while she was still in the womb; that her nerves were so attuned to the sound of music that at the first notes her limbs automatically began to move to its rhythm. Ballet, tap or modern, waltz, tango, samba or can-can – it made no difference. She loved them all. There was nothing to stop her ignoring her mother's objections and taking the job, of course. But she remembered her anguished expression and knew she would never forgive herself if anything happened to her or Bet while she was away. She could hope for a job that would allow her to stay in town, but she had combed the pages of *Variety* for weeks without seeing any hint of auditions for a new show. Monty was her only chance, and it looked as if she was going to have to turn him down.

Coming downstairs to breakfast, she found Bet weeping over a crumpled sheet of notepaper.

'Bet, what is it?' she exclaimed, going quickly to put her arm round the plump shoulders.

'Oh, it's just me being silly,' Bet answered. 'It's a letter from Billy, that's all.'

'Is there something wrong with him?' Rose asked.

'No, no. He says everything's fine. But I hate them being away from me, Rose. I wish I'd never let them be evacuated. There isn't any danger, after all. It's more than four months since I've seen them and even Billy's letters don't sound like him any more.'

'Let's see,' Rose requested, and Bet handed her the letter. It was written on good-quality notepaper and, from the absence of blots and spelling mistakes, Rose had the impression that it had been copied out, perhaps more than once.

Dear Mother,

This is just to let you know that Sam and I are well and happy and to thank you for the presents. We had a good Christmas with plenty of good things to eat, but we missed you and Gran and Aunty Rose, of course. I am back at school now. There are a lot of children in my class, so we only go in the morning or the afternoon because there isn't room for all of us at once. But when I cannot go to school I do lessons here with Mrs Marshall. Sam sends his love. We hope you are all well. Give my love to Gran and Aunty Rose.

Your loving son,
Billy

Rose laid the letter on the table. 'You're right. It doesn't sound like Billy. He wouldn't call you "Mother", would he?'

'Not when he was living here,' Bet said, rubbing her eyes with the back of her hand. 'He's being taught different ways, Rose. When he comes home he'll be a stranger.'

'Or he's being told what to write,' Rose said grimly.

Bet stared at her. 'You mean that Mrs Marshall who's looking after them won't let them write what they want?'

'Well,' Rose said, 'I reckon that letter's been corrected and rewritten, don't you? Our Billy was never that hot on spelling.'

'Oh!' Bet exclaimed. She was silent for a moment, taking in the implications of the situation. 'Then we wouldn't know if there was anything wrong, would we? Not if she was telling them what to write.' Her eyes filled with tears again. 'Oh, Rose, what are we going to do?'

Rose looked at her sister and the irritation of the previous evening evaporated. Poor old Bet, she hadn't had much of a life. Two kids by the time she was twenty, in a little two-up, two-down house just round the corner from her mother's flat. She had never known anything beyond the small corner of south London where she had grown up. 'We'll go down there and see them, that's what,' she said. 'And if they're not happy, we'll bring them home.'

'How are we going to get there?' Bet wailed. 'It's right out in the country, miles from anywhere. Oh, I wish I'd learned to drive! Reg wanted to teach me, but I was too scared.'

'Me too,' Rose said. 'You know what, Bet? We've depended too much on men, and now they're not around we're blooming helpless. We've got to learn to stand on our own feet.'

'That's all very well to say,' Bet said miserably, 'but it doesn't answer the question.'

'There must be trains, buses, something!' Rose exclaimed. 'Where are they?'

'Little village called Hawkhurst, down in Kent.'

'Well, at least it's not the other end of the country,' Rose said comfortingly. 'We'll go round to Waterloo station and see what we can find out.'

At that moment their mother came running up the stairs from the shop.

'Hey, girls, guess what!'

'What?' they asked simultaneously.

'The river's frozen! Mrs Jackson from up the road just came in to tell me.'

'The Thames?' Rose said incredulously.

'Yes! Mrs J says it's the first time since goodness knows when.'

'Well,' Rose said, 'I told you it was cold last night. I didn't realise it was that cold!'

'What's the matter with you, Bet?' Mrs Taylor demanded, noticing her elder daughter's face for the first time. 'You look like you'd lost half a crown and found sixpence.'

Rose explained. Mrs Taylor nodded emphatically.

'Right! The sooner you get down there and sort it out the better.'

It turned out that there was a train that would take them as far as Etchingham, a neighbouring village, but as far as they were able to discover the bus service from there to Hawkhurst was infrequent at the best of times and did not run at all on Sundays, the only day when Rose was free. It seemed Bet would have to go on her own.

'I shan't know what to say!' she protested. 'This Mrs Marshall sounds like a right old dragon. I've never been much good at speaking up for myself, not like you, Rose.'

'Hang on!' Rose said. 'I've had an idea. I know who might help us out.'

'Who?'

'Monty Prince. He's got a car.'

'Oh, but we couldn't ask him, could we? I mean, he doesn't even know me.'

'He remembers you from when you came down to see the show. He asked after you and Mum last night. And he's a really good-hearted man. He gave me his card. I'll go down to the phone box now and ring him.'

She had not misjudged him. Monty agreed to come over the following Sunday and drive them down to Kent.

Promptly at eleven, the car drew up outside the shop and Rose and Bet climbed in.

'This is really very good of you, Mr Prince,' Rose said. 'You remember my sister Bet?'

' 'Course I do.' Monty twisted in his seat to shake hands with Bet in the back. 'And call me Monty, please. I'm not the boss now.'

'How's Madame?' Rose asked.

Monty shrugged. 'Busy, busy. We're looking after some refugees, relatives from Poland.'

'I didn't know you had Polish relations!' Rose said.

'Oh, distant, you know, distant. But we Jews have a strong sense of family ties. And some of the stories coming out of the country since the German invasion are very disturbing.' He turned to Bet. 'Your old man off in the forces?'

Bet nodded. 'He was called up early on. They want mechanics, people who can maintain trucks and such.'

' 'Course, they would,' Monty said, nodding as he started

the engine. 'Two million called up this month! It's starting to feel like the last shambles.'

They drove for a while in silence and then Monty said, 'You heard anything of the rest of the girls, Rose?'

'Sally and Lucy are in panto in Croydon,' Rose told him. 'Babe is at home, helping her mum and dad. They've got a market garden somewhere down in Dorset, you know. And Pam's working in a munitions factory. I get letters from them all when they can find time to write.'

'Pam in a munitions factory!' Monty said. 'It's hard to imagine, somehow.'

'Well,' Rose said with a grin, 'she reckons she's earning better money than she'd ever have made in the theatre. And it said in the paper the other day that women doing war work are demanding equal pay with the men.'

'Equal pay!' Monty chortled. 'Whatever next! Don't suppose you've any idea what happened to Chantal?'

'None at all,' Rose said, trying to keep her voice neutral. The less she thought about the company soubrette, who claimed to be the love child of a Scottish aristocrat and a French ladies' maid, the better for her own peace of mind. There had never been anything definite but she had been aware of the nudges and winks, immediately suppressed when she appeared. She told herself that she had only herself to blame. She had told Richard he must wait until they were more certain of their feelings, so she could hardly blame him for seeking consolation elsewhere. Sally Castle had tried to warn her, but then Sally's morals were no better then Chantal's and she had no intention of descending to their level.

The weather was still bitterly cold and as they left the city the roadside hedgerows were stiff with ice. The sky was overcast so there was no glitter or sparkle to the frost. The land was steel grey, as if the fields themselves had been camouflaged for war. Occasionally they had to pull over to allow a long convoy of tanks and trucks to pass, but apart from that there was very little traffic. Petrol for private motoring was in short supply and most people hoarded it for essential journeys.

Monty insisted on buying them both lunch at a pub, so it was early afternoon when they reached their destination. The house where the two boys had been placed turned out to be a mile or so outside the village in a narrow country lane. It was a tall, rather forbidding red-brick building, half hidden behind a thick laurel hedge. Bet was suddenly seized with panic.

'We ought to have written,' she murmured. 'Let them know we were coming.'

'Well, we're here now,' Rose said firmly, 'and we're not going home till we've seen the boys.'

She marched up the garden path and rang the doorbell. Bet followed hesitantly, with Monty tagging along at a discreet distance. There was a pause long enough for Bet to whisper, 'Perhaps they're out.'

Then they heard the sound of movement inside and the door was opened by a gaunt middle-aged woman, whose grey hair was drawn back so tightly into a bun that it appeared to pull the corners of her eyes out of shape.

'Yes?' she enquired.

'Mrs Marshall?' Rose knew it was no good expecting Bet to take the initiative.

'Yes.' The same flat, unwelcoming tone.

'I'm Rose Taylor. And this is my sister Bet . . . Mrs Barker. We've come to see Billy and Sam.'

For a second the woman's face remained blank, then her lips stretched in a smile that seemed to have no relationship with the rest of her face.

'Billy and Sam's mother! You'd better come in.' She stepped aside and they moved past her into a dim hallway. 'This way.' She opened a door and showed them into the front room, where an aged white-haired man wrapped in a tartan shawl was crouched over the single bar of an electric fire. Rose could understand why, for the room struck her as being scarcely warmer than the street outside.

'This is my father,' the woman said. 'I'm afraid he's rather deaf. This is Billy and Sam's mother and aunt, Father,' she said, raising her voice. 'They've come to visit.'

The old man glanced up and mumbled vaguely, but then relapsed into his former position staring at the fire and took no further notice of their presence.

'And is this the boys' grandfather?' Mrs Marshall enquired, with the brightness of a cracking icicle.

Monty looked slightly embarrassed and Rose said quickly, 'No. This is Mr Prince, a family friend. He drove us down.'

'Are the boys here?' Bet asked timidly.

A strange expression passed over the woman's face and her eyes darted from one side of the room to the other. 'No, I'm afraid they're not. They're out. What a pity you didn't let us know you were coming.'

'Out where?' Bet asked.

'They've gone out to tea. They were invited . . . Sunday afternoon, you see . . .'

Rose said, 'Perhaps you could give us the address and we could call in. We wouldn't want to miss seeing them.'

Once again the eyes flickered round the room. 'Well, it's a bit difficult. I'm not exactly sure of the address. They were collected, you see . . . by car. It's not people I know very well.'

'You've let them go off with people you don't know, to you don't know where?' Rose said.

'Oh, but they're quite safe. The people who invited them are very reliable. It's all arranged through the church, you know. A nice afternoon out for the poor little chaps.'

'What time will they be back?' Bet asked.

'I couldn't tell for sure . . . quite late, I should imagine.'

'We'll wait,' Rose said grimly.

Mrs Marshall's expression was becoming increasingly hunted. 'I don't know that that would be a good idea. I mean, there's no knowing how long they'll be. They might stay the night.'

Rose's heart was beating fast and there was a chill sense of foreboding in her stomach. She took a step closer to Mrs Marshall. 'You don't actually know where they are, do you?'

The woman stepped back and her nostrils flared. For an instant Rose was reminded of a frightened horse. Then the look of panic was replaced by defiance.

'No, I don't. And you know why? Because they've run away, the ungrateful little brats! After all we've done for them. They arrive here, a couple of dirty little guttersnipes, and I do my best to turn them into decent, well-behaved children with some sense of discipline, and this is what happens.'

For a moment Rose thought Bet was going to faint. The colour had drained out of her face and she took a couple of wavering steps forward. Then a red flush rose from her neck up to her hairline.

'They're not dirty! And they're not guttersnipes! How dare you call them that! What have you done to them, you old witch?'

'Old witch! Old witch!' Mrs Marshall was spluttering with fury.

Rose stepped between the two of them. She was not given to displays of temperament. Years of living and working with volatile 'artistes' had taught her to avoid confrontations. Now, however, her pacific nature had given way to a cold rage. 'How long have they been gone?'

Something in her tone seemed to quell the other woman's bluster. 'Since this morning. I took them to church, like I always do, and they went into the Sunday school. Then, when the service was over, there was no sign of them. I asked the girl who teaches the Sunday school and she said she hadn't seen hide nor hair of them. I thought they'd slipped off home but when I got back I found they'd taken their things and disappeared. And what's more,' the tone of righteous indignation returned, 'they've stolen food from the larder. Bread, and a whole week's ration of cheese!'

At this point Monty, who had been standing in the doorway, stepped forward. 'Have you informed the police?'

'No. There's no need to go bothering them. They'll turn up, soon enough. Once it starts to get dark they'll be back, looking for a warm bed to sleep in.'

Rose ground her teeth. 'Well, they won't be sleeping here, that's for sure! They wouldn't run away for no reason. As soon as we find them we're taking them home.'

'Taking them home!' Mrs Marshall exclaimed. 'At a moment's notice? You can't do that!'

'Oh yes we can,' Rose retorted.

Mrs Marshall drew herself up and sniffed. 'Well, I must say, I've never known such bad manners! Never a by-your-leave or a please or thank you. But I suppose I should have expected no better.'

'You can expect a great deal worse when the authorities find out how you've let them go wandering off without any attempt to find them,' Rose replied grimly.

'Come along, ladies,' Monty interposed. 'There's no point in standing here arguing the toss. Where's the nearest police station?'

'Up on the hill, the other side of the village,' Mrs Marshall said sullenly. 'But you won't get much help there. I happen to know Constable Hitchins is fed up to the back teeth with dealing with these refugee children. They've been nothing but trouble from the word go.'

Monty turned to leave, taking Bet by the arm.

'Just a minute,' Rose said. 'We need their ration books. Get them, please.'

'Ration books?' Mrs Marshall sounded as if she had trouble remembering what the words meant. 'Oh, well, I'm not sure I can put my hand on them right now.'

'Oh yes you can,' Rose said. 'I don't mind betting you and your father have been eating their rations and letting them go short. That's probably why you took them in, in the first place. Now, are you going to find them or do I have to tell the police you've stolen them?'

The threat produced the desired effect. Mrs Marshall disappeared into the kitchen and returned with the two little books of coupons. Rose snatched them from her and followed Monty and her sister out to the waiting car.

Since her outburst, Bet had relapsed into shocked silence, and as soon as they reached the car she burst into tears.

Rose put her arms round her. 'Don't cry, love! We'll find them. They'll be on their way home. They're probably back at your house by now.'

'But I'm not there!' Bet wept. 'They won't know where to go.'

''Course they will. They know where their gran lives, don't they? They'll be all right.'

Monty produced a hip flask of brandy from the glove box and after a sip or two Bet became calmer, but Rose could feel her shivering as they drove through the winter dusk.

Mrs Marshall had been right about the attitude of the local constable. He wrote down the boys' descriptions and grudgingly agreed to circulate them to other forces in the area, but he obviously took the same view as she had, that they would turn up as soon as cold and hunger drove them back. And if they didn't, his attitude seemed to say, so what? It was two fewer problems for him to deal with.

By the time they left the police station darkness had fallen. 'I can't bear to think of them out there in the cold,' Bet wailed.

'I've told you,' Rose repeated, 'they're probably home by

now. We'd best get back and see.' It was the only course of action she could think of.

They were halfway up Wrotham Hill when the dimmed headlights picked out two diminutive figures trudging along the side of the road.

'That's them!' Bet cried. 'It is! It's them!'

Monty brought the car to a standstill a few yards beyond the boys and Bet scrambled out.

'Billy! Sam! Oh, thank God you're safe!'

Rose, following her, was horrified to see the two boys draw back, as if frightened. Bet stood still, her arms outstretched. 'What's wrong? Don't you know me? You haven't forgotten your mum, have you?'

Billy edged away, gripping his little brother by the hand. 'Have you come to take us back?'

'Yes, darling, of course I have. Come along.' Bet moved towards them but they backed farther towards the verge, and Rose saw Billy looking around him as if seeking a way of escape.

'We're not going back there!' he said fiercely. 'We hate that woman. She hits us. She made Sam sleep in the dog's kennel.'

'She what?' Bet seemed to choke on the words.

Rose stepped in quickly. 'Your mum means take you home, Billy. We're not going to take you back to Mrs Marshall.'

Bet's voice was shaking, but it was not with fear now. 'Did you say that woman hit you?'

'Look!' Billy extended his hand. Monty had joined them, carrying a torch, and by its light they all saw the three red weals that crossed the little boy's palm.

'The cow! The cruel bitch! I'll have the law on her!' Bet stammered. 'What was that about sleeping in the dog kennel?'

'When Sam wet the bed she put him in the kennel and put the dog in his bed.'

'Oh my God!' Bet stretched out her arms again. 'I'm so

sorry! My darlings, I'm so sorry. If I'd known what she was like I'd never have let you go.'

Billy was still gazing at her, his small face pinched and pale in the torchlight. 'She said you didn't want us. She said you'd sent us away because we were too much trouble.'

'Oh, the wicked, wicked woman!' Bet sobbed. 'It's not true, Billy. I sent you because I thought you'd be safe from the bombs.'

'There aren't any bombs,' he said woodenly.

'No, but there might have been. Truly, Billy, I only wanted to do the best for you. Your dad said you'd be better off in the country.'

For a moment they all stared at each other in silence, then Sam broke the tension by throwing himself against his mother's legs. 'I want to go home,' he sobbed. 'I want to go home.'

'That's where we're going, all of us,' Rose said. 'Come on, Billy. Gran will be wondering where we've all got to.'

She held out her hand and after a moment the boy took it. Bet reached out an arm to him and a second later he, too, was sobbing against her breast.

In the car, Monty produced a bag of humbugs and soon the boys' cheeks were bulging. He offered the flask of brandy again and Bet took a large swallow, spluttered and began to giggle hysterically. Rose did not care for spirits, but she took a sip and was grateful for the sense of warmth. She realised for the first time that, like the others, she was shivering with cold.

'Here, Bet.' Monty pulled a rug from the boot. 'You and the kids snuggle up under this.'

Bet settled in the back seat with a boy on either side of her and Monty tucked the rug round the three of them. Rose got into the front seat beside him and pulled her coat closer round her. As they drove towards London she could hear Bet and the boys murmuring together, then the sounds ceased and, looking round, she saw that the children were fast asleep and Bet, too, had her eyes closed.

In the comfortable silence her thoughts turned towards the future, and immediately she felt a pang of guilt. She ought to be thankful that the boys were safe and that Bet had her children back – and she was – but the thought that came immediately into her mind was that now they would all move back to their own home. There was no room for all of them in the flat. That meant that her mother would be left alone, unless she stayed. Now she really was trapped.

As if he had read her mind Monty said, 'This ENSA group's coming together nicely. I've got Frank and Isabel signed up and I think Sally Castle's coming on board. It'll be nice to get the old Follies company together again – those of them that aren't in the forces, anyway.'

Rose took a deep breath. 'I'm sorry, Mr Prince. I don't like letting you down but I'm afraid I'll have to back out. I can't leave my mum to cope alone – not while there's a war on.'

Chapter Two

Guy Merryweather woke in the freezing pre-dawn darkness and eased himself into a sitting position. His chest felt as though someone had clamped a vice around his ribs and every shallow breath was a struggle. He had lived with his asthma long enough to recognise the symptoms, but this was worse than usual. His head throbbed and he was starting to shiver. He huddled the rough blankets around his shoulders and listened to the sound of his own wheezing in the silence of the tiny room. His watch showed 4.30. Somehow he must hang on until reveille. He swallowed a couple of pills and tried to relax. The important thing was not to panic. He had learned that years ago.

Waiting for the dawn, he considered his present situation. It was bleak. He *hated* the army, with a loathing that deepened with every passing day. When war had been declared he had had every intention of enlisting in the RAF, not with any ambition to fly – he was pretty certain his health would make that impossible, even if he had any aptitude as a pilot, which he doubted. He simply cherished the forlorn hope that if he was in the RAF he might be able to maintain some contact with Felix. He had gone home to Seaford to say goodbye to his father and had discovered to his dismay that the colonel had assumed that his son would enlist in his own old regiment and had started to pull strings accordingly. He was not only determined that Merry should go into the army, but that he should go in as an officer, and Merry had quickly realised that if he demurred and insisted on the RAF instead it would break the old man's heart. He knew only too well that he was an abiding disappointment to him, with his love of music and the theatre and his complete lack of interest in what his father regarded as proper masculine pursuits. Now he felt he owed it to the old man to try to live up to his expectations. He had given in, Colonel Merryweather had pulled a few more strings, and Merry had been commissioned as a second lieutenant in the Sussex Yeomanry.

How he had survived his initial training was as much a mystery to him as it was to his superior officers. His chest had been in reasonably good condition when he attended the preliminary medical and he had seen no reason to mention his asthma to the harassed medical officer. There had been only a couple of minor attacks in the first months and he had managed to make light of them. But in every other respect he had shown himself to be, as he expected, totally inept. His only talent was marching, where his innate sense of rhythm and coordination made him the delight of his drill sergeant. Everything else about the army filled him with despair.

He hated the innate snobbery of the officers' mess, where the regular army officers looked down on their enlisted colleagues and those who had been to public schools looked down on the 'grammar school boys'. He hated the petty rules and regulations, which seemed designed to eradicate every trace of individuality, and the straitjacket of tradition that governed even the simplest forms of behaviour. He hated the philistinism of most of his fellow officers, which made any form of emotional or artistic expression suspect. He could, he supposed, have won a certain degree of facile popularity by sitting down at the piano and playing a few popular songs, but he refused to cheapen himself in that way and preferred to retain an aloof, sardonic independence.

By the time his batman arrived with the morning tea the pills had taken effect and Merry decided that he could cope without bothering the MO. He had a reason for keeping quiet, though it was one that filled him with dread. He knew that that morning they were all scheduled for a cross-country run and that officers were expected to set a good example. He knew, too, that his fellow officers regarded him as a wimp and that the men under him sensed it and were ashamed. He was determined not to let them down.

At breakfast in the mess a stranger in the uniform of a lieutenant colonel was seated beside their own Colonel Hemingway. When they were all present Hemingway tapped his cup with his spoon for silence.

'I'd like to introduce Colonel Basil Brown from Army Welfare. He's come with a rather unusual request, so I'll let him explain.'

Brown got to his feet. 'It's quite simple, really. I'm sure all you chaps are well aware that morale can suffer in the present circumstances. I know you've all got your work cut out training a lot of raw recruits but with no actual fighting going on you can't blame the men for getting a bit fed up. The War Office feels that what is needed is something to brighten up their off-duty hours in the way of entertainment. And of course, if the fighting does start, it is going to be even more necessary to provide a little light relief, something to take their minds off the war, perhaps to lift their thoughts to a higher plane. So that's what I'm here about.'

'Excuse me, sir,' someone put in, 'isn't that what this ENSA lark is supposed to be about?'

'To some extent, yes,' Brown agreed. 'But the ENSA people are civilians and there are some places where civilians cannot be allowed to go. Areas that are restricted for intelligence reasons, for one thing. The front line, for another. We couldn't have civilians getting captured and perhaps shot as spies. So we need our very own entertainments unit, manned by service personnel, and I've been given the job of putting it together. Now, I know quite a lot of units have put on their own entertainments – Christmas pantos, concerts, that sort of thing – so what I am asking you to do is to pass on to me the names of any men who seem to have a talent in that direction. Some of them may have been professional performers in civvy street. I'm looking for musicians, comedians, singers, jugglers – anybody who can put on an act. I'll be in the adjutant's office for the rest of the morning, so if you think of anyone who might be suitable just let me have his name – or better still, send him along to see me.'

'Looks like a good opportunity to get rid of some of the dead wood,' Merry heard the officer on his right murmur to his companion on the other side.

Leaving the mess, Merry saw Colonel Brown walking up the corridor ahead of him with Hemingway and the adjutant. He quickened his step to catch up.

'Excuse me, sir, I wonder if I might have a word.'

The other men turned and Hemingway frowned at him. 'What is it, Merryweather?'

'I wanted to speak to Colonel Brown, sir,' Merry said breathlessly.

'Carry on, then.'

Brown gave him an interrogatory smile. 'Got someone for me?'

'I just wanted to say, I'm a musician – if you're interested.'

'Amateur or professional?'

'Professional, sir.'

'What's your instrument?'

'Piano, sir. But I can also conduct and arrange music. I used to be the musical director for a concert party before I joined up.'

'MD of a concert party, eh?' Brown's smile broadened. 'You could be just the sort of chap I'm looking for. What was the name again?'

'Guy Merryweather, sir.'

'I'll make a note of it. At present I'm just on a scouting mission, but once things get under way I'll be in touch with you. You can depend on it.'

As Brown moved away with the adjutant, Colonel Hemingway paused and glared at Merry. 'Surprised at you, Merryweather. That's no life for a man – not in wartime.'

As he turned away Merry restrained an impulse to put out his tongue. To hell with Hemingway and his like! Here was the chance of a job he was good at, one where he could make a real contribution to the war effort.

There was no respite for the time being, however, from the demands of army life, and half an hour later Merry was slogging through the mist after the rest of his company along a country track. Within a few hundred yards he could feel the band tightening around his chest and there was a sharp stabbing pain under his ribs with every struggling breath. Soon he was aware of nothing but the pounding of the blood in his ears and the desperate wheezing of his lungs. He knew that he was getting left behind but he forced himself to stagger on. *What am I doing?* he asked himself. *Me, the man who always regarded competitive sport as the occupation of the mentally defective and war as an obscene extension of the same activity?* Was it pride, he wondered, which kept him going, or fear . . . the fear of being seen as inadequate, less than a man? The track was rising up a slight slope. He told himself that when he got to the top he would pause and try to get his breath back. Behind him he heard the thud of feet. The second company was catching him up. He tried to put on a spurt, and then there was nothing but blackness . . .

Merry came round briefly in the ambulance, with a medic leaning over him holding an oxygen mask to his face. The next time he surfaced he was in hospital and a doctor was listening to his chest through a stethoscope. Then there was the stab of a hypodermic and the familiar racing of his pulse as the adrenalin took effect, and at last his congested lungs relaxed and he was able to breathe. He closed his eyes and sank back gratefully into oblivion.

There was an interval during which he was vaguely aware of night following day, of the routine attentions of the nurses, of the arrival of meals and someone trying to persuade him to eat. Then one day he awoke to find the same doctor looking down at him.

'You gave us a nasty scare, old man. We thought for a while we might lose you. What the hell were you doing out there running, in your condition?'

'I don't like to let it get the better of me,' Merry croaked. A deep breath still produced a sharp pain in his side.

'Let what get the better of you?'

'My asthma.'

'It was more than asthma this time, you know. You're suffering from a nasty bout of pleurisy. You should have been hospitalised days ago, not running around in the cold. Still,' the doctor straightened up, 'you're out of the woods now. A few more days and we'll be able to discharge you to a convalescent home. But I'm afraid that's the end of your career as a fighting soldier. I'm going to write you off as unfit for active service.'

'What will that mean?' Merry asked in alarm. 'Will I be discharged?'

'Oh, probably not. I expect the army will find a desk job for you. There's always room for one more pen-pusher in the War Office.'

When the doctor had gone Merry lay staring at the ceiling. 'One more pen-pusher . . .' He had always had a horror of being confined to an office. He thought of his father's reaction when he heard the news. Colonel Merryweather had never made a secret of the fact that he regarded Merry's asthma as purely psychosomatic – though he would never have used the word. In his opinion it was a device to allow him to get out of activities he did not enjoy, such as sport. It was one more piece of evidence of his son's lack of manly qualities. Merry knew now who he had been trying to prove himself to on that run.

Something was nagging at the back of his mind; something important had happened that he could not quite recall. Then it came to him. Colonel Brown's visit! He had promised to get back to him about the job. Merry groaned aloud. How long had he been here? Days, certainly. Suppose the colonel had contacted his regiment and been told he was no longer available? Merry had been in 'the profession', as all those involved in the theatre called it, long enough to know that if one person was unavailable there were always half a dozen others willing and able to take his place. The offer would not come again.

Sunk in despair, his mind turned, as it always did when he was not policing his thoughts, to Felix. Where was he now? It was only after he had watched his blue Lagonda pull away along the promenade in Fairbourne that he had realised he had not left a forwarding address. He had comforted himself with the thought that Felix knew his and had waited in vain hope for a letter, but after a few weeks he had been obliged to accept that he was not going to get one.

There was a locker beside his bed. With an effort that sent the pain stabbing through his chest again, Merry leaned over and opened it. His wallet and his other personal possessions were inside on the shelf. The movement brought on a bout of coughing that left him gasping and exhausted. When the spasm had passed he took out a creased photograph cut from one of the Follies programmes. It showed Felix in the costume he always wore for his stage act, a top hat tilted rakishly on the side of his head, a scarlet-lined opera cloak thrown back from one shoulder. You had to imagine the scarlet lining, of course, but Merry's memory had no difficulty in supplying the rest of the colouring – the corn-gold hair visible under the hat and the vivid blue of the eyes. For the rest, the black-and-white picture almost did justice to the classic bone structure and the slightly-too-wide mouth with its enigmatic smile. Night after night, Merry had stood in the orchestra pit and watched him work his magic, magic that consisted not so much in the white doves that appeared from the top hat or the sleight of hand that caused cards to change their positions and bouquets of flowers to vanish, skilled though that was, but in the personality of the magician himself. On stage, Felix had a charisma that ensured that whenever he asked for a young lady to help in one of his illusions he was almost trampled to death in the rush. Merry had experienced it offstage, as well, alternately basking in the charm and accepting without complaint the apparently casual cruelty of Felix's barbed wit. He put the picture back in his wallet. It was over. It was obvious that Felix did not want to keep in touch and the chances of ever running into him again were negligible.

Two days passed and the pain in his side subsided but nothing could lift the depression that seemed to suck him down like a bog. The doctor spoke cheerfully of a convalescent home in the Cotswolds and an eventual return to health. Merry felt only weakness and lethargy. On the third day the doctor came into his room looking puzzled.

'I've just had a signal from the War Office, passed on from your HQ. You're required to report immediately to a Colonel Brown. Of course, I've replied saying it's quite out of the question at the moment. You're in no condition to go anywhere yet.'

Merry started up in bed. 'But I must go! It's something very important. I really need to go at once!'

The doctor patted him on the shoulder. 'Take it easy, old chap. If it's that important they'll wait for you. Maybe in two or three weeks you'll be fit enough for light duties but right now all you need is rest and good food.'

As soon as the doctor had left Merry swung his legs cautiously out of bed and looked round the room. He was thankful that his status as an officer had meant that he was given a private room but he was unsure what had happened to his clothes. The effort of standing up made him giddy, but when that passed he opened a cupboard and was relieved to find his uniform hanging up inside. It took him some time to get dressed and he had to sit down to put his trousers on but he managed it in the end. He splashed his face with cold water at the basin in the corner, combed his hair, collected his possessions from the locker and quietly opened the door. To his left open double doors gave him a view of a long ward. Nurses were moving around there but no one was looking in his direction. To his right was another set of double doors, which he guessed led to the rest of the hospital. He closed the door of his room silently, straightened his shoulders and marched down the corridor.

After that it was easier than he had imagined. The doors gave on to a wider corridor running at right angles, which in turn led him to the main reception area. Nurses and porters were hurrying backwards and forwards but no one took any notice of him. A doctor passed him, wearing a white coat over his uniform. Merry saluted and the doctor nodded in return and went on his way. In a few more paces he was outside the main doors. He had to sit down on a low wall until his head stopped swimming but as it cleared he saw a taxi draw up and deposit an elderly man in civilian dress. Merry waved to the driver to wait and forced himself to his feet. He felt as if he were walking in slow motion as he headed for the cab, and as he climbed into the back seat he realised that he had no idea where he was. The station seemed a reasonable destination to ask for and to his relief the driver responded with a cheerful 'Right you are, guv'. Half an hour later he was in a train heading for Paddington.

It was mid-afternoon when Merry presented himself in Colonel Brown's office. He had snoozed on the train and treated himself to a decent lunch at a hotel near the station and the sense of extreme weakness had passed, though he suspected that he was still running a temperature.

A very good-looking young corporal in the outer office rose to attention as he announced himself. 'Lieutenant Merryweather, sir! We were told you were on the sick list.'

'Well, I'm better now,' Merry said. 'Is the colonel free?'

'I'll find out, sir.'

He disappeared through a communicating door and Merry reached out to support himself on the back of a chair. The half-bottle of wine at lunch had been a mistake. His throat was parched and he was definitely feverish. *You fool!* he berated himself. *What sort of impression do you think you're going to make, turning up in this state?*

The corporal came back and from the other room Merry heard Brown's voice, a rich baritone. 'Merryweather? Come in, come in.'

He stepped past the corporal, who was holding the door open, and Brown rose from behind his desk.

Merry came to attention and threw up a salute. 'Second Lieutenant Merryweather reporting for duty, sir.'

The colonel came round the desk and extended a friendly hand. 'Good to see you. But we were told you were in hospital. Are you sure you're quite fit?'

'Yes, thank you, sir,' Merry replied, still standing to attention.

Brown waved him to a chair. 'Do sit down. I expect you could do with a cup of tea, couldn't you?'

Merry hesitated. After the rigid formality of the regiment he found Brown's relaxed manner disconcerting. 'Thank you, sir.'

Brown turned to the door. 'Get us some tea, will you? Do you take milk, Guy?' And, on Merry's nod, 'Two teas with milk, please, Jimmy.'

As the corporal disappeared Brown turned back to Merry. 'Please, do sit down and relax, Guy,' he repeated. 'You don't mind if I call you Guy, do you?'

'Merry,' Merry said. 'I'm usually called Merry.'

'You are?' The other man looked into his face for a moment and his eyes twinkled. 'Yes, of course. I can quite see why.'

Merry found himself smiling in response. He secretly enjoyed the ironic contrast between his nickname and his normal manner. He relaxed and dropped into the chair. 'I think I ought to confess something right away. The fact is, I've gone AWOL.'

'Absent without leave? How come?'

'The MO didn't want me to leave hospital. But I couldn't miss the chance of working with you – if you still want me.'

'My dear chap, of course I want you! It seems to me that you are exactly the sort of chap we need. But there was no need to rush here when you're still not fit. I thought you were looking pretty rough when you came in. Are you sure you want to go ahead with this?'

'Yes, please,' Merry said. 'It's just too good an opportunity to miss.'

'Well, I'm glad you see it that way.' Brown seated himself behind his desk. 'But, look, there's no desperate hurry. Take some time off, get yourself well again. Then we'll talk.'

'What about the MO? He's probably got the redcaps looking for me by now.'

'Oh, don't worry about that. I'll square it with him, and your CO and the regiment. I've pretty well been given a free hand when it comes to recruiting personnel.'

The tea arrived. Merry sipped his. He could hardly believe that all difficulties could be smoothed away so easily. He said, 'What exactly do you have in mind for me to do, if you don't mind me asking?'

Brown put down his cup and leaned forward. 'If I were to ask you to get together a small concert party, from army personnel with suitable talents and experience, and to rehearse a show that could be taken to France and performed in some pretty improvised situations, what would you say?'

Merry gazed at him for a moment. 'I'm not being interviewed for some kind of undercover work, am I?'

Brown laughed uproariously. 'No, good heavens, no! It's absolutely straightforward, I assure you. No strings attached.'

'Well, then,' Merry said. 'I can't think of anything I'd like more.'

'Good man! Now, I've collected a few names of men I think might be suitable. I've been going round attending some of the concerts and variety shows being put on in the camps and making notes of the available talent. Take this list away with you and look it over. See who you'd like to work with. Then report back to me and I'll get them transferred. Now, you need to take some leave. I'll make out a pass for you. Where would you like to go? Got any family?'

Merry thought of his father down in Seaford. That was the last place he wanted to go to recuperate. 'My father lives on the south coast but he's not very fit – dicky ticker, you know? I'd rather stay in town if it's all the same to you.'

'You'll need somewhere to stay,' Brown said. 'We don't have any accommodation available here, I'm afraid, but I can arrange a sleeping-out pass for you. Is there anyone you can stay with – someone who'll look after you?'

Merry thought. 'Well, there is one couple, but I don't know if they'll be at home, or if they have any extra rooms. It's Monty Prince and his wife. Have you ever come across them?'

'Monty Prince? Yes, of course. Know him well. Lovely chap. Not so sure about his missus, though.'

Merry laughed. 'Oh, Dolly's all right when you get to know her. You just have to show you're not going to be browbeaten. But they may not be there. For all I know they could be touring with ENSA.'

'Well, look,' Brown said, 'go and see if they can put you up. If they're not at home come back here and we'll fix you up somewhere. Corporal! See if you can find a taxi for the lieutenant, will you?'

Chapter Three

It was almost 5.30 and Rose was about to shut the shop for the night. As she was bolting the door she felt someone push it from outside.

'Sorry, we're closed,' she called. 'Come back tomorrow.'

'I'm looking for Mrs Taylor,' a man's voice called back. 'I'm a friend of her daughter's.'

Rose pulled aside the blackout curtain and peered out. 'Who is it?'

'My name's Guy Merryweather.'

'*Merry!*' She opened the door, and pulled him inside, closing it again behind him.

'Rose!' he exclaimed as she turned to face him. 'I wasn't expecting you to be here.'

'I didn't recognise you for a minute,' she said. 'And I don't know if I would now, if you hadn't said your name.' She checked herself. He looked terrible, thin and pale with great shadows under his eyes and a hectic flush on his cheekbones. 'Fancy you an army officer!'

'Only a sham one, I'm afraid,' Merry said. 'I feel as if I'm walking round in costume all the time.' Then, changing his tone, 'It's good to see you, Rose.'

'And you,' she answered warmly, and kissed him on the cheek. 'But what are you doing here?'

'I could ask you the same,' he responded. 'I thought you were in panto.'

'Oh, you're out of date,' she told him. 'The show closed last month. I'm helping out in the shop until something else comes up. Come on upstairs. Mum'll be pleased to see you.'

Her mother was up in the kitchen, getting tea ready.

'Look who's here, Mum,' Rose called. 'You remember Merry, don't you?'

She had no doubt about her mother's reaction. Mrs Taylor always referred to Merry as 'a perfect gentleman', and Rose had been careful not to drop any hints that he might not quite fit her image of perfection. Her mother took one look at him and forgot all pretensions to gentility.

'Oh, you poor man! Whatever have you been doing with yourself? Are they feeding you properly? You look really peaky.'

'I've been in hospital,' Merry explained. 'A touch of pleurisy. But I'm on the mend now.'

'Well, sit yourself down,' Mrs Taylor said. 'I'll get another cup and saucer.'

'So, what brings you to Lambeth?' Rose asked, as Merry settled himself at the table.

As she listened to Merry's explanation she tried to hide the turmoil that it raised in her own feelings. She sympathised with his frustration with army routine and was glad that he had been offered a way out, but how she wished that she could be given the same opportunity!

'Any girls wanted in this new outfit?' she asked.

He shook his head. 'I'm afraid not, from the look of the list I've been given. It seems to be men only.' He hesitated. 'The thing is, I need somewhere to stay for a week or two. I've got some leave but I'll still be in town when I start this new job, for a while at least. I went to see Monty and Dolores but they've got a house full already. He suggested you might be able to put me up. The army will pay for my keep, of course.'

'Goodness me, why didn't you say so straight away?' Mrs Taylor exclaimed. 'Of course you can stay. We'd love to have you, wouldn't we, Rose?'

'Of course we would,' Rose agreed. 'That way we can make sure you get properly looked after.'

When they had finished eating Rose got up to clear the table but her mother stopped her. 'I'll do that, Rose. You sit down and talk to Merry.'

Rose sat down again, puzzled. Her mother had taken to spoiling her recently, which was an unfamiliar experience. It was only small things – cups of tea at unexpected moments, her favourite meals, as far as rations would allow – but it meant something. Either her mother was trying to make her so comfortable that she would not want to leave, or she was feeling guilty. This evening, however, there was a good reason. It would be rude to leave their guest sitting alone.

'Did you say you've been to see Monty Prince?' she asked.

'Yes. It was extraordinary. They've filled their house with Jewish refugees. There were three or four kids, sent over from Poland by their parents, and the top floor has been converted into a flat for an elderly couple who are distant relatives of some sort.'

'Monty said Madame had got her hands full. I can't imagine her coping with a house full of children. I feel sorry for the poor kids.'

Merry smiled. 'That was the strangest part. I know she was a real dragon with you girls, but you would not believe the change in her. She's stopped dyeing her hair, for one thing, and gone quite grey. And she's lost that rigid, buttoned-up look.'

'You mean she's stopped wearing a corset,' Rose said with a laugh.

'I suppose that's it. And she's given up the phoney foreign accent.'

'Poor old Madame! What a come-down.'

'On the contrary, I got the impression she's enjoying it, in a way. She looked . . .' He hesitated. 'She looked like anyone's granny.'

'Really? Well, good for her. I think it's noble of them to take on so much – especially if Monty's going off on tour.'

There was a brief silence. Then Merry said, 'Have you heard from Richard lately?'

Rose felt herself blush. She always blushed when anyone mentioned Richard, though she couldn't think why. After all, she had done nothing to be ashamed of.

'I had a letter last week,' she replied. 'He told me he had heard from you.'

'Yes, we write fairly regularly. I don't think he's enjoying himself out there.'

Rose laughed. 'Funny. He said the same about you.'

Merry made a grimace. 'He wasn't far wrong there. But . . .' She saw him sit back and draw a breath, as if someone had lifted a weight off him. '. . . 'hopefully things are going to get better.' Then he leaned forward again and put his hand over her wrist. 'Rose, what's all this about you turning down an offer of a job in this new outfit of Monty's?'

She lowered her eyes. 'He told you about that, did he?'

'He's very disappointed. He wanted you, particularly.'

'Can't think why.'

'Because you're good!' His fingers tightened on her arm and she was forced to meet his eyes. He had unusual eyes, of a very clear light hazel that could appear almost colourless in certain lights. 'That's always been your trouble, Rose. You're too self-effacing. You don't realise how much better you are than the average run-of-the-mill dancer. Oh, I know I'm no expert but I've stood in enough orchestra pits and watched enough dance troupes to recognise talent when I see it. And so has Monty. You shouldn't be wasting your life serving in a shop.'

'I'm not,' Rose protested. 'It's only temporary. I just can't leave Mum on her own.'

'But she's been on her own every summer, while you were with the Follies.'

'But this is different. That was peacetime.'

His expression was sombre. 'Rose, this war could go on for years. If you don't dance for all that time, what chance will you ever have of getting back?'

'I am dancing,' she protested. 'I'm still going to class twice a week.'

'It's not the same thing as working professionally – and you know it.'

She sighed and shook her head. 'What can I do? She needs me to help in the shop.'

'Surely there must be someone else who could do that.'

'Well, yes, there is.' Rose hesitated for a moment but the look in his eyes encouraged her to go on. 'As a matter of fact, I found out the other day that Joan Johnson from up the road actually asked Mum if there was any chance of a job, just before I finished with the panto. And Mum turned her down.'

Merry sat back. 'Well, that tells you something, doesn't it?' When she did not respond he went on, more intensely. 'Rose, we can't always do things to please our parents. You have a great talent! It's a crime not to use it – particularly now, when this country is going to need people like us more than ever. If things get really bad – and they still could – people are going to need something to remind them that there's more to life than just survival. That's where we come in.'

Rose looked at him. 'You've really thought about this, haven't you?'

'I've had plenty of time, lying in bed over the last few days. Am I right?'

She nodded slowly. 'Yes, you're right.'

'So, will you do something?'

'I'll think about it.'

*   *   *

The next morning Rose asked her mother for the morning off and was mildly surprised when the request was granted without questions being asked. She returned to the shop just as it was time to close for the lunch hour.

Rose bolted the door and stood for a moment, gathering her courage. Then she said, 'Mum, I've found someone to take my place in the shop.'

Her mother straightened up, a discarded pair of shoes in her hand. 'Oh?'

'It's Joan Johnson. I know she's only young but she's a bright girl and she's very presentable. She'll soon pick things up.'

'I see.' Her mother put the shoes back in their box. 'I suppose that means you're off.'

'I'm taking up Monty Prince's offer. I went to see him this morning and there's still a place for me in his company. I'm sorry, Mum, but I've got to do this. I've got a good career. I can't just throw it away. And this way I can be doing something useful – something other people wouldn't be able to do. You do understand, don't you?'

Her mother turned away to put the shoebox back on the shelf. 'And that's more important than your own family, is it?'

'It's not that you're not important.' Rose clenched her fists so that the nails dug into her palms. 'But why does it have to be a choice? You've never minded me going away before.'

'That's right. You go. I shouldn't be trying to keep you back. I'm just a selfish old woman.'

Her mother's back was turned but Rose could hear tears in her voice and for a moment her resolution wavered. She knew that life had not been kind to her. Her marriage had been blighted first by the tension and anxiety of the First World War and then by years of caring for the husband who had returned from it with his lungs ruined by the effects of poison gas, at the same time as bringing up two small daughters. That had been followed by more years of widowhood and the struggle to make ends meet on her widow's pension and the meagre proceeds from the shop. Rose was aware that her own lot had been so much easier, but it had never occurred to her until now that, while she was away pursuing her career in summer shows at the seaside or in pantomime in some northern city, her mother might be lonely.

She went and put her arm round her. 'Don't start that, Mum. You're the least selfish person I've ever met. God alone knows the sacrifices you've made over the years to pay for my dancing lessons. That's another reason why it's a shame to let them go to waste.'

There was a moment of silence. Then her mother looked into her face. 'Yes, you're right. Don't worry about me. You go and do what you need to do. I've seen you pining away here, these last weeks, and I've kicked myself for trying to keep you. I thought it was too late for you to change your mind – the chance would have gone. I'm glad it hasn't. I'm really glad for you, Rose.'

Rose hugged her and hid her face for a moment in her plump shoulder. 'Thanks, Mum!'

'Well, if it ain't the one and only Rose Taylor! I thought Monty said you'd turned him down.'

Rose recognised the sardonic drawl. Sally Castle was draped over a trestle table at one side of the church hall, a cigarette poised elegantly between scarlet-tipped fingers. She went across with a smile. She and Sally had had their ups and downs over the past couple of seasons but usually they got on all right and it was nice to see a familiar face.

'Hello, Sally. I changed my mind. How are you?'

'OK – apart from being chilled to the marrow. It's freezing in here.'

'It is cold, isn't it?' Rose hugged her coat closer and looked around. 'Where's Monty?'

'Round the back with a couple of the boys from the band, looking for oil heaters or something.'

'Are we the first, apart from them?'

'Looks like it.'

'Isn't Lucy with you?'

'No. The silly cow's only gone and joined the ATS, hasn't she?'

'Really?'

'Really. I wish her joy of them – and them of her. She won't last long.'

Rose understood the bitterness in Sally's tone. Ever since she had known them Lucy had existed in her elder sister's shadow. Now, she guessed, Sally was finding it hard to come to terms with the idea that Lucy could strike out on her own.

'Who else is coming? Do you know?'

Sally stretched her long legs. 'Well, Frank and Isabel are signed up, according to Monty.'

'Oh no!' Rose sighed. 'I've got nothing against her, she's rather sweet. But he's such a creep. And he can't keep his hands to himself. I don't know why she puts up with him.'

'She knows which side her bread's buttered, that's why,' Sally responded. 'I gather they've been making quite a name for themselves. My mum said she heard them on the wireless the other day.'

'Trust Frank!' Rose grunted. 'If there's something good going you can rely on him to grab a bit of it. Who else?'

'I don't know. Not many, I don't think. Monty says we all have to be able to fit into the back of a truck.' She paused for a moment and then went on. 'Hey, I know what I wanted to ask you. Do you still hear from Richard?'

'Oh yes,' Rose said, deliberately casual. 'He writes from time to time. He's in France. Oh, but I'll tell you who I have seen lately,' she added, in an attempt to deflect the inquisition she sensed was coming, 'Merry.'

'Merry! Where?'

Rose explained and Sally asked, 'Is he still sweet on Felix?'

'I don't know. He hasn't mentioned him. I don't think they're in touch.'

'Just as well. It was a hopeless case, anyway.' Sally sighed. 'Now, if there's one person I'd like to see walk through that door right now, it's Felix Lamont.'

Rose laughed. 'Forget it. You know you haven't got a hope. You tried hard enough last summer.'

'Well, a girl can dream, can't she?' Sally said.

'Anyway,' Rose went on, 'he's got a lady friend – a real lady. Lady Harriet something or other. Don't you remember he invited me and Richard to join them for one of those tea dances at the Palace Hotel?'

'Oh, yes! What's she like?'

'OK. Quite nice, really. Not a bit stuck up. Beautifully dressed, but still looks as if she's more at home on a horse. You know the type.' Rose grinned. 'Tell you one thing, though. She can't dance to save her life. Felix practically had to carry her round the floor. But she must be pretty well off. That dress she was wearing probably cost more than we'd earn in a month.'

'Trust Felix! Expensive clothes, swanky car, posh lady friends. I'd love to know how he does it. I asked him once, you know – how come he'd always got money to spare when the rest of us were stony broke most of the time.'

'You didn't! What did he say?'

'Oh, he made some crack about a maiden aunt dying and leaving him a legacy. But I never know how much to believe of what Felix says.'

'Mr Mysterioso offstage as well as on,' Rose agreed.

The door opened to admit Franklyn Bell and Isabel St Clair. He was wearing an elegantly cut tweed overcoat and a trilby hat tipped rakishly on the side of his head, and she had a fox fur draped around her shoulders.

Frank raised his hat. 'Hello, girls. Looking lovely as usual.'

Isabel drew the fox fur closer round her neck. 'It's freezing in here. We can't possibly work in these conditions.'

At that moment Monty hurried in, followed by two of the men Rose remembered from the orchestra of the original Follies. All three were carrying oil heaters.

'Here we are,' Monty cried. 'These will take the chill off the place and once we get to work we'll soon warm up. Now, who are we waiting for?'

'What about the dancers?' Rose asked Sally. 'It's not just us, is it?'

'There are supposed to be four of us, but I've no idea who. Hang on, here's someone.'

A tall, blonde girl had come in and stood by the door looking around her. Monty spotted her and called out, 'Vera! Come along in and meet the gang. Everybody, this is Vera Ellis, one of our dancers. The other girls are over there, Vera. I'll leave them to introduce themselves.'

Vera came over with a friendly smile. 'I recognise you both from auditions for various shows. You're Rose, aren't you . . . and you're . . . Susie, is it?'

'Sally. Nice to meet you.'

'I say, isn't this exciting?' The new girl had lively blue eyes and a vivacious manner. Rose decided she was going to enjoy working with her.

There was a small commotion at the door as another member of the band struggled in lugging a double bass. He was followed by another man carrying a trombone. Then Sally grabbed Rose's arm.

'Oh no! I don't believe it. Look!'

Rose looked. A slender girl with raven-black hair, wrapped from chin to ankle in a mink coat, stood in the doorway.

'It's Priscilla!' Rose whispered. 'What on earth is she doing here?'

'Our very own poor little rich girl,' Sally murmured in reply. 'I dread to think!'

The girl saw them and came quickly across the room. 'Hello, Rose. Hello, Sally.' Her eyes went from one to the other, begging for a welcome and finding none. 'I bet you're surprised to see me.'

'You could say that,' Sally responded drily.

'Have you come to join us – as one of the troupe?' Rose asked hesitantly.

'Yes.'

'But I thought you gave up dancing – after what happened.'

'Oh no! I could never give up dancing. I swore I would never set foot on a stage again, professionally. But this isn't quite the same as being in a professional show, is it?'

'It is as far as I'm concerned,' Sally said.

Priscilla rattled on. 'I mean, it's not as if the audiences will be paying to watch us. And anyway, I really have improved since last summer. You'll see. I've been going to classes every day and I wanted to do my bit, you know, for our boys. So I got in touch with Frank and he fixed it for me.'

'I bet!' Sally muttered, not quite under her breath.

'Oh, there he is! I must go and thank him.' Priscilla flashed a last ingratiating smile and moved away.

'Who is that?' Vera enquired. 'And where did she get that coat?'

'Bet somebody's missing their cat!' Sally muttered.

'That is Priscilla Vance,' Rose explained. 'And the coat will be a present from her doting guardian, dear Uncle Lionel.'

'What did you mean – "after what happened"?' Vera looked at Rose.

Rose wrestled unsuccessfully with a desire to giggle. 'Prissy was in the Follies with us last year. She's terribly keen but not really very good.'

'Not very good!' Sally broke in. 'She's useless. Monty only

took her on because her uncle offered to put money into the show.'

'It's true, probably,' Rose agreed. 'Early in the season we weren't doing too well. Audiences were very thin and Monty often couldn't pay us our full wage at the end of the week. We used to do a ballet sequence, an excerpt from *Les Sylphides*, and we had a Russian ballerina as the soloist – Irena Tereskova . . .'

'My God! Tereskova!' Sally cut in again. 'She was a pain in the you-know-what. Made out she used to dance with the Bolshoi. *I don't think!*'

'No, she was good,' Rose insisted. 'She was getting a bit past it, poor old thing, but she still thought she was a big star. Anyway, after a few weeks she got fed up and walked out and Prissy's uncle offered to bale Monty out again provided his little darling got the star part.'

'That's not fair!' Vera said.

'You can say that again!' Sally took up the story. 'You can imagine how the rest of us felt. Anyway, come the first performance, Miss Moneybags there only turns up with a brand-new pair of pointe shoes and goes on stage in them.'

'We should have warned her,' Rose said remorsefully.

'No we shouldn't. She should have known you don't wear any shoes for a performance until you've broken them in. So, you can imagine the rest. She comes onstage, turns one pirouette and falls flat on her face.'

'No!'

'Oh yes! The audience thought it was hilarious – so did we.'

'But poor Priscilla was absolutely mortified. She ran off-stage and swore she'd never dance again,' Rose said.

'Pity she didn't stick to it,' Sally retorted.

'What's he got to do with it?' Vera nodded towards Frank, who was holding Priscilla's hand and smiling down at her.

'Oh, Frank's always got an eye for the main chance,' Sally

said. 'She's pretty *and* rich – so he's only too pleased to act as a go-between. Just look at him sucking up to her now.'

Monty cut off any further conversation by clapping his hands. 'Right, boys and girls. We're all here so let's get started. I've roughed out a programme but it's going to be up to you to fill in the details. We'll want an ensemble number to open the show, something rousing. I want three dance numbers, and Frank and Isabel will have two spots for their duets. I'll compère and do a couple of stand-up routines and then we'll have another ensemble number for the finale. Frank, I need to discuss the ensembles with you and Vince here, who's going to be our MD. Girls, you need to put your heads together and decide what you want to do.'

'Isn't Madame going to be with us?' Rose asked, taken aback.

'Unfortunately not. She feels she has other more pressing duties to attend to. You four will have to work out your own routines. Nothing too airy-fairy. Eyes and teeth and plenty of leg. You know the sort of thing. One last point. We need a name for the company and as most of us were in the Fair-bourne Follies I thought it would be nice to keep that, but make it a bit more – what can I say? – more military. So from now on we're the Front Line Follies. Anyone have any problems with that? No? Right. Let's get to work.'

For the next three weeks Rose got home every evening exhausted but happier than she had felt for months. She and the other three girls had agreed without difficulty on the three dance numbers. They would do a tap routine, a number based on an Arabian Nights theme which would allow a good deal of provocative wiggling of bare midriffs, and the inevitable can-can. But none of them had ever had to choreo-graph a dance before. They could all suggest individual steps, or sequences of steps, but Rose found that she was the only one with the vision and the organising ability to weld them together into an artistically satisfying whole. Halfway through the rehearsal period Monty came to watch what they were doing.

'Great little number,' he exclaimed. 'Well done, girls.'

'It's all down to Rose, really,' Vera said. 'We were just floundering until she took over.'

Monty looked at Rose and nodded. 'Always knew you were more than just a pretty face. Good work, Rosy. Keep it up.'

Rose hugged the words to herself on the way home. It was not just Monty's approval. It was the fact that she had discovered a talent she had not known she possessed.

Monty had passed over a hamper full of costumes, and when they were not dancing the girls spent their time altering and refurbishing them to suit their needs. At the end of the rehearsal period Rose felt with some satisfaction that the dance numbers were as slick and polished as it was possible to make them. Even Priscilla was not the liability she had feared, though she had an infuriating habit of turning up late and wanting to leave early, to keep up with what appeared to be a very hectic social life. All that remained to be learned was where their masters in the War Office were going to send them.

'Well, this is what you've all been waiting for,' Monty said, rubbing his hands. 'Monday morning, six thirty a.m., we embark at Newhaven for Dieppe. We've got a three-week tour of army bases in Normandy.'

Rose clung to the rail and retched as another wave crashed into the side of the ferry. There was nothing left in her stomach except a bitter trickle of bile, but still she could not stop vomiting. Her hair and face were wet with spray and her eyelashes were caked with salt and the voyage seemed to have lasted for ever. She had been so excited at the prospect of

going abroad, but right now she would have welcomed a
return to the shoe shop – anywhere as long as it was on
dry land.

Eventually the ferry crept into the harbour and the terrible
bucking and rolling eased. Rose looked along the deck. The
ship had been commandeered by the War Office to transport
troops, and on both sides of her men in army uniform hung
over the rail in the same condition as herself. She straightened
up and made her way unsteadily below to try to repair the
damage to her face and hair. Sally was sitting in the saloon,
smoking and playing poker with some of the band, Vera was
stretched out across three seats, apparently asleep, and Priscilla was sitting up at the bar drinking brandy as if she were in
the cocktail bar of the Ritz. Rose waved groggily and headed
for the Ladies.

By the time they had disembarked she was feeling better.
She had never been to France before but friends who had
toured there before the war had given her a mental image of
breakfast on a balcony overlooking gardens filled with bou-
gainvillea, eating feather-light croissants and sipping coffee
out of cups the size of soup bowls. The reality was disappoint-
ing. As the army truck bumped over the roads in the direction
of their first venue all she could see in the grey morning light
were tall grey houses with peeling paintwork and faded
advertisements for products whose names she could not
pronounce. The army breakfast that awaited them, of greasy
bacon and reconstituted scrambled egg, did nothing to lift her
spirits.

Their first performance was to be staged in the *mairie*, which
had a hall with a proper stage. The audience was drawn from
the staff at headquarters and there were several senior officers
present. Rose had recovered by the time the curtain went up
and the enthusiastic reception banished the disappointment

she had felt in the morning. After the show there was a party in their honour and the four girls found themselves in great demand as dancing partners. Rose had found very few men who could dance to her satisfaction. They either steered her round the floor as if they were manoeuvring a machine of some kind or they clutched her so tightly that she felt more like their prisoner than their partner. Tonight was no exception, but she made use of the chance to talk to ask the question that had been uppermost in her mind ever since they embarked for France.

'Do you happen to know where the South Lancashire Fusiliers are?'

She got no useful information, however. The response was either a blank 'Sorry, I've no idea' or a suave 'I can't tell you that, I'm afraid. It's classified information'.

As the tour continued Rose approached each new venue with a flutter of nervous excitement, but no one seemed to have had any contact with the South Lancs and she began to think that they must be stationed in a different part of the country altogether.

After the first night in Dieppe conditions deteriorated. They performed in schools and church halls and sometimes in large marquees on improvised stages, and slept wherever they could find a bed. Sometimes camp beds were erected for them in the hall where they had been performing, sometimes in tents. Once they were put up in a hotel that Sally insisted was nothing more than a glorified brothel. Before long the constant travelling over bad roads in unsettled weather and the nightly performances began to take their toll.

One night they were due to perform to a detachment of the Royal Engineers encamped outside Le Tréport. The show was to take place in a Dutch barn, so at least they would have a roof over their heads, even though the sides were open to the weather. The engineers had rigged up a stage for them by lashing together a series of trestle tables and had set up some lights. The stage was small and not the ideal surface for dancing on.

'It's going to be very cramped,' Rose commented to the other dancers. 'Frank will have to restrain himself in the big ensemble numbers.'

An initial rehearsal proved her point. In the finale Frank and Isabel took centre stage and he had a habit of making expansive gestures with both arms.

'Watch it, Frank!' Sally exclaimed. 'You nearly took my eye out then.'

He merely smiled at her. 'Well, you'll just have to keep out of the way, won't you?'

As the time for the performance approached Rose felt flat and out of sorts, and the other three were no more cheerful. It was cold and damp inside the tent they had been given as a dressing room and she knew it would be even colder in the barn. The thought of stripping down to the skimpy costumes they had created made her shiver in anticipation. She pulled on some long woollen socks over her tights and started her warm-up exercises. Soon the noise of the audience filing in came to them, a good-natured, expectant hubbub. The men were looking forward to the show. Rose pulled herself together and smiled at the others.

'Come on, girls! Let's give them something to remember.'

As soon as the band struck up and they walked out to begin the first number her mood lifted. 'Dr Theatre' was a great healer, and she forgot the hollow feeling in her stomach. The cheer that went up when the lads in the audience saw them was enough to warm her.

The performance went without a hitch and the audience shouted and stamped and whistled their approval. By the time they reached the finale Rose was thoroughly enjoying herself. Monty and Frank had chosen the 'champagne chorus' from

The Merry Widow as a suitably upbeat finish, and while Frank and Isabel sang their hearts out in the centre of the stage the dancers whirled around them. At the conclusion, they were in two pairs, one on either side of the stage, with linked arms as they spun on the spot, high-kicking as they turned. Rose had paired herself with Priscilla, knowing that either of the other two might object. They were in the middle of this manoeuvre and Frank was making the most of his big moment, forcing them out to the extreme edge of the platform, when all the lights went out. Priscilla screamed and let go of Rose's arm, and at the same instant there was a deafening roar from an engine just above their heads and a sound like hail on the tin roof of the barn. Rose struggled for balance and felt an agonising wrench to her left leg. The next moment she was lying across the lap of an officer in the front row.

The laughter and applause had turned to shouts of alarm. The roar, which she now recognised as the sound of an aero engine, came again, and once more there was the rattling hail on the roof. Whistles were blowing and voices shouting, 'Take cover! Take cover!'

The man she had fallen on grabbed her round the waist. 'Come on, under the stage!'

She screamed as her foot touched the ground and a second wave of pain shot up her leg. He scooped her up and half crawled, half rolled with her under the stage.

'What's happening?' she gasped.

'Jerry fighter,' he replied. 'Must have been stooging around up there looking for a target and spotted the lights. Thought he'd have a pop at them and got lucky.'

They lay for a few minutes in the darkness. Rose could smell crushed grass and damp uniforms and sense the bodies of other soldiers all around her. She called out, 'Sally? Priscilla? Vera? Are you all right?'

Sally's voice answered, 'We're OK over here. You?'

'I don't know. I've hurt my leg. Where's Priscilla?'

A small, tearful voice responded. 'I'm here. I'm sorry, Rose. I'm so sorry.'

The noise had stopped by now and a voice called, 'All clear! All clear!' Torch beams were moving in the area where the audience had been sitting. Orders were shouted and the men around her began to crawl out from the shelter of the stage. Rose's saviour said, 'Come on. We'd better get you over to the MO and see what the damage is.'

He crawled out and she attempted to follow but any movement of her leg made her yelp with pain. He reached back and more or less dragged her out into the open, then picked her up in his arms and carried her out of the barn and across open ground to a large marquee marked with a red cross. Inside, he laid her on a stretcher and straightened up.

'You'll be OK now. The medics will look after you. I must get back to the men.'

Looking around her, Rose was horrified to see that there were eight or nine men already in the tent and they were all wounded. One man was clasping his arm, blood dripping between his fingers, another lay flat on his back, coughing and moaning. From behind a partition screening off the rear of the marquee a man screamed in pain.

An orderly with a Red Cross armband knelt beside her. 'What's happened to you?'

'I fell off the stage. I've hurt my leg.'

He ran his hands down her calf, making her gasp, and said, 'It looks like a nasty sprain. Maybe broken. But it's not life threatening. I'm afraid you'll have to wait until some of the urgent cases have been dealt with.'

He gave her a blanket but by the time the doctor was ready for her she was shivering violently and almost weeping from the pain in her leg. He cut away her tights and examined her ankle, asking her to move her toes and turn her foot.

At length he nodded. 'I think you've probably broken something but I'd need an X-ray to be sure. We don't have the facility here, so I'm going to strap you up temporarily and get you transferred to the hospital in Dieppe.'

'But I've got another performance tomorrow,' Rose protested.

He gave her a small, grim smile. 'Not on that ankle you haven't.'

Two days later Rose was back in London, in the Charing Cross Hospital. When the orthopaedic consultant came on his rounds she asked, 'Excuse me. How long will I be here, please?'

Matron, who was accompanying him, tutted audibly and the consultant frowned as if he were not sure how to address such a lowly being as a patient. 'Several weeks, I expect. And then you will require a long period of convalescence and intensive physiotherapy. But at the end of that time you should be able to walk quite normally.'

'And dance?' Rose asked. 'How long before I can dance again?'

His look of puzzlement deepened and Matron broke in, 'Now then, Mr Sanders hasn't got time to stand chatting to you. There are other patients, you know.'

'But I need to know!' Rose insisted.

'Dance?' the surgeon repeated. 'You mean ballroom dancing?'

'No. Ballet, tap, that sort of dancing. I'm a professional.'

He looked at her in silence for a moment and she had the impression that for the first time he was seeing her as an individual. Then he said abruptly, 'I'm afraid that's out of the question. You've torn several ligaments and cracked one of your metatarsals. The ankle will never be strong enough to support that sort of activity.'

With that, he turned away and headed for his next patient.

Rose turned her face into the pillow and clenched her teeth. She refused to let the other women in the ward see her crying. In the hours that followed she found herself repeating the surgeon's words over and over again in her head. She tried to envisage some form of alternative future but she could not get beyond that one sentence. It was like a blank wall on which she battered until her fists bled.

When her mother arrived at visiting time Rose repeated what the doctor had said, her voice cracking with the effort of self-control. Mrs Taylor took her hand.

'Oh, Rose! Oh, luv, I am sorry.' Then her face cleared. 'Well, there's one mercy. It's just as well there's always a job for you in the shop, isn't it.'

Rose closed her eyes and swallowed hard. She was used to her mother's knack of drawing something positive out of the most disastrous events and recognised it as a mechanism for dealing with the many tragedies of her life. But at this moment it seemed very cruel.

A possible escape route occurred to her. 'But what about Joan Johnson? I thought she was helping out.'

Her mother smiled. 'You needn't worry about that. Joan will understand that family comes first. Anyway, I don't think she'll be sorry. She said the other day she didn't like dealing with people's smelly feet. Found she could get more money behind the counter at Woolworths, more likely. So, it all works out. We'll all be together after all. I've told you before, everything happens for a good reason.'

Rose turned her head away. She could feel the prison bars closing in around her again.

Her mother went on, 'Did he say how long you'd be in here?'

'Several weeks. And then he said I ought to have physio-therapy.'

'Physiotherapy? I don't know how we'd afford that. I've got a bit put by, and of course there's Merry's rent, as long as he stays with us, but after that I don't know . . . The shop's not been doing well lately . . .'

Her face was puckered with anxiety. Rose said, 'If the shop's not doing well, you don't need an assistant, whether it's me or someone else.'

'Oh, bless you, there will always be a job for you. I didn't mean it like that. We'll manage.'

Rose felt the tears she had been suppressing all day welling up in her eyes and spilling on to her cheeks. She threw herself into her mother's arms. 'Oh, Mum, I feel so useless! I've let Monty down and now I'm going to be a burden on you. I don't know what to do.'

'Don't be so silly!' her mother chided her. 'You haven't let anyone down. You couldn't help the accident. And you don't need to worry about being a burden to me. You're my little girl. You could never be a burden. We'll work things out, you'll see. It will all come right in the end.'

When her mother had left Rose hid her face in her pillows and let the tears flow at last. She had cried herself to exhaustion and was drifting into a doze when she became aware of a ripple of surprise and curiosity running down the ward. A tall man, very smartly dressed, was walking towards her carrying a huge bouquet of flowers. It was a moment before she recognised him as Sir Lionel Vance, Priscilla's guardian. She rubbed her face hastily on the pillowslip and sat up.

He stopped at the foot of the bed and laid down the bouquet. 'I do hope you will forgive me for coming out of visiting hours. I was held up at a meeting but I persuaded Sister to let me in. How are you feeling?'

'Not too bad,' Rose replied warily.

'I had a telephone call from Priscilla this morning. She's very upset about your accident and seems to feel she may have been responsible for it in some way. She asked me to come and see you and give you her most profound apologies.'

'It wasn't her fault. All the lights went out and it was chaos.'

'It's kind of you to say so. How bad is the damage?'

Rose was tempted to tell him that it had ruined her career but she could not bear the idea that he might feel he had to make himself responsible for her in some way. She did not want to be beholden to him, or to Priscilla. Instead she said, 'It'll heal, given time.'

'I'm delighted to hear it. Now, if there is anything I can do, anything at all, please ask.' He looked round the ward. 'Wouldn't you be more comfortable in a private room? At my expense, of course.'

'I'm quite happy where I am, thank you. I like the company,' Rose said primly. Then, remembering her manners, she asked, 'Is Priscilla all right?'

'Yes, I'm happy to say. A few bruises, apparently, but nothing serious.'

Rose thought bitterly that Priscilla should have been where she was. She could have afforded the private room and all the little luxuries – and she did not have a career to speak of that could be ruined. Aloud she said, 'And the other girls?'

'They're all fine, according to what Prissy tells me.'

'Oh, that's good.'

There was a silence. Sir Lionel fidgeted and looked at his watch. 'I shall have to go. I'm meeting dear Ninette de Valois for tea. Priscilla has talked me into becoming a patron of her Sadler's Wells Ballet. So, just remember, if there is anything you need, I'm only too happy to help.' He took a card from his card case. 'Here's my number. Please don't hesitate to call.'

When he had gone the woman in the next bed leaned over to Rose with a confidential leer. 'Them flowers must have cost a pretty penny. You want to hang on to him, ducks. Loaded *and* nice looking with it!'

At evening visiting time Merry arrived, bringing a box of chocolates from the NAAFI. He sat by her bed and put his hand over hers. 'Your mother told me what the doctor said. I'm so sorry, Rose. It's a rotten thing to have happened.' Sympathy was the last thing Rose felt able to cope with at that moment and she felt her eyes beginning to fill up again. Merry went on, 'She told me about the physiotherapy you need and I know she was worried about the cost, so I made some enquiries. You belong to the Variety Artiste's Association, don't you? There's a Variety Artiste's convalescent home in Eastbourne, with a resident physiotherapist, where you can go when you're discharged.'

Rose sensed the first faint crack of light in the wall confronting her. 'I never thought of that. Thanks so much, Merry. You're a real pal.'

He smiled at her. 'As for this business of never dancing again – don't take the medic's word for it. They don't know as much as they'd like you to believe. We'll soon have you back on your feet. You're a fighter, Rose. You won't let this beat you.'

Chapter Four

Merry reported for duty at Colonel Brown's office determined not to expect too much. Experience had taught him that life did not always deliver what it seemed to promise. He was grateful for being freed from the tedium of routine army life but quite prepared to discover that he had only exchanged one form of servitude for another. On the other hand, the ideas Brown had outlined at that first meeting had fired his imagination and he could not quench a small flame of excitement as he made his way along the corridor.

He had spent two weeks being cosseted and mothered by Mrs Taylor – an unfamiliar experience for him. As a result he was feeling better than he had done for some months. To begin with, he had been content to spend most of his time sitting by the fire, reading and dozing. The weather was still bitterly cold, but with the beginning of March came occasional days when the sun shone and there was a hint of spring in the air. On those days he had gone walking, down to Kennington Park or up past the Oval cricket ground to Vauxhall and the river. It was not a beautiful part of London, but he found he warmed to the cheerful, friendly character of the locals and began to feel quite at home. But when Rose started coming home in the evenings, full of enthusiasm about the new show, he grew restless. He realised that it was months since he had touched a piano and that he was badly out of practice. The thought that Brown might ask him to play, by way of an audition, brought him out in a cold sweat.

When he mentioned these worries to Mrs Taylor she went straight across the road to the Queen's Arms pub and returned with the message that he was welcome to use the piano in the saloon bar whenever the pub was closed.

To Merry's surprise the old upright turned out to be quite a good instrument and it was even more or less in tune. He spent the first hour playing scales and arpeggios, trying to work the stiffness out of his fingers. Then, as a treat, he allowed himself to embark on Beethoven's Moonlight Sonata. He had no need of music. Every note was engraved on his memory. For nearly ten years, he had earned his living as an accompanist and, latterly, a conductor in the world of musical theatre, playing mostly popular songs or items from operetta. But his first love had always been the classics and he had once cherished ambitions as a soloist. His mother's early death and his father's total lack of sympathy with such aspirations had meant that he had left home at the first possible opportunity and had been forced to earn a living where he could.

At the end of the first movement he heard a sound behind him and turned to discover that the publican and his wife had crept into the room.

'I'm sorry,' he said. 'Did you want to get on in here?'

'Oh, no!' his hostess replied. 'Don't stop. We just came in to listen.'

'I'll say this for you,' her husband put in. 'You can certainly tinkle them ivories! Do you play anything else – popular stuff, like?'

Merry smiled to himself and responded with a lively rendition of 'The Lambeth Walk'.

'Right!' said the publican. 'If you fancy popping in one evening during opening hours and playing for a sing-song you'll be more than welcome – and there's all the beer you can drink, on the house.'

So he had become a regular at the Queen's Arms. He liked

the atmosphere of genuine good nature after the forced bonhomie of the mess, and it was all good practice. But now his leave was up and it was time to find out what Colonel Brown had in store for him.

The notice on the door said CENTRAL POOL OF ARTISTES. Brown greeted him with a warm handshake. 'How are you feeling?'

'A lot better, thanks.' Merry cocked an eyebrow quizzically towards the door. 'Is that what they're calling us?'

'Not very snappy, is it,' Brown said. 'I've been trying to think of something better. Any ideas?'

'Not at the moment,' Merry admitted.

The colonel ordered coffee for both of them and seated himself behind his desk. 'Now, have you looked through that list of names? See anybody you fancy working with?'

After some consultation Merry selected a small group of performers, musicians, singers and a comedian, to make up his concert party. 'What about some dancers?' he suggested. 'I'm sure the sight of a few girls would cheer the men up.'

Brown shook his head. 'Sorry, no can do. The High Command won't hear of girls being sent to the sort of areas we're aiming at.'

Merry was allotted an office and the services of a typist, and by the end of the first day he was aware that he was as happy as he was likely to be for the duration of the war. Rehearsal space had been found for them at the army base in Greenford, and over the next week the men arrived in ones and twos, puzzled, confused and sometimes downright suspicious, but invariably delighted, when the scheme was explained to them, at the opportunity to employ their particular talents instead of being faceless cogs in the army machine. One or two were newcomers just starting their careers, but several of them were already well-known names, with a large following of fans.

It soon became clear that one thing they all had in common was a healthy disrespect for the rules and regulations of army life. Since they were still serving soldiers, however, and none of them had aspired to a rank higher than corporal, they were required to go through the correct motions, which included morning parades. On the day that they were all due to report for duty Merry arrived in good time, spruce and correct in his officer's uniform, determined to set a good example. Since there was no accommodation available on the base all his new recruits were 'living out', some in hotels or boarding houses, the lucky ones in their own homes. First to arrive was Dave Shadwell, who in civilian life was the saxophonist in the band at a very smart nightclub. A slightly overweight figure, he had obviously succeeded in evading the attentions of the army barber and his thick dark hair curled luxuriously over his battledress collar. Next to appear was a crooner who was already a national heart-throb. He was tall and willowy in build and clad in battledress so immaculately fitted that it must have been tailor made. A neatly rolled umbrella and suede shoes completed the ensemble.

Merry watched with incredulous amusement as the others wandered across the parade ground and formed up in an approximation of a straight line. Willy Banks, the comic, had a long hand-knitted scarf wrapped round his neck, another man wore a silk scarf tucked into his collar, a third had what looked like gym shoes on his feet. By the deadline for roll-call all were present except one and Merry was beginning to think with a sinking heart that his first action was going to be to report someone for being absent without leave. Just then a large car drew up at the end of the parade ground and a dapper figure, whom many of London's 'bright young things' would have recognised as the trumpet player in a popular jazz club, climbed out and strolled over to join the others.

Merry looked along the line, gripped by indecision. Should

he 'bawl them out' and demand proper attention to uniform regulations? Perhaps they were testing him, waiting for him to exert his authority. But instinct told him that if he began like that he would never be able to establish the kind of working relationship that he required. After a brief hesitation he grinned at them.

'Good morning, gentlemen. Shall we get to work?'

He saw looks exchanged along the line and there was a visible relaxation. He was over the first hurdle.

As rehearsals proceeded a new relationship developed, based on mutual respect for fellow professionals. Individualists they might be, but they were all imbued with the discipline of the theatre, which was based on the simple premise that the show came first. Just the same, there was a good deal of laughter and some of the company delighted in practical jokes. Even if he had wished to, it would have been impossible for Merry to preserve any distance between himself as an officer and the others. Indeed, for long stretches of time he forgot that there was supposed to be a difference.

The group shared the base with other, more conventional units, which led to occasional problems. One morning, on his way across the parade ground to the Nissen hut where they rehearsed, Merry fell in with one of the officers. He seemed a pleasant enough character and was very interested in what was going on but, as they were talking, they were overtaken by Dave Shadwell. The day before, the band had substituted for Merry's baton one of those trick wands that will only stand up straight if it is held in a certain way.

Dave glanced round as he passed and drawled, 'Morning, Merry. Still having trouble keeping it up?'

The officer beside Merry froze. 'You there! Halt!' he barked.

The saxophonist stopped and turned enquiringly towards them.

'How dare you address an officer like that?' Merry's companion demanded. 'And look at you! Stand to attention when you're spoken to. And get your hair cut! What's your number?'

The saxophonist swivelled his eyes in Merry's direction and raised his eyebrows suggestively, then returned his attention to the other officer. 'You don't waste much time, do you? Knightsbridge 374. Do give me a call if you're free, but I should warn you I'm not at home much these days.'

It took the combined efforts of Merry and Colonel Brown to prevent their musician being put on a charge.

'How are you getting on?' Brown asked when Merry reported to him at the end of the first week. 'Finding the men all right, are you?'

Merry paused for thought. 'Put it this way,' he said. 'I've just spent six months being treated as an officer but not quite a gentleman. Now I'm being treated as a gentleman but not quite an officer, and on the whole I find I much prefer the latter.'

Brown gave a guffaw of laughter and slapped him on the shoulder. 'You'll do!' he said. 'You'll do!'

Merry's contentment with his new existence was shattered by the news of Rose's accident. He had always kept a little distance between himself and the girls in the Follies chorus, as a precaution against any misunderstandings, but he sensed a sympathy in Rose that was unusual in his experience and he was genuinely fond of her. Her distress at the doctor's prognosis upset him. He could imagine how he would feel if he were to be told that he would never play the piano again. He visited her every evening and amused her with descriptions of his new cast and their jokes, but he could sense that even in her laughter there was pain at the thought that she was now excluded from that world for good.

When the time came for her to be discharged he managed to borrow a staff car through Colonel Brown and drove her down to Eastbourne to the convalescent home.

'Will you still be around when I come home?' she asked as he prepared to leave.

Merry lifted his shoulders. 'I can't say. I've no idea where we might be sent once the show's ready. But I'll try to get down for a visit before then.'

Rose balanced herself on her crutch and reached up to kiss him on the cheek. 'Thanks for everything, Merry. You're a good friend. Take care.'

After three weeks' rehearsal Merry and his cast were informed that their show was to be vetted by some high-ranking officers before being deemed suitable for performance to the rank and file. The morning after this rather nerve-racking 'first night' Merry received a summons to Colonel Brown's office. Brown greeted him with an expansive smile.

'Well done, Merry! Thoroughly professional show. You did us all credit.'

'Not me, especially,' Merry demurred. 'I only stand in front waving a stick.'

'Nonsense,' Brown exclaimed. 'I've been in and out of rehearsals and I've seen how much you've done to pull it all together. It's not easy to get a lot of highly talented individuals who have been used to being stars in their own right to work together, but you've shown just the right measure of tact and firmness. Good show!'

Merry murmured his thanks and the captain went on, 'So, now you're ready for your first tour. You'll be going to France, probably very soon. I'm working out the details now. One important thing. I've agreed with the powers that be that all the cast should be made up to the rank of sergeant, so that they can use the non-coms' mess.'

'Oh, that's good,' Merry exclaimed. 'I don't feel comfortable outranking them all. At least this lessens the discrepancy.'

'Well, that's the point I'm coming to,' Brown said with a smile. 'I don't want you feeling you've been passed over, after all the work you've put in, so I'm getting you made up to full lieutenant.'

'Oh!' Merry was at a loss for words for a moment. Then he said, 'I'm not really officer material, you know. I only got my commission because my father was a regular officer in the regiment until he retired.'

Brown's smile broadened. 'You underrate yourself, my friend. You may not be exactly what the regular army is used to, but you have powers of leadership nonetheless. Anyway, you're going to be in charge of this forthcoming tour, so you'll have every chance to prove yourself. Now, let's get down . . .'

There was a tap on the door and the nice-looking corporal put his head in.

'Excuse me, sir, but there's a telegram for Lieutenant Merryweather. I thought I'd better bring it in, in case it was something urgent.'

Merry took the telegram with a sense of foreboding. His first, crazy thought was that something had happened to Felix, rapidly followed by the recognition that if anything had happened no one would have any reason to let him know about it. He slit the envelope and read quickly, then looked up at Brown.

'I'm sorry, sir. They want me to go down to Seaford. My father's been taken ill. It seems to be serious.'

Rose had been grateful for the offer of a place at the convalescent home but within two days she was bored. Most of the other residents were considerably older than she was and since they were all artistes of one kind or another their conversation consisted almost entirely of reminiscences about their days 'on the halls'. At any other time she would have been fascinated by these anecdotes, but now the last thing she wanted was to be reminded of life in the theatre – the life she had loved and lost. And she rapidly tired of listening to the repeated accounts of old jealousies and internecine feuds that seemed to obsess most of her companions.

Her salvation was the library, which had a good stock of novels. She had always loved reading. In fact, her friends had often teased her about always having her head in a book. Her favourite stories were romances, but now she found that these, too, evoked too many unhappy thoughts. She had had her chance at romance and lost it, through her own lack of courage. If only, she thought, she had followed her heart instead of her head things might have been different. Richard wrote a long, tender letter expressing his sympathy and wishing her a rapid recovery, but words on paper were no good to her in her present mood. She wanted to feel his arms around her and be assured that their love was real and tangible, not just a fantasy to which they both clung because they were lonely. The longer they were apart, the more convinced she became that they were both attempting to blow life into a flame that had sunk to faintly glowing embers. She put the romantic novel back on the shelf and turned to Agatha Christie.

Her mother and Bet came to visit on the Sunday, with the two little boys, and she tried her best to put on a cheerful face for their sakes. When the boys were outside exploring the garden she asked, 'How are they now, Bet? Have they got over that awful business with Mrs Marshall?'

Bet sighed and shook her head. 'Not really. Sam still wets the bed and Billy's turning into a right little tearaway. I found out last week he's been bunking off school. I gave him a good telling-off, of course, but I don't think he takes much notice of me any more. If only Reg was at home, it'd be different. He'd soon teach him a lesson.'

'With his belt, I suppose,' Rose said. She tried to conceal it, but she had never really liked her brother-in-law. She thought him vain and pigheaded, too cocky by half, and not nearly good enough for Bet. 'Is that the right way, do you think?'

'I dunno,' Bet said. 'But he needs taking in hand somehow. Boys need a father, Rose.'

'How is Reg?' Rose asked. 'Have you heard from him lately?'

'Oh, he's fine. To be honest with you, I think he's having the time of his life. The army seems to suit him. He's coming home next week – embarkation leave.'

'So he's going to France?'

'Looks like it. He says he's looking forward to it.'

Rose's mood improved slightly when the plaster was taken off her leg and she was able to start physiotherapy. The therapist was a brisk woman who obviously did not intend wasting her sympathy on minor injuries. When Rose explained, tearfully, what the doctor had told her, her response was curt.

'Well, if that's what you choose to believe there's no point in me giving you exercises, because you won't do them.'

'Do you mean he might be wrong?' Rose asked. 'That I might be able to dance again one day?'

'I'm not making any promises. I'm just saying that if you want it badly enough you'll do anything to make it happen. I can give you the exercises. The rest is up to you. There is such a thing as mind over matter, you know.'

Rose promised faithfully to do whatever exercises she was given and she kept the promise. To begin with it was a painful process and she often felt that she was getting nowhere, but she persisted and day by day she began to detect that her muscles were growing stronger. After that, she spent so much time on the exercises that the physiotherapist had to warn her against overdoing things.

Towards the end of her third week at the convalescent home she had a pleasant surprise in the shape of a visit from Monty Prince.

'You're back from France!' she exclaimed. 'So the tour's over?'

'Finished at the end of last week,' he said. 'And I can't say I'm sorry.'

'So what next?'

'We've got a few days' rest, then we're off up north to tour the factories making armaments.'

'You look tired,' Rose commented.

He nodded. 'I expect the girls have told you it's all good fun, and it is in a way. The audiences have been marvellous. But it's been hard work, moving on all the time, never knowing quite what you're going to find when you arrive. And after what happened to you there's always the thought that there might be another enemy plane up there. It's a big responsibility.'

'Of course it is,' Rose agreed. She paused, then asked, 'Did you manage to find someone to replace me?'

He looked uncomfortable. 'Yes. Did you ever work with a girl called Kathy Blake? She's a nice little mover – not as good as you, but good enough. She's fitted in very nicely.'

Rose knew it was ridiculous to feel jealousy but she could not suppress the notion that this girl had somehow usurped her position. There was no shortage of talented dancers and it was a fact of life that if you fell out there was always someone to take your place. She ought to be used to that by now. Just the same, it hurt to feel that she was hardly being missed.

She was looking forward to Merry's promised visit and was disappointed when, on her next visit, her mother told her that he had been called away to Seaford to see his sick father.

When her mother came down the following Sunday she asked, 'How's Merry?'

'Your guess is as good as mine,' her mother replied. 'All I can tell you is, night before last – it was late, gone eleven, I was in bed – I heard him come in. First time he's been back since he went down to Seaford. Next morning, about half past six, I heard him up and about again. Before I could get dressed I heard him go downstairs and the front door slammed. When I got to the kitchen I found this on the table.'

She held out a sheet of notepaper, on which was written:

Leaving for France today. All news when I get back – whenever that might be! Take care.
Love,
Merry

'I hope he'll be all right,' Rose said.

''Course he will,' her mother responded. 'Nothing's happening over there.'

'Something happened to me,' Rose pointed out.

'But that was just bad luck. There's no reason why it should happen to Merry.'

'But suppose the war starts in earnest?'

'If you ask me, the Germans have got cold feet. They're sitting there, looking at that French Maggot line or whatever it's called, and wondering how they can get out of fighting without looking like cowards. I don't mind betting it'll all be over in a couple of months.'

Chapter Five

W edged into the corner of the tiny café with its zinc-topped tables and air thick with the smoke of Gauloise cigarettes, Richard Stevens was trying to concentrate on writing a letter. Around him, packed in so tightly that they could scarcely lift their glasses, were the rest of his platoon, and underlying the smell of tobacco was the odour of sweat and of battledress uniforms that had been soaked, from without and from within, dried and soaked again too many times. Richard took a mouthful of the rough, ink-flavoured *vin ordinaire* in his glass and returned his attention to the letter.

May 10th 1940

Dear Merry,

Well, summer is icumen in, as they say, and the word along the trenches is 'When is this bleeding war going to start?' Or better still, 'Why don't we all just pack up and go home?' At least it's warm now, so conditions are not quite so grim as they were.

He paused and scratched the back of his neck, shorn and prickly from the attentions of the army barber. It was hard to find things to write about. He had already described the monotony of army routine, the terrible food, the flat, uninspiring countryside and the poverty of the nearby villages. He had recounted the occasional flare-up of hostility between the 'Tommies', who even on the scale of basic army pay had money for cigarettes and drink, and the locals, who by and large had not. There was really very little else to talk about. He succeeded eventually in finding one or two anecdotes to fill out the letter and added:

> I'm so glad you are staying with the Taylors. I'm sure Mrs T must be glad of your company, under the circumstances. I feel so sorry for Rose. Why do these things always happen to the best, sweetest and most talented people? Please give her my love, if you manage to visit her in the convalescent home.
>
> Write when you get the chance. I hope the asthma is not giving you too much trouble.
>
> Yours,
>
> Richard

He put down his pen and looked around the table, allowing the din of voices to penetrate his consciousness again. These were the accents he had grown up with, the speech of the lads he had played with as a child and the men he had briefly worked among as an apprentice before he went to Italy, the accent that had been rigorously drilled out of him by his ambitious mother. The men of his platoon had taken the mickey out of him to begin with, but the long winter months of working and drinking together had brought a tolerant acceptance that had left him with the nickname of 'Prof', because of his education, or sometimes 'Caruso', because he was occasionally heard singing snatches of Italian opera. It was useless to point out that Caruso was a tenor and he was a baritone. As far as they were concerned it was all the same.

He had just addressed the envelope when the table was shaken by a violent tremor and there was a distant detonation, felt rather than heard. A sudden silence fell over the crowded café. Then young Charlie Watts, sitting next to Richard, said, 'Blimey! What was that?'

As if in answer there came another thud, and again the glasses on the table rattled.

'Thunder?' queried someone.

Bob, one of the few regulars in the platoon, lifted his head like a dog scenting the air. 'Nay, lad. That's not thunder,' he declared. 'That's gunfire. If you ask me the balloon's gone up.'

In confirmation there were two more distant crumps.

Richard hastily folded his letter and shoved it into his breast pocket. 'I think we'd better get back to base.'

As they rose, fumbling for coins to pay for their drinks, there was a rattling roar, like an express train passing overhead, followed by a closer and much louder explosion.

'Streuth!' squeaked Charlie. 'What the 'ell was that?'

''S all right,' Bob reassured him. 'That'll be our fellows firing back.'

Behind the counter Madame was crossing herself repeatedly and exclaiming '*Mon Dieu! Mon Dieu!*'

Richard put his money on the bar and summoned his best French. '*N'ayez pas peur, madame. Les Boches n'arriveront pas ici. Nous sommes ici pour vous protéger.*'

She gathered up his money with one hand while continuing to bless herself with the other. Her lips moved but he could not make out what she was saying.

Outside, the sky was laced with searchlight beams and the far horizon was lit with momentary flashes. As they made their way at the double up the rutted lane towards the dark bulk of the old factory where they were billeted, Charlie panted, 'D'you think this is really it, Prof?'

'Looks like it,' Richard replied.

The courtyard of the building was crowded with running figures carrying kitbags or items of equipment and loud with the revving of lorry engines. When they reported to their corporal he said, 'Get your kit together. We're moving out.'

'Moving out?' Charlie exclaimed. 'Where to?'

'Timbuktu, for all I know. Shift yourself!' was the succinct reply.

'But why?' Bob wanted to know. 'We've spent all bleeding winter digging trenches here. What's the point of leaving them now?'

'You want to go and discuss it with the colonel?' the corporal enquired. 'Just do as you're friggin' told, will you?'

By dawn they were in the back of a lorry, bumping and swaying over the potholes as part of a long convoy of vehicles.

'Where d'you reckon we're headed?' Charlie asked. He was the boy who had played Aladdin in the pantomime. It had been his first experience of the theatre and had turned him from the butt of everyone's jokes into a kind of regimental mascot. He had not forgotten who was responsible for this transformation and had since attached himself to Richard with a dog-like devotion.

Richard, seated nearest the tailboard, peered out at the brightening sky. 'We're headed roughly north-east.' He frowned, trying to visualise the map of Europe. 'I guess that means Belgium.'

'I thought Belgium was neutral,' Charlie said.

'I doubt whether that would matter much to Hitler,' Richard replied.

The lorry swayed to a halt and he hauled himself up on to the tailboard and looked over the roof. The head of the convoy had arrived at a red-and-white striped barrier beside which was a small white building. Richard could see an officer engaged in some kind of altercation with a bemused-looking official. He leaned down into the lorry, laughing incredulously.

'It's Belgium all right. We've just arrived at the border and there's some kind of argument going on. I reckon the customs officer wants to check all our passports!'

The ensuing comments were interrupted by the sound of a shot.

'Bloody 'ell. He's blown 'is bloody 'ead off!' somebody said.

Richard pulled himself up again in time to see the officer replacing his revolver in its holster while the border guard scrambled to raise the barrier. A couple of minutes later they were on the move again.

Richard gazed out at the flat, marshy fields with their intersecting canals. Flanders! *In Flanders fields the poppies blow/Beside the crosses, row on row.* The lines came unbidden into his mind and he tried to shut them out again. His father had fought in the last war and, though he rarely spoke of his experiences, what he had said was enough to fill Richard with an abiding horror of trench warfare. Around him the other men were napping, but every time he allowed his eyes to close he found his mind besieged by such recollections. His mouth was dry and there was a nauseous feeling at the pit of his stomach which he tried to tell himself was the result of too much alcohol and a night without sleep.

Eventually he fell into a fitful doze, from which he was roused by the noise of shouting. The others started into consciousness with curses and exclamations of alarm and Richard, leaning out of the back of the lorry, realised that they were passing through a town and that the streets were lined with cheering people. Bob stumbled to the opening, hanging on to the overhead struts that supported the canvas awning, and looked out too.

'Well!' he exclaimed. 'By 'eck, it's good to know someone's pleased to see us!'

Several others scrambled to the back as well, shoving each other aside in order to wave to the crowd, which consisted mainly of women and children. The lorry slowed and a girl ran forward and thrust a bunch of purple lilac into Richard's hand, provoking mocking cries of 'Hey up, Caruso! You're on to a good thing there'. Then a large woman pushed through the throng and held up a bundle wrapped in a white cloth to Bob.

'Here, Tommy,' she called. 'For your *petit déjeuner*.'

'For my what?' Bob asked.

'Breakfast,' Richard said. 'What has she given you?'

Bob unwrapped the napkin. Inside were a dozen rolls, warm from the oven. They shared them round and realised for the first time that they were hungry.

By noon that day they were in position beside a narrow canal as part of the British force deployed along the course of the River Dyle. A few miles ahead of them was the front line, where the Belgian army was endeavouring to stem the advance of the German tanks. In the event of a breakthrough, their job was to hold a bridge over the canal. They dug themselves in, patrolled the canal bank, and waited.

As darkness fell, someone farther along the trench began to play a harmonica – a haunting tune stolen, or borrowed, from the Maoris of New Zealand – and a voice called, 'Give us a song, Caruso!' It was a familiar request and the song was one which Richard knew well and had sung often. He straightened up, leaned his rifle against the side of the trench and began, half-consciously transposing 'I' for 'you' to fit the mood of the moment:

> *Now is the hour that we must say goodbye*
> *Soon I'll be sailing far across the sea.*

From around him other voices joined in softly:

> *While I'm away, oh please remember me!*
> *When I return, I'll find you waiting here.*

The following morning, over mugs of tea, Bob said suddenly, 'Do you know what day it is?'

Richard thought briefly. 'Twelfth of May.'

'Apart from that.'

'Sunday?'

'*Whit* Sunday, that's what. It's a bloody bank holiday weekend.'

'Good Lord!' Richard murmured. Somehow it seemed impossible that in another world, away from the war, people still had bank holidays.

Bob blew on his tea nostalgically. 'This time last year me and the missus took the kids to Morecambe. Wonder what they're doing today.'

Richard thought back. Last Whit Sunday he had been rehearsing a new number with Merry in the empty darkness of the pier-head theatre. Afterwards the whole company had gone for lunch at a country pub up on the downs. He could picture it now, bright and unreal like an illustration in a child's picture book.

Wally Miller, known to everyone, inevitably, as Dusty, pushed his way along the trench.

'Here, have you heard the latest?'

'The Boches have surrendered and we're all going home?'

'No such luck! But maybe we'll get back a bit sooner than we thought. They've made Winnie prime minister.'

'Churchill?' Bob looked up with the first spark of optimism he had shown since the start of hostilities. 'By 'eck, that's good news! Mebbe we'll get some action now.'

All day they listened to the guns pounding the Belgian lines, while flight after flight of heavy German bombers droned overhead. By evening the horizon behind them was aglow and still the planes came over.

'Where's the bloody RAF?' Bob demanded, over and over again. 'We're letting the buggers have it all their own way.'

Richard noticed the young lieutenant who commanded their company studying a map by the light of a hurricane lamp. He moved closer and the officer looked up and smiled. They were much the same age and over the months there had been these occasional moments of recognition, of tacit acknowledgement that they were closer in background and education and had more in common with each other than with men of their own rank. When he had first joined up it had been suggested to Richard more than once that he might apply for a commission, but he had always refused, giving as his reason the fact that he could never bring himself to order men into a battle in which some of them, perhaps many of them, might lose their lives. But when he examined his conscience he knew that it had more to do with what his father had told him of the life expectancy of young subalterns during the carnage of the Great War. Since then he had had to live with the lurking suspicion of cowardice.

'Who do you reckon is getting that lot, sir?' he asked, nodding towards the reddened horizon.

'Probably Louvain,' the lieutenant returned. 'Poor devils!'

'Civilians?' Richard exclaimed.

The officer nodded. 'Looks like it.'

'The bastards!' Richard muttered.

Later that night he and his platoon were on duty, patrolling the canal banks. The bombers were no longer flying and even the guns had fallen quiet, and somewhere in a thicket on the far side of the canal a nightingale was singing. It was a warm, sweet-smelling early summer night, with an almost full moon dodging in and out of high, fast-moving clouds. As the watch drew to an end they found themselves at the top of a short slope leading down from the road to the canal. At the bottom, by the canal bank, was a low wall. The corporal looked at his watch.

'Ten minutes, lads. Time for a quick fag.'

They wandered down to the water's edge and sat down, some of them on the wall, others, Richard included, on the far side of it with their feet over the canal bank and the wall at their backs. Cigarettes were lit and there were murmurs of conversation, but then they all fell quiet. It was a night for silence and contemplation. Richard sat between Bob and Charlie. Somehow the three of them always gravitated together.

Richard appreciated the dour common sense of the older man, and where Richard went Charlie followed. Suddenly Bob hissed, 'Hey up! Listen!'

The others heard it too – the sound of feet coming along the road above them, not marching but the uneven tread of men who no longer cared how they appeared to others. Richard raised himself above the wall and peered over. Beside him Bob readied the Sten gun. The corporal hissed, '*Quiet!*'

The moon had gone behind a cloud but enough light remained for Richard to see the shadowy figures of men, perhaps thirty of them, advancing along the road. He could make out the outlines of helmets and rifle barrels against the sky but could get no hint of colours or insignia. The men were parallel with them now. In a minute they would have passed.

At that moment the clouds cleared away and Richard heard a muffled exclamation and then a cry of alarm. A shot rang out and a bullet ricocheted off the wall a yard or so to his right. Then all the men on the road swung round to face them, unslinging their rifles as they did so, and fired a ragged volley in the direction of the canal. Someone screamed and fell backwards off the wall and at the same moment Bob opened up with the Sten gun beside his right ear. Richard grabbed his rifle and took aim. There was no time to reflect that these dark figures were real people, not the painted targets he had trained with. He fired three or four rounds and then, above the bedlam, he heard a voice screaming, '*Ah, mon Dieu! Mon Dieu!*'

He grabbed Bob's arm and yelled in his ear, 'Cease fire! Cease fire!' Then he scrambled along behind the wall to where the corporal lay. 'They're not Germans!' he yelled. 'Stop firing!'

The corporal stared at him for a minute, then pulled out his whistle and blew it. Up on the bank another whistle blew, followed by a few ragged shots and then silence. Richard hauled himself to his feet and shouted, '*Ne tirez pas! Nous sommes anglais.*'

A pause, then a voice harsh and cracked with exhaustion. '*Anglais?*'

'*Oui. Vous êtes français?*'

'*Non. Belges.*'

Richard turned back to the others. 'Oh Christ! They're bloody Belgians!'

The corporal got to his feet. 'Come on. You parlay the lingo. Come and help me sort this out.'

The Belgians, it transpired, were retreating. The line was broken. No one, they said, *no one*, could withstand the German tanks. Exhausted, thinking themselves safely back in friendly territory, they had been marching half asleep. Then one of them had caught the glint of moonlight on steel helmets. It had been easy to assume that they had walked into a German ambush.

When the casualties were counted seventeen of the Belgians lay dead along with two Englishmen. Back at base Richard clasped shaking hands around a mug of tea and muttered, 'What a shambles! The first shots we've fired in the whole war and we end up shooting our own side.'

'Well,' Charlie said, 'they fired first.'

'Any road up,' commented Dusty Miller, with evident satisfaction, 'we got the best of it. Reckon we showed them how it's done.'

There was a general murmur of agreement and Charlie added, 'Serves 'em right for running away. I reckon they're deserters.'

Richard gazed from one face to the other. None of them reflected the despair in his own heart.

The next day it became obvious that the group they had encountered were not an isolated band of deserters. The

Belgian army had collapsed and was in full retreat. All day they watched as bands of dispirited men, some of them almost too exhausted to walk, trudged through their lines, equally oblivious to catcalls and to shouts of encouragement. The Germans, they declared, could not be more than a few hours behind them.

In the early hours of the next day they were shaken by a series of explosions close at hand. Word spread quickly. British sappers had blown up the bridges over the Dyle to delay the German advance. As the light grew they crouched in their trench, watching the countryside on the far side of the canal. To their right was a low hill, on which cattle were grazing. Beyond it they could see a short section of road. It was deserted. Then, after an interminable wait, Richard noticed movement. He touched Bob on the arm.

'Look at the cows.'

On the far hill all the cattle were moving in one direction, away from the road. Then they heard a low, throbbing rumble that seemed to vibrate deep in their own chests. A moment later the first tank appeared beyond the flank of the hill. It was followed by another and another, until the whole stretch of road that was visible from their position was filled with them, and as the leaders disappeared behind the first houses of a village others took their place at the rear of the line. Richard started to count them, but gave up when he reached twenty. Somewhere down the line artillery opened up and there was a cheer along the trench as one tank exploded in a gout of flame and oily smoke. Another swerved off the road and came to a standstill with its gun turret pointing into the ditch, but still the line came inexorably on, filling up from the back and disappearing at the front.

Bob grunted uneasily. 'I don't like it. Where are they headed? We don't want to end up being outflanked.'

A few minutes later there was a stir along the trench. The lieutenant pushed his way towards them.

'Right, men! Listen. Grab your gear and get ready to move. We're pulling out.'

'Pulling out!' Consternation battled in Bob's voice with the ingrown habit of respect. 'But we only just got here!'

'I know.' The lieutenant gave a taut grin. 'Unfortunately the Boches have broken through farther east and with the Belgian line on our left collapsing we run the risk of being surrounded. We have to make a strategic withdrawal. And it's Shanks's pony for now, I'm afraid, men. All the lorries are needed for transporting wounded and essential equipment.'

Within the hour they were trudging back down the long, straight road over which they had advanced only three days earlier. Before long they passed a farm, where the farmer and his family were loading their belongings on to a cart drawn by a knock-kneed horse. Shortly after that they overtook a man pushing a bicycle, on which rested a feather bed and sundry cooking pots, topped off incongruously by a gilt-framed mirror. In front of him walked his wife, a baby in one arm and a small child holding her other hand, together with a girl of about nine, who was pushing a pram loaded with the rest of their possessions. Before long the road was crowded with other refugees, some on foot, others in horse-drawn carts or trailers pulled by tractors. The few cars honked ineffectually in the middle of the crush. Among them the columns of khaki-clad men had difficulty in maintaining their cohesion and broke up into smaller and smaller units.

Suddenly, from above and behind him, Richard heard a banshee-like wail and then the scream of aero engines. Looking round, he saw a dark shape swooping over the road, and before he could call out sharp stabs of flame broke out along the forward edges of the wings and the crowd on the road a hundred yards away flattened like wheat in front of the harvester. As he stood paralysed with shock, Bob smote him on the shoulder.

'*Down!*' he yelled.

Released by the blow, Richard flung himself into the ditch bordering the road, and as he did so he heard the bullets smack like lethal hail into the sandy surface behind him.

As the scream of the engines faded he raised his head and slowly dragged himself up to the level of the roadway. All along its length the dusty surface was strewn with dark, huddled shapes. As he watched some of the shapes moved and attempted to rise. Others lay still. There was a moment of terrible silence and then the crying began, a terrible wailing sob that seemed to come from a single throat and swept along the road from far behind him to a point in the distance ahead. Richard got to his feet. His legs were shaking so much that he could hardly stand. Beside him Bob was staring skywards, crying out words of scarcely articulate rage.

'You bastard! You stinking, cowardly bastard! I hope you rot in hell, you devil!'

A short way off an old lady was sitting in the dust, staring down in numbed silence at her shattered leg. Richard stumbled over and knelt beside her, his tongue formulating useless, idiotic words of reassurance.

'*N'ayez pas peur, madame. Ça ne fait rien. Je vous aiderai.*'

The blood was pumping from somewhere under the old woman's skirt. He realised confusedly that an artery must be punctured. He began to fumble with his belt, with the idea of making some kind of tourniquet. As he did so someone screamed, 'Look out! He's coming back!'

He looked round and saw that the plane had made a steep turn and was now sweeping back up the road, its guns blazing. Without rising to his feet he dived frog-like for the shelter of the ditch. This time, when he crawled back to the road, the old woman lay still, her black dress ripped into bloodied shreds. Richard sat down in the road and put his head in his hands.

He was roused by a kick at the base of his spine. The sergeant stood over him.

'Come on, on your feet! What do you think you're going to do? Sit here till Jerry comes back for you? Up!'

He staggered to his feet and saw the rest of his unit forming up into marching order. There were some gaps in the ranks, and one or two of the men wore hastily applied field dressings. All were pale with shock at the enormity of what had happened. Somehow Richard found himself in his usual place, between Bob and Charlie, his legs automatically falling into step with the sergeant's barked commands. 'Left, left, left!' The rhythmic movement took the place of thought.

As the day progressed they learned to listen for the first faint scream of the dive-bombers coming in to attack. They became practised at diving for cover and inured to the bruises and abrasions that resulted. They also learned to avert their eyes from the bodies that each attack left lying along their route. Women, children, old men, sometimes whole families, lay sprawled where they fell. Some were dead, others called out for help. Once Richard stopped when a young boy, his shirt soaked with blood, cried out for water as he passed. He took out his water bottle and held it to the lad's lips, but before the boy could take more than a sip Bob gripped his shoulder.

'Come on, son! You can't help them all. You must leave that to their own folk. Save your water. You may need it yourself before the day's out.'

Late in the afternoon they flung themselves off the road for the seventh or eighth time. By now they were wise to the tactics of the Stukas. They would make one dive along the length of a stretch of road, then pull up into a steep turn and come back to finish the job. After the first pass Richard looked up to see what carnage had been wrought. There were fewer bodies now, as people began to learn the enemy's intentions, but in the middle of the road was a single figure, still upright. A small child, about three or four years old, stood howling beside the body of its mother. From the ditches on either side voices called out to him, begging him to come to them, but the child was oblivious. Richard looked up. In the distance the Stuka had completed its turn and was dipping its nose for another dive. He looked at the plane, and then at the child, some part of his brain engaged in calculations of relative distance and speed. Then, without being aware of a conscious decision, he sprang forward, bent low and running as fast as his legs would carry him. With a speed and dexterity that would have amazed and delighted his old rugger master he swept the child into his grip and rolled with him into the ditch on the far side of the road. The plane roared over his head and bullets thudded into the ground inches away.

The almost hysterical gratitude of the child's relatives was cut short by the sergeant's voice.

'Well done, lad. But we'll have no more heroics now, if you don't mind. We've got a job to do.'

As the long summer evening was fading into dusk they crossed another small canal and received orders to dig in along its bank. Weary beyond words, Richard took out his trenching tool and began to hack at the soft ground. On either side of him Bob and Charlie dug with the same grim endurance. No one spoke until there was the sound of a door slamming violently behind them and a woman's voice screamed something incomprehensible.

'What the . . .?' Bob demanded, and they all turned to look in the direction of the sound. A short distance away there was a small cottage, belonging perhaps to a lock-keeper. A thickset, elderly woman was advancing towards them from it, waving her arms and yelling at the top of her voice. It was not until she reached them that Richard was able to make out what she was saying. He glanced at his companions and said, mirthlessly, 'She wants to know what we think we're doing digging up her onions. She says this is her garden and we've no right to dig here without her permission.'

Bob turned away with a grunt. 'Tell her where she can put her onions!'

Richard looked at the irate woman and lifted his shoulders. '*Pardon, madame, mais nous avons nos ordres.*' Then he turned his back on her and resumed digging.

Later, when the trench was finished, an orderly came down the line with mugs of tea and hunks of bread and jam.

'Is this all?' Charlie exclaimed. 'We've marched all day, had nothing since breakfast, and this is all we get?'

'Think yourself lucky,' was the reply. 'We're practically out of rations and Gawd knows what's happened to the field kitchen.'

As they ate, rumours and questions passed along the trench. 'Anybody seen Dusty?' 'What happened to old Bert?' In the course of the day the column had become fragmented. One or two men were known to have been killed during the air attacks. Others had simply disappeared. Then came another piece of news, at once more distant and more disturbing. 'They're saying the Dutch have surrendered. The Nazis have flattened Rotterdam.'

The young lieutenant came along the trench, exchanging banter, offering words of encouragement. When he reached Richard he said, 'Saw what you did this afternoon, saving that kid from getting strafed. Well done, Stevens. I'll see it's reported.'

Richard looked at him. His face, under the grime of the day, was white with fatigue. Richard wondered whether, if he had been in the officer's shoes, he could have found the energy to go round cheering his men. He doubted it.

Once the meagre rations had been consumed the men settled down to sleep as best they could. Richard wrapped himself in his greatcoat, pillowed his head on his kitbag and closed his eyes. He slept immediately but was awakened almost at once, or so it seemed, by Bob nudging him in the ribs.

'Quiet, lad. There's others trying to sleep, tha knowst.'

Richard realised he had been dreaming. It was a recurrent nightmare that had plagued him since the outbreak of war. He was in the trenches, knee deep in liquid mud that made every step a heart-bursting effort. All along the trench bodies lay half submerged in the filth and, as he passed one, it stirred and cried out to him. He stooped to turn it over and found himself looking at Rose. He struggled to lift her but a hand caught hold of his sleeve and dragged at it and he turned to discover Chantal gazing up at him in entreaty. As he floundered between the two of them, unable to lift either clear of the clinging mud, he was aware of a man standing near by. They were about the same age but Richard recognised his father from the photograph of him in uniform in the family album. He gazed at Richard and shook his head. 'Tha canna tek 'em both, lad. Tha mun mek up thy mind.'

Awake now, he lay wide eyed, staring at the sky. The night was overcast. There were no stars to look at. He was hungry and weary beyond sleep, and he could find no single comfortable thought on which to rest his mind. He tried to picture Rose, with her huge violet eyes and her delicate, elfin face under its cap of dark, wavy hair. He had thought of her so often but as the months had passed he had found it more and more difficult to summon up a clear image of her, and this evening she seemed more distant and insubstantial than ever. By contrast, his memory of Chantal was still so vivid that in spite of his exhaustion he felt a stir of arousal. He could feel her long-limbed, suntanned body against his own and see the amber eyes and the tawny hair. It had been like embracing a golden cat. But that had been lust, not love. They had both understood that. It was Rose he longed for now, with her gentle smile, her common sense, the feeling she gave him that it was good to be alive. There was nothing good about life tonight. Today had been terrible, and tomorrow would be no better. He had no control over his circumstances. There was nothing he could do to improve his conditions. He had no alternative but to endure. Oddly enough, this thought brought a kind of peace and he slept.

It seemed as if scarcely more than a few minutes had passed before he was roughly shaken awake to the sound of the corporal's voice yelling, 'Come on, up! Up you get, all of you! Grab your gear. We're moving out.'

Richard forced his eyes open and blinked around him. It must be morning, yet it was still dark. With a sense of incredulity he realised that there was only the faintest hint of dawn in the eastern sky. He had slept for perhaps three hours of the short summer night.

Around him men were struggling to their feet. 'What does he mean, moving out?' Bob demanded. 'We spent half the night digging bleeding trenches. What's the point if we're not stopping?'

Richard got up and found himself having to choke back tears of pain and self-pity. Every muscle in his body ached and his feet were blistered from the previous day's march. Beside him Charlie was still curled into a fetal position, muttering semicoherently. 'Not going anywhere . . . too tired . . . bloody stupid . . .'

Bob bent over him. 'Come on, lad. Make the effort. You'll be OK when you get moving.' He looked up at Richard. 'Give me a hand with him.'

Between them they hauled the protesting boy to his feet and the three of them staggered out on to the road, where the column was already forming up. Minutes later they were off, tramping down the pale ribbon of road between the misty shapes of the trees that lined the way. They were not the only travellers. Many of the refugees had not stopped at nightfall and they passed one pathetic little group after another: old men pushing handcarts where children slept on top of the family's household goods; mothers carrying whimpering infants; teenagers supporting elderly grandparents. Sometimes they all had to move off the road for a convoy of trucks or artillery, all heading in the same direction – away from the front and the advancing Germans.

At some point Richard found the lieutenant beside him.

'You're a singer, aren't you, Stevens – in civvy street?'

Richard blinked at him. 'Yes, sir.'

'Then sing, for Christ's sake! Give the men something to keep them going.'

Sing! How could he sing now? His throat was as dry as dust, his lips cracked, his head throbbing with exhaustion. He unhooked his water bottle and took a swallow. What should he sing? It should be something heroic, something jaunty, with a swing to it. His mind was blank. The only song that came to him was the one resurrected from the previous war, to which his comrades delighted in adding scurrilous extra verses. He drew a breath and began,

> Mademoiselle from Armentières, parlez-vous,
> Mademoiselle from Armentières, parlez-vous,
> Mademoiselle from Armentières,
> She hasn't been kissed for forty years,
> *Hinky-dinky parlez-vous.*

Other voices joined his own.

> Oh, Mademoiselle from Armentières, parlez-vous,
> Oh, Mademoiselle from Armentières, parlez-vous,
> She got the palm and the croix de guerre,
> For washin' soldiers' underwear,
> HINKY-DINKY PARLEZ-VOUS.

Suddenly he was back on stage in the Follies. He could see Merry in the pit, grinning up at him encouragingly, and he heard the applause, the shouts of 'Encore'. He gave them Rudyard Kipling's 'Boots' next, and then 'It's a Long Way to Tipperary'. Then he was back on that endless French road, and his feet hurt and his throat was sore, but the men were singing with him and the boots thudded in rhythm in the dust.

When the sun was fully up the Stukas came back. Sometimes now, instead of diving with that terrible banshee howl, they adopted a different tactic, sweeping low along the road from behind so that the first warning of their presence was a sudden rushing noise and the patter of bullets striking the ground. As before, the dive for cover became a reflex action not dependent on conscious thought.

The days that followed passed in a numb haze of confusion, hunger and exhaustion. Richard lost count of the number of times they were ordered to dig in, only to be moved on a few hours later. There was no longer any pretence of maintaining regular rations. They foraged for food wherever it was to be found. Once they came upon an abandoned lorry, its engine riddled with bullets and its driver dead in the cab, but its load of tinned sardines untouched. They ate all they could and carried away as much of the rest as they could manage. The fish helped to fill their stomachs but did nothing to assuage their thirst. Even drinking water was in short supply. Few of the villages they passed through had mains water and wells and springs were either exhausted or polluted. In one village they raided the local *estaminet* and many of the men slaked their thirst with bottles of local wine and brandy, which only made things worse.

One afternoon, marching in a semi-trance, Richard felt Charlie stumble against him. 'Watch it!' he growled, but Charlie seemed not to hear. Looking at him, Richard saw that his eyes were shut. Bob, on the boy's other side, turned his head without breaking his stride.

'He's asleep on his feet,' he said. 'Grab his other arm, Dick.'
Then, as Richard did as he was told, he added, 'OK, Charlie
boy, you have forty winks. Just keep your feet moving, that's
all. Dick and I'll see you don't stray off the road.'

And so they marched, the three of them with linked arms,
Charlie fast asleep between the other two, stumbling sometimes but keeping up. After that, they each took it in turn to
doze, while the others guided their steps. Whenever the
column halted men fell asleep where they stood, leaning on
walls or on each other. Some slunk off into corners and were
left behind when the rest moved on. No one had the energy to
call for them, or report their absence. Indeed, sometimes they
were not missed until hours later.

Five days after leaving their positions along the River Dyle,
and a mere ten days after the beginning of the German
offensive, Richard and the rest of his platoon found themselves digging in once more along the bank of another river,
the Escaut. This time, mercifully, it seemed they were to stay
put. The river at this point was bordered by an artificial
embankment produced by dredging and the South Lancs
trenches were dug behind this convenient rampart. Foraging
parties sent out into nearby villages came back with meagre
supplies and reports of cows standing in the fields, lowing
pitifully to be milked, and abandoned dogs still chained in
farmyards or wandering the streets in packs. One lad, who had
worked on a farm in civilian life, volunteered to try to milk one
of the cows. The poor animal was so distressed that it took four
men to hold her still, but that night they all had milk in their tea
for the first time in days.

Towards afternoon on the following day they were all
brought to their feet by the sound of rifle fire. Two of their
number, who had been on watch lying on top of the embankment, came scrambling back down to the trenches.

'Jerry!' one of them spluttered. 'Just the other side of the river! Strolling along large as life, as if he owned the place.'

The other grinned. 'Not any more!'

'You shot him?' exclaimed the sergeant. 'You blithering idiot! Why don't you just stand up there and tell the whole bleeding German army where we are?'

Not long after that the shelling started. They huddled in their trenches as the shells whistled overhead and waited for the tanks to come. Nothing happened. The world contracted to a few yards of muddy earth in either direction. As usual, rumours were rife. The Germans had broken through and were already advancing on either side of them. The British army had made a stand round the Channel ports. Not so – the British army was being evacuated. The Germans were in Paris. The French had surrendered. No one knew what was true and what was mere speculation. The lieutenant confessed to Richard, in an unguarded moment, that the chain of command had broken down and he was no longer in touch with his senior officers.

At the end of a week the bombardment suddenly stopped and an eerie silence fell. A scouting party reported no sign of the German forces. The landscape on all sides was a scene of silent devastation in which nothing moved. The lieutenant called them together.

'Right, men. It seems we're on our own and it's up to us to use our initiative. There's no food or water and we seem to have lost touch with the rest of the regiment. Let's get out of here.'

They set off to trudge across country, heading as nearly as they could tell towards the coast. They foraged as they went, but the fields were empty except for one planted with rhubarb. Some of the men pulled sticks of it and ate them, with predictable results.

Late the following evening they came to a road so clogged

with refugees and abandoned vehicles that movement was virtually impossible. By keeping to the fields and following the line of the road they eventually reached a junction. Here the chaos was even greater. From north and south the remnants of two armies, British and French, were struggling to reach the Channel. Tanks bulldozed derelict vehicles out of their way, only to find themselves blocked by armoured columns moving in from the opposite direction. Staff cars hooted uselessly, their occupants leaning from the windows to engage in angry exchanges with their opposite numbers. Men slumped along the side of the road or slept where they stood. In the centre of it all a British officer was attempting to direct the traffic and to divert some of it on to a side road.

Converging on the mêlée, Richard and his companions fell in beside a group approaching from the south.

'What the hell's going on?' Bob demanded. 'Where have you lot come from?'

'Abbeville,' was the dispirited reply. 'All hell's broken loose down there. The panzers came through the Ardennes. There's no stopping them. They rolled us up like an old carpet.'

Farther down the road they encountered an officer.

'What regiment do you lot belong to?' he demanded.

'South Lancs, sir,' the lieutenant told him. 'We got separated somehow.'

'Join the club!' the officer retorted bitterly. 'But I happen to know where your lot are. They're with Twelfth Brigade holding the line at Nieuport. Keep heading down that road there. You'll find them.'

By nightfall the little group was reunited with what remained of the regiment, but it was small comfort. There still seemed to be no food or water and shells were once again beginning to whistle overhead. Richard slumped to the ground and wondered whether he would ever find the strength to get up again. It was four days since he had eaten and in the last two he had drunk nothing but a few mouthfuls of foul-tasting water from a trough in an abandoned farmyard. As far as he could remember he had not had more than two hours of uninterrupted sleep at a stretch in the last eight or nine days, and he had not had his boots off since they left Belgium. Looking around him, he could see that none of the other men was in any better condition. Even the officers were swaying on their feet, hollow cheeked and red eyed with exhaustion.

It was a pep talk from the CO, Brigadier Clifton, which got them all moving again. The army, he told them, was being evacuated from Dunkirk and the beaches around it. Every vessel that could be pressed into service was on its way, but even so the evacuation would take several days. Meanwhile, the German panzers were advancing from all sides. It was their job to hold the line here until their comrades could be lifted to safety. As soon as that had been achieved they, too, would be taken off from the beach at La Panne.

All the next day they manned the trenches under continuous heavy bombardment. Casualties mounted and beyond the River Yser they could see the German forces massing for an attack. For the first time Richard faced the stark fact that in all probability he would not survive the next twenty-four hours. It occurred to him that he ought to make a will, or at least write a last note to his parents. Fumbling in his pocket for something to write on, he discovered the letter he had been writing to Merry in the café when the attack started. He began to reread it and was suddenly overwhelmed with sadness at the thought that Merry would never receive it. He turned to Bob, who was still beside him.

'If you get back to England and I don't, will you post this for me, please?'

'Give over, will you?' Bob said, his broad, solid face still managing a grin. 'We're all going back. Tell you what. I'll look after it for you. Then when we get home I'll give it back and you can post it.'

Thinking of Merry brought Rose to Richard's mind for the first time in days, and the thought struck him with devastating force that if he were to be killed no one would tell her what had happened to him. He had never told his parents about her, knowing that his mother would not approve. He began to search in his pockets again.

'Got a pencil, Bob?'

'Sorry, lad.'

'Listen, there's a girl in London . . .'

His words were drowned in a sudden roar of engines, and they all instinctively ducked, but this was not the satanic whine of the Stukas but a deeper, heavier note, and the planes were coming in from the sea behind them. Someone yelled, 'It's the RAF, boys!'

'About time too!' someone else answered, but the men were on their feet, waving and cheering.

'Ten, twelve, sixteen, eighteen,' Richard counted aloud. 'What are those, Blenheims? And six more little ones – fighters of some kind, I suppose.'

The squadron flew low over their lines and on towards the German positions. In a few seconds the first bombs exploded, shaking the ground beneath their feet. More followed.

'By jingo, they're getting a right pasting!' Bob exclaimed.

As he spoke a huge cheer went up farther along the line. Richard scrambled up on to the rim of the trench, hunger and weariness forgotten for the moment.

'They're running!' he yelled. 'The Huns are on the run!'

They cheered and waved until the aircraft were out of sight, and then fell back into their trenches. That night there was an uneasy silence, but soon after dawn the shelling started up again, though the opposite bank of the river remained deserted. Dusk was falling again when the order to withdraw arrived.

Richard was thankful to discover that this time there were lorries to transport them, but it was a slow and nerve-racking journey. There was no let-up in the bombardment and the roads were so choked with debris that the vehicles often had to leave the carriageway and grind and skid their way across the fields. Eventually, they reached the little seaside town of La Panne – or what was left of it. Most of the buildings were wrecked and the roads were cratered with shell holes. As they formed ranks in the square shells were falling all around them.

'This is bloody daft!' Bob muttered.

As if his words had been heard a voice shouted above the din, 'Every man for himself! Head for the beach!'

Richard began to run down the street, Bob at his side and Charlie panting behind. From above and behind them came the familiar whistle of a shell, and they all flung themselves sideways into a narrow alley. The blast from the explosion threw them against the wall and almost stunned them, and when they looked out into the street they saw that a new crater had appeared at exactly the point they would have reached a few seconds later.

'Too close for comfort,' commented Bob. 'Best stay here for a bit.'

They huddled in the shelter of the alley for a long time, deafened by the noise of the bombardment. Then, suddenly, the shelling stopped. Richard looked at the other two and they exchanged doubtful shrugs. The silence endured for a minute or two longer and then was broken by a new sound – the clatter of hobnailed boots on cobblestones as the surviving men ran for the beach.

'Come on!' Richard urged, and the three of them joined the race.

Richard ran with a speed and urgency he would not have believed himself capable of an hour earlier, but the sense that at any second the shelling might start again, that the ground beneath his feet might disintegrate and himself with it, drew out some last reserve of stamina. Along with the rest, they thundered across the promenade, and then there was a sudden eerie cessation of sound as their feet hit the sand. They ran on, until they were up to their knees in the sea, and then they stopped and gazed about them, like stampeded animals no longer certain what had started them running. Around them were the shadowy outlines of hundreds of others. Behind them the horizon smouldered with the light of the burning town; ahead the sky was clear and milky with starlight. There was no sound except for the lapping of the waves. The sea was as flat as a mirror and empty of ships.

Slowly it sank in that they were not about to be rescued, and slowly they turned and plodded back towards the shore. Richard stumbled up beyond the line of debris that marked high water and collapsed on the sand.

He must have slept immediately, because the next thing he was aware of was Charlie shaking his shoulder and shouting, 'Ships! Ships! Wake up, they've come for us!'

All along the beach men were wading out into the water. Offshore Richard could make out the shape of a destroyer lying at anchor, and nearer the beach four small boats were pulling towards them. Bob was heading towards the sea and Richard and Charlie followed. Already one of the boats was close in and men were wading up to their shoulders to reach it. Richard watched as they swarmed around it, trying to haul themselves aboard.

'They'll capsize it if they don't watch out!' he exclaimed.

He ducked involuntarily as a shot rang out. A naval officer in the bows of the whaler was brandishing his revolver and shouting commands. Reluctantly the men fell back and formed a line and the sailors began the task of hauling them aboard.

A second boat was coming in, closer to where Richard and his two friends were standing. They began to move forward. An army officer waded towards them.

'Form a line, men! There will be room for you all. Get into line.'

Docilely, they did as they were told. Richard looked ahead. How many men in front of him? And how many would the boat hold? He found it hard to estimate. Slowly the line moved forward. Bob was just in front of him, Charlie immediately behind. The sun was up now and he could feel its warmth on his shoulders. The water was getting deeper. He was up to his chest now, carrying his rifle above his head. His arms ached with the weight of it. The rest of his kit had been abandoned long ago. Ten men ahead of him now – nine – eight.

Then he heard the Stuka. It was coming in low across the water, its guns blazing. He saw a bomb drop and a huge gout of water rose and engulfed the line of men still being lifted into the first boat. He felt the shock waves and saw the plane swooping towards him. He took a deep breath and submerged himself and heard the bullets smack into the water around him. When he came up he saw that the line had broken and men were struggling and thrashing in the water. Near by a body floated, face down. He looked around and saw Bob shaking water out of his hair like a dog, but there was no sign of Charlie. Richard stared wildly up and down the line and shouted his name, but there was no response. With an animal howl of anger he ducked once again under the surface of the water. The sand had been so churned up that it was impossible to see anything, but his groping hands encountered the rough-ness of army battledress and he grabbed it and hauled it to the surface. Charlie was choking and gasping, but conscious. Richard saw that there was blood in the water around him.

'Are you hit?' he demanded. 'Charlie, are you wounded?'
The boy nodded and sobbed in assent.

'Where? Where did it get you?'

'I don't know. My chest. It hurts when I breathe.'

Richard looked around. The last few men ahead of him were being dragged into the boat. He took a firmer grip on Charlie's tunic.

'Come on. One last effort, Charlie. We're going home.'

He dragged the boy, half walking, half floating, towards the boat. Ahead, he saw Bob being lifted over the gunwale. Hands reached down to him. He pushed Charlie up to them and shouted, 'Careful with him. He's wounded.'

He heard Charlie scream as he was pulled up and then a strong hand gripped his wrist and he looked up into a weather-beaten, friendly face. At that moment a voice above him shouted, 'Sorry, that's the lot! We can't take any more without running the risk of capsizing.'

For a second or two he gazed up in mute entreaty into the sailor's blue eyes, but the hand released its hold on him and the man said, 'Sorry, mate. Orders is orders.' Then, as the boat began to move away, he called back, 'Don't worry! We're like London buses. There'll be another one along in a minute.'

For a long time Richard stood in the water, staring after the departing boat. Then he turned and waded back to the beach. He found his way back to the place where he had lain before and stretched himself out. He could not believe that he had been so close to safety and that it had been snatched from him at the last second. He would not let himself think that Charlie had been behind him in the queue. He turned on his face and let misery engulf him.

When the Stukas came over again he did not even try to take cover. There was nowhere to shelter on the beach and he was too tired to dig himself a hole, as some others had done. He felt the bullets strike his legs like hammer blows and felt the warm blood begin to flow. Then the pain came and he lost consciousness.

Some time later he came round to find an officer stooping over him.

'Can you walk, Private?'

He tried to speak but his tongue was swollen and his throat seemed to have closed up. He could only shake his head and mumble.

'Don't think so,' was what he tried to say.

The officer patted his shoulder. ' 'Fraid we'll have to leave you here, old chap. We can only take those who can stand on their own feet. Sorry about that, but don't worry. The Huns are pretty close now. They'll take care of you.'

He moved away and Richard let his head drop back on his arms. He was too weak to protest or argue. Too weak even to care very much.

Chapter Six

Rose returned home towards the end of May just as news started coming through of the German advance. The bulletins on the wireless gave little detail but she sat by the set, trying to work out what was happening and where, her imagination sketching different scenes of disaster with every hour that passed. She knew that it was foolish to imagine that anything she might hear would give her any clue about Richard's fate, but she listened to every report as if it might contain a message from him.

She worried, too, about Merry. Almost a month had passed since he had left for France and during that time they had had only brief, hastily written notes. Where, exactly, he had been performing she had no idea, but it seemed inevitable that he and his company had been caught up in the fighting.

On the evening of 30 May Rose and her mother had just sat down to tea when they heard a taxi draw up outside. Rose jumped up with a pounding heart and hobbled to the window, but even as she moved she knew that it could not be the one person she longed to see. Merry was paying off the driver. She limped downstairs and flung open the front door.

'Oh, Merry! Thank God you're all right! We've been so worried! Whatever's happened to you?'

He was filthy and unshaven and hollow eyed with fatigue and seemed almost incapable of speech. She took him by the arm. 'Come on, come upstairs. You look done in.'

It was hard to be sure who was supporting whom as they

made their way to where Mrs Taylor was waiting. 'Heavens above!' she exclaimed. 'What's going out there?'

Merry shook his head and croaked hoarsely, 'It's chaos. Complete bloody chaos.'

'Sit down. There's tea in the pot. I'll get another cup and plate.'

Merry sank into a chair and Rose saw his eyes focus on her plate of Spam and mashed potato. Without comment she put it in front of him and watched as he devoured it. Her mother, returning with the extra crockery, took in the situation at a glance and went back to the kitchen to fetch the remains of a loaf and all that was left of their weekly ration of margarine, together with a small tin of condensed milk she had been saving for 'emergencies'. Merry ate two doorsteps spread with the sweet, sticky substance and then sat back and looked at them.

'I seem to have eaten you out of house and home. Sorry! I'll make it up to you.'

'Never you mind about that,' Mrs Taylor said. 'There's always someone around here who'll lend a bit of bread and marge.'

Rose leaned towards him. 'Merry, what's happened to you? What's going on?'

'You haven't heard?'

'Only that there's heavy fighting.'

He shook his head despondently. 'I don't know about that. The Germans have broken through the French defences in the Ardennes and there seems to be no stopping them. They're driving us into the sea. If you ask me, we've had it.'

Then Rose saw that his eyelids were drooping. His head slumped forward and only her quick reaction in pushing his plate aside prevented him from falling face down into the remains of his meal. Between them, she and her mother helped him into his bedroom and pulled off his tunic and his boots. He collapsed back on the bed and closed his eyes.

'Dear Lord! Look at the state of his feet!' Mrs Taylor cried.

Merry's socks were bloodstained and sticking to his feet where the blisters had broken but he was already asleep. Rose fetched a bowl of water and dabbed at the encrusted blood until she was able to peel the socks away. Merry moaned once or twice in his sleep but seemed otherwise unaware of what she was doing. She washed his feet as best she could and asked, 'Should we put plasters on those blisters, do you think?'

'No, leave the air to get to them,' her mother replied. 'We can bandage them up tomorrow.'

All next day they divided their time between the shop and the wireless set, but there was still no confirmation of what Merry had told them. Rose looked in on him once or twice but there seemed no point in disturbing him. He slept for almost twenty-four hours. In the afternoon he came into the sitting room as they were sitting down to tea again. He was still pale and seemed to have lost what little spare flesh he had ever had, but he had bathed and shaved and his eyes were clear.

'Thanks for last night,' he said. 'I'm afraid I must have given you a bit of a shock.'

Rose leaned across the table and put her hand over his. 'Poor Merry! It sounded dreadful.'

He gazed at her in silence for a moment, then said, 'I can't begin to describe it. I've never seen such confusion.'

'What exactly happened?' Rose asked. 'It's not true that the Germans have beaten us, is it?'

Mrs Taylor came in with fresh tea and Merry took a swallow.

'I don't know. I can only tell you what happened to us. We were near Abbeville, playing to a Royal Artillery unit. It was extraordinary. We were playing in the open air, as usual. It was a lovely early summer night and the gunners were really enjoying the show. We were in the middle of "Rhapsody in Blue" when suddenly all hell broke loose. Sirens started sounding and whistles blowing and the lights went out. The audience all jumped up and went rushing off to man the guns and we were left standing there in the middle of an empty field with artillery shells thundering over our heads. Then an officer came along and said we'd better get out while the going was good because the German tanks had taken the French by surprise and broken the line. Apparently no one thought it was possible for tanks to operate in the thick forest of the Ardennes so the line hadn't been very strongly defended there.'

'Go on,' Rose said.

'Well, we crammed our gear into the lorry and set off back towards Boulogne, but the roads were choked with refugees and army traffic and we had to keep stopping and taking cover because the Luftwaffe were strafing the roads. Willy, the comic, got a bullet in his leg and Dave, the saxophonist, had the screaming habdabs every time we heard a plane coming over. Then we were stopped by a patrol and told that the Germans were nearly in Boulogne and we would have to make for Dunkirk instead. Not long after that the lorry went into a shell hole and broke an axle or something. Anyway, it was completely u/s so we had to start walking.' He broke off and gave one of his wry grins. 'Well, I know we're all supposed to be serving soldiers, but quite honestly I don't think some of those chaps had ever walked farther than from the theatre to the nearest bar. Several of them weren't wearing regulation army boots so before we'd gone many miles they had blisters the size of half-crowns. Added to which, we'd run out of food and there was nothing to be had in any of the villages. They'd been stripped bare already.' He shook his head. 'Some of the men were pretty near to giving up. I think they'd have sat in a field and waited for the Huns to catch up with them, if I'd let them. Not all. Most of them were real troopers. But there were one or two. I don't blame them. I can tell you, there were times when I didn't think we'd make it.'

'But you did,' Rose encouraged him. 'Goodness knows how you did it, but here you are.'

He smiled at her wearily. 'Yes, thank God.'

'But how did you manage it? What with one man with a wounded leg and the others with blisters and all,' Mrs Taylor asked.

Merry hesitated and looked down at his plate. 'It's not a very pleasant story, I'm afraid. We came across this group of refugees, all part of one family, I should guess. An old man, two women, a couple of kids. All dead, killed by the strafing. They had a handcart full of stuff and a bicycle. Well, it was no good to them any more. We emptied all the gear out of the cart and put poor old Willy into it and the others who were the worst off took turns on the bike. And somehow we got to Dunkirk and on to a ship. Believe me, I've never been so glad to see the Royal Navy! But I don't know how it's going to end. There were thousands of our men there. The beaches were full of them, all waiting to be taken off. The whole thing seems to be a complete disaster.'

There was a brief silence in the room, and through the open window they heard a cheery cockney voice singing 'We're going to hang out our washing on the Siegfried Line . . .'

Merry sighed heavily. 'Some hopes!'

'If our army's beaten,' Rose said slowly, 'does that mean Hitler will invade?'

Merry lifted his shoulders. 'Who knows? If he does, I don't see how we are going to stop him.'

'We'll stop him!' Mrs Taylor said grimly. 'If I have to join up myself and hit him over the head with a broomstick, we'll stop him.'

The image she conjured up was so ridiculous that they all laughed, releasing the tension. Rose was unable to hold back the question at the forefront of her mind any longer. 'I don't suppose you came across anyone from the South Lancs, did you?'

Merry looked at her sympathetically. 'No, I'm afraid not. We didn't perform for them, that's for sure, so they may not have been in that sector at all. Oh, I've just remembered. Isn't Bet's husband out there?'

'No, thank goodness,' Rose's mother replied. 'Last week he phoned the garage where he used to work and asked them to give Bet a message, saying he was back in England and he hoped to get leave soon.'

'Well, that's one thing to be grateful for. I'm glad.'

'So,' Mrs Taylor said briskly, 'what about you? You don't have to go back to work straight away, do you?'

Merry shook his head. 'No, I've got a week's leave.'

'I should think so!' She began clearing the table. 'You just make yourself at home. You need a good rest.'

'That's very kind of you.' Merry got up and wandered over to the window. 'But I have to go down to Seaford.'

'Of course!' Rose exclaimed. 'You haven't seen your father. You have let him know you're all right, haven't you?'

Merry turned and his bleak expression sent a chill through her.

'I'm sorry. I forgot you didn't know. My father died just before we left for France. That's why I had that week off.'

Rose went to him and laid her hand on his sleeve. 'Oh, Merry, I am so sorry! Why didn't you tell us?'

'There didn't seem to be a chance. I got back here late one night and I had to be off to France first thing next morning. I had intended to come and see you in the convalescent home. I'm sorry I didn't make it. And I haven't even asked you how your ankle is.'

'It's getting better, but never mind about that,' Rose said. 'Tell me about your father. How did it happen?'

'He had a heart attack. His heart's been dicky for years, although he would never admit to it. He survived the first attack. That's when they sent for me. But a couple of days later he had another. It happened in his sleep. They said he wouldn't have known much about it.'

'In between,' Rose asked, 'was he . . . were you able to talk to him?'

'Yes, he was conscious. In fact, we thought he was going to get over it.' Merry touched the shoulder of his tunic. 'I was able to tell him I'd been promoted. I think that pleased him.' He looked away and dropped his voice. 'I didn't tell him I'd been transferred to the entertainments section.'

Rose gripped his arm. 'Merry, you're doing a wonderful job. You mustn't feel ashamed of it. I've seen how much it means to those boys to have something to brighten their lives a bit.'

Merry answered without looking at her. 'I know. But men were fighting and dying out there, Rose, and we just scuttled for the coast. We should have stayed and fought.'

'It wouldn't have made any difference, would it?' she pointed out. 'By the sound of it, they had to give up and scuttle for the coast themselves. And you got those men back to safety. You said yourself some of them would have just given up, if you hadn't made them carry on. You saved them, Merry.'

He looked at her then and for the first time she saw in those transparent eyes a faint stirring of pride.

'Yes,' he said, 'I did manage that, didn't I.'

Twenty-four hours later he left for Seaford, pointing out that he must check the house and deal with various bits of legal business that were outstanding, though he added with a wry smile, 'Not that that will matter if Herr Hitler's going to take over.'

While he was gone Rose sat glued to the wireless as little by little the story of the débâcle in France came out. One afternoon her mother came up from the shop to find her in tears.

'Oh, Mum! They've just appealed for anyone who's got a

boat – even a little boat – to go across the Channel to help pick up our boys from Dunkirk. They'll never get them all out!'

Five days later Merry was back, bringing a gift of new-laid eggs from 'a farmer friend'. He noticed the previous day's newspaper, which lay on the table, and pointed to the head-line: 'MIRACLE OF THE SMALL BOATS – BRITISH EXPEDITIONARY FORCE EVACUATED'.

'You see? They got them all out in the end.'

Rose nodded and turned away so he would not see the tears in her eyes. 'Yes. I expect we'll hear something soon.'

Richard came round to find himself lying on a mattress on the floor of a huge, echoing room. His throat was parched and there was a throbbing pain in his left leg. With a struggle, he lifted his head and looked across the room. On either side of him other men lay in long rows. Grimy, bloodstained faces were turned to the ceiling or pillowed on a sheltering arm. Nurses were bustling about with trays of implements, and opposite where he lay a priest in a cassock and purple stole was kneeling over one of the patients, murmuring a prayer.

Richard let his head fall back. *So they got me out after all*, he thought. *I wonder where I am. It must be a casualty clearing station of some sort.*

Feet approached along the narrow pathway between the mattresses and he summoned all his strength to call, 'Nurse!'

A girl stooped over him, her face framed by the white nurse's coif. He muttered huskily, 'Can I have a drink of water, please?'

She frowned. '*Tut mir leid, ich spreche kein Englisch.*'

She put a hand under his head, however, and held a cup of water to his lips. He drank and sank back on the pillow. So he was not in England. This was a German casualty station, and he was a prisoner of war. He remembered the officer saying, 'The Huns will be along soon. They'll look after you.' It seemed he had been right, but what sort of care could he expect, as a captured enemy?

The day after his return from Seaford, Merry reported to Colonel Brown's office. The colonel came round his desk and shook his hand warmly.

'Merry! Welcome back. How are you feeling?'

'I'm OK, thanks.'

'Good. You certainly look a lot better than when I last saw you, when you got back from France.'

Merry rubbed his chin. 'Sorry about that. Not much chance to shave under those conditions.'

'My dear fellow, don't apologise!' Brown exclaimed. 'You did a marvellous job getting the company back home. Marvellous! I've had a chat with several of them, and they all insist it was you who kept them going. Well done!'

'Oh well,' Merry murmured, 'I didn't fancy spending the next God knows how many years in a German POW camp. I've never cared much for Wagner.'

Brown laughed and moved back to his chair. 'Sit down, old chap. I want to talk about the future.'

Merry sat. 'What do you think will happen now? Will the French hold out?'

Brown lifted his shoulders. 'Who knows? The Germans are advancing on Paris. There seems to be no stopping them at the moment.'

'And if the French can't hold him up, will Hitler invade us, do you think?'

'We'll be in a bad way if he does,' Brown replied. 'We've got bugger all left in the way of weapons after the débâcle at Dunkirk. Still, you heard Winnie the other day, I suppose? "We will fight them on the beaches . . . we will never surrender."'

Merry nodded. 'Stirring stuff. I think he's right, but imagine the cost . . .'

They were both silent for a moment, then Brown took a deep breath and straightened his shoulders. 'Anyway, that's not our problem at the moment. We have to decide what to do to entertain people while we wait to see what happens. That's where you come in. Right now the army is far too busy reorganising and taking stock to want to cope with a concert party descending on them and needing staging, etcetera. On the other hand, if there was ever a need for a bit of distraction, it's now. So what I'm proposing to do is to send out individual artistes who can perform with the minimum of fuss and equipment. People like you, who need nothing but a piano. How do you feel about that?'

'I've never seen myself as a solo performer,' Merry objected.

'Why? Because you think you aren't good enough? Take it from me, you are. I've heard you play and you're good enough to give a lot of people a lot of pleasure.'

'What do you want me to do, exactly?' Merry queried.

'I'll sort out a list of venues for you – hospitals, particularly. There are a lot of wounded, traumatised men, men who've been through hell and back again, who desperately need something to take their minds off what's happened. You can probably do some NAAFI canteens and maybe officers' messes as well. We'll give you transport of some sort and after that it will be up to you to organise yourself. OK?'

Merry considered. 'I'd be sorry to lose the contact with the rest of the company. We'd grown pretty close over the last few weeks.'

'I can appreciate that,' Brown said. 'But right now I'm not proposing to put another concert party together. For one thing, several of your chaps are on sick leave. Later on, when things settle down a bit, you can take your pick of the available talent. How about it?'

'Of course, if that's what you think is best. What sort of programme do you want me to do?'

'That's up to you. You can vary it according to where you happen to be. But concentrate on the classical side. These people are getting a lot of popular music on the wireless. We want to give them something a bit more – what shall I say? – uplifting.'

Merry took a long breath. 'When do I start?'

'Not for a few days. I have to arrange a schedule for you. You concentrate on getting a repertoire together, and I'll let you know as soon as I can.'

Merry passed the next week in a strange suspension between two worlds. He would spend hours in the empty rehearsal room, immersed in the transcendent beauty of Beethoven and Mozart, and then come out to find all his colleagues huddled around the wireless, their faces grave and drawn as each successive bulletin told of further disasters. By 10 June the Germans were within thirty-five miles of Paris. The same day Mussolini brought Italy into the conflict on the German side. Three days later the Nazis entered Paris in triumph.

On the 16th Merry arrived back at the Taylors' flat to find Rose white faced and her mother in tears.

'What's happened?' he asked.

'We've just heard the news on the wireless,' Rose said. 'The French have surrendered. Reynaud has resigned and Pétain has taken his place. He's suing for peace.'

'Dear God!' Merry said softly. 'We're on our own, then.'

Chapter Seven

For Rose the following days had an unreal quality. The whole country seemed to be holding its breath as people waited for the seemingly inevitable invasion. The Germans were reported to be massing on the other side of the Channel, and already the Channel Islands were in enemy hands. The newspapers reported attacks on Atlantic convoys by German submarines. Food shortages worsened and queues for basic rations grew longer.

Winston Churchill broadcast a rallying call to the nation. 'Let us so conduct ourselves that, if the British Commonwealth and Empire last a thousand years, men will still say "This was their finest hour".'

As if in ironic contrast June lived up to its reputation in a succession of cloudless, brilliant days, but Rose hardly noticed the weather. Every morning she tried not to watch for the postman, and every morning when he arrived she shuffled through the letters with a hollow feeling in her stomach, looking for the familiar handwriting and knowing it was not there. Whenever she saw someone in army uniform coming down the street her heart turned over, though she knew it was not him. The lack of information gnawed at her like an ulcer. She had never known his home address, so she could not write to his parents. She looked up Didsbury on a map in the library and it seemed a very long way away. She considered going there and searching the telephone directory for all the Stevenses. She was certain his family would have a telephone, but

Stevens was not an uncommon name. And if by any chance she found the right ones, what could she say? 'I'm your son's girlfriend'? A 'girlfriend' he had been ashamed to mention, let alone introduce. She tried writing to the War Office and the Red Cross to ask for news but received the same terse reply from both, stating that they were unable to give out information except to next of kin. She had no official standing, was nothing more in the eyes of the world than a casual acquaintance.

One evening she was alone in the kitchen, preparing the supper, when Merry came in. She sensed at once, from a tautness in his expression, that he had news.

'What is it? You've heard something!'

He laid a hand on her arm. 'It's not what you think, Rose. Sit down a minute.'

She sat at the kitchen table and gazed up at him in mute appeal. He seated himself opposite her and took an envelope from his pocket. She caught her breath as she recognised the handwriting.

'This arrived this morning, at my HQ. But don't jump to any conclusions. It's dated May the tenth. That's the day the fighting started and this was obviously written before anything happened.'

He handed her the letter and sat quietly while she read it through.

'But why has it taken so long?' she asked at length.

'I imagine he didn't have any opportunity to post it, in the circumstances.'

Slowly the implications dawned on Rose. 'Where was it posted?'

'In Southampton.'

'Then he got back!'

'Possibly.'

'What do you mean, possibly?'

'He could have given it to someone else to post – if he thought he might not make it.'

She absorbed this in silence for a moment. Her throat was aching, as if someone had clamped a hand around it. One thought hammered away in her head. *Why has he written to Merry and not to me?* Then common sense intervened and she remembered that she had only replied to his most recent letter early in May. It was quite possible that he had not received it by the 10th – which meant that he had probably never received it at all. What mattered now was the letter in her hand, not who it was addressed to.

'If he posted it himself,' she said, 'that means he's safe. So that's something to be grateful for.'

She did not add 'but in that case he could have written to let me know', but Merry read her thoughts. He put his hand over hers. 'There could be all sorts of reasons why he hasn't been in touch. He may be wounded. Perhaps he can't write, at the moment.'

Rose shook her head. 'He could have asked someone else to write. He could have found some way to get in touch – if he wanted to.'

'Rose.' His eyes held hers. 'There could still be reasons we don't understand. All we really know from this letter is that he was alive and well on May the tenth. We mustn't jump to any conclusions.'

She jerked her head up and swallowed. 'Well, it's all the same really, isn't it? If he's alive he obviously isn't keen to keep in touch. And if he's not – well, he's not and that's that.'

Over the following days Rose lapsed into a deep depression. Her common sense told her that it was time she stopped living in the past and took control of her life again. But her heart still ached with longing for what might have been and was not prepared to listen to reason. Her ankle was strong enough now to allow her to walk normally, so she had no excuse for not helping out in the shop, but, in truth, there was hardly enough work for two people.

As July followed June and the heatwave continued she drooped listlessly around the flat until her mother exclaimed, 'For goodness' sake, Rose! I'm fed up with the sight of you moping about the place. There are folks around here who have a lot more to grieve over than you, you know.'

It was true, as Rose knew well enough. Several of their neighbours had lost husbands and sons at Dunkirk. She made an effort to pull herself together and be pleasant to customers, and filled her spare time looking after her two young nephews to give Bet a break. Bet's husband, Reg, came home on leave for a week, looking brown and healthy, and spent his evenings in the pub giving lurid accounts of his unit's part in the battle. He seemed quite happy to go back when the time came.

Merry appeared only rarely these days, though they kept a room for him and some of his civilian clothes still hung in the wardrobe. He spent most of his time on the road, sleeping wherever his latest concert had taken him. When he did show up his face was drawn and there were lines at the corners of his eyes which had not been there before. Long days driving from one hospital to another, struggling to find his way on roads from which all signposts had been removed in order to confuse an invading army, followed by a performance and then a night in a strange bed, were taking their toll. He often gave six or even eight concerts in a week and, from something he let slip on one of his rare days off, Rose knew that in between he spent time in the wards, sitting by the beds of wounded men whose families were unable to visit them.

In London everyone was waiting for the threatened air raids to begin. Periodically, the warning siren would wail and Rose and her mother would gather up their gas masks and a book and make their way down to the shelter at the end of the road.

Usually, after an hour, the all-clear would sound and they would return to the upper world and pick up where they left off. Nothing ever happened. Before long people became irritated with the false alarms and stopped bothering to take shelter when they heard the warning.

Everyone's attention was focused on the battle being fought in the skies to the south of them over Kent and Sussex. The Luftwaffe was concentrating on bombing the airfields and day after day the fighter pilots of the RAF were scrambled in an effort to prevent them. One day, Rose was walking in the park with Billy and Sam when people around them started craning their necks and pointing upwards. Following their gaze, she saw two planes, like silver insects against the blue.

'Look!' Billy shouted. 'A Spit and an Me-109! It's a dog-fight!'

They watched the planes whirling in what looked to Rose like a lethal mating dance, each aircraft unfurling a long banner of white vapour behind it as it moved, climbing, diving, twisting, first pursuer and then pursued.

'Which one's which?' Rose demanded.

'That one diving now, that's the Messerschmitt.' Billy was hopping up and down with excitement. 'Go on, Spit! Don't let him get away!'

The plane zoomed low over their heads, pulling up when it was only a few hundred feet from the ground so that they could clearly see the black crosses on the underside of its wings. A universal jeer sounded from the throats of the onlookers. The Spitfire had circled, waiting to pounce, and the fight was resumed until one of the combatants broke away, smoke trailing from a wing.

'Which one is hit?' Rose asked. Her heart was thumping.

'Not sure. I think it's the Jerry. Yes, look, there's the Spit! Hurrah! Got the bastard!'

'Billy!' Rose reproved, but her eyes were on the stricken

plane. A cheer went up from the crowd, followed by a growl of hostility as a parachute blossomed beneath it. In spite of the circumstances Rose could not suppress a twinge of pity for the luckless German pilot.

On 19 July *The Times* carried the headline 'GERMANY'S HEAVIEST AIR DEFEAT: 140 Machines Shot Down out of 600'.

Merry, back in London for a brief respite in his wanderings, gathered round the wireless with Rose and her mother to listen to Winston Churchill.

'The gratitude of every home in our island . . . goes out to the British airmen who, undaunted by odds, unwearied in their constant challenge and mortal danger, are turning the tide of the world war by their prowess and by their devotion. Never in the field of human conflict was so much owed by so many to so few.'

Rose was on her way to meet Sally Castle. It had been some time since she had heard anything from her so she had been surprised to receive a brief note stating: 'I've got some news I must tell you! Meet me at Lyons Corner House, in Piccadilly, Sunday 25th, at four. I'll wait half an hour. Be there!' She was a trifle annoyed by the peremptory tone, but the invitation was irresistible. What on earth could Sally have to impart that was so important? Probably nothing much, Rose reckoned, but it made a break from her usual routine and it was a long time since she'd been 'up West'.

Sally was sitting at a table near the door. Her make-up was immaculate and her peroxide blonde hair gleamed like a helmet under a chic little hat. Dressed in a simple cotton frock and a headscarf, and aware that her hair needed a professional shampoo and set, Rose felt dowdy in comparison. It struck her that over the last months she had 'let herself go'.

'*Rose!*' Sally shrieked, and jumped up to kiss her. 'It's been simply ages! How are you?'

'Not too bad,' Rose replied, seating herself. 'You look well.'

'Mustn't grumble,' Sally said, grinning. 'All things considered.'

The waitress came and Rose ordered tea and toast. It was about all that was available these days.

'So,' Sally said. 'What are you up to?'

'I told you, nothing much. I've been helping my mum in the shop since I hurt my leg.'

'You mean you still can't dance?'

'No.' Rose paused. She had not told any of her friends what the surgeon had said. She had a feeling that once she did it would be admitting defeat and making his prediction come true. She temporised. 'It's going to take time.'

'Well, don't leave it too long,' Sally said. 'You know what this profession's like. Once people have forgotten you it's very hard to get back.'

Rose bit her lip. Sally did not mean to be cruel. 'Yes, I know. I'm working on it.'

That, at least, was true. She had never let up on the exercises, but although her ankle was definitely stronger the moment she tried any dance steps it gave way under her.

'Poor you!' Sally said.

Rose looked at her. She sounded sympathetic but Rose had a feeling that she was not really listening. She just wanted to get round to talking about her own news.

'So, how are things with the Front Line Follies?' Rose asked obligingly. 'Still going strong?'

'Oh, I'm not with them any more,' Sally said. 'I'd had enough after a couple of tours – all that performing on rickety stages and sleeping in tents! If I'd wanted to do that I'd have joined the Girl Guides.'

'But have you heard from Monty or any of the others? They weren't caught in France when the Huns attacked, were they?'

'Oh, no. They were touring up north somewhere.'

'Thank goodness for that.' Rose realised, with a stab of guilt, that she had been so worried about Richard that she had not even thought about them. 'So, what are you doing? Are you working?'

'Boy, am I working!' Sally exclaimed. 'I should say so!'

'Where?'

'You'll never guess.'

'Won't I?'

'You won't believe me when I tell you.'

'Why not?'

Sally leaned across the table and lowered her voice. 'I'm at the Windmill.'

Rose gasped. 'Sally, you're not! I mean, you aren't . . .'

'Not as one of the strippers!' Sally said, scandalised. 'What do you think I am? I'm one of the dancers. They do have a proper show, you know, as well as the nudes.'

Rose frowned. 'You mean they have dancers who keep their clothes on, and other girls who . . . who take them off?'

'Well, they have to, don't they? Have both, I mean,' Sally pointed out. 'You know the Lord Chamberlain's rules. The nudes have to stay completely still. It's all very artistic, really. They have these tableaux. Cleopatra and her ladies, Greek goddesses, that sort of thing. All in very good taste.'

'I'm sure,' Rose murmured sceptically.

'And then in between they have other turns – comics, singers, dance numbers, just like we had in the Follies. And the costumes are really gorgeous!'

'You sound as if you're enjoying it,' Rose commented.

'I am,' Sally returned, on a note of defiance. 'Mind you, it's hard going. Six shows a day.'

'*Six!*' Rose exclaimed.

'Non-stop,' Sally confirmed. Then she giggled and leaned forward again. 'It's really funny. All the blokes want to sit in the front rows, so they can get a really good look. So those seats fill up first and the ones who come later have to sit farther back. Then, at the end of each show, the ones at the front leave and the others all climb over the backs of the seats to get to the front. We call it the Grand National!'

'That's awful!' Rose said, trying to sound scandalised, but she was giggling too. 'Oh, Sally!' she exclaimed when she finally got herself under control, 'you do me good. I haven't laughed like that for a long time.'

Sally looked at her shrewdly. 'You heard from Richard lately?'

Rose looked at her cup and shook her head. 'Not since Dunkirk. I don't know whether he just doesn't want to write, or something has happened to him.'

Sally reached across the table and took her hand. 'That's terrible, Rose. I'm so sorry. Can't you find out somehow?'

Rose shook her head. 'I've thought and thought but there's no way. Anyway, whichever it is I guess that's the finish. I'm never likely to hear anything now.'

'Don't you believe it!' Sally said sternly. 'One of these days he'll come marching up to your door. You mark my words.'

Rose took a deep breath and changed the subject. 'How's Lucy? Does she like the ATS?'

'She *says* she's loving every minute, but I think she's just putting on a brave front,' Sally declared.

'More tea?' Rose poured, and when the cups were full Sally looked at her with a strange gleam in her eye.

'Right! Now for my big piece of news!'

'You mean there's something else?'

Sally leaned down and picked up a newspaper from the floor by her chair. 'You obviously haven't seen this, or you'd have mentioned it by now.'

'Seen what?'

Sally folded the paper carefully and held it out to Rose. In the centre of the page was a photograph of a young man in the uniform of a flight lieutenant in the RAF, but the caption beneath it had been folded back so that it was hidden.

'Who's that?' Sally demanded.

Rose leaned closer and examined the picture. The young man's face was partially obscured by his officer's cap but there was no mistaking the features.

'It's Felix!' she exclaimed delightedly.

'Ah-hah!' Sally said triumphantly. 'That's what you think!'

She unfolded the paper so that the caption became visible and handed it back to Rose. Underneath the picture was the legend

Air Ace Awarded DFC

Flt. Lieut. The Hon. Edward Alexander Mountjoy, younger son of Lord and Lady Malpas, yesterday received the Distinguished Flying Cross for his exploits in shooting down seven enemy aircraft during the recent action over southern England.

Rose looked up at Sally in consternation. 'There must have been a mistake. That's definitely Felix. They must have got the pictures muddled up somehow.'

'You mean it's definitely the man *we* know as Felix,' Sally said. 'But didn't you ever wonder who he really was? I mean, all that spare cash he always had and the posh friends.'

'It's true,' Rose said thoughtfully. 'He never quite seemed to fit in and we could never get him to talk about his family. So you think he really is this . . .' She consulted the paper. '. . . this Edward Alexander Mountjoy?'

'*The Hon.* Edward Alexander Mountjoy,' Sally corrected her. 'Rosy, my girl, we've missed our chance. We've been consorting with the aristocracy and we never knew it.'

'But why?' Rose asked. 'Why would he do it?'

Sally shrugged. 'Just fancied going on the stage, I suppose, and didn't want to drag the family name in the dust. You know what snobs these people are.'

'I don't think Felix was a snob,' Rose said. 'He had his bad points but he wasn't a snob.'

'Well, he's dropped all of us now, hasn't he?' Sally pointed out. 'Bet no one's heard anything from him since he went back to being the Hon. Edward.'

Rose did not answer. There was only one thought in her mind. Had Merry seen that picture?

Chapter Eight

Richard picked up his crutch and hobbled painfully down the long ward. At the window he paused to look out. Inside, the ward could have been part of any hospital, anywhere in Europe. It was only when you looked out, at the high barbed-wire fence surrounding the grounds, that you realised where you were. He gazed beyond the fence, at the fields on the low hill that bounded his field of vision. When he had arrived the wheat had still been green. Now it had been harvested and the fields were clothed in bronze stubble. He turned and resumed his slow, uneven progress towards the door.

Once in the privacy of the bathroom he laid aside his crutch and began the series of exercises he had devised for himself a few weeks earlier. Over the two-and-a-half-month period since his capture he had undergone a series of operations to remove bullets from his legs and repair the damage. He could not complain about his treatment, which had been as good as any he might have received in a British hospital, but his recovery had been slow, hindered by weakness and general debility. Exactly why he had chosen to preserve the illusion that he still had not regained the full use of his left leg he was not sure. The surgeon who treated him had hinted that perhaps the reason for his disability might be largely psychological and he had been quite happy to allow him to go on believing that, while maintaining outwardly that he simply did not have the strength in his leg to manage without his crutch.

He had no definite plan, simply the gut feeling that the longer he was thought incapable of rapid movement the better his chances of escape.

When he returned to the ward, being careful to maintain his exaggerated limp, he found an orderly waiting by his bed.

'The Herr Major wishes to speak with you in his office.'

Major von Pebel was the surgeon in charge of the hospital, a tall, thin, grey-haired man who looked perpetually weary. Richard stood to attention, still supported by his crutch.

'Tomorrow,' said the major, 'you will leave here.' He spoke English well, almost without an accent. 'You are to be transferred to a prison camp in Germany.'

'But I was told I could stay here until I was fit,' Richard protested.

'You are well enough to travel,' the major said. 'The hospital is no longer required for prisoners of war. It will be returned to civilian use. However, since you are unable to walk far, you and some other more severely disabled men will be transferred by ambulance instead of travelling by train. That is all. You may go.'

Back in the ward Richard sat on his bed and tried to think calmly in spite of the racing of his pulse. The man in the next bed, who had developed appendicitis after being captured, said, 'You heard the news? We're all being sent to a POW camp.'

'Yes,' Richard said absently. 'I heard.'

'Well, that's us for the duration, then,' the other man remarked. 'All we have to do is sit it out until the war's over.'

Richard looked at him. 'You're quite happy with that?'

'Better than getting killed, isn't it?'

'Suppose the Nazis win?'

The other man shrugged. 'Nothing we can do about that now, is there? We're out of it.'

Richard turned away and picked up a magazine. Instead of

seeing the photographs on the pages he was seeing the image of the old woman lying in the dust of a French road. 'Yes,' he said indifferently. 'I suppose we are.'

That night he lay awake, formulating and discarding plans for escape. The task was made more difficult by the fact that he had only the vaguest idea of where he was. He had been moved twice since regaining consciousness in the improvised dressing station outside La Panne. Each time he had made a point of noticing the direction, using the sun as a guide, and estimating as closely as he could speed and time travelled. Now he guessed that he was somewhere in eastern Belgium, probably not far from the German border.

The next morning he was shepherded out to an ancient, clapped-out ambulance. It was fitted to accommodate several patients in a sitting position on benches along either side. Richard examined his fellow passengers carefully. They were all known to him by sight, but he could not have called any of them friends. He had not made friends with anyone at the hospital and, with hindsight, it occurred to him that this had been a mistake. All he could do was try to make good the deficit as far as possible.

There was Andy, a big Scotsman who had lost a leg below the knee, and Ginger, a runt of a man who had lost part of a lung and seemed to have a permanent cough. Then there was Steve, whose hands had been so badly burned trying to rescue his mates from a burning tank that they were reduced to blackened claws. Opposite them sat 'Pinky' Pinkerton, who shook all the time with shell shock, and Dave, who had retreated into a state of catatonia and neither spoke nor seemed to hear what was said to him. They were not a promising crew for the enterprise Richard had devised during a long, sleepless night.

Two German soldiers came out to the ambulance. One, a

grossly fat man whose stertorous breathing Richard could hear from inside the vehicle, climbed into the driver's seat. The other, a pale, lanky youth with pinched, undernourished features liberally decorated with acne, got into the back, his rifle across his knees. Obviously they were both regarded as being unfit for active duty and had been relegated to this comparatively undemanding task instead. Richard said politely, 'Good morning. Are you escorting us to the prison camp?'

The boy merely stared at him blankly and made no response. Richard smiled pleasantly and remarked, 'I hear the Germans are losing the war.'

The boy ignored him.

'You're an ugly-looking little bugger, aren't you?' Richard commented cheerfully. There was no response.

'He doesna' speak English, mon,' Andy pointed out.

'No, so I gathered,' Richard agreed.

The ambulance coughed into life and jolted out of the hospital gates. Richard grinned at his companions.

'Well, all aboard the *Skylark* for the grand mystery tour. I wonder where we're going.'

'It won't make any difference to us, will it,' Ginger commented morosely.

'I'm Richard, by the way,' Richard said.

The others introduced themselves, except for Dave, who continued to gaze blankly into space. Andy and Steve seemed happy with this small act of sociability and there was some desultory conversation as they traversed the streets of a small town and headed out into the country. Ginger, however, stared gloomily out of the window and said nothing. Richard set himself to be entertaining. He told them several of Monty's old jokes – not the ones he used in his stage act, but the ones he kept for his audience in the pub afterwards. They went down well and even Ginger began to snort with laughter. Richard kept an eye on the spotty guard, but although he occasionally glanced towards them as if puzzled by the sudden outbursts of mirth there was no flicker of comprehension in his eyes.

The vehicle began to climb, grinding along in low gear, and Richard could see that the land outside was heavily forested. He had taken a rough bearing from the sun as they set off and now guessed that they were heading into the Ardennes. Before long they would come to the German border, after which his chances would be considerably diminished. He looked again at the guard and saw that his unhealthy face had become even paler than before and that he was breathing hard through his nose. Richard felt a sudden flicker of optimism. The boy was travel sick! He turned to his companions again.

'Did I tell you the one about the prisoners of war who escaped from an ambulance?' he asked, maintaining the same light-hearted tone as before.

There was a brief silence and then the Scotsman said, 'No. How does that one go, then?'

'Right.' Richard sat forward and grinned encouragingly at the others. 'There were these six prisoners of war who were being taken to prison camp through the middle of a forest. After a bit one of them asked the guard to stop because he needed a piss. When the ambulance stopped all the others decided they needed to pee too, so they all got out. While the guard was trying to keep an eye on all of them, one of them,' he indicated himself, 'got round behind him and cracked him over the head with his crutch. Then they all ran like hell in different directions, and because the driver was too fat to run far, and anyway he couldn't run in six directions at once, they all got away.' There was a stunned silence. Richard, still grinning, added, 'Laugh, bugger you. That was the punch line.'

There was a ragged chuckle from the listeners and then Andy said, 'There's a couple of things wrong with that story.

One, some of us can't run, and two, the driver has a rifle. He may not be able to run but he can still shoot.'

'Look how thick the trees are,' Richard said. 'In a few yards he wouldn't be able to hit anyone.'

'Well, you can count me out,' said Ginger. 'I'm not running anywhere.'

'And there's no way I can run,' the big Scotsman pointed out. 'However, if you want to go ahead I've no objection to distracting the driver's attention for as long as I can.'

Richard looked at the others. He knew that if he was the only one to run his chances of being caught were proportionally greater.

Steve said, 'I'll give it a go. I don't fancy the next few years in a prison camp.'

'Pinkie?' Richard asked.

The man was shivering harder than ever. 'I . . . I don't know,' he stuttered.

Richard looked at Dave. To his surprise the usually blank eyes were fixed on him and he thought he saw an imperceptible nod.

The road flattened out and the engine changed up a gear. Richard had the feeling that time was running out. Suddenly the guard made a convulsive movement and lurched towards them, and for a terrifying moment Richard thought he had understood after all. But he merely thrust himself between Richard and Andy and stuck his head out of the window. Richard caught the smell of vomit on the air.

As the boy returned to his place, muttering an embarrassed apology, Richard decided that he must take his chance. If the rest did not follow his lead then so much the worse. He leaned towards the guard and smiled sympathetically, patting his own stomach and nodding to convey that he understood what he was suffering. An answering smile flickered briefly across the boy's face. Richard tapped him on the knee, pointed outside and mimed undoing his flies. The boy shook his head. Richard grabbed himself and jogged up and down with an anguished expression. The boy looked doubtful. Then Richard saw a new wave of nausea sweep him and he got up and moved to the front of the ambulance, where he hammered on the partition between them and the driver and shouted to him to stop. The ambulance pulled in to the side of the road and came to a halt, and the guard opened the rear door and gestured to Richard to get out.

As he climbed down, being careful to move with difficulty and lean heavily on the crutch, Richard looked around him. There was a shallow ditch on either side of the road and beyond that the forest stretched into the distance, tree upon tree. The guard had unslung his rifle and was pointing it in Richard's direction, jerking it in an indication that he should get on. Richard looked beyond him to the interior of the ambulance. If the others did not back him this far he had no hope. To his relief he saw first Steve and then Andy clamber down. The guard turned and tried to gesture them back but they both indicated that they need to perform the same operation as Richard. Behind them, he could see Ginger and Pinky climbing out too.

Richard limped to the edge of the ditch and unbuttoned his flies. He found Steve beside him. Steve muttered, 'You take the other side of the road. I'll go this way.'

He was fumbling at his buttons with his contorted fingers and Richard wondered briefly whether he should offer to help, then a sound to his right recalled him to the purpose of the exercise. The young guard was leaning against a tree trunk, vomiting helplessly. Richard looked round. The back view of the driver was visible as he climbed ponderously out of his cabin but between them stood Andy, propped squarely on his crutches and barring his way. Richard hobbled back towards the vehicle. The guard was a few feet away, bent over in a further convulsion of nausea. For a second Richard hesitated, prevented by a chivalric instinct from taking advantage of his condition, but then he remembered the bodies on the French road. He took his crutch by the lower end, swung it like a mallet and brought the heavy wooden cross-piece down on the back of the boy's head. He fell forward without a sound into his own vomit.

By the time he hit the ground Richard was running, across the road, over the ditch and into the sheltering trees. He did not stop to look round and see how many of the others had taken their opportunity. It seemed an amazingly long time before he heard the fat man's shout of alarm and then the crack of a rifle. By this time, glancing round, he could only just make out the ambulance through the trees. The bullet, if it had been aimed at him, must have buried itself harmlessly in a tree trunk.

He ran on, gasping for breath, putting as much distance between himself and the road as possible, until he could run no farther. Then he stopped and leaned against a tree, trying to listen for the sounds of pursuit over the rasping of his own breath. The muscles of his leg had gone into spasm and arrows of pain shot up into his groin. Eventually, he eased himself round the tree and stared back the way he had come. The forest was quite silent. He guessed that the fat man had decided, since he could not chase them all, to chase no one. That was, assuming anyone else had run. He spared a passing thought to the hope that those who remained behind would not suffer on his account.

After a brief rest he forced himself to go on, knowing that before long others would be searching for him who would not be so easy to shake off. The land sloped away ahead of him and he followed it down in the hopes that at the bottom of the valley he might find a stream. He suspected that dogs would be brought in to track him and calculated that his best chance of shaking them off was to find water. There was a stream, but it was a miserable trickle rather than the deep watercourse he had hoped for. He stooped and scooped up water to drink, then stepped into it and waded downstream.

After an hour's walking the little stream led him to a larger river. This was more what he was looking for. He hesitated for a moment. If they tracked him this far, which way would they expect him to turn? Downstream was probably the way back into France and towards habitation. He turned and waded upstream. It was hard going. Though the water was only knee deep the bed of the river was rocky and slippery with weeds. Every step sent a stab of agony through his damaged leg, and after several months of forced inactivity he was far from fit. When he felt he could go no farther he struggled across the river and dragged himself out on the far bank.

He lay there for some time, telling himself that this was a stupidly exposed position but unable to summon the strength to go on. At length, he got to his feet and stumbled deeper into the woodland that clothed the hills on this side of the river, as on the other. It was late afternoon and he had eaten nothing since breakfast, his muscles ached and he could hardly bear to put his left foot to the ground. What was worse, he had no idea where he was or how far it might be to the nearest dwelling. He had planned, vaguely, to subsist by stealing food – eggs from farms or scraps from any houses he passed. He intended to keep heading west until he reached the sea. Beyond that he had no idea what he was going to do.

When he could walk no farther he sat down with his back against the bole of an oak tree and rubbed his leg to try to ease the cramp in it. The forest stretched around him in all directions, and he recalled that throughout the day he had not seen a trodden path, much less any sign of a road that might lead to a habitation. He knew from prior experience that he could keep going without food for much longer than he had believed possible, but sooner or later he would have to find something to eat, and he had no woodsman's skill in trapping animals or recognising edible fruits. Accustomed to the woodlands of England, where it was impossible to walk for very long in any direction without reaching civilisation, he began to suspect that in this apparently illimitable forest it would be possible to die of starvation before finding a house. He consoled himself with the thought that, at least, there was no sign of pursuit and that the summer night was mild, even at this altitude. Eventually he curled himself into a ball in the hollow at the base of the tree and fell into a fitful sleep.

He woke from the last and deepest doze with the instant conviction that he was not alone. He lay still, his brain coldly assessing the possibilities. They had found him after all, then. How many of them? What chance was there of making a sudden, surprise move and losing them among the trees? He knew from the feeling in his legs that for some time he would be incapable of rapid movement. He continued to lie still, waiting for the jackboot in his ribs. When it did not come he cautiously opened his eyes. A boy of about fifteen was squatting on his haunches a few feet away, regarding him curiously.

Seeing Richard's eyes open he said, '*Soldat anglais?*'

The accent was unfamiliar but the words, praise God, were unmistakably French. Richard raised himself carefully on to his elbow and looked around him. Apart from himself and the boy the woods were empty and silent. It was early morning and the new-risen sun was slanting almost level rays between the trees.

'*Soldat anglais?*' the boy repeated.

'*Oui,*' Richard responded.

'*Prisonnier?*'

'*Oui.*'

The boy straightened up. '*Venez.*'

Richard eased himself into a sitting position. 'Come where? *Où?*'

The boy stooped and picked up two dead rabbits, holding them by their back legs.

'*Vous avez faim?*'

Richard's stomach rumbled in answer. '*Oui.*'

'*Alors, venez.*'

Richard looked around at the forest. The boy might be leading him into a trap. On the other hand, if he refused to go with him, where else was he to find help? It seemed he had no choice but to trust. He struggled painfully to his feet.

The boy came back to him. '*Vous êtes blessé?*'

'Wounded? *Oui.*'

Without further words the boy took his hand and laid it on his own shoulder and, thus supported, Richard began to limp beside him down the slope of the hill. Before long he noticed that they were following a trodden path, which later joined a wider track and then, rounding a bend, they came in sight of a clearing. In the centre of the clearing was a small, wooden house with a steeply sloping roof. Against one side of it and sheltered by the overhang of the roof was a huge pile of logs. Smoke rose from the chimney, a goat bleated at the end of a long rope and chickens scratched around a few rough sheds. Already the boy was leading him across the open ground, calling as he went, '*Maman! Maman!*'

A door opened and a short, sturdily built woman appeared. She stared for a moment, then threw up her hands in a gesture of dismay and hurried over to them. Richard let her take his other arm and heard the boy explaining how he had found him asleep, while she muttered and clucked like a sympathetic hen. Inside the cottage the single ground-floor room was furnished with tables and chairs of rough wood. A kitchen range glowed in one corner and there was a smell – he could scarcely believe the evidence of his own senses – a smell of freshly baked bread.

The woman and her son helped him to a seat by the table and within minutes she had set before him a long loaf of crusty bread, some curd cheese and a glass of milk. It was the best meal he had ever tasted.

While he ate the boy set to work skinning the rabbits and the woman busied herself around the room, without asking any further questions. When she saw that he had finished she came to him and tapped his left knee.

'*Blessé?*'

He nodded. She mimed washing and he shook his head and rolled up his trouser leg to show her that the wounds, though painful, were healed and in no need of attention.

She exclaimed and clicked her tongue in sympathetic distress. Then she tapped her own chest and said, '*Je m'appelle Clothilde. Clothilde Jumeau. Mon fils s'appelle Stéphan.*'

He smiled. '*Je m'appelle Richard. Vous êtes très gentille, madame.*'

She was delighted to discover that he spoke enough French to converse, although he struggled often to understand the unfamiliar accent. In a series of fractured exchanges he learned that they were a family of woodcutters but that the father, Jean-Claude, had been called up at the beginning of the war and they had no idea what had become of him since the Belgian capitulation. They hoped that he, like Richard, had been taken prisoner and that perhaps he, too, might escape. They wanted to know how Richard had done it.

He told them briefly and then added, 'The Germans will be looking for me, madame. I should go now. If they find me here it will be bad for you.'

She shrugged. '*Les salles Boches!*' Then added, 'You need to rest. Tomorrow, perhaps, you can move on.' She pointed to a ladder that led up to a platform which extended over half the room. 'Stéphan will keep watch. If the Boches come we shall hear them a long way off and have plenty of time to warn you.'

He hesitated. He had two choices. He could leave now and take his chances in the forest, or he could trust them. He opted for the latter.

He climbed the ladder with some difficulty and found that the platform contained two beds, covered in rough woollen blankets and divided by a curtain. Madame directed him to the smaller bed, presumably Stéphan's, and tucked the blanket over him as if he were still a child.

He murmured, 'You are very kind, madame,' and she answered, with a lift of her shoulders and a small smile, 'After all, you are some mother's son.'

Then she went back down the ladder. He saw the door open and close as Stéphan went out and discovered that, lying on his side, he could watch Clothilde as she moved around, clearing the remains of his meal and then chopping vegetables to go with the rabbit. He found himself thinking of his own mother, who was so different in every respect from this rough peasant woman. Where Clothilde was thickset, with large, capable hands that were roughened with hard labour, his mother was tall and thin, with delicate, carefully manicured fingers. Where Clothilde's movements were slow, deliberate, economical, his mother's were rapid, febrile and fastidious. Yet there was something basic and essential that they both shared and that he had sensed as Clothilde bent over him.

He had suffered anguished hours in the hospital at the thought that his parents might not know what had become of him. His recollections of the days immediately prior to his capture were hazy. He remembered giving Bob a letter but could not think who it had been addressed to, and he knew he had intended to give him Rose's address, but could not recall whether he had done so or not. He presumed his parents would have been told that he was 'missing in action' and had imagined their distress as they waited for further news. Then, just a few days before his transfer from the hospital, a representative of the Swiss Red Cross had visited the ward. He had written down Richard's name, rank and serial number and his parents' address and had promised to contact them. He had told Richard that he was entitled to write one letter a month and had offered to post one for him. Richard had wanted to write to Rose, but he knew his first duty was to his mother and father, so he wrote a rapid note, telling them what had happened and giving them Rose's address, with the request that they pass the news on to her. He wondered what his mother would make of the sudden introduction of this hitherto unmentioned girlfriend, but there was nothing he could do to change matters now.

Drifting into sleep, lulled by the sound of Clothilde's movements, he wondered whether his letter had arrived yet and tried to calculate how long ago he had sent it. Then it occurred to him that all the information in it was out of date anyway and might merely serve to set up hopes that would ultimately be dashed. He was very far from being safely tucked up in a hospital bed, as they might imagine.

When he woke it was late afternoon and the cottage was full of the smell of rabbit stew. Over the meal, he learned more about his hosts. He asked how they managed without Stéphan's father and was told that, though times were hard, they did not go hungry. They had the hens for eggs and the goat for milk and a vegetable patch where they grew potatoes and greens and Stéphan was adept at setting snares for rabbits. Although he could not manage alone to cut down large trees or haul big pieces of timber there was plenty of smaller wood in the forest, more than enough for their own needs. Once every two weeks they walked to the nearest village to collect the small pension that the government allowed Clothilde and to barter firewood for essentials such as flour and salt. And out here in the forest no one bothered them. Things could be worse, much worse.

The next morning Stéphan came into the cottage carrying some tools. 'If the Boches come, you will need a place to hide,' he said. 'Are you strong enough to help me?'

Richard nodded and Stéphan led him across the room to where a large chest stood. Together, they moved it aside and the boy began levering up the floorboards underneath. Richard saw that the cottage had no real foundations but the floor was laid on joists that rested in turn directly on the ground. Once the boards were up, Stéphan handed him a spade.

'Dig,' he commanded.

They dug until they had created a long, narrow hole, just deep enough for Richard to lie in. It reminded him horribly of a grave but, as Stéphan pointed out, once the floorboards were in place and the heavy chest on top of them he was unlikely to be discovered. He drilled several holes in the boards, to let air in, and then they replaced them and put the chest back in position. Richard shuddered and prayed that he would never have to make use of the hiding place.

On the third day Richard was sitting in the sun on a bench by the cottage door when Stéphan come running into the clearing. He had taken to working in the woods farther down the track that led to the cottage, so as to get prior warning if anyone was approaching.

'*Les Boches!*' he panted. '*Les Boches viennent! Ecoutez!*'

Richard listened. In the distance he heard the sound of a motorbike. Already Stéphan was hauling the chest out of its place. Richard scrambled into the hole and found himself in semi-darkness as the boards were put in position. Pinholes of light came through the air holes but in a moment they dimmed as he heard Stéphan and his mother pull the chest into position. He was thankful to see that they were not blocked altogether, since the chest had feet and so did not rest flat on the floor. Nevertheless, with the boards only inches above his face, the feeling of claustrophobia was almost unbearable.

He found he could still hear what was going on above him. He heard Clothilde greet the visitors, her voice level, matter-of-fact, neither hostile nor falsely welcoming. What, she asked, could she do for them? A man's voice replied, speaking French with a heavy German accent, and Richard heard the word '*prisonnier*'. It was him they were looking for, then. He closed his eyes and thought of his two protectors, praying that they would not suffer for concealing him.

Steps vibrated on the floor of the room. Voices muttered, speaking German this time, and he heard furniture being moved. His heart hammered harder. They were searching the room. If they moved the chest, would they notice the loose boards? He jumped convulsively as the lid of the chest opened and slammed shut over his head. If they found him he must put up no resistance. That would only endanger Clothilde and her son further. Could he pretend that he had found the hiding place without their knowledge? The Huns would never believe that.

Suddenly a thought came to him, more terrible than his former imaginings. Suppose the Germans decided to arrest Clothilde and Stéphan, or to take them away for questioning? He knew that he would never have the strength to lift the floorboards and push the chest aside from below. He would be buried alive. The only chance of being found would be if his hosts betrayed his hiding place, but why should they do that when it would incriminate them? It took all his self-control to stop himself hammering on the boards to be let out.

Clothilde's voice spoke, casually. Would the soldiers care for a glass of cider? It was a warm day and they had come a long way. Steps moved away from the chest and he heard a cupboard door open and shut and the clink of glasses. Some-one said, '*Santé*.' There was a pause, and then smacking of lips and a genial comment on the quality of the cider.

The voices and the footsteps receded. Richard strained his ears. Had they taken Clothilde and Stéphan with them? He was sweating in the confined space and beginning to pant for breath. He heard the engine of the motorbike start and fade away into the distance. Then there was silence. He had almost convinced himself that he had been left to die alone when he heard steps and the chest was pulled aside.

'I'm sorry,' Stéphan said. 'I waited to be sure they were not coming back.'

Richard scrambled out, trying to conceal the fact that he was shaking all over. 'You were quite right.' He looked across to where Clothilde had imperturbably resumed kneading dough. 'Madame, you were magnificent. I owe you my life.'

She looked across and shrugged. 'Your mother would do as much for my Stéphan.'

For an instant Richard tried to imagine his mother dealing with a similar situation and found it impossible. He crossed the room, took one of Clothilde's flour-covered hands and pressed his lips into the palm.

He stayed on with the Jumeaus for several weeks, waiting for his leg to regain its strength. To begin with he was content just to sit in the sun and watch his hosts at work, his mind and body lulled into a convalescent lassitude. Then he began to find small ways of helping out. He collected the eggs and fed the hens, chopped and carried firewood, drew water from the well. Later still he started to go out into the forest to help Stéphan cut down and drag home timber that he could not have managed on his own. A morning came when, lying in bed in the brief moments between waking and getting up, he discovered a sense of contentment, of pleasure in the prospect of the day ahead. It would be quite easy, he reflected, to stay where he was until the war was over. Clothilde and Stéphan could do with his help, after all.

That evening, coming back from the forest with Stéphan, he felt relaxed and pleasantly tired. As they came to the edge of the clearing the boy suddenly caught his arm and pulled him back into the shelter of the trees.

'What is it?' Richard asked. 'What's wrong?'

'See, on the washing line? My mother's blue apron. That is our signal for danger. We agreed it at the beginning of the war. Someone has come to the house. Perhaps the Germans are back.'

Cautiously, they circled the house, keeping under cover of the trees, until they could see the front. There was no motorbike, but an ancient bicycle was propped by the front door.

'It is Henri Dubois, our local gendarme,' Stéphan whispered. 'What does he want?'

They waited until the policeman appeared, a small, neat man who made an odd contrast with his ancient machine. His parting with Clothilde, who saw him off, seemed affable enough, and the somewhat erratic course he steered across the clearing suggested that he, too, had been drinking cider, but when they entered the house Clothilde's expression was grim.

'Someone has been talking in the village. It is probably Laforge, who keeps the shop. He must have noticed that I was buying more food than usual. He is a *collaborateur*. So is Dubois. He came asking questions – had I seen any strangers, et cetera – but all the time he was looking around. He saw the extra bed.' (Richard had suggested that they make up a bed for him in the living room so that Stéphan could have his back.) 'I told him it was for me. That my rheumatism is bad and I cannot climb the ladder any more. But he knows I do not suffer from rheumatism. He is suspicious. He will tell the Germans and they will come back and search again.'

'Then I must go,' Richard said, with a sudden wrench of nostalgia for the peaceful days now ended. 'I must go at once.'

That night Stéphan conceived a sudden need to go to confession and later the local *curé* arrived in his old Renault, on an urgent pastoral mission.

Chapter Nine

Rose straightened up and looked at the clock. Nearly a quarter to five, only three-quarters of an hour to closing time, and tomorrow was Sunday. Thank heaven! With every week that passed she was growing more and more bored and frustrated with working in her mother's shop. She looked down at the elderly lady seated in front of her.

'How do those feel, Mrs Cleary?'

The woman rose and walked a few steps uneasily in the new shoes.

'I don't know. They're not as comfy as the old ones. Are you sure you can't get the same pattern?'

'We have to take what we can get, Mrs Cleary. Things are in short supply now. New shoes never feel as comfy as the old ones to start with. Perhaps when you've worn them in a bit . . .'

She was interrupted by the wail of the air-raid siren. Mrs Cleary jumped visibly and exclaimed, 'Oh my Gawd! We'd better get to the shelter.'

'I expect it's only another false alarm,' Rose said reassuringly.

'I don't know about that,' the old woman replied. 'I ain't takin' any chances, anyway.'

She grabbed up her handbag and began to shuffle towards the door, just as Mrs Taylor came down from the flat above, carrying their gas masks and Rose's library book.

'Come along, Rose,' she said. 'We'll lock up now and get down to the shelter. There won't be any more customers today.'

'I don't think I'll come down, Mum,' Rose said. 'I hate that smelly, gloomy shelter and it's bound to be a false alarm.' She turned as the bell over the shop door jangled. 'Hey! Mrs Cleary! You've still got the new shoes on!'

She ran to the door but the old woman was already scurrying away along the street as fast as her bunioned feet could carry her.

'Mrs Cleary!' Rose called. 'You haven't paid for those shoes!'

'Oh, let her go,' her mother said. 'I'll catch up with her in the shelter and remind her. Where are her old ones?'

'Here.' Rose put the dilapidated old shoes into a bag and handed them to her mother. 'I'll keep that,' she added, taking the book.

'Are you sure you won't come down, Rose?' Mrs Taylor asked. 'It worries me to think of you up here, in case there really is a bomb.'

'Well, even if the bombers do come over this time,' Rose said, 'why would they bomb Lambeth? There's nothing important here, is there?'

'And what makes you think they know where the bomb's going to drop?' her mother asked.

'Look,' Rose took her mother's arm and led her to the door, 'if it's a real raid and the bombs start to drop I'll come straight down to the shelter. Promise.'

'If you're still able,' her mother grumbled.

'I'll be all right,' Rose assured her. 'Go on. You'll be back inside the hour, I bet.'

Once her mother had gone off down the road Rose locked the shop door and went upstairs to put the kettle on. She was looking forward to a quiet cup of tea and an uninterrupted chance to get on with her book. The sitting room felt stuffy and she went to open a window. It was a beautiful September evening, as warm as high summer still, with a cloudless sky.

She could see over the roofs of the houses to the trees in Kennington Park, their leaves drooping and dusty after the long dry spell. She leaned on the sill and thought of the previous September. It was over a year now since war had been declared, over a year since she had said goodbye to Richard.

As she stood dreaming she became aware of a noise. It was the low throb of approaching aero engines. She leaned out of the window and searched the sky. Over to the east she saw a V formation of planes, their fuselages gilded by the lowering sun. *Ours, or theirs?* she wondered, and for the first time felt a twinge of fear. As she watched the pattern changed. The V formation stretched itself out into line astern and the leader began to describe a tight circle, the others following. The dull thud of the first explosion came a minute later and seconds after that the curtain suddenly blew back into Rose's face on a blast of warm air. Rose gasped but she could not drag herself away from the window. Below the circling planes small white puffs appeared, like dabs of cotton wool. Rose recognised them as anti-aircraft fire, but the planes were far too high to be disturbed. There was another explosion and another and another. The leading plane left the circle and headed away, the others following, but even as they did so a second formation was already moving into position. Rose scanned the streets, trying to work out where the bombs were falling. That way was the river and the East End. Of course, it was the docks! The bombers were attacking London's lifeline, the umbilical cord that connected the city to the outside world, on which it depended for its supplies.

As Rose watched a cloud began to rise above the house tops, as white as cumulus on top, rose red underneath. It was a thing of beauty until she realised that it must be smoke from an enormous conflagration. A few streets away a fire engine roared past, its bell clanging. A minute later another followed.

From farther away she could hear others. Every fire engine in London must be heading east! The sound roused her. She had promised her mother that if it was a real raid she would go down to the shelter. Oddly enough, she did not feel frightened. The spectacle of the glinting planes and the blossoming white cloud was too distant and too beautiful to seem threatening.

In the street the mood was different. People were scurrying towards the shelter at the corner and Rose could see panic on their faces. The ground shook under her feet as a fresh rain of bombs fell. As she entered the shelter her mother jumped up and grabbed her.

'Oh, Rose, you bad girl! I've been worried to death. I thought you were a goner.'

Rose hugged her. 'It's all right, Mum. I've been watching, that's all. It's not us that's getting it. It's the docks.'

Other voices chimed in. 'What's happening? What's going on up there?'

Rose described what she had seen, to murmurs of horror and disbelief.

'Where are the guns?' an old man demanded. 'They told us the bombers would never get near London. They said the guns would get them first.'

'Well, they don't seem to be doing much good at the moment,' Rose said, and explained the ineffectual anti-aircraft fire.

In the windowless underground shelter the people huddled along the benches had no way of knowing what was happening, but they could feel the concussion of the explosions.

A big woman hugged her Pekinese to her and wept. 'What if it's our turn next?'

Mrs Cooper from two doors down glared at her over the head of her five-year-old. 'We'll be all right. We're safe enough down here.'

Time passed and at length the ground stopped shaking.

People became restless. 'How much longer?' was the repeated refrain. Daisy Perks, a pretty fifteen-year-old wearing too much make-up, kept looking at her watch and exclaiming, 'It's not fair! It's Saturday night, and I've got a date.'

'Oh, stop whining, for the Lord's sake,' snapped her mother.

'But he'll think I've stood him up,' the girl protested.

'If he's got any sense he'll been down in a shelter too,' Mrs Taylor pointed out. 'He'll know why you're not there.'

At 6.15 the all-clear sounded. 'Blimey, about time too!' someone exclaimed.

They made their way stiffly up into the daylight and then stopped, staring along the street towards the east. A huge pall of black smoke hung in the sky, its underside lit red by the sunset – or was it by flames?

'Streuth!' said someone. 'The whole bloody docks must have gone up.'

In a strange silence, too shocked for conversation, they dispersed to their various houses. Up in the flat Rose discovered that she had left the kettle on and it had boiled dry.

'Lucky it didn't set the whole place on fire,' her mother remarked drily. 'Save Hitler a job.'

They did not talk much over supper, but as they were clearing up Mrs Taylor said, 'Oh well, look on the bright side. They've probably done what they set out to do. Maybe that'll be the end of it.'

'I wonder,' Rose murmured. 'I hope so.'

They settled for the evening, Mrs Taylor with the wireless tuned to the Light Programme and Rose with her book. Soon after eight the siren went again. They looked at each other and Mrs Taylor exclaimed, 'Oh, not again!', but there was fear in her eyes and this time Rose made no argument about going down to the shelter.

By the time they got there it was already filling up with their neighbours. Men, those beyond the age for call-up or in reserved occupations, were grumbling about being dragged out of the pub, leaving half-finished pints behind them. One woman hurried in with a towel wrapped round her head, her hair still wet from her Saturday night shampoo. The local air-raid warden looked in and attempted to reassure them.

'Don't suppose it'll be a long one, this time. Probably just a recce to see how much damage they did this afternoon.'

'How bad was it?' someone asked.

'Pretty bad. The whole of the docks area is on fire. There have been a lot of casualties. You keep your heads down in here. You'll be all right.'

They felt the concussion of the first bombs a few minutes later, and this time they seemed closer. Suddenly the door opened and half a dozen Saturday evening revellers who had intended to ignore the warning tumbled in.

One woman was screaming hysterically. 'Oh my God! Oh my God! They're coming down like rain out there! The sky's full of planes – thousands of them! They're going to flatten the whole city!'

Outside, they heard the bells of fire engines and ambulances. One of the latecomers said, 'A shelter round the corner got a direct hit. God knows how many killed.'

The woman with the Pekinese set up a wail to rival the hysterical one. Mrs Taylor got up from her seat and marched over to her. 'Now listen here, Mrs Sharp! There are kids down here, and it's frightening enough for them as it is, without you making it worse. So pull yourself together. There's nothing we can do, so we must just trust in God and hope for the best.' She looked at the other woman. 'And you can stop your noise, too. If you hadn't been out drinking instead of down here with the rest of us you wouldn't know any different.'

Both women were so stunned by her verbal attack that they stopped howling and stared at her in silence. For a moment nobody spoke. Then a grey-haired woman at the far end of the shelter began to say the Lord's Prayer. Other voices joined in and after the 'amen' a precarious calm settled over the shelter.

By ten o'clock people were beginning to get restless again. Over-tired children grizzled and fidgeted. Men complained that if it didn't stop soon the pubs would be shut. Rose shivered in her thin summer dress. It had not occurred to her, on such a balmy evening, to bring a coat. The shelter was packed now, and there was not room on the narrow benches down either side for everyone to sit. Some of the men spread newspapers on the bare concrete floor and sat on them. Several of the children had needed to pass water and had done so in a bucket in the corner. The air stank of urine and sweat and stale alcohol. Rose began to be afraid that she might not be able to hold out and would have to make use of the bucket too.

The hours passed. Midnight came and 1 a.m. Still they could hear the endless drone of planes overhead and the crump of explosions. For a time it seemed that they were farther away and they began to relax a little. Someone suggested a sing-song, so they all sang 'Pack up your troubles in your old kit bag' and 'Tipperary' and 'Somewhere over the Rainbow'. Then, in the early hours of the morning, the planes seemed to come closer, as if they were circling directly overhead. There was a whistling scream and then an explosion that rocked the shelter and covered them with dust and flakes of whitewash off the walls. Before they could react there was a second scream and another explosion. Altogether they heard six in rapid succession. Children howled and clung to their mothers, women wept and men swore. Rose and her mother clasped each other in silence, too stunned for speech.

The barrage lasted for half an hour and then the focus of the bombing seemed to move away again. They looked at each other, shaken but beginning to exchange tentative smiles. They had had their baptism of fire, and had survived.

Mrs Taylor gripped Rose's hand and voiced the thought that had been in both their minds.

'Oh, Rose, do you think Bet and the little ones are all right?'

' 'Course they are,' Rose answered, with a confidence she did not feel. 'They'll be in their shelter, like us. They'll be OK.'

It was dawn when the all-clear sounded. Stiff and shivering, they clambered up the steps to the outside world. Rose heard the cries of despair before she got to the top of the steps, and as soon as she came out into the daylight she understood what had prompted them. The world they knew had utterly changed. Where there had been a busy, familiar street with shops and houses, buses and cars and bicycles, there was now a wilderness. Rubble was strewn across the road, broken glass was everywhere and everything was covered in a thick layer of brick dust. When they raised their eyes from this to find its source, the real horror struck them. Where rows of terraced houses had stood there were now huge gaps, like missing teeth, and on each side, still clinging to the walls of the remaining buildings, were the pathetic remnants of the inhabitants' lives – a wall decorated with nursery characters for a child's bedroom, a wardrobe hanging perilously in a corner, its contents scattered, a fireplace and above it a mirror, miraculously unbroken.

Rose dragged her gaze from the destruction in front of her and swung round to look down the street. Her mother turned at the same moment and they gave a simultaneous cry of relief.

'Thank God! The shop's still there,' Mrs Taylor exclaimed. Then she caught Rose's eye and, once again, the same thought entered both their minds. 'Bet! We must see if Bet's OK.'

They set off in the direction of Kennington. The sun was hardly up and Rose felt chilled to the bone after the long night in the damp shelter. She longed for a hot bath and a cup of tea but she knew that neither she nor her mother could relax until they were sure that Bet and the children were safe. In normal circumstances Bet's house was only a ten-minute walk away but today it took much longer. They had to pick their way over or around heaps of fallen masonry or negotiate patches of broken glass sometimes several inches deep. Rescue workers were busy in the middle of the chaos, clawing with their bare hands at fallen doors or lifting away the rubble brick by brick. Once they had to wait while a party of stretcher-bearers negotiated the narrow space between the piles of debris. As they passed Rose could not prevent herself from looking at the burden they carried. She could see nothing but a figure shrouded in an old rug and a wisp of grey hair clotted with blood.

Two streets away from their goal they found their way barred by tapes strung across the road. A policeman on duty said, 'Sorry, ladies. There's a house down here that could collapse any minute. You'll have to find another way round.'

Mrs Taylor said, her voice unsteady, 'Has there been a lot of damage in this area, then?'

'Yes, they got it pretty bad, I'm afraid,' the man replied, and then, seeing her reaction, he added, 'You got relatives round here?'

'In Chiltern Street. My daughter and two little ones.'

'Chiltern Street,' the policeman repeated. 'I think there was a direct hit there, but I haven't heard about casualties.'

They hurried on, tracing a circuitous route through neighbouring roads, and came at last to the end of Chiltern Street. There, once again, they found their way barred. Ahead they could see a huge mound of rubble that almost completely blocked the road. Men in the tin hats of the Civil Defence Corps were clambering over it and two St John's Ambulance volunteers stood by with a stretcher.

Just as they arrived a voice shouted, 'Quiet! Quiet everybody. I think I can hear someone.'

A silence settled over the street as the men stood still, straining their ears. Then came the shout, 'Over here! Everyone over here. There's someone trapped in here.'

As the rescuers converged on the spot Mrs Taylor clasped Rose's arm and murmured, 'Oh no! Oh no!'

'It's all right, Mum,' Rose said, putting her arm round her. 'That's not Bet's place. Her house is farther down the street.'

'But how do we know what's happened farther on?' her mother asked. 'That rubble could go right back to her place.'

Rose screwed up her eyes. The air was still full of dust and it was hard to see clearly more than a short distance ahead. Dimly she made out a moving figure, picking its way around the edge of the debris. As it came closer she could see that it was a woman. An old woman, she thought at first, but then she realised that the white hair was not the result of age but of a thick coating of white powder, dust from falling plaster. The woman carried a bundle wrapped in a bit of old curtain, and as she reached Rose and her mother she looked at them, her eyes startlingly dark against her clown-white face, and said, 'This is all that's left. It's all gone – everything. I've got nothing left.'

Mrs Taylor said urgently, 'What number do you live at?'

The woman looked down at her bundle. 'It's all gone,' she repeated. 'This is all I could find.'

'Do you know the Barkers?' Rose asked. 'Bet Barker and her two little boys? They live at number twelve. Have you seen them?'

Without responding the woman turned away and began to walk down the street. As she went they could hear her mumbling to herself, 'All gone! All gone!'

'Well, really!' Rose's mother exclaimed, her voice sharp with the effort of holding back tears.

'She's in shock, Mum,' Rose answered. 'You mustn't blame her.'

At that moment Mrs Taylor gave a sudden cry of relief. 'Oh, look, Rose! Look!'

Rose turned her eyes towards the blocked street again and saw advancing towards them three figures, one with the ample curves of her sister, flanked by the small shapes of the two boys. Mrs Taylor called out, 'Bet! Bet! We're here. Are you all right?'

Bet did not speak until they were only a few yards away. Then she stared at them as if puzzled. 'Mum? Rose? What are you doing here?'

Rose gazed back at her. All three of them were so covered in brick dust that they might have been figures made out of terracotta. Sam's face was smudged and blotched where he had wept and then rubbed his eyes. Billy stared at her expressionlessly, but there were rings round his eyes too where the skin showed paper white. Bet was clutching a suitcase in one hand and holding tightly on to Sam with the other.

'We came to look for you, of course,' Mrs Taylor answered. 'Thank God you're all in one piece! Are you hurt? What happened?'

'We was all in the shelter,' Bet said. 'Then there was this almighty crash and half the roof came in. Someone said it must have been a direct hit. I think some people were trapped. We got out and got in the cellar of number six for the rest of the night.' She paused and set down the suitcase. Her voice was flat, uninflected, as if she were describing something that had no immediate significance. 'The house has gone – most of it. The stairs were still there and the boys' bedroom. I managed to get a few of their things. All covered in dust, though.'

'Oh, Bet, you shouldn't have!' their mother exclaimed. 'It was a terribly dangerous thing to do. The whole place might have come down on top of you!'

'Gran, can we come and stay at your house?' Billy said. 'We can't sleep in our house any more.'

'Of course you can!' Rose answered for her mother. She ducked under the tape and took the suitcase. 'Come on, all of you. Let's get back home and have a nice cup of tea.'

It took a long time to make their way home. Bet moved as if sleepwalking and Sam began to whine that he was tired and couldn't walk any farther. Rose picked him up but her damaged ankle was already aching and before long she had to put him down again. Then, when they finally reached the flat, there was the business of getting the three of them clean and either washing or disposing of their clothes, which exuded brick dust on to every surface. Regretfully, Rose had to relegate her longed-for hot bath to later in the day, when the tank would have reheated. It was mid-morning before the two little boys, clean and fed, had been tucked up in Rose's bed to catch up on lost sleep and the adults sat down to a meal of bread and marge and tinned Spam. Mercifully, Bet had had the presence of mind to take their ration books down to the shelter with her, so at least when the shops reopened they would be able to buy food, but for the time being they were happy to settle for whatever was to hand.

'Will it happen again tonight, do you think?' Bet asked.

'No, surely not!' her mother answered. 'Haven't they done enough damage?'

'It depends on what they're trying to do, doesn't it?' Rose pointed out. 'If they want to bomb us into surrendering then I suppose they'll keep at it until we do.'

'But we won't surrender, will we?' Bet said. 'So that means this could go on and on.'

'Oh God, I don't think I can go through another night like last,' Mrs Taylor cried.

'Can't we get away?' Bet asked. 'We could go to the country somewhere. All of us, not just the kids like last time.'

'Where would we go?' Mrs Taylor asked. 'We don't know anyone who lives in the country.'

'People take in refugees, though,' Bet said. 'I've heard it on the wireless.'

'We can't just turn up somewhere and expect to be taken in,' her mother protested.

'Well, I'm not putting the kids through another night like last night,' Bet said, with sudden determination. 'I'd rather sleep under a hedge if we have to.'

'Just a minute!' Rose broke in. 'I've had an inspiration. Well, an idea anyway. It may not work but it's worth a try.'

'What is?' asked her mother and sister in unison.

'You remember Babe Willis – Barbara, from the Follies?'

'The little blonde girl?'

'That's the one. Her parents have a smallholding down in Dorset somewhere. I met them once or twice – ever such nice people. I'm sure if they've got room they'd put us up for a bit.'

'Oh, we couldn't ask them to do that, could we?' Mrs Taylor demurred. 'I mean, it's not as though there were just a couple of us. Five's too many.'

'OK,' Rose said. 'If they can't take us all, perhaps they could take Bet and the boys. That would be something, wouldn't it?'

'Oh, it would be wonderful if they could,' Bet murmured wistfully. 'Just to get out of London. We could all share one room, we wouldn't mind. Do you think they would have us, Rose?'

'We can only ask,' Rose said. 'I've got Babe's address somewhere and I'm pretty sure they've got a telephone. I'll have to get the number from Directory Enquiries.'

It took the rest of the morning to find a phone box that was still working and then to get through to an over-stretched Directory Enquiries. By the time Rose finally got a long-distance call connected to the Willises' house she was weary and despondent.

'Hallo, Mrs Willis? It's Rose Taylor. I don't know if you remember . . .'

'Rose? Of course I do. Where are you, dear?'

'I'm in London . . .'

'Oh my goodness! We've just heard on the news about the bombing. It's awful, just awful. Are you all right, dear?'

'Yes, I'm fine. But my sister's been bombed out, with her two little boys.'

'Oh, the poor things! Now look, why don't you all come down here for a bit? Best thing you can do is get out of London till it's all over.'

Rose gulped. 'Oh, Mrs Willis, that's terribly kind of you. It's exactly why I rang. Could you take in my sister and her two?'

'Of course we can, and welcome. But what about you?'

'Well, it's not just me. There's my mother, too.'

'Well, bring her as well. There's plenty of room with Barbara away.'

'Babe, away? Where is she?'

'Oh, didn't you know? She's gone and joined the Wrens. Having the time of her life, by all accounts.'

'Good Lord!' Rose exclaimed. It was hard to imagine the childlike Barbara in one of the armed services.

'So, as I was saying, there's only me and Bob so we've three spare bedrooms. You come, my dear. You're more than welcome.'

Rose returned to the flat flushed with triumph.

'Start packing!' she commanded. 'We're all going to the country.'

She relayed her conversation with Mrs Willis and was about to go to her room to pack when her mother said suddenly, 'But what about the shop?'

Rose stopped dead. The problem of the shop had never crossed her mind.

'I suppose . . .' she said slowly. 'I suppose we can't leave the shop.'

'Yes you bally well can!' her sister exclaimed. 'What's more important? Your lives or a few pairs of old shoes?'

'New shoes, not old shoes,' Rose corrected automatically. 'It's what we live on, Bet. Remember?'

'Bet's right,' their mother put in emphatically. 'And what are we losing anyway? There's not much stock, because we can't get the stuff, and even if we could people aren't buying. We can't do repairs any more, since Will was called up.'

'But how will we manage?' Rose asked. 'Bet's got her allowance from the army, but what about us?'

'I've got my widow's pension,' her mother pointed out. 'And I dare say you can find a job of some sort, or go on the dole if need be. After all, it may not be for long. A few weeks, perhaps. They can't keep this up indefinitely, can they?'

Rose gave in. 'All right. We'll go, and then we'll see what happens. Perhaps we'll be able to come back soon.'

They were halfway through packing when Mrs Taylor said suddenly, 'What about Merry? I know he's not often around these days but we can't just disappear without letting him know.'

'I'll write a note and send it to his HQ,' Rose said. 'He's got a key, so he can still stay here if he wants to, but I should think he'd rather find somewhere a bit safer. I'll leave the Willises' address for him, so we can keep in touch.' It occurred to her suddenly that if, by any remote chance, a letter came from Richard it would not reach her. 'And I'll give Mrs Sear, next door, a key and the address, so she can send on any letters.'

By four o'clock they were at Paddington station, where they discovered to their despair that the whole place was under siege from a vast horde of desperate refugees. Some people were trying to reach relatives, others were simply prepared to get on any train leaving the city, with no idea of what they would find at the other end of the journey. When they eventually boarded a train going to the right destination it was already packed. They struggled down the corridor, burdened with a heavy case apiece, squeezing past others who were already resigned to sitting on their luggage for the whole journey. Eventually they gave up and dumped their cases in one of the few spaces not already filled and sank down on them, Bet and Rose each with a child on her lap. Rose thought she had never been so tired in her life. After a night without sleep and the traumas and exertions of the day she was ready to weep with exhaustion.

The door of the nearest compartment slid open and a friendly voice said, 'Hey up, you look about all in, miss.'

She looked up. A soldier with a lean, sunburned face and bright hazel eyes stood looking down at her. Beyond him the carriage was full of his comrades.

'Why don't you and your family come and sit in here?' the man asked. 'We can take it in turns to stand, can't we, lads? Can't have ladies perched on suitcases while we sit in comfort, can we?'

Within minutes they were installed in the compartment, each boy was accommodated on a soldier's knee and, miraculously, supplied with chocolate. They were infantrymen going home on leave and had only passed through London on their way west. They listened with horror to the Taylors' story of the previous night's bombing.

'That swine Hitler had better look out!' Rose's rescuer declared vehemently. 'We'll be back, as soon as we've got the equipment, and we won't be such a pushover as we were at Dunkirk.'

'You were at Dunkirk?' Rose asked him.

'Oh, ay, we were there,' he said grimly.

Rose questioned him eagerly, but it was clear that none of them knew anything about the fate of the South Lancs regiment.

'Got someone in the South Lancs, then?' the soldier asked sympathetically. 'Boyfriend perhaps?'

'No,' Rose said hastily, 'no, just an acquaintance. Someone I used to work with.'

'Oh, right.' The man grinned and winked at his comrades. 'I might still be in with a chance, then.'

Rose looked at him uncertainly and his smile softened. 'You're OK. Don't worry. I've got a girl of my own back home. You're quite safe with me.'

The journey dragged on. Over and over again the train stopped, for no apparent reason. Once they heard the air-raid sirens and Mrs Taylor murmured, 'Oh no, not again, please God!' but after a few minutes the all-clear sounded and the train chugged on its way. In the carriages, unlit except for tiny blue bulbs, the passengers dozed fitfully, the men taking it in turns to stand in the corridor but refusing to let either Rose or Bet give up their seats.

When they finally drew into the station it was after midnight. They said goodbye to the soldiers and were helped out with their cases on to an empty and darkened platform, the two boys sleepy and querulous.

'What now?' asked Bet.

'There won't be any buses at this time of night,' Rose said. 'We may have to sit in the waiting room until morning.'

A solitary figure advanced along the platform towards them, resolving itself as it came closer into a large, raw-boned man with a weathered face.

'Mrs Taylor?' he asked. 'Rose, is that you?'

'Mr Willis!' Rose exclaimed. 'We didn't expect you to be here at this time of night. You surely haven't been waiting for us?'

'Well, we didn't know what train you'd be on,' the big man answered, his voice deep and untroubled. 'So I thought I'd best hang on till you showed up. Didn't want you stranded on the station all night.'

The relief was the last straw. Rose burst into tears and Bet immediately followed suit. Somehow they were all got into a rickety old truck and by the time they had negotiated the narrow lanes leading to the Willises' house they had regained their self-possession. In the big farmhouse kitchen there was light and warmth from the range and a meal of home-baked bread and home-cured ham and plum crumble laid out for them. Rose remembered little more of that night beyond crawling into a large double bed alongside her sister and the smell of linen sheets dried in the country air.

Chapter Ten

Merry climbed stiffly out of the jeep outside the Jolly Farmers pub and eased his shoulders. He felt as though he had travelled the length and breadth of England two or three times over in the last couple of months. His last tour had taken him to Yorkshire and Lancashire. Now here he was back in Essex, close to the RAF station at North Weald. The saloon bar was quiet as he entered but he felt sure that that would change soon. This was the nearest pub to the airfield and experience had shown him that it was where the pilots would come to unwind after the long daylight hours of tension and danger. He bought himself a pint and retired to a corner to wait.

As the late summer twilight faded he heard the sound of cars pulling up outside and loud, youthful voices. A moment later half a dozen young men in RAF uniform tumbled into the room, the wings on their tunics and the unfastened top buttons proclaiming them as pilots. Spitfire pilots, the elite among the elite. Merry had watched the planes coming in to land earlier and he knew a Spitfire when he saw one. He scanned the faces as they entered, but in some part of him he knew already that the face he was seeking was not among them. Relief mingled with disappointment. He still did not know, after all these pub vigils, what he would say if Felix walked in – as surely he must, one day.

The airmen bought their drinks and settled round a table. After a while, one of them wandered over to the old upright piano in the corner and began, inexpertly, to pick out the tune of a popular song. Merry stood it as long as he could, then he got up and went over.

'Mind if I have a go?'

'Can you play?'

'Yes.'

The boy got up. 'Good show! She's all yours.'

Merry played the tune he had been murdering and the other men crowded round the piano and began to sing. Merry segued smoothly into another popular favourite and then a couple more and the pilots began to call out requests. When he paused, someone said, 'Can you play ragtime?' So he gave them a Scott Joplin selection. As he finished there were cries of 'Encore!' but he sat back with a laugh.

'Do you mind? My fingers are dropping off!'

After that someone bought him another beer and he was invited to join the group. Introductions were exchanged and as soon as he felt a suitable moment had arrived Merry asked the question he had asked of every RAF man he had met on his travels. 'By the way, none of you happen to have come across a chap by the name of Edward Mountjoy, have you?'

The sudden silence caused the blood to drain from his heart.

'Are you a friend of Ned's?' one of the pilots said, his voice taut.

'Yes.' Merry forced himself to speak calmly. 'We worked together before the war but we seem to have lost touch. He's not . . .?'

'Shot down in flames yesterday,' the other man replied. 'He managed to bale out but he's badly burned, we were told.'

Merry discovered he had been holding his breath. He released it in a gasp. 'But he's still alive?'

'Yes. Well, he was this morning when the CO reported. But in a pretty bad way, by all accounts.'

'It's a bloody tragedy!' the boy who had been playing the piano blurted out. 'He was a brilliant flyer – and a bloody nice bloke!'

Another man got up abruptly, muttered an excuse and left the room.

'Chris was Ned's wingman,' the first speaker explained. 'He feels responsible – thinks he should have spotted the Hun before he got Ned. It's rubbish, of course. You can't have eyes everywhere.'

'Which hospital is he in?' Merry asked. 'Somewhere near here?'

'No. He was shot down over Kent. Which hospital did the CO say he was in?'

'Ashford,' one of the others volunteered.

'Yes, that's it. Ashford General.'

Felix was on his own in a side ward and it took all Merry's charm to persuade the sister in charge to let him in. At the door he hesitated for a moment, unsure whether he was in the right room. Felix's whole head and face were bandaged, only the left cheek and the corner of his mouth visible. But as Merry moved closer he saw that above the left ear a few strands of un-mistakable corn-gold hair had escaped the bandage. Then the smell came to him and he had to swallow hard to stop himself from gagging. It was the sweet-sour smell of burnt meat.

Merry felt cold sweat prickle his forehead. Felix was very still and it was impossible to tell whether he was conscious. He thought it would be cruel to wake him. But as he hesitated Felix turned his head on the pillow and mumbled, 'Who's that? Is somebody there?'

Merry forgot the smell and his own nausea and sat on the edge of the bed. 'It's me, Felix,' he said quietly.

'Merry? *Merry!* Thank God!' The voice was a harsh whisper but there was no mistaking the relief in it. Felix's right hand

and arm were shrouded in bandages but his left groped out to touch Merry's sleeve. Merry took it and held it firmly.

'I don't know,' he said, forcing himself to keep his tone light, 'I let you out of my sight for a few months and look what you go and do! Didn't anybody ever tell you the story of Icarus?'

The corner of Felix's mouth twitched in response. 'Flew too near the sun and got frazzled. That's me!'

They were silent for a moment, then Felix croaked desperately, 'I can't see, Merry! It's bloody well blinded me.'

Merry tightened his grip on the slim, long-fingered hand in his own. He could feel that Felix was trembling, a delicate, subtle vibration like an electric current. 'It's the bandages, Felix,' he said. 'You can't see because your eyes are bandaged. The sister told me that they won't be able to tell how bad the damage is until they take the bandages off.'

'When?' The young airman's voice cracked. 'When will they do that?'

'Not for another day or two, she said. You'll have to be patient, old chap.'

'Patient!' Felix gave a short, bitter laugh. 'I don't have much choice, do I?'

Merry waited a minute, then said, 'What happened, exactly?'

Felix twisted his head on the pillow restlessly and Merry regretted asking the question. 'Got into a dogfight over the South Coast. While I was busy with one Jerry another one must have sneaked up behind me. Suddenly realised the tail was on fire. Didn't want to ditch in the sea so I turned back for base, but the fire had got too much of a hold. I went to bale out but something got stuck – don't remember exactly. Just remember struggling with the canopy and the flames . . . Suppose I must have managed it eventually because a farmer found me lying on his muck heap. Might as well have left me there!'

'Self-pity?' Merry said. 'Come on, Felix, that's not like you.'

Felix was silent for a moment. Merry was aware that the hand, which he still held, had relaxed a little. Then Felix said, 'You called me Felix.'

'You are Felix, aren't you?'

'Yes, of course I am, but . . .'

'Thank God!' Merry tried for a note of comic relief. 'For an awful moment I thought I might be lavishing my care and attention on a total stranger.'

'But how did you know it was me?' Felix persisted.

'Well,' Merry said slowly, 'I have to admit it was a bit of an act of faith. To be quite honest, you look more like the invisible man at the moment.'

This time he was rewarded by another twitch of the lips, but Felix was not satisfied yet.

'What I mean is, they don't know me as Felix here. So how did you know it was *me*?'

'Ah,' Merry responded, as if enlightenment had dawned, 'I happened to run into some chaps from your squadron last night in the Jolly Farmer and they told me that Ned Mountjoy had been shot down and was in here.'

'And you knew that was me?' Felix persisted.

'My dear old chap, only a week or two ago, when you got your gong, your name and your face were plastered all over the papers – and it's not a face one readily forgets.'

As soon as the words were out of his mouth Merry regretted them. Felix turned his head away. 'I imagine it will be even more memorable now,' he said flatly.

For once Merry was at a loss for words. It was Felix who spoke next.

'What are you doing here, anyway? Oh God, you're not wounded too, are you? I never thought to ask.'

'No, no, I'm fine,' Merry said soothingly. 'I'm on my way to give a concert in Dover and I thought I'd drop in.'

'A concert?' Felix sounded puzzled. Then, for the first time, he seemed to become aware that his hand was still in Merry's. He pulled it away sharply. 'Oh my God! You're a bloody conchie!'

Merry drew a deep breath and said evenly, 'No, as it happens I'm not. If your eyes weren't bandaged you'd be able to see that I'm in uniform. I joined up the same day you did, but the army instead of the RAF. Unfortunately I had such a bad asthma attack that the powers that be decided I wouldn't be much use on active service. When they found out I used to be in show business it occurred to someone that I might be better employed entertaining the troops than pushing paper back at HQ.'

Felix sounded sceptical. 'You're not talking about ENSA, are you?'

'Good God, no! For one thing I'm still a serving soldier. Anyway, you know what ENSA stands for.'

'Every Night Something Awful,' Felix supplied with another twitch of the mouth. His hand crept out and touched Merry's sleeve. 'Sorry, old chap. Unforgivable of me.'

Merry looked down at the hand but did not take it. 'Oh, not really. Understandable mistake.' After a moment he said, 'Are you in much pain?'

Felix appeared to consider the question. 'Not really. Every so often a nice nurse comes and sticks a needle in my arm. Morphine, I suppose. I seem to sleep a lot.'

'Best thing you can do, for the time being,' Merry told him. He looked at his watch. 'Look, I'm going to have to leave you. I've got to get to Dover and find out what sort of instrument they've found for me to play on. With any luck they might even have got someone to tune it.'

'What are you going to play?'

Merry hesitated. 'Not quite the same sort of repertoire I used to play in the Follies. A bit of Chopin, Mendelssohn, some Beethoven . . . My bosses feel it's part of my job to supply a bit of culture as well as entertainment.'

'Good for you.' Felix's voice was growing drowsy. 'You were always too good for us lot. Wish I could come and listen.'

Merry swallowed a sudden lump in his throat. 'I'll play very loudly,' he promised. Then he added, 'I'm booked up for the next three days, but after that I should have a day off. If I can possibly wangle it I'll come and see how you're getting on.'

'Don't bother if it's difficult,' Felix mumbled.

'*Difficult* won't stop me,' Merry assured him. 'With *impossible* I may need a little help.'

He rose to his feet. Felix said suddenly, 'Merry, will you do something for me?'

'Of course. What is it?'

'There are some things in my locker – papers, letters and so on. Sister told me they'd found them in my inside pocket. Apparently the flying suit stopped them from getting burned. Could you look?'

Merry opened the locker by the bed. On the top shelf was a small pile of personal effects.

'There should be a letter,' Felix said. 'It's from Harriet. Her address and phone number are on it. Could you possibly call her and let her know what's happened? She must be wondering why I haven't been in touch.'

Slowly Merry opened the envelope and drew out the letter far enough to read the address.

'Yes, of course,' he said. 'I'll do that for you. I'll make a note of the number and leave the letter in the locker.' He wrote the phone number in his diary and then said, 'Of course, she may not be there, you know. A lot of people have left town because of the bombing. She may have gone to the country.'

'I don't think so. She was there last week,' Felix said.

'Right. I'll give her a ring, then.' Merry paused, looking down at the bandaged figure, wondering what that exquisite face would look like when the bandages came off; wondering whether Lady Harriet Forsyth could cope with what might be revealed. He laid his hand briefly over Felix's again. 'Keep your pecker up, old man. I'll see you in three days' time.'

Felix mumbled something, as if half asleep, but as Merry reached the door he roused himself.

'Merry?'

'Yes?'

'Thanks for dropping in. I . . . I needed to hear a friendly voice.'

Merry swallowed. 'Glad it helped. Take care.'

Outside in the corridor he found that he was shaking violently. He found a door leading outside and lit a cigarette. He had smoked it down to the butt before he felt calm enough to go back to his jeep.

It was the following day before Merry was able to get through to Harriet. He told her briefly what had happened to Felix. There was a silence at the other end of the line, a silence that went on so long he said, 'Harriet? Are you still there?'

'Yes!' It sounded as if she had been holding her breath. 'Yes, I'm here. Actually, I knew about Felix. One of his squadron rang me the other day and told me. I . . . I just haven't been able to get down to the hospital.'

'Oh,' Merry said bleakly. Then, 'Of course, I know transport is a problem these days.'

'Yes,' she said, 'no petrol for private motoring, and the trains all full of refugees. Merry?'

'Yes?'

'Have you . . . seen him?'

'Yes, yesterday.'

'Is he . . . Does he look . . .? How is he?'

'Heavily sedated, at the moment, fortunately. But quite

lucid. He asked me to get in touch with you.' *Bugger you*, he thought, *I'm not going to make it easy for you.*

'Will he . . .? Alan, the chap who rang, said he'd suffered burns to his face. Is he going to be . . . badly disfigured?'

'Impossible to tell at the moment,' Merry said. 'His whole head is swathed in bandages.' His voice hardened. 'He may have lost his sight.'

'Oh no!' Harriet sounded as if his words had caused her physical pain. 'Oh, how terrible! Poor Felix!'

'Yes, indeed, poor Felix.' Merry went on relentlessly, 'He needs every friend he's got at the moment, Harriet.'

'I know, I know!' She was almost in tears but Merry felt no pity. 'I'll try to get down, Merry. I promise.'

'Good,' Merry said. 'I'll call you again in a day or two to compare notes.'

He called again the following evening, but the butler informed him that Lady Harriet was not available.

Merry had to call in a number of favours and promise several new ones in order to obtain sufficient petrol to reach the hospital on his day off, but he managed it in time to arrive soon after lunch. At the entrance to the main ward he encountered the sister.

'You've come to see Flight Lieutenant Mountjoy?' she said. 'I'm glad. He could do with a bit of company this afternoon.'

'Why this afternoon, particularly?' Merry asked.

'The doctor promised to remove the bandages today, so we can see if his eyes have been affected. Unfortunately we've had several new admissions this morning and Doctor Evans simply hasn't been able to get round to him yet. The trouble is, he's refusing to let us give him any medication until after the doctor's been. He says he wants to keep a clear head.'

'I can understand that,' Merry responded, 'but I see the problem. Is he in a lot of pain, do you think?'

'Quite a considerable amount, I should say,' the sister replied. 'But with Flight Lieutenant Mountjoy it's hard to be sure. He's not one to complain.'

'Has he had any other visitors?' Merry asked.

'His CO came the other day – and a young lady called in yesterday. She didn't stay long.'

I bet she didn't, Merry thought.

Felix was lying very still, but this time Merry had no doubts about whether he was awake. It was not the stillness of relaxation.

As he approached the bed Felix said, 'Doctor?'

'No, sorry,' he replied. 'It's me, Merry.'

'Merry! Thank heaven! Someone sane to talk to at last.' Felix reached out with his good hand and Merry took it in both his own and held it tightly.

'They tell me you're refusing to let them give you an injection.'

'Want to be able to think straight when the damn doctor arrives,' Felix said. His hand was hot, the febrile tremor stronger than before.

Merry said, 'I can understand that, but is it sensible to suffer unnecessarily?'

'He should be here soon.' Felix twisted his head restlessly. 'The sister said after lunch.'

'OK,' Merry replied. 'It's your decision.'

'Give me a drink, can you?' Felix asked. 'There's a drinking cup thing somewhere with water in it.'

Merry relinquished his hand and found an object like a small teapot. Very carefully he slid his hand under Felix's head and raised it so that he could insert the spout into the exposed corner of his mouth. Some of the water escaped and ran down his chin and Merry found a clean handkerchief and gently blotted it away.

As he laid the bandaged head back on the pillow Felix said, 'Thanks for contacting Harriet for me.'

'She came, then?'

'Yes, yesterday. But she couldn't stay long. She had an aged aunt in the car who she was driving down to the country. She might call in again on her way back.'

'She might stay in the country herself,' Merry commented diplomatically. 'They had another bad raid last night.'

'Yes, I told her she should do that,' Felix agreed. 'She said she might.'

Footsteps came along the corridor and Merry saw Felix tense, but they passed without pausing.

'Damn!' Felix muttered. His hand moved and found Merry's sleeve. 'Talk to me, Merry. Tell me what you've been up to. How did the concert go?'

So for the next half-hour Merry set himself to entertain, recounting and embroidering incidents that had occurred during his performances or on his travels.

'Do you ever come across any of the old crowd from the Follies?' Felix asked at one point.

'I was in touch with Richard up until Dunkirk, and I've seen quite a bit of Rose,' Merry told him. 'Rose has had a hard time, poor girl.'

'How so?'

Merry told him the story of Rose's accident and explained how he had come to be staying at the Taylors' flat. 'But now it looks as though I shall have to find somewhere else,' he continued. 'I got a note from Rose the other day saying they were leaving London. Apparently they caught it pretty badly in the Blitz and her sister Bet was bombed out. But guess where they've gone – to stay with Babe Willis's family in Dorset.'

There was the rattle of a trolley outside and the door opened. An elderly man in a white coat came in, followed by the sister and a nurse pushing a trolley of instruments. Felix's hand tightened for an instant on Merry's arm and then withdrew.

The doctor said, 'Sorry to have kept you waiting so long, old man. We had a young lad brought in an hour or so back in an even worse state than you.'

'Who?' Felix asked tensely. 'Anyone I might know?'

The doctor mentioned a name and a squadron and Felix shook his head. 'Not one of ours. Poor blighter!'

Dr Evans looked at Merry. 'Would you mind waiting outside for a few minutes? We shouldn't be long.'

'Of course,' Merry agreed. He looked down at Felix and wished that he could think of something encouraging to say. In the end he just touched his shoulder and murmured, 'See you in a minute.'

Outside he paced the corridor. He had been brought up like most of his contemporaries in the comfortable assumptions of the Anglican faith, but by the time he reached adolescence he had realised that Christianity, or rather the current interpretation of it, had little to offer him. It was many years since he had prayed, but now he found old, half-remembered phrases rising to the surface of his mind. 'Oh Lord, to whom all hearts be open and all desires known – let him see, Lord! At least give him that!' But he had no belief in the efficacy of the prayer. At length he noticed the door that led to the outside. He went out and lit a cigarette, but he had only smoked half of it when he felt impelled to stub it out and return to his vigil. It was as well he did, as very soon afterwards the door to the side ward opened and the doctor and the two nurses came out. Merry opened his mouth to ask a question but the sister was already talking about another case and the three of them hurried away without looking in his direction. Merry drew a deep breath and went back into the room.

The bandages had been renewed, but this time they covered only the right side of the face, leaving the left, and the left eye, exposed. The flesh around the eye was swollen and discoloured and the lid was closed, but as Merry approached the bed, to his enormous relief, it opened and Felix regarded him with a fierce, blue gaze.

For a moment they looked at each other in silence, then Felix said, 'Good Lord, Merry! What are you doing dressed up as an army officer?'

Merry choked back a sob of relief and replied in kind. 'I'm auditioning for a production of *Journey's End*.'

'Wrong war,' Felix pointed out.

'It's a modern-dress production,' Merry told him. Then he abandoned pretence and sat down on the edge of the bed. 'Thank God, Felix!'

'Yes,' Felix replied soberly. 'I must say, it is a merciful relief.'

'Do you know what I did just now, out in the corridor?' Merry said, his voice suddenly unsteady. 'For the first time in years, I prayed.'

'For me?'

'Yes, of course, chump! Who else? Herr Hitler?'

Felix fixed him with his eye. 'You prayed for me, Merry?' he repeated. He reached out and touched Merry's sleeve. 'Thank you.'

Merry looked down at the hand on his arm but for some reason, now that Felix could see, he felt inhibited from taking it. After a moment he said, 'What about the other eye?'

'Too early to tell,' Felix replied. 'Apparently the lids are still too swollen for me to be able to open it. But at least this one is OK. At least I'm not in the dark any more.'

There was such exultation in his voice that Merry smiled in spite of himself.

'There's one thing that puzzles me,' he said. 'Why is only half of you affected?'

'Not even that,' Felix said. 'It's only my face and one hand. It seems my flying suit protected the rest of my body. They reckon the flames must have caught me down one side as I struggled to bail out. I wasn't wearing my goggles and I vaguely remember taking off my right glove to wrestle with the catch on the cockpit cover. I wish to hell I hadn't. In the long term the hand is going to be the worst problem. I suppose I can manage with half a face, provided the eye is OK, but you can't fly a plane with one hand.'

'Christ, Felix!' Merry exploded. 'You're not thinking of flying again!'

'I'm sure as hell not going to sit on my backside for the rest of the war,' Felix responded fiercely.

Merry looked at him. The unbandaged side of his face was deathly pale. He decided not to pursue the argument. 'Why don't you let them give you a jab now?' he suggested.

'They already have.' Felix drew a long breath. 'It's just beginning to catch up with me. 'Fraid I'm not going to be very good company for a bit.'

His voice was already beginning to slur. Merry said quietly, 'Don't worry about that. Just take it easy.'

The one open eyelid drooped and closed for a moment, then reopened.

'Merry?'

'Mmm?'

'Thanks for this afternoon. I don't know if I'd have been able to cope without someone to talk to.'

Merry laid his hand over the one that still rested on his sleeve. 'You'd have coped. But I'm glad I was able to help.'

Felix closed his eye again. Merry sat still, feeling the hand under his own relax and listening as Felix's breathing slowly deepened. When he was quite sure that he was fast asleep, he leaned forward and very lightly brushed his lips across the exposed temple. Then he got up and tiptoed out of the room.

It was ten days before Merry was able to return to the hospital, days during which he continued to quarter the south of

England, playing in army barracks and works canteens, hospital wards and officers' messes. Sometimes he was listened to in rapt silence, at others he played to a background of rattling dishes and murmured conversation. He accepted both with equanimity. He telephoned the hospital several times to be told that Felix was 'as well as could be expected' and left messages of encouragement, messages that he could never be sure would be delivered.

Finally, on the eleventh day, he managed to divert his journey to take in the hospital. When he entered the ward the sister greeted him with relief.

'I'm glad you're here. Flight Lieutenant Mountjoy is in a bit of a state.'

Merry's heart sank. What sort of emotional turmoil, he wondered, was covered by that euphemistic phrase. 'Why's that, Sister?' he asked.

'The doctor removed the bandages a couple of days ago. Obviously, in cases like this, we try to make sure that there are no mirrors around. There's a barber who comes round and shaves them, when required. But of course the flight lieutenant is able to get out of bed now. This morning he found his way to a bathroom where there is a mirror. I'm afraid it was a bit of a shock.'

Merry swallowed. 'It's bad, then?'

'Well, of course, it looks worse than it is at the moment. Once it's properly healed it won't be so bad and I keep telling him they can do wonders now with skin grafts. But I can see that it isn't easy to believe that, as things are. And that young woman who came in yesterday didn't help matters!'

'What happened?'

'I wasn't on duty at the time so I don't really know. I was just told that he was very distressed after she left.'

Merry mentally consigned Harriet to the worst torments of hell.

'Have his family been informed?' he asked.

'Oh yes, of course,' the sister responded. 'I specifically asked his CO about that. He said he had spoken to Lady Malpas on the telephone. Apparently Lord Malpas is in America on some kind of diplomatic mission, and the elder brother is in the navy. Lady Malpas is trying to run the estate single handed and cope with a house full of refugees. And, of course, Cheshire is a long way away.'

Farther than you realise, Merry thought. They had reached the door of the side ward.

'Shall I tell him you're here?' The sister asked helpfully.

Merry shook his head. 'Thanks, Sister. It's all right. I'll announce myself.'

He took a deep breath and tapped on the door.

Felix's voice answered sharply, 'Who is it?'

'It's me, Merry.'

'Just a minute!' There was a brief pause, then, 'Come in.'

Felix was sitting on the far side of the bed so that his back was to the door. Before Merry could speak he said harshly, 'I'm afraid you're in for a bit of a shock.'

Merry kept his voice level. 'I'm not easily shocked. I've worked at the Windmill, remember?'

He walked round the bed, but Felix kept his head lowered and turned away so that he could see only the undamaged left cheek. Merry took him firmly by the shoulders.

'Look at me, Felix,' he commanded.

Slowly Felix raised his head. Merry forced himself to look him steadily in the face. It was not hard to see why the sight of his reflection had had such a devastating effect. The image that came to Merry's mind was of a grotesque carnival mask, one side of it pale, regular, unblemished, the other blackened and distorted so that the features were hardly recognisable as human. The mask-like impression was reinforced by the fact that the right side of Felix's face seemed to be coated in a dark brown veneer, almost as if it had been lacquered.

'Well?' Felix challenged him. 'How do I look?'

Merry considered him judiciously. 'It's a remarkable transformation, but I can't say I like it. What are you going to do for your next trick?'

Felix made a sound that was perilously balanced between a laugh and a sob. 'Sarky bastard! Thank God for someone with a sense of humour!'

Then the tears started, welling up in the swollen eye sockets and running down the one unscathed cheek and the grim travesty of the other's former perfection, while the shoulders between Merry's hands suddenly heaved convulsively. Merry gulped, hesitated, and then sat on the bed and pulled Felix into his arms. For a dizzying moment he was almost swamped by contradictory emotions, anguished pity on the one hand and on the other sheer physical delight as Felix burrowed his head into his shoulder and gave way for the first time to helpless sobs. The weakness did not last long. After a minute or two he drew two or three shuddering breaths, sniffed and sat back.

'Sorry!'

'Nothing to apologise for,' Merry said.

Felix winced. 'Ouch! Somehow I don't think tears are the best ointment.'

'Here.' Merry handed him a clean handkerchief and waited while he dabbed carefully at his damp face. After a moment Felix said, without looking up, 'At least you didn't burst into tears and run out of the room.'

Merry made no reply. So that was what Harriet had done. Once again, he condemned her to eternal damnation. Aloud he said, 'What about the other eye, Felix?'

Felix sniffed again and raised his head. He had himself under control now.

'OK, thank God. At least, things are a bit blurred at the moment, but the doc says that should clear up in time.'

'Splendid!' Merry forced an encouraging smile. He looked at Felix more closely, and added, 'What's this brown stuff?'

'Tannic acid,' Felix told him. 'Apparently it's the standard treatment to keep out infection.'

'I see. So what happens next?'

'They want me to see some quack – what was the name? Mac something. McIndoe, that's it. He's supposed to be the bee's knees when it comes to skin grafts.'

'That's good. Sister says they can do wonders now.'

'So she keeps telling me.' Felix managed a wan smile.

'You must believe her,' Merry said earnestly. 'It will get better, Felix.'

'Better, perhaps,' Felix conceded. 'Not right, though. It'll never be like it was before.'

'Is that so terribly important to you?' Merry asked.

Felix looked down at his right hand and for the first time Merry saw that it, too, had been left unbandaged. The fingers were curled into claws and it seemed that most of the flesh had been burnt away.

'Not if he can do something to make this work again,' Felix said. 'I can live with the rest.'

Merry felt tears prick at the back of his own eyes. 'Well, we'll just have to hope for the best.' It was all the encouragement he could think of. To change the subject he said, 'Have you had any other visitors?' and instantly regretted the question.

Felix, however, seemed undisturbed. 'Just the CO. The chaps from the squadron sent their best wishes. They'd come over too, if they could, but they're all a bit tied up right now.'

'I bet they are!' Merry said.

Felix's eyes brightened a little. 'Did you hear the news last night? One of the nurses brought me in a wireless so I could listen to it. A hundred and eighty-five German planes shot down. Bloody marvellous!'

'Yes,' Merry agreed, and then added, in a reasonable imitation of Churchill's growl, ' "Never in the field of human conflict was so much owed by so many to so few." That includes you.'

Felix caught a breath. 'It did – once. Good old Winnie!' There was a pause, then he said brightly, 'Well, what have you been up to? I haven't seen you for days.'

'Sorry,' Merry said. 'I did try. Didn't you get my messages?'

Felix grinned, a lopsided grin but a genuine one. 'It all right. Little Nurse Wilson brought them all faithfully. I was only teasing. So, tell me all about it.'

So once again Merry found himself rifling his memory and his powers of invention in order to entertain, and was rewarded by hearing Felix chuckle. He went on until a nurse looked in.

'Excuse me, but Sister thinks perhaps the flight lieutenant ought to get some rest now.'

Merry rose. 'Yes, I'm sure she's right.' He touched Felix on the shoulder. 'I don't know when I'll get back, but I'll make it as soon as I can.'

Felix lifted his ravaged face and smiled at him. 'Yes, do that. But don't worry about me. I'll be OK.'

Merry nodded. 'Of course you will. See you soon.'

When he looked back from the door Felix was settling himself on the bed as if preparing for sleep. Outside, the nurse said softly, 'Well done! That's the first time I've seen him smile.'

Chapter Eleven

Richard sat at a small table in the corner of the crowded café, an almost untouched glass of beer in front of him. In his shabby, working man's clothes, among all the other men talking and drinking, there was no reason why he should feel conspicuous, yet he had never felt so naked or so alone. The reason for his unease was not hard to identify. All the best tables were occupied by parties of German officers.

He had been on the move for over two weeks now and the strain was beginning to tell. He had left the Jumeaux' cottage in the boot of the *curé*'s car and spent the night in the priest's house. The following day he had travelled in the same uncomfortable fashion to the village of Musson, where he was handed into the care of another cleric. Father Goffinet was a much younger man, who greeted him with a reassuringly warm handshake and a promise that he need have no further anxieties as he was now 'in good hands'. From there, dressed as a visiting Franciscan friar, he was driven over the Franco-Belgian border and deposited in the precincts of the Convent of Poor Clares.

He spent several days there, while his over-stretched nerves relaxed under the influence of the serene kindness of the nuns. In conversation with the Reverend Mother it became clear that he was by no means the first fugitive they had sheltered, yet as they crossed the border he had seen the posters that proclaimed the death penalty for aiding the enemies of the Nazi occupiers. One evening he raised the subject with her.

'Madame, you and the sisters are taking a terrible risk. You know what the penalty is for helping people like me. Why do you do it?'

She smiled and laid a hand on the book on her desk. 'You are a Christian. You know your Bible. You must recall this passage from the Gospel of Matthew. "I was an hungred, and ye gave me meat: I was thirsty and ye gave me drink: I was a stranger, and ye took me in: Naked, and ye clothed me: I was sick, and ye visited me: I was in prison, and ye came unto me . . . Verily I say unto you: Inasmuch as ye have done it unto one of the least of these my brethren, ye have done it unto me." '

Richard lowered his eyes and found that he had to clear his throat two or three times before he could answer. 'Madame, you make me feel very humble. I just hope and pray that you will get your just reward.'

She lifted her shoulders slightly. 'If we do God's will, that is its own reward, is it not?'

Eventually the local doctor had come to the convent, on the pretext of visiting a sick sister, and Richard had been driven away, dressed now as a simple labourer. The doctor bought him a railway ticket for Lille and saw him to the train.

'No one is likely to question you, but if they do tell them you are a refugee from Belgium. There are plenty of those wandering about these days. Say that you lost all your papers when your house was shelled in the invasion. When you get to Lille go to the Café Bleu in the Rue de la Paix. Sit at a table in the far corner opposite the door and tell the waiter you are looking for Gaston. Someone will contact you. The password will be "I will wait for you" and you must reply "It will be worth the wait". Do you understand?'

The journey was nerve-racking. The train seemed to be full of German soldiers but they were obviously not interested in the sullen, conquered civilians in the other carriages and no one asked for his papers. In the station he consulted a local map and was astonished and wryly amused to discover that he was now only a few miles from Roubaix, where his regiment had been quartered before the beginning of the German offensive. After five months and everything he had endured it was ironic to find himself almost back where he started.

The Café Bleu, however, was a very much more sophisticated place than the local *estaminet* he had frequented with his comrades. It had polished tables and heavy velvet curtains and in the centre of the room was a piano set in a small clear space that formed a stage. As Richard sat, with his eyes lowered, he was suddenly aware of movement in this area and a ragged splutter of applause. Looking round, he saw that a man had taken his seat at the piano and a woman in a close-fitting black dress, slit to the thigh, was standing beside him. From the reaction of the German officers it was apparent that this was their main reason for choosing this bar to drink in. The pianist began to play. The woman had her back to Richard, but from the moment she began to sing he recognised the smoky, seductive tones that had beguiled him in Fairbourne over a year ago. As she turned in his direction he twisted in his seat, propping his head on his hand to hide his face. What malign fate, he demanded in silent, fruitless anger, had brought to this bar the one person in France who would undoubtedly recognise him?

Chantal was moving among the tables now, making a point of picking out those occupied by German officers. He watched her out of the corner of his eye, leaning provocatively over the backs of chairs, touching a shoulder here, a cheek there, no longer innocently flirtatious as he remembered her act in the Follies but charging every movement, every intonation, with a sexual invitation that had the Germans almost visibly salivating. Chantal, a *collaboratrice*! Well, perhaps it was hard to blame her in the circumstances, but he remembered the courage and faith of the nuns and the others who had helped him and felt sickened.

The song came to an end, amid enthusiastic applause, and then the pianist began a new number.

'*J'attendrai*,' sang Chantal, '*la nuit et le jour, j'attendrai toujours . . .*'

She was moving again, this time away from the tables with the officers and out into the rest of the room. To his horror Richard realised that her wanderings, though apparently aimless, were bringing her steadily nearer to where he sat. He sank his head in both hands, hoping that he looked either sick or half asleep. Her voice was close above him now and then, beneath his fingers, he saw her slide a silken thigh on to the edge of his table. Her fingers curled under his chin and raised his face to hers and her incomparable amber eyes smiled into his own.

'*J'attendrai* . . .' she sang again, and then in a throaty murmur that might still have been part of the number, '*J'attendrai, mon brave!*'

And then, with a flood of relief, he comprehended. '*J'attendrai* . . . I will wait for you!' He cleared his throat and managed to mutter in French, 'It will be worth waiting for.'

She smiled at him and moved on to continue her song at another table. At the end of the number she disappeared, leaving him to wonder what was supposed to happen next. Before long a waiter came over with a glass of beer that he had not ordered.

'Mademoiselle's compliments, monsieur. She said to tell you that she has to sing again soon but when she has finished she asks you to visit her in her dressing room. It is over there, beyond the curtain.'

He gave a complicit leer whose meaning was as subtle as a nudge in the ribs and departed. After a while Chantal reappeared and sang two more numbers without coming near his table. When she had finished he waited for a few minutes and then got up and wandered casually over to the curtained archway indicated by the waiter. It led, among other places, to the toilets, so there was no reason for anyone to see his movement as suspicious. Beyond the curtain was a short, rather dark corridor. The first doors led to the toilets, then another curtained archway gave access, from the noises coming from beyond it, to the kitchen. At the end of the passage was another door. Richard took a deep breath and knocked.

'*Entrez*,' came Chantal's voice. Then, as he entered, she went on loudly in French, 'So! It is the shy boy from the corner! Come in, *mon ami*. Do not be afraid. Chantal will not eat you.'

As soon as he had closed the door she came to him and laid her fingers on his lips. 'Speak only in French, *mon cher*,' she whispered in his ear. 'The walls are thin.' Then she slid her arms round his neck and kissed him. He held her while every nerve in his body quivered with recognition, of the taste of her mouth, the pressure of her slender, agile body against his own and that same perfume that he had found so exciting last summer. He had not slept with a woman since that last time with her. There had been some unsatisfactory gropings with a girl he had met during his basic training, and once, desperate, he had joined the queue outside the tiny, officially sanctioned brothel that served the troops based in Roubaix, only to give up in disgust before his turn came. Since then stress and general debility had kept him quiescent, but now her touch released in him so much pent-up desire that he had difficulty restraining himself.

She drew back after a moment and said out loud, '*Eh bien, mon brave*, you will come home with me for a little supper, yes?'

'You are very kind, mam'selle,' he replied, in what he hoped was a suitably diffident tone.

'Good. Give me a moment to dress, and we will go. Sit there, have some wine if you like. I shall not be long.'

She had taken off the black dress and was wearing a dressing gown. Now he watched as she shed the gown, revealing the long, elegant legs, the trim waist and the full breasts, which were burned into his memory like a seal stamped on hot wax. She put on a simple dress, a light jacket and a beret and turned to him with a smile.

'*Allons, chéri*. It is not far.'

She tucked her arm into his and led him through the kitchen, where a couple of pot-boys and a chef stopped what they were doing to watch them pass with the same meaningful leer he had seen on the waiter's face. Undisturbed, Chantal bade them a cheerful goodnight and Richard felt that, if he was blushing, it was wholly in keeping with the role he had been given.

Outside he murmured, 'Those men, the staff in the kitchen, don't they wonder what's going on?'

She laughed softly. 'They think they know what is going on. Chantal is a promiscuous woman who likes to pick up young men and take them home for the night. They call me La Tarantelle – you know, the spider who eats her mate when she has finished with him? – because the young men are never seen in the bar again.'

In spite of himself Richard shivered and she laughed. 'But you know otherwise, *chéri*. Or have you forgotten?'

'I could never forget,' he answered with feeling.

They came to a door set in a long wall. Chantal opened it and led him into a dim courtyard. Opposite was a stone staircase and to one side a small cabin with a lighted window, framing the head of an elderly woman, who peered at them curiously.

Chantal called out, '*Bonsoir*, Madame Raymond.' Then she added softly to Richard, 'She is the concierge. She thinks I am a bad woman also but as long as there is no trouble with *les flics* she will not say anything.'

On the second floor she opened the door and led him into a small apartment which, like the house she had inhabited in Fairbourne, was as clean and tidy as any bourgeois housewife could have wished. As soon as the door was shut he caught her arm and pulled her into another embrace.

'Am I to stay here?' he whispered, when his mouth was free again.

'Of course,' she answered. 'Are you hungry? Do you want an omelette?'

'Later!' he breathed. She slipped off her jacket and drew him towards an inner room. 'Much later,' he added.

It was all over very quickly, much too quickly, but after such long abstinence that was not surprising. He apologised and she kissed him gently and went to cook. Later, when they had eaten, they made love again, this time with a dreamy relaxation that left them both satisfied, and then he slept until late the following morning.

Upon rising he found her in the sitting room, writing a letter.

'To my *maman*,' she said. 'Do you want coffee?'

'Your mother is not here with you, then?' he queried, as much for something to say as for any other reason.

Going to the kitchen she cast him an amused glance over her shoulder. 'Obviously not. She is still working for the same family, in Normandy.'

He said, 'Chantal, how did you get mixed up in all this? I mean, I'm not the first, am I? That is, not the first escaping soldier you've helped.'

'No, there have been others before you,' she agreed. 'It started when I was staying with my mother. The family, the Dubreuils, are very Anglophile. When the British evacuated their troops at Dunkirk they were heartbroken. Then we found two British Tommies hiding in a barn. They had become separated from their comrades and had been left behind. The Dubreuils took them in and we realised that there must be others in the same predicament. M. Dubreuil and I went looking. We found some being cared for in farms round about, others were still out in the fields. They were all starving and some were wounded. We took them all back to the château and at one time we had ten men hiding there. Then we began to look for ways of getting them out of the country. M. Dubreuil has many contacts. He made some very careful enquiries and discovered that others were doing the same thing. It was impossible to send the men back across the Channel. The ports were too well guarded. But we thought it might be possible to send them south, into unoccupied France and then over the border to Spain. That is the way you will go.'

'All the way to Spain?' Richard exclaimed. 'Is it possible?'

'*Bien sûr*! Many have already gone that way.'

'How will I go?'

'The exact route has to be worked out. Each batch of "parcels" is delivered by a different courier and a different route. Soon you will meet Paul and he will decide what is best.'

'Paul?'

'Paul Cole. He organises the line. He is an English captain, but he has chosen to stay here and help to get other evaders and escapers out. He is a strange man, but he has a gift. He can talk his way into, or out of, anywhere. You will see. He will be here soon.' She handed him a cup. 'It is ersatz, I am afraid. There is no real coffee to be had.'

'Don't worry,' he said, 'I'm used to it by now.'

'So, tell me.' She sat down opposite him. 'Where have you been? What has happened to you since Dunkirk?'

He related his story, leaving out, as he had been warned to do, the names and precise locations of those who had helped him. It was not because they did not trust each other, it had been emphasised, but it was known that the Gestapo routinely tortured those who were arrested for helping escapers and what they did not know they could not be forced to reveal.

At the end of the story he said, 'Tell me about the unoccupied part of France. I only found out it existed a few days ago. I thought the whole country had surrendered.'

'They might just as well have done,' Chantal remarked contemptuously. 'But Marshal Pétain has managed to hang on to the southern portion of the country. He has set up a government at Vichy but, of course, he is a puppet of the Germans. Do not suppose that you will be safe when you reach there. Many of the police are pro-German and they will hand you over without thinking twice about it.'

He was silent for a moment. Then he said awkwardly, 'Chantal, when you bring other escapers here, do you . . . do they . . .?'

She smiled indulgently and leaned across to pinch his cheek. 'Do I take them all to bed with me? Well, that depends. Some are much more attractive than others.'

'But you do sleep with some of them?' he persisted.

'You are jealous?' She sat back and surveyed him sardonically. 'But why should you be? We have always understood, you and I, that we take our pleasure when it suits us but there is no commitment on either side.'

He felt himself blushing. 'I know. I know I've got no right to be jealous but . . . I can't help it.'

She laughed. 'Well, perhaps I am glad. I think if you were not I should be disappointed. And, if it helps at all, there has only been one other. He stayed here for several days and he begged me so prettily I could not refuse. But the rest have slept there on the couch, like perfect English gentlemen.'

There was a knock at the door, three sharp taps, and Richard jumped, but Chantal said reassuringly, 'It is Paul. Don't worry.'

Paul Cole was a sandy-haired man, a few years older than Richard, with a heavily freckled face, a moustache and an energetic, bouncy manner. He strode over to Richard as Chantal introduced them and shook hands effusively.

'Good to meet you, old chap. Don't worry about a thing. Everything's taken care of. Trust your Uncle Paul! Now, tell me how you fetched up here.'

Once again Richard told his story. Cole questioned him closely about his regiment and where he had been during the fighting and Richard guessed that he was trying to make certain that he was genuine and not a double agent sent to infiltrate the organisation. After a few minutes Chantal interrupted.

'Paul, you can stop interrogating him. We know each other from before the war. I can promise you he is who he says he is.'

'Really? Why didn't you say so sooner?' Cole grinned at him. 'Sorry, old boy. Can't be too careful, you know. OK. Let's get down to business. Do you have any documents?'

Richard shook his head. Paul went on, 'Right, we need to create a new identity for you. How's your French?'

'A lot better than it was six months ago,' Richard said, 'but I'm not sure I could convince a Frenchman.'

'You speak Italian, don't you?' Chantal said suddenly.

'Fluently?' Paul asked.

'Oh yes. I lived there for three years. But what good is that?'

'I just thought,' Chantal suggested, 'that as Italy is now an ally of the Nazis, that might be a good cover.'

'Certainly less chance of being caught out,' Paul agreed. 'And the guards will be less familiar with Italian identity documents. It's worth thinking about. But what's an Italian doing in France?'

'Trying to get home?' Richard offered.

'Back to Italy, to enlist!' Cole exclaimed. 'Yes, I like it! But why are you here in the first place?'

'Because he has been singing here, of course,' Chantal said. 'Richard is a professional singer.'

'That seem reasonable to you?' Cole asked.

'Yes, I suppose so. I might have been working with an opera company here, or in Belgium.'

'And when the invasion came your opera company folded, leaving you short of cash for your fare back to Italy.' Cole was beginning to catch Chantal's enthusiasm.

'So,' she took up the story, 'you came here to Lille to find your old friend Chantal and ask for help.' She stopped, gave a little gasp and then went on, 'Oh, I have an idea – a beautiful idea! We shall perform together, *mon ami*! In order to earn the money for your fare back to Italy we shall become a double act. I have a friend in Paris who owns a nightclub. He will give us a booking. And he may know someone farther south, who will invite us to perform there.'

'Hang on a minute!' Richard protested. 'I can't do your kind of act, Chantal. I'm not a cabaret artiste.'

'Pouf!' she exclaimed dismissively. 'Of course you can. You have a wonderful voice and you are used to performing. I shall teach you the rest.'

Richard looked at Cole. 'What do you think?'

'Don't ask me about the artistic side of it,' Cole replied. 'I'm no judge of that. But if you can pull it off it would be a wonderful cover. Once you have a letter from somewhere in the south inviting you to go there, you will be able to apply for a pass to cross the demarcation line without arousing any suspicion. It couldn't be better.'

'But what about Chantal?' Richard said. 'It would be putting her at risk.'

'That's her business.' Cole shrugged and smiled. 'She goes backwards and forwards as a courier anyway. This'll be, what, your third trip, Chantal?'

'It is true,' Chantal said. 'I shall come with you anyway and like this it will be safer than usual. Better than escorting Englishmen who cannot speak French and have to pretend to be deaf and dumb or half-witted!'

'Is that what you do?' Richard marvelled.

Cole chuckled. 'It has been known.' He produced a pencil. 'All right. I'm going to leave it to you two to sort out the details. I'll see to the paperwork. What shall we call you?'

Richard produced the first Italian surname that came into his head. 'Benedetti? My old landlady in Milan was a Signora Benedetti.'

'First name?'

'Ricardo.'

'Place of birth?'

'Milan.'

'Parents' names?'

'Do I need those for a passport?'

'No, but you may need to know them if the Huns start asking questions. What's your address in Italy?'

And so it went on, until they had constructed a complete life history for Ricardo Benedetti and invented an imaginary opera company based in Louvain, complete with a repertoire and the name of the conductor. At length Cole sat back and smiled at them.

'OK, kiddies. I'm going to leave you to it now. Chantal, get him to the photographer this afternoon, but get his hair cut first, for pity's sake! I'll pick up the pictures tomorrow and get them down to the father at Abbeville. I hope he knows what an Italian passport is supposed to look like!'

'He'll know,' Chantal said. 'The abbé is a genius.'

At the door Cole turned to Richard. 'Better you don't leave the flat except to get your picture taken this afternoon.'

Richard nodded. 'I understand.'

'Right,' said Cole. 'Cheerio, then. See you tomorrow.'

When he had gone Richard said curiously, 'Who's the abbé?'

Chantal shook her head. 'You should know better than to ask that by now. He is a good man, a saint, and a brilliant forger! You will see.'

Later, over a frugal lunch, he said, 'What do you know about this Cole chap?'

'Only that he was left behind by the army, like so many others. Why?'

'I don't know.' Richard frowned. 'There's something about him. He doesn't sound like an army captain.'

She pursed her lips and shrugged. 'Surely there must be all sorts of people in the army now who are not regular soldiers.'

'I suppose so,' Richard said. 'I mean, yes, of course there are. It's just . . . Well, put it this way. I shouldn't have been surprised if he had started trying to sell me a second-hand car.'

Chantal laughed. 'You English! You are such snobs! Paul is a brave man. He risks his life to get people like you out of France. I promise you can trust him.'

'Yes, I'm sure you're right,' Richard said apologetically. 'I didn't mean it to sound like that.'

That afternoon Chantal accompanied him to a barber and a photographer, both of whom she assured him could be trusted, and then he was left alone in the flat while she went to work at the bar. She returned later than he expected and by the time he heard her key in the lock he was pacing the floor. She laughed at his anxiety and explained that some German officers had insisted on buying her drinks.

'Look!' she exclaimed, opening her bag. 'One of them brought me a present.'

'Chocolates!' Richard exclaimed. 'I haven't seen a chocolate for months and months.'

She laughed. 'So! We shall eat them in bed, no? It will be

amusing to eat that stupid man's chocolates while we make love.'

The next morning they began work on the cabaret act. Chantal had a stack of sheet music of popular songs and it was not hard to adapt some of them as duets, though Richard found it harder to change his singing style to match hers. There was no piano in the flat but they both had a good sense of pitch and, with Chantal's coaching, they began to make a good duo. It helped, too, Richard realised, that they were both so strongly attracted to each other. Blending his voice with hers became a sensual experience, an extension of their love-making.

One afternoon she said, 'You should have a solo. Look, this will go down very well with any Germans in the audience. It's a song all the soldiers sing and it has quite a haunting tune. I usually sing it, but it is better for a man really.'

He took the music and read the title. ' "Lili Marlene"? Do I have to sing in German?'

'They will be a big part of our audience. We mustn't antagonise them.'

He began to sight-read the music, humming the tune. She joined in, translating the words into French. It was, as she had said, haunting, capturing the longing of the soldier confined to barracks for the girl waiting outside under the lamplight.

'OK,' he said. 'I'll learn this one.'

Most of the music she gave him was in the wrong key for his voice, and as Chantal had no formal musical training it was left to him to transpose it. She bought him some manuscript paper and he occupied his time when she was out with the tedious task of rewriting the music. It was a job he had disliked even as a student, and as he worked he frequently found his thoughts turning wistfully to Merry, who seemed to be able to do it by instinct. Thinking of Merry naturally led him to Rose, and he experienced a sudden lurch of anguish. Had his mother passed on his message or was Rose still waiting for news of him? And if she knew what was going on, how would she feel about his relationship with Chantal? He found himself physically breaking out in a sweat at the thought. All through his captivity and his recent adventures he had comforted himself with dreams of Rose, yet now he was betraying her as he had done that first summer. It was all very well for Chantal to insist that it was possible to divorce sexual attraction from real love, but for him it was not so simple. However attractive he found Chantal, however much he enjoyed sex with her, it was Rose he loved, and it was to see her that he longed to get back to England. It was important to get back into the fight, but until he had found Rose and proposed to her properly the war could wait.

After five days Paul Cole reappeared with a complete set of documents for the mythical Ricardo Benedetti, so perfect that Richard found it hard to believe they were forgeries. He also brought what he considered to be a suitable costume for his act with Chantal – tight black trousers and a red shirt. Looking at himself in the mirror, Richard burst out laughing.

'Look at me! All I need is a carnation between my teeth!' He struck a pose and sang, 'List' to me while I tell you/Of the Spaniard who blighted my life, tra-la-la!'

Chantal laughed and kissed him. 'Well, I think you look very romantic, *chéri*. You will have all the women in love with you.'

After a few days a letter arrived saying that the proprietor of the Chat Qui Rit nightclub in Montmartre would be happy to give them a spot in the show whenever they liked. At the beginning of October they caught the train for Paris.

Chantal took him to a small hotel on the Left Bank, where she seemed to be known. It did not take him long to realise that it was, in fact, a *maison de rendez-vous*, one of those establishments that let out rooms by the hour for amorous assignations. But when he mentioned the fact to Chantal she only laughed.

'*Bien sûr*. But the rooms are clean, it is cheap and they don't ask too many questions. *Ça suffit, n'est-ce pas?*'

Changing the subject, he confessed uneasily, 'I don't feel at all happy about performing tomorrow night without ever having had a proper rehearsal.'

'Don't worry,' she told him. 'In the afternoon we will have a run-through with the pianist. He will expect it.'

Le Chat Qui Rit was small and rather shabby but obviously very popular with the occupying forces. After a reasonably straightforward rehearsal Richard felt more confident, but as he waited for their turn to come he had to admit to himself that he had worse stage fright even than on his first night with the Follies.

Chantal leaned up and kissed his ear. '*Courage, mon brave!*'

Two minutes later they were on.

Richard came offstage with a sense of amazement. They had got away with it. Not only that, but it seemed from the reception they got that the act was very popular. In particular, his rendition of 'Lili Marlene' had gone down extremely well with the German officers. Nevertheless, he was stunned when a waiter approached him and told him that a certain Hauptmann Schumacher requested that he join his party.

'What shall I do?' he hissed to Chantal.

'You must go, *chéri*,' she answered. 'Go and make yourself pleasant. It is the only way.'

Reluctantly he allowed himself to be conducted to a table at which sat three young officers, all blond with close-cropped hair and pale blue eyes. He was offered champagne and congratulated on his performance but, what with the effort of following their heavily accented French and trying to speak himself in the same language but with an Italian accent, it was several minutes before he realised that he was being propositioned. When he did, the shock was so great that he was able to put on a fine display of affronted Latin manhood. The Germans, slightly taken aback, apologised and tried to pass the whole thing off as a joke.

'It's this damn shirt!' he exclaimed to Chantal, back in the dressing room.

She laughed. '*Pauvre petit!* Were you so shocked?'

'Listen, there's a lot I'm prepared to do to get home,' he said. 'But I draw the line at sleeping with a bloody German.'

She looked at him and for a moment her eyes were serious. 'Do you? I wonder. If it were that or surrender to the Gestapo . . .'

'Don't!' he said, and took her in his arms.

When the club closed Chantal led Richard up a narrow flight of stairs to the manager's office. It was clear from his manner that he understood what was at stake and sympathised. Chantal explained that they needed to go south and the manager immediately offered to write to a friend who ran the Tour Blanche nightclub in Marseilles. He would write to him and suggest that he might like to employ this very successful new act. A few days later they received a letter, formally requesting them to appear at the Tour Blanche in three weeks' time.

Carrying this letter, they went to apply for passes to cross into the unoccupied zone. The official studied Richard's passport and then looked up at him. 'Why are you not at home, fighting for your country?'

'I am going home,' Richard explained. 'But I have to pay my way. From Marseilles it will be easy to cross the border.'

The man asked a few more questions, looked at the letter and finally produced the necessary passes. Outside, Chantal squeezed his hand. 'There, that is the most difficult part over. Now we shall have no more trouble.'

He looked at her and forced a smile, but inwardly he was unable to share her confidence.

Chapter Twelve

For Rose and her family the first weeks with the Willises felt like a long holiday. In the warm early autumn days they took the boys for long walks and picked blackberries and gathered baskets full of creamy white, earth-scented mushrooms. They helped their hosts to harvest apples and pears and took turns at digging over the beds where beans and lettuce and other summer vegetables had been growing. Mrs Taylor and Mrs Willis became bosom pals, spending their days in the kitchen happily bottling damsons and making chutney and bramble jelly and elderberry wine.

It was wonderful to be away from the bombing, though they were never able to forget the war for long. Night after night Rose lay listening to the chugging drone of the bombers heading for Southampton or Bristol and the wailing of the sirens that marked their passage across the countryside. Sometimes, though not so often now, they would all stop work to watch a dogfight overhead. Every evening at nine the whole household gathered around the wireless to listen to the latest news. It was not encouraging. The London Blitz continued and there were daily reports of the damage it was causing. Early in October they were horrified to hear that the high altar in St Paul's Cathedral had been destroyed by a bomb. Abroad, the Italians under Mussolini attacked Greece and British troops were rushed in to fight alongside their Greek allies. It seemed that the invasion of Britain, however, which had seemed so inevitable after Dunkirk, was not going to materialise – at least, not immediately.

The happiest result of their move to Wimbourne was the change in Bet's two little boys. After growing up in the shabby streets of Lambeth, the countryside was a revelation to them. The Willises had a dog and two cats and kept chickens and pigs. The boys were allowed to collect the eggs and Jack Willis took them with him when he went shooting rabbits for the pot. In between times they were allowed to run wild in the fresh air. They were eating better too because, although rationing was just as strict here, there were always eggs and plenty of fresh vegetables and fruit to eke out what they were allowed to buy, and sometimes ham and bacon from the pig Jack had slaughtered a month ago. Perhaps more important than all this was the fact that they were all together, and the threat of another separation from their mother was fading from their minds. Billy was no longer watchful and hostile and Sam, to everyone's relief, had stopped wetting the bed.

When it became obvious that they would not be returning to London in the near future Bet decided that the two boys must be enrolled at the village school. She and Rose went, with some trepidation, to interview the local headmistress. This lady turned out to be a straight-backed spinster with a severe expression that was constantly undermined by the twinkle in her eye. The school was already overcrowded with refugees, so that lessons had to be taken in shifts, but she assured them that two more could be fitted in somehow.

The boys' reaction was predictable. 'Why do we have to go? I hate school!' Billy's face was mutinous.

'We won't know anyone. And they all talk funny. It's not fair!' Sam whined.

'Well, you're going, and that's that!' Bet said, as she and Rose marched them down the lane. But once they had disappeared into the school her expression changed. 'I hope I'm doing the right thing. Poor little scraps. They look so lost. I hope they won't be bullied.'

'They'll be fine,' Rose assured her. 'Can you see our Billy putting up with any bullying? And he'll look after Sam.'

At four o'clock two small boys burst into the kitchen with scratched knees and glowing faces.

'Guess what!' Billy crowed triumphantly. 'There's a whole crowd of us refugees and we challenged the local kids to a game of football and we won!'

'And Billy scored the winning goal,' Sam added loyally.

'And another thing. Some of our lot are living up at what they call the Big House and we've been asked to tea on Sunday.'

'Up to Squire's House?' Mrs Willis put in. 'Well, there's a thing! You'll get a good tea there, I should think.'

'I bet it won't be any better than what you make us,' Billy said, and Mrs Willis turned back to the sink with a smile.

For Rose, however, the idyll began to wear thin as the days shortened towards winter. There was not enough work to keep them all busy and she felt guilty about not contributing financially. Most of all she missed dancing and the excitement and comradeship of belonging to a theatre company. One afternoon, she raised the subject with her mother over a cup of tea.

'I was thinking, Mum. About now, any other year, I'd be auditioning for pantomime.'

Her mother looked up from her knitting. 'Will there be any pantos this year? I mean, what with the bombing and everything . . .'

'The theatres are still open,' Rose pointed out, 'but that's not what I'm talking about. I couldn't audition for anything at the moment.'

'Well, of course not. Not with that ankle of yours.'

'But that's the point,' Rose said, trying to keep the urgency out of her voice. 'It's much, much better. I've been going for long walks and helping in the garden, and it only gives me the occasional twinge. I reckon I could start practising again.'

'I suppose you could use the back of a chair to hold on to, and do your exercises in here, like you did when you were first learning,' her mother said doubtfully.

'Yes, I could, but it wouldn't be enough. What I really need is to go back to class again. I thought I might go home and see if I can arrange some lessons with the Levines.'

The Levine School of Dancing was where Rose had had her initial training and she had fond memories of the two sisters who ran it.

Mrs Taylor put down her teacup with a clatter. 'Back to London! Oh no, Rose! You can't go back there while the Blitz is on. I shouldn't have a minute's peace, knowing you were there in the middle of that. And anyway, the surgeon told you you couldn't dance any more. It's one thing walking on it. If you start getting up on your points or tap-dancing again you could end up crippling yourself.'

There were tears in her eyes and Rose decided it would be best to leave the topic for the time being. That evening, in the bedroom she shared with Bet, she set a chair in the middle of the small space between the bed and the wall, and tried out some of the exercises she had learned as a child. For a few minutes it seemed that the surgeon might have been wrong, but when she tried to rise on the toe of the damaged foot her ankle collapsed under her, sending pain shooting up her leg. She hobbled to the bed and sat rubbing it, and when Bet came in a moment later she had difficulty in hiding her tears.

She was afraid that she might have done some real damage but the next morning there was nothing but a slight stiffness to remind her of her disappointment. It seemed that her ankle could stand up to any normal activity, as long as she did not try to dance.

'Well, I can't just stay here doing nothing,' she said aloud as she dressed. 'There's a war on. I've got to make myself useful somehow.'

After breakfast she took the bus into Wimbourne and went to the labour exchange. The acid-faced woman behind the counter looked up at her and snapped, 'Yes?'

'Er . . . I'm looking for a job. Some kind of war work.'

'What sort of job?'

'I don't know,' Rose stammered. 'What can I do?'

'Can you type?'

'I'm afraid not.'

'Ever done any nursing?'

'No.'

'Have you got any qualifications at all?'

'Not really.'

'I suppose you aren't considering joining up?'

'Well, no, not really.'

'In that case it will have to the Women's Land Army. That's the only kind of work available round here. Or you could get a job in a factory, making munitions. But that would mean moving away, to Bristol probably. Which would you prefer?'

Rose gazed at her, stunned. She wanted to say 'neither' but her conscience would not let her. The last thing she wanted to do was leave her family, so she said, 'Well, the Land Army, I suppose.'

'Right,' the woman replied crisply. 'Their office is just three doors down. You'd better go along and sign up.'

In the WLA office Rose found herself facing a large woman in a tweed suit.

'Can I help you?' she enquired, in what Rose mentally termed a 'plum-in-mouth' accent.

'I've been told to come and sign up for the Woman's Land Army,' Rose said.

'Told to?' The woman's voice swooped upwards in a long-drawn octave of disapproval. 'By whom?'

'By the lady at the labour exchange,' Rose answered.

'Ah!' The tone suggested that 'Madam' was not impressed. 'So what makes you think you're cut out for life on a farm?'

'Nothing, really.' Rose was beginning to feel distinctly antagonistic. 'I just don't want to work in a factory.'

'I see. You're not from round here, are you.' It was a statement, not a question.

'No, I've come down from London.'

'And what did you do in London?'

'I was helping in my mother's shoe shop. But I'm a dancer, really.'

'A dancer?' The words were a staccato exclamation of dismay. 'What sort of a dancer?'

'Tap, ballet – a bit of everything, really. I worked in a concert party.'

The woman surveyed her with a wintry eye.

'I don't suppose you have any idea of how hard and dirty farm work can be. It isn't just romantic milkmaids and harvest suppers, you know.'

'I didn't suppose it was,' Rose said coldly.

The woman went on regardless. 'You'd soon find all your nails were broken and your hands and face all red and chapped. You'd be mucking out the cowsheds and feeding the pigs and carrying heavy loads. You'd be expected to do a man's work, in fact.'

Rose straightened her shoulders. 'I'm not afraid of hard work and I don't mind getting my hands dirty.' She looked at the woman's immaculate suit and manicured fingernails. 'Unlike some people!' she added.

The other woman looked up sharply and her nostrils flared like those of a horse about to bolt. For a moment they held each other's gaze. Then the woman turned her attention to the papers on her desk.

'I really don't think you'd be at all suitable. I'm sure they can find you a job sewing uniforms for our soldiers, or folding parachutes or something. Good morning.'

Rose stood looking at her bent head for a moment, then she turned and marched out of the office. Back at the house she described the encounter with a mixture of humour and exasperation.

At the end of her tale Jack Willis said, 'Well, if you're serious about farm work, I know someone as'll be grateful for an extra hand.'

'Are you serious, Rose?' her mother asked. 'I didn't think it would be up your street at all.'

'Nor did I, before I met that woman,' Rose replied. 'But I'm serious now, all right.'

'But what about your ankle?'

'If I can help out here, digging and so on, I don't see why I can't manage a bit of farm work.'

'OK, then,' Jack said. 'We'll go up and see Matthew Armitage this evening. I know he's short-handed since young Ben Cowley went off to join the navy.'

'Oh yes, that's a good idea!' his wife put in. 'You'll be all right up at Ashbrook Farm. Matt's a nice chap, a widower. His wife died in an accident after they'd only been married a few months, poor chap. But it's a good farm, well run, everyone says so.'

'But what about that old cow at the recruiting office?' Rose queried. 'Won't she stop me?'

'Old Mrs Heatherington-Smythe?' Jack chuckled. 'Don't you worry about her. Her bark's worse than her bite, as they say. She and Matt are old cronies. If he decides he wants you he'll sort her out all right. You wait and see.'

That evening Rose borrowed Mrs Willis's bicycle and she and Jack rode up the hill to Ashbrook Farm. Matthew Armitage was in the dairy, cleaning up after milking. Rose's first impression was not encouraging. Matthew was younger than she expected, in his early thirties, she guessed, with fair hair bleached almost silver by the sun and blue eyes set in a network of wrinkles that made him look as if he were constantly screwing them up against the light. He must have been attractive once, she thought, but his expression was bleak and he greeted them without a smile.

Jack explained their errand and Matthew's look became more wintry than ever. 'I'm sorry. I don't mean to be rude, but this is tough work. It wouldn't suit a town girl.'

'She may look a slight young thing,' Jack said, smiling, 'but she's a good worker. I can vouch for that.'

'Have you ever milked a cow?' Matthew asked her.

Rose shook her head.

'Come up at half past five tomorrow morning and we'll see how you get on. Now, if you'll excuse me, I've got to finish up in here.'

Rose had never got up at five o'clock in the morning in her life but Armitage's sceptical look, combined with the reception she had received at the recruiting office, had made her determined to prove that she could do anything a country girl could do. At 5.30, bleary eyed and shivering in the early morning chill, she rode into the farmyard. Armitage was just coming through the gate, the herd of black-and-white cows behind him, two dogs at their heels. When he saw her, his eyebrows shot up in surprise.

'You're here, then. I thought you'd have changed your mind by now.'

'I don't change my mind when I've set it on something,' Rose said firmly.

For the first time she saw the hint of a smile and he nodded. 'Good for you. Right, let's see how you get on.'

He opened the door of the cowshed and the cows plodded past him, their full udders swinging. Rose followed, trying not to gag at the smell and the sight of the cows' excrement-streaked rumps. She had not stopped for breakfast and her stomach felt hollow, but she could not decide whether that was a good thing or not, under the circumstances. Matthew took up a bucket full of disinfectant and a cloth.

'First thing to do is wash them down, see. I'm very particular about hygiene – unlike some people in this business.'

When he had finished he fetched a stool and a fresh bucket and settled himself beside the cow. Rose watched his hands, expertly squeezing and pulling, as the milk hissed into the bucket.

'Like this, see.' He turned his head to look at her. 'Come on, it's no good hanging around there. Come closer.' Then his face softened. 'It's all right. This old girl won't kick you. She's as gentle as a lamb, aren't you, my beauty?'

Reluctantly Rose edged forward, wishing she had chosen a job in a factory. After a moment Matthew stopped and looked up.

'Right, now you have a go.'

He stood up and made room for her and she sat herself down gingerly on the stool and took hold of the dangling teats. It felt like an invasion, to touch an animal so intimately. The cow seemed to agree, stamping a hind foot impatiently. Rose pulled and squeezed, as she had seen Matthew do, but only a few drops of milk fell into the bucket.

'It doesn't work,' she said, dropping her hands.

'You keep at it,' Matthew responded. 'It'll come. She's not used to you, that's all.'

Rose kept at it until her hands ached and at last she was rewarded with a thin stream of milk. By the time Matthew said, 'Right, that'll do for this one,' she was wishing she had never seen a cow.

If she thought that he meant that her ordeal was over, she was mistaken. There were twenty cows to milk in all and he set her to work on another one while he got on with the rest. Then he told her to start on a third. By the time she had finished that one he had milked all the others, but at least she felt that she was beginning to get the hang of it. Not that the work was finished, even then. The cows had to be turned out, the pails of milk lugged to the dairy and emptied into the churns and the churns carted down to the farm gate to be collected. Then all the equipment had to cleaned and disinfected. By the time they were finished Rose felt she had done a hard day's work – and it was only eight o'clock in the morning.

As she stood drying her red hands after swabbing out the last bucket she suddenly realised Matthew was looking at her. He nodded. 'OK, you'll do. You can start properly on Monday. Now, how about some breakfast?'

Rose was tempted to tell him that she had changed her mind but then she remembered the condescending expression on Mrs Heatherington-Smythe's face and instantly decided that she would not give her the satisfaction of being proved right.

'OK,' she said. 'Monday it is, then.'

It was agreed that Matthew would speak to Mrs Heatherington-Smythe. As Jack had predicted, she made no further objections and Rose was asked to provide her measurements for her uniform for the Women's Land Army.

When this arrived it provoked so much hilarity in the Willises' kitchen that a pan of potatoes was left to boil dry and supper was delayed by half an hour while they cooked some more. There were a pair of breeches that stuck out on each side of her thighs as if she had left a couple of coat hangers in them, heavy black leather boots so big that Rose declared she could turn round in them without moving the boots, a green Aertex shirt, a green sweater, bib-front overalls and a pair of wellingtons. But the pièce de résistance was the hat, a felt pudding basin with a wide brim. Rose, posing in the outfit while her family fell about in helpless mirth, did not know whether to laugh or cry.

'Never mind, love,' her mother said, when she could speak through her giggles. 'Get out that old sewing machine and we'll see what we can do.'

Miraculously, by bedtime that night the breeches had been taken in and the hat steamed into a jaunty trilby style. There was nothing to be done about the boots except to wear two pairs of socks inside them, but Jack produced a tin of dubbin and assured Rose that after a week or so of treatment with that the leather would soften.

On the Saturday before she was due to start at the farm, she received a letter.

> Dear Rose,
>
> I should have written to you before this but life has been even more hectic than usual lately. Please forgive me.
>
> The most important thing to tell you is that I have found Felix. As we knew, he had been flying Spitfires but tragically he was shot down towards the end of September. The plane caught fire and he was badly burned, particularly on the right side of his face and his right hand. By pure chance – or the operation of Divine Providence if you believe in such a thing – I happened to run into some members of his squadron, who told me which hospital he was in. I've visited several times and offered what comfort and distraction I can, though God knows it's little enough. He's in a pretty bad way, poor chap. His right hand is more or less useless and for a while we were not even sure if he would ever be able to see again. However, our worst fears in that direction were not realised and his general health seems

to be improving so he is being sent to a convalescent home near Bournemouth. He's waiting to go for plastic surgery but apparently they won't start that until he's fully fit again.

I have a heavy schedule of concerts up north for the next two or three weeks so there is no chance of my getting down to Bournemouth for a while. It has occurred to me that you are not too far from there. Do you think you could possibly manage to go and see him? I hesitate to ask, because I know you and he were never particularly close when we were all at Fairbourne and obviously it's not going to be easy, but I know he would appreciate seeing a familiar face. Harriet ran out on him when she saw what the burns had done to him and, as you probably realise, he doesn't have any contact with his family. He really needs all the help and support we can give him.

He's in what used to be the Belleview Hotel. If you can get over there I know he will be delighted to see you and I shall be eternally grateful. Just one warning. He may look horrendous but he's still the same old Felix – in other words proud and fiercely self-reliant. Just try to behave as normally as possible. I know he would hate pity – or even sympathy. Oh – and don't forget, as far as the RAF is concerned, he's Flt. Lt. Edward Mountjoy.

Write soon and let me know how you are – and if you can bear to visit, how he is.

Regards to your family.

Love,

Merry

Rose got off the bus outside the Belleview Hotel. The October sun was still warm but she felt as if a chill wind was blowing down her spine as she walked up the drive. She had always been slightly in awe of Felix, with his handsome face and his easy, confident manner, and the thought of confronting him now, helpless and disfigured, disturbed her profoundly. The Sunday train service was even more erratic than the weekday ones had become and it had taken her several hours to make the journey. Her mother had insisted on putting up some sandwiches and a flask of tea for her but in spite of that she felt tired and hungry and quite inadequate for the task ahead of her.

At the reception desk she remembered to ask for Flight Lieutenant Mountjoy and felt even more intimidated by the recollection of Felix's real identity. An orderly led her out to a terrace at the back of the hotel where a number of men were sitting in deckchairs in the sunshine. Rose was aware of their eyes following her as she passed them, but she kept her own gaze lowered. She was unsure whether this was tact, a desire not to embarrass any of them by taking notice of whatever wounds or disabilities they might have, or an attempt to protect herself.

The orderly said, 'If you'll just wait here a minute, miss, I'll go and find him for you.'

She saw him approach a man sitting some way away from the rest with his back to her and bend to speak to him. There was an exchange of words and she thought she saw the man shake his head. The orderly spoke again and after a moment the figure in the deckchair rose and came towards her.

'Rose! What a wonderful surprise!'

The debonair manner was exactly as she remembered but she could hear the tension behind it. Felix offered his left hand and she forced herself to look him full in the face. The blue eyes held hers unwaveringly. He was smiling, or at least half his face was smiling, but the eyes conveyed something else – something that was both a challenge and an appeal. In that moment Rose forgot her own nervousness. She took his hand and leaned up to kiss the undamaged cheek.

'Hello, Felix. I had a letter from Merry to say you were here, so I thought I'd pop over and visit you.'

'Of course!' Felix said. 'I remember now. Merry told me you'd been evacuated because of the Blitz. You're staying somewhere near here, aren't you?'

'Wimbourne. With Barbara Willis's family. They've been wonderful.'

'And how is everyone? How's Babe?'

'Fine, as far as I know. She's joined the Wrens.'

'Babe, in the Wrens? But she's just a kid!'

'Old enough to join up, though.'

'Of course. It's over a year now. One forgets.'

The rapid-fire conversation had got them over their initial awkwardness but Rose was aware that they were chattering in order to avoid what could not be said.

Now he asked, 'Would you like a drink of some sort? Tea? Lemonade?'

'A glass of lemonade would be lovely.'

'Shall we go and sit over there?'

He indicated a table a little separated from the rest and laid a hand on her arm to shepherd her in that direction. Rose had a sudden vivid recollection of dancing with him at the Palace Hotel two summers ago. He was a good dancer, not as intuitively sympathetic as Richard but more flamboyant. She remembered the expressions on the faces of other couples on the floor and knew that the women had envied her. She wondered whether Felix would ever feel able to ask a woman to dance again.

They reached the table and she carefully seated herself so that, by turning his chair to look out towards the distant sea, he could present his undamaged profile. He sent an orderly for the drinks and said, 'How are you? You look well.'

'Yes, I'm fine, thanks.'

'So, what are you doing with yourself these days? Are you working?'

Rose grimaced. 'I shall be, from tomorrow.'

'Which theatre? Here, in Bournemouth, or are you touring? It's a bit early to be rehearsing for panto, isn't it?'

She shook her head. 'Oh, I'm not dancing. I'm going to be a Land Girl.'

'A Land Girl!' For a moment he gave her his full face. 'Oh God! I've just remembered. Merry told me about the accident. I am so sorry!'

Rose felt herself blush. The idea that Felix could feel sorry for her made her ashamed. 'Goodness, it's nothing compared with . . . what some people are having to put up with.'

'So, how is the ankle?' he asked. 'Will you be able to cope with working on a farm?'

'It's much better, thanks. Most of the time it's fine, it's only if I try to dance on it it gives way.'

He gave her a quizzical look. 'Rose, I can't imagine you on a farm.'

'Nor could I until a day or two ago.'

'But it's such a waste! You were a lovely dancer.'

She registered a double impact – pleasure at the compliment and dismay at his use of the past tense.

'Oh well, you have to do what you can, don't you? After all, there is a war on.'

'So they tell me,' he remarked with grim irony.

She said, 'I haven't congratulated you on your medal. We saw your picture in the papers. We're all so proud of you, Felix.'

He twitched a shoulder dismissively. 'I'm just glad I was able to be of some use before . . .' He let the sentence trail into silence.

Rose hesitated. 'We all ought to be grateful, too. Mr Churchill was right – about what we owe to you and the other boys.' He made no response, and after a moment she went on. 'Oh dear! I've been calling you Felix. It ought to be Edward, oughtn't it?'

He looked round at her and smiled. 'Stick to Felix. After all, we're both used to it.'

She longed to ask him why he had changed his name but knew that he would not answer.

He said, 'So you're still in touch with Merry. I gather he stays with you when he's in town. How is he?'

'OK, I think. We don't see much of him now, of course. Anyway, he's touring most of the time. He's tired, but I think he's rather enjoying himself – as far as one can tell.'

Felix grinned. 'As far as one can tell – that's about it with Merry, isn't it? Do you know who he reminds me of?'

'Mrs Mopp in *ITMA*,' Rose said promptly. Then, assuming the quavering tones of the popular comedy character, 'It's being so cheerful as keeps me going.'

He chuckled. 'I see what you mean. But actually I was thinking of someone else. Eeyore in *Winnie-the-Pooh*. You know, that long-suffering look, as if he accepts that fate is always going to kick him in the backside when he isn't looking, but he keeps going just the same.'

Rose said nothing. It was on the tip of her tongue to remark that if anyone was responsible for Merry's pessimistic outlook, it was Felix himself.

As if his mind was running on the same lines he went on, his voice softening, 'I'm glad they found something sensible for him to do. It would have been a terrible waste of a talent like his if he'd been left to unravel red tape in some army back room – or worse.'

'Yes, it would,' she agreed. 'But he hasn't been completely out of danger, you know. Did he tell you how he got his company out of Dunkirk?'

He looked at her sharply. 'No! Merry was at Dunkirk?'

'He was leading a concert party up at the front line when the Germans broke through. They got out just a day or two before the final evacuation.'

She told him the story Merry had related to her and he listened with a concentrated attention that surprised her. When she had finished he turned away and gazed out to sea.

'He never mentioned it. Trust him!' She saw his throat work as he swallowed. 'Good old Merry!'

She said, 'I'm so glad he found you. He was very upset at losing touch, you know.'

'I know. My fault. It was lucky for me that he happened to come along. He's been . . .' His throat worked again and he went on, almost too quietly for her to hear, 'He's been a good friend.'

Rose looked at her watch. 'Oh dear! Felix, I'm going to have to go. My bus leaves in a few minutes and if I miss it I shan't catch the train back to Wimbourne.'

He rose immediately. 'Of course. I don't want you to be stranded. I wish I could offer to drive you home but . . .' A slight gesture indicated his distorted right hand. 'I'm confined to barracks at the moment.'

'Of course. Don't worry. I'll be back in Wimbourne in time for supper,' she said, with an optimism she did not feel.

'I'll walk you to the front door.'

He took her arm again and again the touch sent a tingle through her body. She wondered why she had felt so uncomfortable with him when they were in the Follies.

At the door he stopped. 'I won't come down to the road, if you don't mind.'

'No, that's fine. The bus will be along any minute.'

'Thank you so much for coming, Rose. It's given me a real lift to see an old friend.'

'I've enjoyed it, too,' she responded, and realised that she meant it. 'How long are you likely to be here?'

'A few weeks, I suppose.'

'I'll try to come again, if I can get the time off.'

'That's sweet of you, but don't put yourself out. I can see

that you'll have your work cut out on the farm. I don't want to add to your burdens.'

'It isn't a burden.' She held out her hand and reached up to kiss him again. 'All the best, Felix. I hope . . . I hope you feel better soon.'

'Oh, don't worry about me. I'm as fit as a flea. Just getting bored hanging about here. Take care of yourself, Rose. And watch out for those cows!'

'I will!'

Halfway down the drive she looked back and he raised a hand in salute. At the gate she turned again but he had disappeared inside.

Chapter Thirteen

It took Merry several weeks to rearrange his schedule in order to fit in a concert at the Belleview, so it was late October when he finally drove up to the imposing front entrance. After announcing himself and giving the piano a cursory inspection – it was, he was glad to see, a better instrument than many he had encountered – he asked where he might find Flight Lieutenant Mountjoy and was told that he would be out in the grounds somewhere. The brilliant summer weather had segued almost imperceptibly into a mild, sunny autumn, and the wide lawns overlooking the sea were dotted with men. Merry paused on the terrace and looked around. Some of the men were in wheelchairs, others on crutches. One or two stared sightlessly ahead of them. Felix was not among them.

Merry wandered across the grass until the sound of shouts and laughter drew him aside, through an archway in a yew hedge. He found himself at the top of a short flight of steps leading down to a tennis court. The net had been removed but half a dozen young men in shirtsleeves were engaged in an impromptu but energetic game of volleyball. At one end of the court, to Merry's right, was Felix. For a few seconds Merry experienced a dislocating sense of time having reeled back on itself, for this was the Felix of summer games on the beach at Fairbourne. Positioned as he was, only his left profile was visible and his right hand was tucked into a pocket. His movements were exactly as Merry remembered them, agile and graceful as a cat, with that deftness of touch that had made him such a brilliant performer. Briefly Merry found himself wondering whether he had imagined the extent of his injuries; then Felix turned and saw him and came running over and the illusion was dispelled.

The brown glaze had vanished but in its place the skin was taut and shiny, pulling the outer corner of the right eye down and the lip up in a permanent sneer, while the right nostril appeared to be missing altogether. For the moment, however, Felix appeared unaware of his disfigurement. He was breathing hard and his eyes – both eyes – were bright with pleasure.

'Merry! You made it. Good to see you!'

He extended his left hand and Merry took it briefly. 'Good to see you too, old chap. You look very fit, but then the sea air always did suit you.'

Felix sobered. 'Nothing wrong with most of me – fit as a fiddle, in fact. Unfortunately this is still pretty useless.' He extracted his right hand from his pocket and held it up briefly.

'Give it time,' Merry said, trying to sound encouraging.

Felix seemed to put the thought out of his head. 'I was delighted to get your letter. We're all looking forward to the concert.'

'I hope you won't be disappointed,' Merry replied. He had long since lost his nerves about solo performances but tonight would be different.

'You're kidding!' Felix exclaimed. 'I've heard you play, remember? You'll be terrific.'

Someone shouted a query from the tennis court and Felix turned.

'Sorry, chaps! Got a visitor. You'll have to manage without me.' Turning back to Merry he said, 'Come on up to the house. I expect you could do with a drink, couldn't you?'

As they strolled back across the lawns Merry asked, 'So, how's it going? I must say, I didn't expect to find you so full of beans.'

Felix jerked his head towards the other figures around them. 'Can't sit around feeling sorry for yourself when you see these chaps. It made me realise how bloody lucky I am. They brought in a kid from my squadron the other day. I never really knew him. He only joined us a few days before I copped my packet. Came straight out of training school, lasted about five days. Shot down, couldn't bail out because his legs were trapped. Lost them both above the knee. Nineteen years old, Merry! What sort of a world is it when kids of that age get maimed for life?'

'A bloody cruel one,' Merry said quietly. 'So what happens next for you?' he pursued.

'Plastic surgery. McIndoe came to see me in hospital. He reckons they can do a lot to improve the hand and patch up the face but apparently the tannic acid treatment was about the worst thing I could have had. He can't do anything until the skin has softened up a bit, so he won't look at me for a month or two.'

'And until then?'

Felix shrugged. 'Not sure. Stay here until they kick me out, I suppose.'

They reached the terrace and Felix ordered tea for Merry and lemon barley water for himself. They sat in cane chairs in the last rays of the sun and looked out to sea. Felix said suddenly, 'Oh, I had a visitor. Guess who!'

Merry drew a long breath. 'Harriet?' he hazarded.

'Harriet? No. Rose.'

'Of course! I was forgetting. She wrote and told me. How is she?'

'She seemed very well. Country life seems to suit her. I think she's probably put on half a stone.'

'That'll make it even harder for her to go back to dancing,' Merry commented, then added thoughtfully, 'But how many of us will be going back to what we did when this is all over?'

He could have bitten off his tongue a second later as Felix looked down at his damaged hand and said, 'Well, I don't think I'll be performing feats of prestidigitation for the entertainment of an appreciative audience again.'

For once Merry could think of nothing to say. The tea arrived. As he poured it he asked, 'Have you had any other visitors?'

'No. It's too far for any of the chaps in the squadron. But Harry wrote. Here's something else you'd never guess. She's become an ambulance driver in London.'

'An ambulance driver? But I thought she was . . .' Merry trailed off. 'I wouldn't have thought she was suited to that sort of work,' he finished.

'No, nor would I,' Felix said, with a hint of grimness. 'I gather she was sort of shamed into it.'

'How?'

'You know she's a keen amateur photographer?'

'Yes, I remember you saying something about it.'

'Apparently she decided to make a photographic record of the effects of the Blitz. One morning she was taking pictures of a bombed-out house and the ARP were still working to get someone out. One of them came over and said, "There are people in there who are going to die if we don't get them out soon. Stop poncing about with that camera and come and give us a hand" – or words to that effect.'

'So she did?'

'Yes. And that same day she went and volunteered for the ambulance service. Of course, it means she can't get away to come down here, but at least she's doing her bit.'

'Of course,' Merry echoed. 'Well, good for her.'

Felix reached into his pocket and drew out a cigarette packet, fumbled it open and extracted a cigarette with his lips and passed the packet to Merry. Then he reached into his pocket again and fished out a lighter but the flint refused to spark.

'Damn!' He looked at Merry. 'Got a light?'

Without thinking Merry offered a box of matches. Felix shook his head. 'Sorry, old chap. Experience has taught me that striking a match is a strictly two-handed operation.'

Merry felt himself flushing with embarrassment. 'God, what an idiot I am!' He struck a match and leaned across the table to light Felix's cigarette.

'Not at all,' Felix responded. 'It's actually quite comforting that you can forget my limitations.'

After tea Merry went to his room to rest and change. The concert was to begin immediately after dinner and following the long drive he knew he needed to relax for a while if he was going to give of his best. As he unpacked a clean shirt he became aware of a familiar tightening in his chest. He drew a careful breath and heard the wheeze as he expelled it. He swore softly and sat down on the edge of the bed. 'Not tonight!' he begged some unseen power, but at the same time he knew that it was when he was most keyed up that his asthma was most likely to strike. He eased himself on to the bed and propped himself up with pillows, trying to relax his shoulders and breathe deeply and evenly. He considered taking a pill, but he knew that one of the side effects would be to increase the flow of adrenalin and make his heart pound and his hands shake. He could not play well under those conditions – and tonight he wanted to play better than he had ever played in his life. He closed his eyes and tried to make his mind a blank and, to his enormous relief, little by little, he felt the tightness easing. The attack was passing off.

At dinner in what had once been the hotel's elegant dining room Merry became fully aware for the first time of the immense tally of human misery represented in this one con-valescent home. There were young men who had lost their sight, others who had lost limbs or were paralysed, a few who had suffered worse burns than Felix. Yet the atmosphere was one of cheerful comradeship. Sitting next to Felix while they tackled some rather tough roast beef, he was embarrassed once again when Felix's neighbour on the other side reached across and without comment cut his meat up for him so that he could fork it up with his good hand. Later, as they moved into the lounge for the concert, he watched as Felix unobtrusively took the arm of a boy who was feeling his way with a white cane.

By the time he sat down at the piano Merry was breathing freely. He smiled inwardly as he remembered the old theatrical saying about 'Dr Theatre'. He should not have worried. He never suffered from asthma when he was performing.

For once he was listened to in total silence, though he suspected that this had as much to do with respect for Felix as enjoyment of the music. Encouraged, he threw himself into a rendition of Chopin's Grande Polonaise. After a few bars he was disconcerted to hear chairs scraping and people getting to their feet. Glancing round, he saw to his surprise that two young airmen had risen and were standing to attention. Then he recognised the insignia on their uniforms. They were Poles who had fled their country in order to enlist with the RAF, and for them this piece of music had the force of a national anthem. A moment later two or three other men got up and within seconds the whole audience was on its feet in a gesture of solidarity. As the music came to its crashing conclusion the applause was thunderous.

When the concert was officially over there were repeated requests for an encore. Then Merry was persuaded to return to the piano while they all joined in a sing-song. They sang 'Roll Out the Barrel' and 'It's a Long Way to Tipperary' and 'Look for the Silver Lining' and then, as the mood grew more mellow under the influence of a steady flow of beer, they became sentimental and sang 'Roses Are Blooming in Picardy' and 'If You Were the Only Girl in the World' – all the old songs of the First War that had somehow become part of everyone's consciousness and now returned as if they were the natural form of expression for a nation at war. Finally, when there were only half a dozen of them left and Matron was making disapproving noises about the lateness of the hour, they harmonised dreamily to the plaintiff melody of the Whiffenpoof Song.

> *We're poor little lambs who have lost our way*
> *Baa, baa, baa.*
> *Poor little lambs who have gone astray*
> *Baa, baa, baa.*
> *Gentleman songsters off on a spree*
> *Doomed from here to eternity,*
> *Lord have mercy on such as we,*
> *Baa, baa, baa.*

On the way to bed Merry and Felix paused on the landing before going their separate ways. Felix said, 'That was terrific, old chap. You really play extraordinarily well, you know. Why on earth weren't you a concert pianist in civilian life, instead of footling around with us lot in the Follies?'

Merry grimaced. 'Have you any idea how difficult it is to become a concert pianist? I have a living to earn, remember?'

'Well, anyway,' Felix persisted, 'as far as I'm concerned Dame Myra Hess couldn't have done better. You had all those chaps eating out of your hand. Thanks very much.'

Merry turned his head away. 'For God's sake, Felix, don't thank me! When I sat there in front of all those men who've lost arms and legs, men like you who've suffered so much fighting for their country, I wondered how I had the bare-faced effrontery to even pretend to entertain them. God knows, I should be thanking you, not the other way round.'

'You mustn't think like that,' Felix said quietly. 'Everyone here knows that the reason you're not in the front line is because of your asthma. I made sure of that.'

'What sort of an excuse is that to a man with no legs?' Merry enquired bitterly.

'Listen,' Felix said, 'I'm not very good at putting this sort of thing into words, but the point is this. All these men have suffered, yes, and it's not over yet. For some of them it never will be over. The physical wounds are healing now but it isn't only bodies that need healing, Merry. Souls need healing too. And that's your job. Tonight you gave us all a break from the war, a chance to forget the pain, the loss. A chance to remember that there are still beautiful things in this world, things worth living for. You must have felt it, the atmosphere! And afterwards, the camaraderie, the sense of togetherness. You wouldn't blame a doctor for being back at the casualty station instead of in the front line. He's got more important duties than fighting. Well, so have you. And don't ever let anyone tell you otherwise.'

For a moment or two Merry was unable to speak. Then he turned and looked at his companion and said simply, 'Thank you, Felix. I shan't forget that.'

Felix gave him a lopsided smile. 'Good. Now go to bed. Sleep well. God bless.'

'And you,' Merry responded.

The following morning at breakfast Merry broached the topic that had been at the back of his mind for days.

'I've got a week's leave coming.'

'Oh? When?'

'Second week in November.'

'Got any plans?'

'Well, yes, sort of. Nothing exciting but . . .' Merry paused and gathered his thoughts. 'Did I tell you my father passed away last year?'

'No!' Felix looked aghast. 'Oh, Merry, I am a selfish bastard! I never thought to enquire. I'm sorry!'

Merry smiled at him. 'It's all right. As you know, we were never what you'd call close. And he'd not been well for some time. He went all through the last war, of course. Quite honestly, when this lot started I don't think he could face the prospect of going through it all again, even as a civilian. He sort of gave up and died just before I went out to France.'

'I am sorry,' Felix said sincerely. 'It must have been a jolt, even if you didn't see eye to eye.'

'Well, yes, I suppose so,' Merry agreed, 'but I'm over it now. The point is, he left the house in Seaford to me. I was thinking of spending my leave there and I was wondering . . .' He hesitated, nerved himself and went on, 'I was wondering, if they'll let you out of here, if you'd like to come and keep me company.'

He watched Felix's face and saw a variety of emotions chase each other across it. Then Felix looked away. 'It's nice of you, old chap, but I don't think I'm really ready to go out into society yet. Don't want to frighten the horses, what?'

'I wasn't thinking of introducing you to the fleshpots of the South Coast,' Merry persisted. 'Just a very quiet week going for walks, if the weather's anything like decent, reading, listening to music, maybe the odd game of chess. But you'd probably find that pretty boring.'

Felix turned back to him. 'I think that sounds like exactly the sort of holiday I need. Thanks, Merry.'

'You'll come, then?'

'Yes, please. If you really don't mind having my frightful phiz around for a week.'

'My dear fellow, I shall be delighted!' Merry knew that the truth of that must show in his face. 'Do you think there will be any objections here?'

Felix shook his head. 'I can't see why. After all, I'm pretty fit now and I can manage most things for myself – as long as you don't mind helping out with the odd fiddly button.'

'That won't be a problem,' Merry assured him.

Felix rose. 'Right. Let's strike while the iron's hot, shall we?'

On the way to Matron's office Felix suddenly checked his stride. 'I've just had a thought!' he said.

'What?' Merry asked with sudden misgiving.

'The old Lagonda's still laid up at the airfield. Been there ever since I got shot down. Do you think there's any chance you could get over there and pick her up? You could drive down here and collect me, and then we'd have the use of her while we're at Seaford.'

'Well, yes,' Merry said, relieved. 'I think I can manage that. As long as you're sure you want to trust me with her.'

Felix gave him a sideways grin. 'Oh, I think so – she is a lady, after all.'

Chapter Fourteen

Rose emptied the last pail of milk into the cooler and straightened her aching back. She stood for a minute, looking around the spotless dairy, and then glanced at her watch: 8.20! She was getting quicker. Not long ago this job would have taken her until nearly nine. She still found it hard to believe that she, who until a year ago had never dreamed of getting out of bed before ten o'clock in the morning, could be rising at 5 a.m. in the pre-dawn November chill and cycling to work through the dark lanes. Nor that before breakfast she would have milked a dozen cows and cleaned the dairy.

'You need any help in here, Rose?'

She turned to look at her employer.

'No, thanks, Matt. I'm all done.'

It was not often that Matthew smiled. He smiled now and Rose noticed, not for the first time, that it took ten years off his age. 'Well done! You've really got the hang of this now, haven't you? OK, then. I'll get these churns down to the gate. You go and put the kettle on.'

Rose cherished his words as she hurried over to the farmhouse. She had 'got the hang of it'. There had been times when she never thought she would. Not that it was always easy, even now. She soon learned which cows would munch away placidly while she milked and which would fidget and attempt to make her job as difficult as possible. Sometimes one would kick out, knocking over the bucket she had so painstakingly filled or even putting a foot right in it, and once a particularly irritable animal had sent her and her bucket flying. Matthew's obvious concern had, however, more than compensated for her injured dignity on that occasion.

In the farmhouse kitchen Rose set the kettle on the range and started to make porridge. She had been told by Mrs Heatherington-Smythe, who had apparently forgotten how unsuitable she was, to remember that she was employed to work outside and not as a domestic help, but she was perfectly happy to take her turn at the stove and the kitchen sink. After all, there was no farmer's wife to cook for them. She would have turned up her nose at porridge in the old days but now, steaming hot and laced with honey and the cream she had brought over from the dairy, it had become a treat to look forward to.

They were joined at breakfast by old Fred Philips, the ploughman and general farm help, and then after they had eaten Rose and Matt returned to the cowshed to clean out the stalls and scrub the food troughs. It was hard work, wheeling the loaded barrows of muck to the heap, and, as she had been warned, Rose's hands were red and chapped from scrubbing out with cold water, but she did not grudge the effort since she saw that Matt worked even harder than she did. How he had ever managed on his own she did not know.

Later, she went out to the fields to bring in Pippin, the big shire horse that provided most of the motive power on the farm. She had been terrified of him at first, until she learned from experience that he was a docile monster who would never tread on her feet or knock into her unless she got in his way out of clumsiness. Now, working with the big horse was one of her favourite jobs. She harnessed him to the cart and headed out to the field of mangel-wurzels. Pulling mangels was one of the worst, most back-breaking jobs, but the cattle had to be fed and someone had to do it. She stuck at it until it was time to go back to the house for lunch.

At three Matt brought the cows in again and the whole process of milking and cleaning up began all over again. It was after six before the three of them sat down to a high tea of boiled eggs and bread and honey. The meal over, Fred set off for home on his ancient bicycle and Rose began the washing up. She lingered over the job, enjoying the warmth of the kitchen and the sense of relaxation at the end of a hard day. Matt stood beside her, drying dishes, and for some moments neither of them spoke. Rose was suddenly aware of how much the atmosphere between them had changed since her arrival. Working side by side they had developed an unspoken comradeship, and though Matt was still taciturn his manner had lost the grimness that she had found so off-putting at first.

As if his mind had been running along the same lines, he said suddenly, 'I hear there's a good film on at the Odeon in Wimbourne. *Goodbye Mr Chips*, or something. Don't suppose you fancy going?'

Rose answered immediately, without thinking, 'Oh, I'd love to, Matt. I haven't been to the flicks for ages.'

'You would?' He looked genuinely surprised. 'Well, that's great. We could go tonight, if you like.'

'Oh no,' she protested. 'I must go home and have a bath and change. I can't go out like this.'

'Well, how about tomorrow, then?'

She hesitated for a moment this time, realising that, for him at least, there was more at issue than a simple visit to the cinema, but she saw how his usually serious face had lit up and hadn't the heart to disappoint him.

'All right. Tomorrow will be fine.'

The next day he insisted that she should finish work early so as to have plenty of time to get ready. Fuel was short, so hot water was at a premium in the Willis household, with two active little boys to keep clean and Jack Willis and Bet working outside most of the time. That night no one grudged her a little extra to wash her hair, however, and for the first time in weeks she changed into a skirt and put on some make-up. Suddenly she realised that she was looking forward to the evening. It was a long time since she'd been out on a date.

Matt picked her up in his battered old Ford, looking smarter than she had ever seen him in a tweed jacket and flannels. They enjoyed the film, though it made Rose cry, and afterwards he insisted on taking her for a drink in the lounge bar of the Crown Hotel. The room was almost empty, except for an elderly couple silently sipping sherry in a corner, but as Matt was coming back with the drinks she heard someone call out to him from the open door of the public bar. He stopped and shook his head, but his answer was drowned in a sudden outburst of laughter from the other room.

When he came back to the table Rose said, 'We could go into the public bar, if you like. If you've got friends in there.'

He shook his head. 'Oh no we couldn't. I couldn't take a lady in there. They're a rowdy lot.'

Rose smiled at him. 'I'm not a lady, Matt.'

'Oh yes you are,' he replied. 'I don't care about where you were born or where you went to school. You're a lady as far as I'm concerned.'

When they reached the Willises' house he came round the car to open the door for her and walked with her up to the front door. She hesitated.

'I expect they'll all be in bed by now. But if you want a cup of cocoa or something . . .'

He shook his head quickly. 'No, no. That's very kind of you but it's late enough now and we both have to be up early.' There was a pause. Then he said, 'I've enjoyed this evening very much. Thank you, Rose.'

'Oh no,' she said quickly. 'I should thank you. It's been

lovely.' Again they were both silent, until she repeated, 'Thank you, Matt. Goodnight.'

He shifted awkwardly, half turning to leave, then bent quickly and kissed her cheek. She hesitated for a second, then hurriedly put her key into the lock and let herself into the darkened house.

The next morning he made no reference to their outing until Fred had left after tea and they were washing up again. Then he said, 'That was a good night out last night. We must do it again some time.'

She surprised herself by replying. 'Yes, it was. I'd like that.'

He dried up in silence for a minute and then said, 'Wimborne Young Farmers have got a dance on Saturday week. It's usually a good do, I'm told. Would you fancy that?'

Rose stopped what she was doing and wrestled with conflicting impulses. Her first instinct was to accept eagerly. She understood, however, that in some undefined way to appear at the dance as Matthew's partner would involve crossing the line between casual friendship and something much more significant. If she went, she would be seen hereafter as Matthew's girl and that was a commitment she was reluctant to make.

Eventually she said slowly, 'I don't know, Matt. I'm not sure what I'm doing Saturday week.' Then, realising how silly that sounded when he knew quite well how limited the opportunities were for social life of any sort, she said honestly, 'I mean, I'd like to think about it. Is that all right? Can I give you an answer tomorrow?'

'Of course,' he answered gravely, but she could see the disappointment in his eyes. He was already assuming that the answer would be no. 'You let me know when you're ready. I can get tickets any time.'

In their bedroom that night, Rose took Bet into her confidence. Bet, busy putting her hair in curlers, turned from the mirror to look at her. 'Want to know what I think?'

'No,' said Rose satirically. 'I was just talking for the pleasure of hearing the sound of my own voice.'

'No need to be sarky,' Bet said calmly. 'If you want to know what I think, I'd say go and enjoy yourself. It's time you had a bit of fun.'

'What about you?' Rose said. 'You're not having much fun either. Why don't you come with us?'

'And play gooseberry all evening? No thanks very much! Anyway, I'm a married woman with kids. I'm not supposed to have fun.'

'Oh dear,' Rose said, only half joking, 'is marriage as bad as that?'

'You know what I mean,' Bet retorted imperturbably. 'The point is, there's Matt, who's a really nice chap, taken a shine to you. You want to take your chances while they're there, girl. They don't come round that often.'

'Bet, you know why I'm hesitating, don't you?' Rose persisted.

'Because you're still carrying a torch for that Richard,' her sister said. She got up and came to sit on the edge of the bed beside Rose. 'Look, love. You've got to face up to facts. There are only three possibilities. Either he's dead, or he's a POW, or he's back in this country and he's just not bothered to write. Well, if he was a POW I reckon you'd have heard something by now. They are allowed to write letters home. We know that because Mary Kitchen had one from her feller before we left London. So, whether he's over there or over here, he's not writing, and if he's neither . . . well, you know what I'm trying to say. After all, you said yourself there was never anything definite between you. My advice is, cut your losses. Forget Richard, and go to that dance with Matt. He won't ask you twice.'

Before Rose could prevent it a tear fell on her sister's hand and Bet impulsively put her arm round her shoulders. 'Oh,

Rose, love, I'm sorry. I know it sounds awful put like that, but I'm only trying to be cruel to be kind.'

Rose sniffed. 'I know, I know, Bet. And I expect you're right. It's just that Richard was . . . he was special, and I didn't realise how special until it was too late.'

'I think perhaps you've made him out to be more special than he was, now you haven't seen him for a long time,' Bet said sagely. 'And if he was really serious about you I reckon he'd have wanted to tie the knot before he went away. And you like Matt, don't you? He's a nice bloke, and quite attractive – very attractive, I'd say.'

'Oh yes,' Rose agreed, 'he is, and he's kind and considerate . . .'

'And what's more he owns his own farm,' Bet put in. She paused for a moment and then went on. 'Look, it's just a dance. It's not as though you were promising to marry the man, is it? Go and enjoy yourself, and let him have a bit of fun too. He's not had much chance for the last year or two, by all accounts.'

Rose straightened up and blew her nose. 'Yes, you're right, Bet. After all, why not. Like you say, it's only a dance.'

So the next morning she told Matt that she would accept his invitation and the delight in his eyes swept away the last of her doubts.

The dance itself was very different from the decorous tea dances at the Palace Hotel in Fairbourne. It was held in a local village hall, which had been decked out rather prematurely with paper chains and Christmas decorations, and music was provided by a band scraped together from those musicians still left in the area after the call-up and was distinguished by enthusiasm rather than finesse. There were probably more youngish men in civilian clothes than might have been found at other functions, farming being a reserved occupation, but many of the local farmers' sons and other workers had volunteered rather than be left at home so the numbers were made up by a group from the nearest air base. They were a lively lot but the locals matched them with equal exuberance and Rose found herself much in demand. Matt raised no objections, declaring that he was not much of a dancer himself, but he insisted on having every waltz with her, on the grounds that this was the only dance he could do.

It was not until the band struck up the national anthem at the close of proceedings that it occurred to Rose that, apart from a slight ache, her ankle had given her no pain, although she had danced all night. She quelled a sudden surge of hope by reminding herself that ballroom dancing was a very different activity from ballet or tap.

At the end of the evening Matthew walked her back along the frosty lanes to the Willises' house, there being no petrol to spare for such relatively short journeys.

'Well,' he said, taking her hand, 'I knew I was taking a pretty girl to the dance, but I didn't realise I'd found myself the belle of the ball.'

'Oh, nonsense,' Rose exclaimed, blushing. 'There were lots of pretty girls there.'

'But not one of them who could dance like you,' he pointed out. 'It was a fair treat, just watching you glide round the floor.'

'Oh, well,' Rose said, self-deprecatingly, 'it is my job, after all. At least, it was.'

When they reached the house the inevitable happened. He drew her to him and kissed her properly for the first time. For a second she froze and then, as if a switch had been thrown, her body responded and she felt herself flooded with desire. She experienced a mingled sense of surprise and relief. Relief because she had been dreading the idea of enduring, or trying to fend off, kisses and caresses that she found repugnant; and surprise because she had always thought that Richard was the only man who could awake such passion in her.

They stood kissing for some time until he whispered, 'I must let you go in. And don't worry about the early milking tomorrow. I can cope.'

In the darkened bedroom, undressing quietly so as not to waken Bet, Rose interrogated her conscience. Was she being unfaithful to Richard? Bet's words came back to her. *Whether he's over here or over there, he's not writing.* Was she falling in love with Matt? It was true that she felt at ease in his company and tonight had proved that there was a strong physical attraction. But was that being in love? It was very different from the way she had felt about Richard, but then if she was never going to see him again . . . Her thoughts became confused and she drifted into sleep, to dream that Matt came galloping up on one of the cows and grabbed her up to ride behind him.

In spite of what Matt had said, and her heavy eyes and aching head, she made a point of being at the farm at the usual time.

One result of the dance was that, having met a number of Matthew's friends, she found her social life considerably expanded. Not that she had much time or inclination for socialising after a long day at the farm, but Matt insisted that she took Sunday off once the early morning milking was finished and increasingly she found herself being invited to other farms for Sunday tea. Very often the invitation was extended to include Bet and the two boys, who already knew the children of the various families from school. Billy and Sam had become regular visitors to Ashbrook Farm, where they watched, fascinated, as Rose demonstrated her new expertise at milking, and begged to be allowed to ride on Pippin's broad back when the big horse was taken back to his pasture. Now they discovered children who had ponies of their own and who offered to teach them to ride.

Rose struck up a friendship with Jane, the squire's daughter, and often went up to the 'Big House' on Sunday afternoon. One day, while Jane was grooming her bay mare and Rose was leaning on the stable door, watching, the other girl said, 'You're very good for Matthew, you know. He's been a different person since you started to work there.'

Rose said, 'I know he's had a very difficult time since his wife died, but I've never liked to ask him what happened. How did she die?'

'It was tragic,' Jane said, shaking her head. 'They'd only been married six months, and she was pregnant. She took the tractor up to fetch hay from one of those steep fields at the top of the farm and it turned over on her. The worst thing is, she was probably lying there for quite a long time, alive but injured. Matt was busy with the cows and he didn't miss her till teatime. By the time he found her it was too late. That's why he won't have a tractor on the farm and does everything with the horse.'

'How awful!' Rose whispered. 'No wonder he looks so sad sometimes.'

'He doesn't look nearly as bad as he did a couple of months ago,' Jane said. 'Like I said, you've done wonders for him.'

It was a subtle hint, but not lost on Rose.

Chapter Fifteen

Merry eased the Lagonda cautiously through the gates leading to the Belleview. He had been delighted to discover that the car had an almost full tank of petrol, since fuel was becoming harder and harder to obtain. Felix was waiting for him in the foyer with his suitcase, as eager as a schoolboy going home for the holidays. At the sight of him Merry felt a surge of elation that was quite foreign to his normally cynical turn of mind.

'Thank God!' Felix exclaimed as they drove away. 'I'd have gone crazy shut up in that place much longer.'

Merry's bubble of optimism burst. 'You're not shut up,' he said, curtly.

Felix turned his head away. 'Might as well be,' he muttered, and Merry was instantly flooded with guilt.

'Cheer up. We've got a whole week to relax and do as we please.'

Felix looked round and smiled with the good half of his face. 'Yes. Thanks, Merry. Good of you to put up with me.'

'My pleasure,' Merry murmured.

The journey proceeded without incident for the first half-hour or so. Then, on an almost deserted stretch of country road, Felix said suddenly, 'Pull over a minute, will you?'

Merry did as he asked, assuming that he needed to answer a call of nature. Instead, Felix walked round to his side of the car and opened the driver's door. 'Hop out, old chap, and let me drive for a bit.'

'Felix, you can't!' Merry expostulated. 'You can't drive with one hand.'

'Why not?' Felix asked. 'There's nothing wrong with my left hand, so I can change gear all right.'

'And how are you going to steer while you do it?' Merry demanded.

Felix lifted his damaged right hand. 'I've been working on this. I can get enough grip now to steady the wheel while I change gear.'

'And suppose you need to turn a corner, or avoid something?'

Felix grinned happily. 'Then you'll just have to lean across and steer for me, won't you.'

Reluctantly, Merry shifted across into the passenger seat and Felix took his place. They proceeded soberly enough for the first mile or so but then Felix began to gain confidence and they were soon bowling along at close on fifty miles an hour.

'For God's sake, Felix,' Merry pleaded. 'Slow down! I don't like going fast, even when the driver's got two good hands.'

Felix laughed in answer. 'Relax! This old girl can do a lot better than this. She hasn't even got into her stride yet.'

'That's not the point!' Merry said, but Felix ignored him and the speedometer crept up towards the sixty mark. Merry gripped the edge of his seat and prepared for sudden death.

It seemed as if his fears were unfounded, until they rounded a bend and found the road almost blocked by a haywain, trundling along at the steady pace of the shire horse pulling it. Felix slammed the car into low gear and stamped on the brakes, at the same time wrenching the steering wheel over, but the effort proved too much for his injured hand, which dropped uselessly on to his knee. The car veered wildly until Merry reached over and desperately swung the wheel to the right. The car mounted the opposite bank, tilted dangerously, recovered and then they were past, with the vision of an irate farmer and a startled horse in the rear-view mirror.

Neither of them spoke until they turned a corner into a wider road. Then Felix drew the car into the side and stopped. 'I think you'd better drive the rest of the way,' he said.

As they approached Seaford, Merry turned the car into a narrow lane. 'I want to call in on a farmer I know,' he said. 'I used to do odd jobs for him when I was a kid and last time I was home he let me have some fresh eggs. I thought we might try it again.'

Felix looked uneasy. 'OK. So long as you don't mind if I wait in the car. Might stop the hens laying altogether otherwise.'

Merry glanced at him. He was tempted to point out that he couldn't go on indefinitely avoiding the eyes of people other than nurses or his wounded comrades, but he decided to let it go for the time being. 'Fine,' he said. 'I shan't be long.'

When he came out he was carrying a box that contained a dozen eggs, a packet of butter, a fresh homemade loaf, a rabbit and an assortment of fresh vegetables.

Felix looked at the contents and said slyly, 'You sure it was only odd jobs you did for him?'

Merry ignored the jibe. Felix's digs no longer had the power to hurt him. 'As a matter of fact,' he said, 'these are all for your benefit. The farmer wasn't there, but I told his wife I had a wounded air ace in the car.'

The house where Merry had spent most of his childhood was a typical flint-and-brick cottage in a pretty lane just outside the town. He led Felix through the neglected garden where a few rain-blotched roses still hung on the leggy, unpruned stems and in through the front door.

'Sorry,' he said, 'the place smells a bit damp and musty, but that'll soon go when we get the fires going.'

He showed Felix round. There was a front room with deep armchairs covered in faded chintz and an upright piano. Behind that was a dining room, which gave on to an extension housing the kitchen. Merry dumped the box of food on the kitchen table and led his guest upstairs.

'You'd better have the spare room,' he said, opening the door of one of the back bedrooms. 'I could put you in Father's old room, but it's still got a lot of his things in there. I think you'll be more comfortable here.'

The room had a double bed with a floral-patterned eiderdown, a square of faded Axminster carpet and a washbasin in the corner.

'This looks fine,' Felix said.

Lest he should be under any misapprehension, Merry opened the door of the room opposite. 'This is my room.'

Felix passed him and looked into the tiny third bedroom where Merry had slept since he was a child. Apart from the narrow single bed, a wardrobe and a dressing table there was little room for anything else. The walls were painted white and were unadorned, except for signed photographs of members of the Follies above the bed.

'Very monastic,' Felix commented.

Merry shrugged. 'I took down all my old pictures and turned out the toys and things after Father died. You know . . . "when I was a child," et cetera, et cetera, "but when I became a man I put away childish things." '

'A new beginning – a rite of passage,' Felix said, and Merry thought, not for the first time, that his offhand manner concealed a remarkably perceptive character.

They went downstairs and Felix pottered around, putting things away under Merry's direction, while Merry busied himself lighting the boiler and the coal fire in the living room. By the time they had finished the winter dusk was well advanced and Merry carefully drew the blackout curtains before switching on the lights. He put the kettle on and cut slices of bread, and when he brought in the tea he found Felix crouched on the hearthrug making toast with a long-handled toasting fork. Later, when he went into the kitchen to prepare dinner, Felix followed him and stood leaning against the door jamb.

'You sure you know what to do with that?' he enquired, eyeing the joints of rabbit suspiciously.

Merry laughed. 'I think I can manage a rabbit stew without too much difficulty.' He sliced into an onion and then looked up again more soberly. 'My mother died when I was thirteen, you know. We couldn't afford servants. Oh, we had a woman from the village who came in most days, but when she wasn't around we had to fend for ourselves. My father's culinary expertise didn't extend much beyond grilled chops and mashed potatoes, so when I was home for the holidays I taught myself to cook in self-defence. It's surprising what you can do with a bit of common sense and a copy of Mrs Beeton.'

'Fried or boiled?' Felix enquired. Then he added, 'Sorry. I didn't know about your mother dying when you were so young. You must have missed her.'

'I still do,' Merry said.

They ate the stew in front of the fire, listening to the wireless and discussing the progress of the war. Then Felix looked at the piano.

'Play something.'

Merry shook his head. 'That instrument hasn't been tuned in years, and it was never very good in the first place. OK to practise on when I was learning, but nothing more.' He rose and went over to a gramophone in the corner. 'We could put a record on, if you like, but I'm afraid the choice is limited. Father's taste ran mainly to operetta and military marches.'

'You must have some of your own, though.'

'A few – mostly classical, though.'

'What makes you think I don't like classical music?'

'I don't know.' Merry hesitated. 'I always somehow thought that dance music was more your style.'

Felix smiled. 'Well, perhaps neither of us was sailing under our true colours when we were in the Follies.' He joined Merry by the gramophone. 'What's this? Beethoven?'

'The Moonlight.'

'Wonderful! Put it on.'

Later, as he lay trying to coax elusive sleep, Merry was jolted to full alertness by the eerie wail of the air-raid siren. He lay still for a while, listening tensely, until he heard the drone of the bombers. Then he got up and went to tap on Felix's door.

'Don't put the light on,' Felix warned him as he entered. He was standing by the window. He had lifted the blackout curtain and was staring out into the night. Merry joined him, as the deep throbbing of the enemy planes grew louder.

'Dorniers,' Felix said.

'On their way to give London another pasting,' Merry added.

'Poor buggers! The Londoners, I mean.'

'I didn't think you were sympathising with Jerry.'

Felix craned his head, staring up into a sky bright with stars. 'Where the hell are our fighters!' he demanded.

'Waiting for them, I expect,' Merry responded. Then he added, 'I'm told that there have been very few bombs dropped here. Occasionally, if one of them hasn't been able to unload them on the target, they dump them around here on the way home, but there hasn't been a lot of damage. But if you'd rather, I believe the next-door neighbours have an Anderson shelter in the garden. I know there would be room for us . . .'

'Bugger that!' Felix interjected. 'If I'm going to buy it I don't want it to happen in some dank hole in the ground. You go, if you want to.'

'No thanks,' Merry replied. 'I happen to feel the same way.'

Felix glanced at him. 'Good!'

The first wave of bombers was overhead now, shaking the window panes with their noise. Looking up, they could see the outlines of the huge planes filling the sky.

'Bloody hell!' Felix exclaimed. 'There are hundreds of the bastards!'

They stood in silence until the planes had passed over. Merry glanced at Felix and saw that he was shivering.

'You're cold,' he said. 'Put something warm on.'

Felix shrugged the remark off. 'I'm OK.'

Merry picked up a discarded sweater from the back of a chair and draped it across his shoulders.

'For God's sake, Merry!' Felix responded irritably. 'Stop behaving like an old hen!'

'Sorry,' Merry responded evenly.

Felix was silent for a moment. Then he said, 'No, I'm sorry. That was uncalled for.'

Merry wandered over to the bed and sat on the edge of it. Distantly they could hear the sound of a fresh wave of bombers heading towards them.

Suddenly Felix said, 'Haven't you ever wondered why Edward Mountjoy was masquerading as Felix Lamont, illusionist extraordinaire? You've never asked.'

'No,' Merry said, keeping his tone carefully neutral.

'Don't you want to know?'

'Only if you want to tell me.'

There was a pause. 'The fact is,' Felix resumed, 'my family disowned me, kicked me out and told me never to darken their doors again.' He waited, but Merry remained silent. 'You see, I was caught in flagrante on the banks of the Cam – with a boy I'd picked up in the town.' The words were coming quickly now. 'I was drunk, of course, very drunk. But I knew what I was doing – and it wasn't the first time. I'd been to a party and on the way home I came across this boy . . . God, I can't even remember his name now! The police found us and I spent the night in a cell. The family solicitor told me I could be looking at two years' hard labour. I was bloody terrified, Merry! My father must have pulled some strings somehow and in the end I got off with a charge of drunk and disorderly and a hefty fine. But I was sent down by my college, of course, and once the pater had made sure the family name wasn't going to be dragged through the courts he gave me my marching orders.' He hesitated and half turned. 'I made up my mind I was never going to be caught like that again. I was going to lead a *normal* life – whatever that means! From now on I was going to stick to the opposite sex. After all, I didn't dislike girls. I mean, I could *do* it with girls. I was going to get married and have a family.' He gave a brief, bitter laugh. 'So much for the best-laid plans!'

He fell silent. Merry sat still. He was scarcely breathing, but this time it had nothing to do with his asthma. Felix was looking out of the window again.

'So now you know.'

Merry got up and went over to stand beside him. 'What makes you think I didn't know already?'

Felix swung round and stared at him. 'How could you?'

'It wasn't difficult,' Merry said. 'An afternoon spent rifling through old copies of the *Tatler*. A photograph of the Hon. Edward Mountjoy attending a Cambridge May Ball. Then a day trip to Cambridge and a few hours going through the back files of the local paper, a chat over a drink with a college porter, the judicious exchange of the odd half-crown . . .'

'But why?' Felix sounded as if someone had punched him in the stomach.

'Do you need to ask? Shall we say you had aroused my curiosity?'

'You've known all this time. Since when? That first season at Fairbourne?'

'Yes.'

'But you've never let on. Why not?'

'What would have been the point?'

'But don't you see?' Felix exclaimed. 'You only needed to drop the slightest hint and you could have had anything you wanted.'

Merry eyed him coldly. 'Such as?'

Felix looked at him, then dropped his gaze. 'Me. You did want me, didn't you?'

Merry said very quietly, 'Do you really think I would have wanted you on those terms?'

Felix turned away. After a moment he said, 'No. I'm sorry. That was unforgivable.' Suddenly he lifted his face to the starlight and cried out, 'Oh, what a bloody mess! All that wasted time, trying to pretend, trying to be something I'm not and never can be, when we could have . . . And now, now that it's too late . . .'

Merry took a step closer. 'What do you mean, too late?'

Felix turned his ravaged face towards him. 'Oh, for Christ's sake, Merry! Do I have to spell it out? You don't want this, do you?'

Merry felt as if he had stopped breathing altogether. Forcing himself to keep his voice steady, he said, 'It doesn't make any difference.'

Felix lurched towards him, thrusting his face in front of his eyes. 'Don't be bloody stupid! You don't want to take this to bed with you!'

Very slowly and carefully Merry raised his arms and took the damaged face between his hands. 'It doesn't make any difference,' he repeated, and kissed him. He felt Felix tense and pull back, and thought for a terrible instant that after all he had misjudged the moment, then the hard lips softened and the taut body relaxed into his embrace. Somewhere in the distance the all-clear sounded, but Merry was only dimly aware of it. His senses were inundated – touch, taste, smell overwhelmed with the ecstatic recognition of Felix, and through it all the triumphant awareness of an avid, unconditional response.

After a long while he lifted his head and murmured, 'Bed?' and Felix answered shakily, 'I thought you'd never ask!'

A long time later, lying loosely entangled in each other's arms, they heard the warning siren wail again and immediately the drone of the returning planes.

'Jerry on his way home,' Merry murmured.

'Sod him!' Felix answered drowsily. 'He can drop his bomb for all I care. At least we'll go together.'

Merry laid his cheek against the fair head on his shoulder and experienced a moment of total happiness. 'I'll settle for that,' he said.

When Merry woke the next morning it was to a sensation he had not felt since he was a schoolboy, waking to the first morning of the long summer holidays. He rolled over cautiously and looked at Felix. He was sleeping on his side, his face towards Merry and his right cheek buried in the pillow so that only the perfect left side of his face was visible, and Merry felt the familiar catch at the pit of his stomach that the sight of him had always evoked. He longed to reach out and touch him but reasoned that it would be unkind to wake him. In a minute or two, however, as if called into wakefulness by the power of Merry's thoughts, Felix stirred, yawned and opened his eyes. A slow smile curled the left side of his mouth.

'So I wasn't dreaming.'

'No,' Merry said, smiling in answer.

'And did we really do what I think we did last night?'

'We certainly did.'

Suddenly the smile faded. Felix turned on his back, his eyes slanted sideways to watch Merry's face.

'Bet you can't do it again in daylight!'

When Merry had proved, comprehensively, that he could, he got up and went downstairs, whistling softly. He boiled eggs and made tea and toast and carried the whole lot back upstairs to where Felix was lying, drowsily contemplating the ceiling. They ate sitting up side by side in the big bed.

Felix licked butter off his fingers and remarked, 'This is the ultimate in decadence.'

'Mmm,' Merry agreed. 'Good, isn't it.'

'You're teaching me bad habits,' Felix said reproachfully.

Merry grinned happily. 'I have every intention of so doing, at every opportunity. More tea?'

'No, thanks.'

'Toast?'

'No, really. I couldn't eat another mouthful.'

Merry disposed of the trays and leaned back against the headboard, while Felix settled down again on his pillow.

'There's one thing I'm not entirely clear about,' Merry said. 'How did Edward Mountjoy metamorphose into Felix Lamont, illusionist extraordinaire?'

'Ah,' Felix said, stretching himself. 'Long story.'

'We've got all day.'

'Well,' Felix looked up at him, 'you see the relevance of the name, of course.'

'Felix being the Latin word for happy – hence happy mount, Mountjoy.'

'Good!' said Felix approvingly. 'Most people seem to think it has something to do with cats.'

'But why the magic act?' Merry prompted.

'OK. When the old man cut me off without the proverbial I wasn't totally destitute. An elderly great-aunt died without issue and left me a trust fund that brings in a small income.'

'Ah!' Merry interjected. 'I thought there must be something like that.'

Felix glanced up at him. 'I felt rotten sometimes, watching you all struggling on that pittance Monty paid us. But I figured that if I started flashing money around, making loans, and so on, first it would result in a lot of awkward questions and second it would cause bad feeling in the long run.'

'I'm sure you're right,' Merry agreed.

'Anyway, I had this money, but it wasn't enough to live on. And I was determined not to end up loafing around London hoping someone would buy me a drink, if you see what I mean. Besides, too many people knew me. I wanted to get away, literally to disappear. And that's what gave me the idea. I'd always been keen on magic and conjuring. I had an Uncle Percy who was mad on the subject. He had no children of his own, so he spent a lot of time teaching me. By the time I went to Eton I was able to entertain my friends with a selection of tricks – and my enemies, too, which was probably more valuable.'

He glanced up again and Merry nodded drily. 'Quite.'

'Percy had got to know quite a few professionals over the years and he'd introduced me to some of them. And I was a member of the Junior Magic Circle. There was one old chap, used to perform under the name of the Great Stupendo, who took a fancy to me . . .' He caught Merry's eye. 'Totally platonic, I hasten to add, at least on my part. He showed me some of his illusions and once or twice during the holidays he let me act as his assistant. So I wasn't exactly starting from scratch. When the idea occurred to me it seemed so neat, somehow. My greatest trick of all. Edward Mountjoy vanishes and Felix Lamont appears in his place. I worked up an act. Then I went to see old Stupendo and he gave me a few contacts in the profession. To start with I was just doing children's parties and that sort of thing. Then I got a spot on the bill at the Holborn Empire. That's where Monty saw me. He offered me the summer season at Fairbourne in 'thirty-eight – and the rest you know.'

'The rest I know,' Merry echoed. 'Just one thing, Felix . . .' He stopped abruptly. 'Should I be calling you Felix?'

'Good heavens, yes! What else would you call me?'

'Edward, I suppose.'

'No thanks!' Felix shook his head vehemently. 'The chaps in the squadron call me Ned, because they don't know me by any other name, but in here,' he tapped his chest, 'I'm Felix Lamont. Edward Mountjoy no longer exists.'

'But you chose to revert to that name when you joined the RAF,' Merry pointed out.

Felix sighed. 'Well, it just seemed simpler. I thought there might be all sorts of trouble if they found out I wasn't who I said I was. And I suppose . . .' He left the sentence hanging in the air.

'Suppose what?' Merry prompted.

'I suppose I thought it might go some way towards removing the blot on the old escutcheon, if you see what I mean.'

'I should think you've done that pretty comprehensively,' Merry said.

'Yes,' Felix returned soberly. 'You might think that, mightn't you.'

Merry looked down at him with a sudden pang of sympathetic anguish. 'You haven't heard anything from your family?'

'No.'

'Not even when you got your gong?'

'No, not a word.'

'Nor after you were shot down?'

'No.' Felix was silent for a moment, then he added, 'Of course, my father's abroad, so I'm told, and brother Anthony is at sea somewhere. Not that we've ever had much in common.'

'And your mother?' Merry queried.

'Busy, I believe.'

'She could have written.'

Felix shook his head. 'My mother is a very religious woman. Takes her wedding vows very seriously – you know, love, honour and *obey*. She wouldn't dream of going against my father's wishes – whatever the circumstances.'

Merry did not pursue the subject, but reached out and sympathetically tousled his lover's hair. After a moment Felix said, 'What are we going to do today? The sun's shining. Let's go out.'

Later on, striding out across the downs in the crisp autumn air, Merry said, 'Incidentally, does Harriet know who you are?'

'Oh God, yes!' Felix answered. 'I've known Harry since I was a kid. She's one of the very few people who do know, but she's sworn to secrecy.'

'Does she know why you were sent down?'

'Yes. But she thinks it was a momentary aberration.'

'Last summer . . .' Merry hesitated, but felt compelled to ask. '. . . were you having a love affair?'

'An affair, yes,' Felix said judiciously. 'Whether you could call it a love affair is an open question. I was trying very hard to fall in love with her, but it wasn't working – for obvious reasons.'

'And her?'

'I don't know. It would seem not.'

'Do you mind?'

Felix stopped walking and grinned at him. 'Did it seem last night – and this morning – as if I minded?'

Merry laughed with relief. 'No, I must say it didn't.'

They stopped at a country pub for lunch. The place was almost deserted and Felix found a table in the far corner while Merry went to the bar to order.

'On leave?' the landlord asked.

'I am,' Merry said. 'My friend's convalescing. He was shot down and badly burned in the summer.'

The landlord looked across at Felix. 'One of the Few, eh?' He placed a second pint alongside the one he had already drawn. 'Have these on the house. I'll see what the missus can rake up in the way of food.'

Shortly afterwards he came over to the table with two steaming plates of liver and onions and insisted on shaking hands with Felix.

'Mr Churchill's right,' he said, his voice thickening. 'We'll never be able to repay what we owe to lads like you.'

After that Merry made a point of coaxing Felix into situations where he had to meet people. One or two of them stared or turned away but by and large they made a point of meeting his eyes and shaking hands, often expressing the same sentiments as the landlord of the pub. And wherever they went, as Merry laughingly remarked, Felix was worth his own weight in free pints. At the same time, he was aware that Felix was watching him, judging the way in which publicans and shopkeepers and casual acquaintances responded to him. It was a considerable relief to know that he could pass that test. In the more liberal atmosphere of the theatre he had occasionally permitted himself to indulge in what was increasingly becoming known as 'camping it up', but he had never been flamboyant. Outside that environment he had always been careful to maintain a strictly man-to-man demeanour, and now he was glad of the fact. He wanted Felix to know that he was quite safe in his company.

For that week they seemed to be suspended in a magic bubble, outside of time, away from the war. After that first night they were not disturbed again by the air-raid warning. The skies remained eerily quiet. Listening to the news on the wireless the next day, they understood why. Hitler had switched his attention to the industrial cities of the Midlands. Coventry was devastated in a single, pitiless night. Birmingham and Liverpool followed. The only comfort was the news that Hamburg had been treated to a similar bombardment.

The sense of unreality extended to Merry's inner feelings. He knew that they both faced, at best, an uncertain future, and that for Felix it held the prospect of renewed pain and distress. Yet nothing could impinge on his own sense of total, ineffable happiness. He told himself it was selfish to feel that way, but his guilt was assuaged by the ever present evidence that Felix was happy too. He took some pleasure in the thought that, whatever happened in the future, if he never did anything else of any worth, at least he had given him one week's respite from his suffering, both mental and physical.

On the last evening he asked, 'What next, Felix?'

Felix lifted his shoulders. 'I don't know. They won't want me cluttering up the place at the Belleview much longer.'

'When does McIndoe want you?'

'Not till after Christmas.'

'So what will they do with you till then?'

'Give me a rail warrant for Cheshire and send me home, I expect.'

'Will you go?'

'Heavens, no!'

'Then what?'

'I'll find somewhere. A hotel or something. Don't worry about me.'

On the way back to the convalescent home Felix said suddenly, 'Look, you might as well hang on to the Lagonda for the time being. She's no good to me at the moment.'

'Well,' Merry replied, 'I must say I'll be easier in my mind knowing you haven't got the temptation of seeing her sitting there. I'll look after her till you're ready.'

They said goodbye as unemotionally as they could manage in the foyer of the Belleview and Merry headed back to his base.

Chapter Sixteen

'Marseilles!' Richard breathed, gazing from the window of the hotel bedroom across the harbour to the blue of the Mediterranean. 'I never really believed we'd make it, but here we are. And it's been so easy!'

It *had* been easy, incredibly so. They had bought first-class rail tickets in Paris and had crossed the demarcation line into the unoccupied zone with only the minimum of formality. From there everything had run as smoothly as if it was still peacetime, and now here they were, breathing in the balmy, salt-tasting air of the Côte d'Azur.

Chantal came and put her arms round him from behind. 'Don't relax too soon, *mon cher*. This is only the first part of the journey, and probably the easiest part. From here on it will be different.'

He turned to her, his mood sobering. 'What happens next?'

She took his hand and drew him to sit beside her on the bed. 'Tomorrow you have to see the doctor.'

'But I'm not ill!' he exclaimed.

She smiled. 'But you must pretend to be. The good doctor is the next link in the chain. He will tell you what to do next – or he will introduce you to someone who can. I don't know exactly how it works.'

'Who is he, this doctor?' Richard asked.

'His name is Rodocanachi. He is Greek, but a naturalised Frenchman. He has lived here in Marseilles for many years but I believe he has family connections in England. He is a great

Anglophile – and a great humanitarian. You can trust him absolutely.'

Richard was thinking of something else. 'Does this mean that we have to part company?'

She sighed and nodded. 'But you knew that this was going to happen.'

'I hate the thought of leaving you here,' he exclaimed. 'Come with me. Come back to England.'

'You know I can't do that,' she said. 'I have my work here.'

'Singing in nightclubs?'

'No, you know that is not what I mean. I must go back to Lille. Paul will need me to bring other Englishmen south.'

'But haven't you done enough?' Richard demanded. 'After all, there can't be many soldiers from the BEF left wandering about after all these months.'

'And what about others who escape, as you did?' she asked. 'And the airmen who are shot down or have to bale out? Already we have returned several of them, and there will be more. I must go on.'

'I can't bear the thought of you being in such danger!' he said.

She lifted her shoulders gently. 'We shall both be in danger, *chéri*. You are returning to your regiment, to fight again. And anyway, if I came to England I should be *de trop, n'est ce pas*? You are going back to find your Rose – and this time you will not take no for an answer.'

Richard sighed. They had spoken of Rose on several occasions and Chantal was well aware of his feelings, but in spite of that he had a guilty feeling that he was cheating on both women.

The next morning Chantal led him to the old part of the city. They had not gone far before Richard suddenly stopped and stood rooted to the spot, staring at an approaching figure.

'What is it?' Chantal enquired.

'Look! Can't you see? There's a British officer in full uniform coming towards us.'

She slipped her hand under his arm and gripped it. 'Ignore him.'

'But he's walking around as if he owns the place,' Richard stammered.

'Ah!' Chantal made a small exclamation of comprehension. 'Of course, I should have told you.' She began to walk on, taking him with her. 'There are many British soldiers here who have been caught by the authorities. Because this is the unoccupied zone they have not been sent to German prison-of-war camps. Instead, they are interned in the old Fort St Jean, across the harbour there. The officers are allowed out on parole as long as they return for roll-call.'

They were almost level with the British officer now, and Richard had to make a conscious effort not to come to attention and salute. Then he realised that his curious stare had attracted the other man's attention and he forced himself to look at Chantal instead.

'So what are they doing? Surely they're not content to loll around here until the war finishes. Why don't they escape?'

She shook her head at him. 'This is not something to discuss in the street. Anyway, they have been given their parole. If they break it, then all the others must suffer.'

'Paroles can be withdrawn,' Richard said.

'And so they are, sometimes,' she agreed, and winked at him.

In the square there was another shock in wait for Richard. A group of German officers were drinking at a café table.

'What are they doing here?' he demanded.

'On leave, I expect,' Chantal said. 'Now that winter is coming this coast is very popular with officers who have two or three days off.'

'I thought we'd seen the last of them,' Richard muttered.

'Don't worry,' she told him. 'They are not going to bother looking for escapers. It is the police you have to watch out for. Some of them are all right, but a lot are working for the Nazis. And then there are Gestapo agents in civilian dress. You must trust no one.'

She led him to a road junction and pointed. 'That is the Rue Roux de Brignoles. The doctor lives at number twenty-one. It is an apartment on the second floor, which is also his consulting room, so the concierge is quite used to seeing people going in and out. Don't take the lift. You can find yourself stuck in a lift with people who may ask too many questions, or remember your face too well. Take the stairs and look as if you know where you are going. Ring the bell and when someone answers just say you want to see the doctor. When your turn comes to go into the consulting room, tell him who you are and what you want and he will do the rest.' She looked at his face and added, 'Don't worry. It is quite safe. I shall wait for you over there, in that café.'

He followed her instructions and found himself standing outside the door of an apartment in a rather old-fashioned but spacious block. It was opened by an elderly woman in a maid's uniform who led him into a waiting room. He took a seat and picked up a magazine, glancing surreptitiously at the other occupants. They were an old man with a continuous, painful cough and a woman who had a small, sickly-looking child on her knee. Richard cleared his throat, having decided that, if challenged, he would say that he had laryngitis.

In due course the old man was called into the consulting room and then the door opened to admit two new patients – a stout, middle-aged woman and a much younger man wearing a long trench coat. Richard looked at him covertly and did not like what he saw. There was something unmistakably

Germanic about the aquiline features and the pale blue eyes. Richard applied himself to his magazine again.

The woman with the child went in and then, after what seemed a very long wait, the door opened again and the elderly maid called, '*Au suivant, s'il vous plaît.*'

Richard rose and followed her across the hall and through the door, which she held open. An elderly man with black hair liberally powdered with grey, a luxuriant moustache and piercing dark eyes under formidable brows looked up from his desk and then rose courteously and extended his hand.

'I am Doctor Rodocanachi,' he said in French. 'And your name is . . .?'

Richard found that his throat really did seem to have closed up. The idea of baldly announcing his true identity, after so many weeks of concealment, and to a complete stranger, seemed ludicrous.

'Benedetti,' he muttered thickly. 'Ricardo Benedetti.'

If the doctor was surprised he did not show it. 'Please sit down, Monsieur Benedetti. What can I do for you?'

Richard sat, and realised that it was pointless to keep up the pretence. If he was to continue his journey he must do as Chantal had bidden him and trust this man. He cleared his throat again and said, in English, 'I'm sorry. That wasn't the truth. My name is Richard Stevens. I'm a private in the South Lancashire Regiment and I was told you could help me get home.'

The doctor smiled. 'I thought perhaps that might be the case. Now, tell me, who told you to come here?'

'Chantal. She's a singer. She brought me from Lille.'

The doctor nodded. 'I know about Chantal. How did you come to be separated from your unit?'

Richard told him briefly of his capture at Dunkirk and his subsequent escape. Apparently satisfied, the doctor rose.

'Come. There is someone you must meet. This way.'

He led him across the room to a second door and opened it. Richard advanced warily, half expecting to find the young man in the trench coat or someone in the uniform of the Gestapo on the far side. In fact, what he saw when he entered the room was far more surprising. He stood still in utter amazement and disbelief.

The room was furnished as a bedroom, but to one side was a table with some papers on it and two chairs. Standing by the table was an extremely tall man in the full uniform of a captain in the Seaforth Highlanders, complete with kilt.

The doctor said, 'May I present Captain Garrow. Ian, this is Richard Stevens. He needs our help.'

Richard came to attention and then remembered that as he was not in uniform he could not salute. The Scotsman came forward and extended his hand but the blue eyes in the handsome face were coolly assessing.

'Good morning. Welcome to Marseilles.' The accent was broad and unmistakable.

'How do you do, sir?' Richard responded.

'What outfit are you from?'

'South Lancashires, sir.'

The doctor said discreetly, 'I'll leave you to talk. I have patients to see.'

The door closed and Garrow said, 'Have a seat. Now, name, rank and serial number?'

Richard supplied them and Garrow looked at him for a moment with raised eyebrows, as if something surprised him. He went on without comment, however.

'Got any identification with you?'

'Yes, sir.' Richard reached into his jacket and tugged free a shoulder pad, which was attached only by a few threads. 'Do you have a knife, or a pair of scissors, please?'

A penknife was supplied and Richard quickly slit open some stitching and emptied out on to the table his identity disc and regimental insignia, which Chantal had carefully sewn into the shoulder pad before they left Lille. Garrow studied them carefully and then looked up.

'All right. Where were you during the retreat?'

Once again Richard repeated his story and Garrow questioned him closely about the disposition of forces and the course of the battle. Richard answered in as much detail as he could, but had to admit that the events of the last few days before his capture were hazy in his memory. He went on to explain how he had been wounded and how he had eventually escaped.

Garrow listened and nodded from time to time. At length he said, 'You look remarkably sleek and prosperous for someone who's been on the run for the last couple of months, if you don't mind my saying so.'

'I had a stroke of luck,' Richard told him. 'I ran into an old friend.'

He explained how he had met Chantal and of the stratagem she had devised to get the two of them through France, and as the story progressed Garrow's eyes widened and a glint of amusement came into them. Finally he threw back his head and gave a shout of laughter.

'You're telling me that you are singing your way through France for the entertainment of German officers?'

'I'm afraid so,' Richard admitted.

'Well,' the Scotsman exclaimed, 'I've heard of some barefaced cheek in my life, but that takes the biscuit! I congratulate you.' He became serious again. 'OK. One or two more questions. Where were you born?'

'Oldham, sir. Near Manchester.'

'And your home address now?'

Richard supplied it and Garrow looked at him, his eyes narrowing.

'You don't sound like a Lancashire lad. If you don't mind my saying so.'

Richard found himself smiling. 'That's my mother's fault, I'm afraid.' Then, reverting to the accent of the streets where he had grown up, 'Happen she liked to think we were a cut above t'other folks round about, tha knowst.'

Garrow laughed. 'Well, speaking as a Scotsman, that sounds like a genuine Lancashire accent to me. School?'

'Manchester Grammar.'

Garrow sat back and studied him for a moment. 'Last question. Why a private? Why didn't you apply for a commission?'

Richard dropped his eyes and hesitated before giving the answer he always gave to that question. 'I didn't feel I was officer material, sir.'

'Well,' Garrow returned, 'it strikes me that someone with your obvious intelligence and initiative is exactly the sort of officer the army needs. Take a tip from me. When you get back, put in for a commission. I'm not saying you'll have a more enjoyable war, but you might find it less of a waste of time than you otherwise will.'

'Thank you, sir,' Richard murmured. 'I'll bear that in mind.'

'Right!' said Garrow, his tone becoming practical. 'This is the situation. You'll be sent south with a party of others and put into the charge of a Spanish guide who will take you over the Pyrenees into Spain. But don't think your troubles are over when you cross the border. Spain is neutral, but they have a nasty habit of interning escaping British personnel and it takes the diplomats some time to winkle them out again. Try to avoid being picked up by the Guardia Civil and get to Barcelona. If you can make it to our consulate there they'll see you get home safely. Oh, and get these sewn back in safely otherwise the Spanish can do what they like with you.' He pushed Richard's insignia back across the table to him. 'OK?' Richard nodded and Garrow went on, 'Did you say you were wounded in the leg?'

'Yes, sir.'

'Let's have a look.'

Richard rolled up his trouser leg and the captain examined the scar tissue carefully, though Richard was not sure whether he was looking for proof of his story or checking to see how bad the damage was.

It seemed it was the latter, as Garrow resumed, 'Does this give you any trouble now? You've got a long and arduous walk ahead of you.'

'It's fine, sir,' Richard assured him. 'It gives a twinge every now and then, but not enough to worry about.'

Garrow looked sceptical. 'I hope you're right. If you can't keep up you'll have to be left to fend for yourself.'

'I understand that,' Richard said. 'When do I go?'

'I can't tell you that at the moment. We're in the process of organising the next transfer. But it should be within the next week or ten days.'

'But I'm booked to sing at the Tour Blanche for two weeks,' Richard responded, without thinking.

Garrow stared at him, his eyes widening. 'You're not a professional entertainer now, you know! You'll go when you're bloody well told to go, and bugger the Tour Blanche.'

Richard felt himself flush. 'I'm sorry, sir. Force of habit, I suppose. How will I know when the time comes?'

'Where are you staying?'

Richard told him. Garrow nodded and went on, 'The day before you're due to leave a bouquet of white carnations will arrive at the hotel for you "from an admirer". As soon as you get that you must come straight here and the Rodocanachis will give you a bed for the night. You have to leave at the crack of dawn. The train to Toulouse goes at six thirty a.m. so you need to be at the station by six. Bring one small bag with you – essentials only. Understood?'

'Understood, sir,' Richard agreed.

'Meanwhile, if you're going to be out on the loose in the town, for God's sake be careful.'

'I will,' Richard promised.

Garrow rose and accompanied him to the door. 'Where did you say you were performing?'

'La Tour Blanche.'

Garrow grinned. 'Wish I could come and watch you. Unfortunately there's a little problem called a curfew.'

Richard hesitated. 'Can I ask you one thing, sir?'

'You can ask. I shan't necessarily answer.'

'Why haven't you escaped yourself? You obviously could, quite easily.'

'More important work to do here,' Garrow said simply.

The performances at the Tour Blanche went as well as those in Paris and Chantal was moved to remark, with wistful humour, 'What a pity there's a war on. We could really go places, you and me.'

Richard nodded and sighed. Incredibly, he was enjoying himself. During the day they explored the city, making the most of the mild, sunny weather. In the afternoons they retired to their room for what they euphemistically termed a siesta, but which was really an opportunity for making love with a passion that was more intense for the knowledge that each time might be the last. Then came the evening performance, and Richard had to admit to himself that, however far the material was from his usual repertoire and whatever his feelings for some of the people who listened to him, it was great to be in front of an audience again. He had not realised until then how addicted to applause he had become after that one season with the Follies.

Early on in their stay Chantal took him to a building near the docks, which housed the Seamen's Mission, where they were greeted by the priest who ran it, another Scot called Donald Caskie.

'My friend is going on a journey,' Chantal said. 'He will need some stout boots and a good coat.'

Without asking further questions the priest led them upstairs and opened a large cupboard full of second-hand clothes.

'We often come across people who need a change of clothing,' he remarked with a meaningful glance at Richard. 'So I try to keep a good store. Help yourself.'

After some time rummaging through the store Richard was provided with an oilskin coat and a pair of boots in the correct size. They felt strange, having been worn in by other feet, but the leather had been well cared for and he hoped would give to fit him.

The days passed with no summons from Garrow. Richard began to worry, not about having to cut short his contract with the nightclub, but about what would happen if there was no sign of the promised escape by the time it finished. They could hang around in Marseilles for a day or two, perhaps, without arousing suspicion, but after that it would become increasingly difficult.

On the Wednesday of the second week, at the end of their performance, a waiter approached them with a request from someone in the audience for Richard to join him at his table. Richard murmured to Chantal, 'It's this damn shirt again!' and she replied with a laugh, 'Don't worry. I'll come and find you in a few minutes and act as chaperone.'

It was a considerable shock to discover, when the waiter pointed out the table in question, that the request came not from a German officer but from a man in the uniform of a captain in the Italian army. For a moment Richard was tempted to withdraw. His Italian passed well enough among the French and Germans, but was it good enough to fool a native? But it was already too late. The man at the table had seen him and was waving him over.

Portly, rubicund and bright eyed, his host was an unlikely-looking army officer. He greeted Richard effusively.

'Signore, I'm delighted to meet you. Massimo Parigi, at your service. Please, sit down and take some wine. I must tell you I have enjoyed your performances enormously.'

'*Piacere, signore,*' Richard murmured in reply. He sat down and for a few minutes they chatted about the club, about Marseilles, about the songs Richard had chosen. Then Parigi fixed him with a mischievous look.

'But you, my friend, are an impostor, I think.'

In that instant Richard understood the full force of the cliché about blood running cold. But the tone had been light hearted and he forced himself to reply in the same manner.

'An impostor, signore? What makes you say that?'

The rotund Italian chuckled happily. 'Ah, you cannot fool me so easily. Others, yes, perhaps, but I know about these things. You are not a cabaret artiste.'

'I'm not?'

'Of course not. I have heard you sing, and that is a trained voice. You have been taught to sing opera. What are you doing wasting your time here?'

Richard felt sweat suddenly break out along his hairline and in his armpits. He smiled as engagingly as he knew how. 'Of course, you are obviously a man of taste, signore, a connoisseur. You are quite right, but these are difficult times. One does what one must.' And he launched into his prepared tale of the failed opera company and his desperate need for cash to fund his journey home.

The captain listened sympathetically and then commented, 'Louvain? I had no idea there was an opera company in Louvain.'

'It was a very new venture,' Richard explained quickly. 'That's why they went bust so rapidly when the war came.'

Captain Parigi was not finished with the mythical opera

company yet. He wanted to know which operas they had performed and what roles Richard had played, and Richard was thankful that Paul Cole had insisted on constructing such a detailed background to his story. He had, he said, sung Rigoletto and also Figaro.

'In *The Barber* or *Nozze?*'

'*Il Barbiere.*'

'Ah-ha!' exclaimed Parigi delightedly, and sang 'Figaro, Figaro, Figaro . . .'

'*Una la volta, per carita!*' Richard finished obligingly.

'So, you see, I am right,' chortled the Italian. 'But what are you doing here in Marseilles when you should be at home in Italy?'

Richard explained that he hoped to go home as soon as his contract at the Tour Blanche expired.

'Perhaps I can help you there,' said the captain. 'I am attached to the German-Italian Armistice Commission. We are based in the Hotel Louvre et Paix. Couriers go backwards and forwards regularly across the frontier. I am sure I could find you a lift with one of them.'

Richard gagged on his wine and had to feign a choking fit. When he recovered he could only mumble, 'That's extremely kind of you, signore. But I wouldn't want to put you to any trouble.' He looked around the tables, hoping to see Chantal coming to his rescue, but she had been intercepted by some other members of the audience and was engaged in animated conversation.

'It's no trouble,' the captain insisted. He leaned forward, confidingly. 'But perhaps I can persuade you to do me a small favour in return.'

Richard had the sense that he was getting into ever deeper waters, but he could think of no excuse to get away. 'What is that, signore?' he asked.

'Next Friday happens to be my birthday,' said the chubby

Italian. 'I am planning to have a small dinner for friends at the hotel, in celebration. I should like you to sing for me.'

Richard searched his mind for some excuse. 'I'm flattered, signore, but my voice is rusty. I'm out of practice – and I have no music. It was all lost in the rush to leave Belgium.'

'But surely you have no need of music. You must have arias in your repertoire. Figaro's aria, for example.'

'But my accompanist – there is no one to accompany me.'

The Italian sat back in his seat, beaming. 'That will not be a problem. I have not introduced myself properly. In civilian life I am répétiteur and rehearsal pianist at the Bologna Opera House. I shall accompany you myself.'

At that moment Chantal finally managed to detach herself and came over. Richard introduced her to Parigi and explained who he was.

'The signore has done me the honour of asking me to sing for him at a dinner on Saturday.'

'You must come too, of course,' exclaimed the captain. 'Your performance here is not until what time? Ten o'clock? You could sing perhaps at eight, my friend? And then I will have a car bring you back here in plenty of time.'

By the time they were able to escape to their dressing room it had all been settled, down to the details of Richard's programme.

'What am I going to do?' he demanded, distraught.

'Go, of course,' Chantal answered. 'Why not?'

'Because I haven't sung most of that stuff for two or three years! He thinks I've been singing it until six months ago. I'm hopelessly out of practice, and I'm not sure I can remember the words.'

'Then make an excuse. You can always tell them that you have a cold or something.'

'You haven't heard the worst yet,' he said, and told her about the proposal to get him a lift across the border. 'Suppose

I hear nothing from Garrow and then Parigi comes up with the offer of a lift?'

'Then you go into hiding until Garrow can get you out,' Chantal said.

Richard was silent for a moment, thinking. Then he gave a short, exasperated laugh. 'The ironic thing is, under normal circumstances I'd give my eye teeth to sing for that man. A répétiteur with a famous opera company! It's a chance in a million. Just my bloody luck!'

Chantal stroked his cheek. '*Pauvre petit!* But perhaps after the war the chance will come again.'

Richard shook his head. 'I can't see myself singing for an Italian company after the war, can you? Whoever wins.'

On Friday morning a bouquet of white carnations was delivered to the hotel. Richard and Chantal faced each other across it in their bedroom. She said, 'So. It is time for you to go, *chéri.*'

'But what about Parigi and his party?' Richard asked. 'If I don't turn up he's going to smell a rat.'

'I shall go and see him tomorrow afternoon,' she said. 'I shall be distressed and very angry. I shall tell him that you met some woman in the club last night and went off with her and I haven't seen you since. I shall suggest that she may have been Italian and that I think you have gone to Italy with her. I shall offer to sing for him and his friends instead.'

He reached out to her. 'I don't like you doing this. You put yourself at risk for me.'

'Pouf!' she said. 'What risk? To them I shall just be a cheap nightclub singer who has been jilted by her lover – and you will be a faithless Italian rat! And at least if they start looking for you they will be looking in the wrong direction, checking the wrong border.'

'I suppose that's true,' he agreed. 'What about the club?'

'I shall tell them the same story.'

He moved round the table and drew her close to him. 'I suppose this is goodbye.'

There were tears in her eyes. 'Not for a few minutes. You have to pack. I will help you.'

He collected his razor and toothbrush and a spare set of underwear and packed them into a small bag. She opened the wardrobe and got out the waterproof jacket and boots. He took her in his arms. 'Oh, Chantal, what would I have done without you?'

'You would have managed, as you did before. But it has been fun, no?'

'Yes. It has been fun. I'll never forget these last weeks.'

'No, nor shall I.'

He kissed her, a long kiss into which he tried to pour all his gratitude and regret . . . and, yes, love. 'I wish I could stay with you,' he whispered into her hair, 'or that you would come with me.'

'No you don't,' she murmured in return. 'When you get home you will see that it had to be this way. Now go, *chéri*. You must go.'

'What will you do now?' he asked, turning to pick up his bag.

'I shall take the train back to Lille and go back to my old job.'

'And to bringing people like me south.'

'British soldiers and airmen, yes. But not like you. It will never be like this again.'

'I'm glad,' he murmured, and kissed her for the last time. 'Take care, *ma chère*.'

At the door he turned again. 'When all this is over, I shall come and find you.'

There were tears on her cheeks now. 'Yes, do that,' she answered huskily. 'And bring your wife – your Rose.'

* * *

He was almost at the door of Dr Rodocanachi's flat before he had himself fully under control.

The elderly maid admitted him and this time, instead of showing him into the waiting room, she led him straight to a bedroom at the rear of the flat. Garrow was there and with him were two other young men in civilian dress.

Garrow said, 'Two travelling companions for you, Stevens. This is Flight Lieutenant Roger Baird and this is Flight Sergeant Wilf Mitchell.' As they shook hands he added to the others, with a grin, 'Get Richard to tell you how he made his way down here. It'll amuse you.' He turned to Richard. 'Glad to see you've got yourself some sensible footwear, but for the moment put these on. We can't have the people underneath wondering why there are men clumping about in boots all day.'

'These' were a pair of large felt slippers, and Richard saw that the other two men were similarly shod. As he changed into them Garrow went on, 'Roger and Wilf have been here for a week already. They'll tell you the house rules. Keep the blinds down, and don't open the bathroom window in case you're spotted by residents on the other side of the courtyard. You will all need to shave this evening. There won't be time in the morning. Be ready at five and for God's sake don't oversleep.'

When Garrow had gone Richard exchanged stories with the two airmen. They were the pilot and wireless operator of a bomber that had been shot down near Calais. They had baled out but had been separated from the rest of the crew, whom they guessed were now either dead or prisoners. From then on their story was much like his own early experiences on the escape route, being transferred from one safe house to another, sometimes by train, sometimes by bicycle or on foot. The main difference was that they had crossed the demarcation line by swimming a river in the dark. Richard thought once again how lucky he had been, but his two companions insisted that they would far rather have done what they did than stand up in front of an alien audience.

Both of them had been cooped up in the Rodocanachis' flat for eight days and were understandably bored and restless. There were English books and packs of cards, but neither they nor Richard felt able to concentrate with the prospect of the next day's journey ahead of them. It was some relief when, in the afternoon, they were invited to sit with Mme Rodocanachi. A striking woman with a classically Greek profile and elegant clothes, she spoke perfect English, a necessary accomplishment in the circumstances since it became clear that neither of the airmen spoke French. She spent some time relaying what she had gleaned of the progress of the war from the clandestine broadcasts on the BBC. The news was not good. The London Blitz had resumed. Richard now had to add to his concern for Chantal a deep anxiety over Rose's safety.

Later, when the surgery was closed for the evening, they were invited to go to the room that was used as a waiting room, now returned to its proper use as the '*petit salon*', where their host and hostess were waiting. To Richard's amazement, the Rodocanachis had dressed for dinner, and on their entry the doctor remarked, 'Richard, since you are our newest guest, perhaps you would care to take Madame in.'

Richard swallowed his incredulity and said gravely, 'Of course, I should be honoured. Madame?'

He offered his arm and together they progressed through the communicating doors into the dining room. The table was laid with fine silver and cut glass and in the centre of it was one single large dish, tastefully garnished. When served, this proved to consist mainly of macaroni, but the conversation that went with it was such as might have accompanied any sophisticated pre-war dinner party.

Madame's only concession to the frugality of the fare was to murmur to Richard, 'I regret that we cannot offer you something tastier. But it would not do to be seen buying rations for four or five. I have to take what I can get and I do my marketing in batches, so that I am never seen carrying home more than I would normally need.'

'Please don't apologise, madame,' Richard answered. 'I am full of admiration for what you and your husband are doing. We shall never be able to thank you adequately.'

He slept little that night, wondering about Rose and his other friends from the Follies and nervously anticipating the journey ahead of him. At 5 a.m. he was ready to jump out of bed when the doctor tapped on his door. In the kitchen he and the two airmen drank ersatz coffee and shivered. With winter approaching the nights had turned cold and there was no oil for heating. After a short time they heard voices in the hall and the doctor came in with a dark, impeccably dressed young man.

'This is my nephew, Georges Zarifi,' the doctor said. 'He will be your courier on the first part of your journey.'

They made their way quietly down the stone stairs and out into the deserted street. At the station they met two other young men, dressed in ill-fitting civilian clothes and looking extremely uncomfortable. Richard gave them a friendly greeting in French. They merely smiled at him nervously in response.

Zarifi murmured in his ear, 'They speak no French. I shall sit with them. You sit with the other two, then if the need arises you can speak for them.'

It was a long journey and, unable to talk to his companions, Richard found that the time passed slowly. He would have liked to sleep but every time his eyelids drooped he jerked himself awake, afraid that he might miss the first signs of some approaching danger. They changed trains at Toulouse and eventually arrived at St Jean de Luz, the last stop before the

Spanish border. Leaving the train, Richard and his companions followed Zarifi and the other two at a short distance. He was disturbed to see that the police were carefully checking everyone's papers at the exit from the station. He knew that his documents would pass the closest scrutiny, but wondered what reason he could give for the fact that he was heading for the Spanish border rather than the Italian. It occurred to him that he might be mistaken for a deserter from the Italian army.

Zarifi must have had the same thought, because he dropped back from the queue and wandered casually over to him. 'Go to the *pissoir* over there. There is a back way out into the station yard. Walk across there to the road and then follow me.'

Richard did as he was instructed and, having urinated to give the move credibility, strolled casually out of the rear door. All the way across the yard he expected to hear someone shouting at him to stop, but he reached the road without incident and saw Zarifi and the others a short distance ahead. He followed them until they disappeared into a doorway. Richard glanced around him. The street was empty expect for an ancient woman with her head shrouded in a black shawl. He ducked quickly into the doorway and found the others in a small courtyard being greeted by a small, wiry man who shook their hands energetically and led them into a large kitchen.

Over a meal of spicy garlic sausage and rough red wine, Richard and his companions were able to introduce themselves to the other two. They, too, were RAF men, fighter pilots who had been forced to bale out over enemy territory. They were both very young, scarcely out of their teens, and pathetically grateful to encounter other Englishmen. Their journey down the line had been so swift that it was only just over two weeks since they had left England, and Richard noticed that they seemed to find the situation much more intimidating than Baird and Mitchell, who had spent much

longer in hiding. Perhaps, he reflected, you could get accli-
matised to anything, given time.

They spent an uncomfortable night, the two young pilots
sharing the only bed and the rest of them lying on old
mattresses in the same room. Richard lay awake, listening
to the sounds of the other men breathing and stirring, reminded of the nights he had spent the previous winter in the
disused factory at Roubaix, waiting for the war to start. Then
he remembered the sound of Chantal's soft breathing beside
him in their hotel room in Marseilles. He wondered how she
had got on with Captain Parigi and whether she was now on
her way back to Lille and feeling as lonely as he was. He closed
his eyes and sent up a heartfelt prayer for her safety.

The next day Zarifi went out, saying that he had to arrange the
next stage of their journey, and they were left to occupy
themselves as best they could in the little house. Their host
spoke only the heavily accented French of the Languedoc so
that even Richard had trouble understanding him, and there
seemed to be nothing to eat except bread and the highly spiced
sausage, which was already playing havoc with his digestive
system.

Zarifi returned in the afternoon and told them to prepare to
leave. They collected their few belongings, said goodbye to
their host and set off on foot up a pleasant valley. The sky was
blue and here, not far above sea level, the air was still quite
mild and very quickly their spirits began to lift. Zarifi had to
reprimand the two boys several times for chattering in English.
The valley appeared to be deserted but, as he pointed out,
sound carried a long way in the mountains.

As dusk fell they reached a small village and Zarifi led them
into the local bar. A huge man with skin like leather and
exuberant moustaches got up from the table and embraced
him.

'This is Florentino,' Zarifi explained. 'He's a Basque and he knows every goat path over these mountains. He'll be your guide from here on.'

They were given glasses of wine so dark it was almost black and which would have made, in Richard's estimation, a very effective paint stripper. With this came more bread and a dish of goat's cheese.

By the time they had eaten night had fallen and Florentino rose to his feet. 'Time to move.'

Richard shook Zarifi's hand. 'I know you've risked a lot bringing us here. Thank you – and take care.'

'Don't worry,' he assured him. 'I'll see you all in England one day. I intend to cross over myself very soon, to join de Gaulle and the Free French.'

They said goodbye and set out in single file along a mountain path.

With nightfall had come a change in the weather. The sky was black and starless and a light rain had begun to fall. Richard was glad of the jacket and boots Chantal had acquired for him, but what concerned him most was the discomfort in his guts. He began to be afraid that he would have to drop out of the party in order to relieve himself.

After some time Florentino raised his hand in a signal to halt. Ahead of them they could hear the sound of running water. Florentino pointed ahead and managed to convey to Richard, in almost impenetrable French, that they should lie low among the trees until he came back. Richard took the opportunity to disappear among some bushes bordering the track. He was just pulling up his trousers when he smelt the unmistakable tang of cigarette smoke. A moment later he heard voices. He froze, his heart pounding, while two soldiers, rifles slung casually over their shoulders, passed him by within a few feet.

When they were safely out of hearing he scrambled back to

the others. 'For God's sake keep quiet!' he whispered. 'There are guards patrolling the river bank.'

Shortly afterwards Florentino reappeared and beckoned them to follow. He led them to a point where the river bank was broken down, perhaps by animals coming to drink, and waded into the water. Richard waved the others past him and brought up the rear. It occurred to him for the first time that, although the other men outranked him, he had somehow assumed a position of responsibility. The water was icy and he had to suppress a gasp as it rose round his knees and then up to his waist. Ahead, Florentino turned and made a downward movement of his broad hand, indicating that they should move slowly. Very cautiously, trying not to make any splashing that could be heard above the normal sounds of the running water, they waded across to the far bank.

On reaching the other side Florentino immediately set off up a steep scarp and they scrambled after him, panting and slipping on the stony ground. Their wet trousers clung to their legs but the rapid movement prevented them from feeling the cold and Richard was grateful that, for the time being at least, the cold water seemed to have eased the cramps in his stomach. They gained the top of the slope at last but were given no time to rest. Florentino was already pressing on up a narrow valley. After that, it became a simple matter of endurance. None of them had had much opportunity for strenuous exercise in recent weeks, though the two young pilots were probably fitter than the rest of them. Florentino, on the other hand, was a man of the mountains, accustomed to walking tirelessly in this steep and rocky terrain, and he showed them no mercy. Richard soon found difficulty in keeping up. His injured leg had begun to ache so that every step was painful and, to add to his misery, his stomach was churning again. There were times when he contemplated telling the others to go on ahead without him.

As dawn broke they came to the crest of a mountain pass and Florentino stopped. This, he indicated, was as far as he went. He warned them, in his guttural French, to continue to move carefully They were now in Spain but there were customs officers who patrolled the mountains looking for smugglers and they would be arrested if they were seen. He shook their hands and disappeared back the way they had come.

By the time it was fully light they were standing on a small plateau, looking down to the vineyards and fields of the foothills. In the distance they could see a huddle of white houses and far away a trail of smoke where a train was making its slow way across the landscape.

'Where now?' asked Roger Baird.

Richard was doubled up on a rock. He looked up and for a moment the panorama of mountains and valleys swayed around him.

'I'm sorry,' he said, speaking with difficulty. 'You're going to have to push on without me. I shall have to rest up for a bit until my guts stop aching.' He looked around him despairingly, spotted a small outcrop of rocks and added hastily, 'Excuse me.'

When he returned the others were still where he had left them. Roger said, 'We've had a pow-wow and come to a decision. We can't leave you here on your own but it seems silly for all of us to hang about. Wilf and the other two are going to press on and I'll stay with you.'

Richard tried to argue but Roger was adamant, and before he could summon up the strength to insist that he should go with the others the rest of the party had shaken hands with them and set off down the mountain. He and Roger stayed where they were, lying on the short grass and allowing the rising sun to warm them. Little by little the pains in Richard's stomach began to subside and he dozed in spite of himself. At length, he felt Roger's hand on his shoulder.

'Feel up to moving on?' the airman enquired.

Richard sat up and nodded groggily. 'Which way are we heading?'

'I thought we might make for the railway. You obviously can't walk all the way to Barcelona. We can use some of those Spanish pesetas Zarifi gave us to buy a ticket, if we can find a station.'

It seemed as good a plan as any and, as the day wore on and the paths grew less steep, Richard began to feel better. They reached the railway in the afternoon and began to walk westward along it, heading towards the village they had seen from higher up. After walking a mile or two they came in sight of the first houses. They left the railway line and cut across the fields to a road, then sauntered as casually as they could into the station. Amazingly, there were people waiting on the platform, as if a train was due any minute. Neither of them spoke any Spanish but on the walk they had rehearsed what they were going to say and decided that Richard could manage '*Dos*, Barcelona' fairly convincingly.

The ticket clerk handed over the tickets almost without looking up and they went through on to the platform. In the distance the smoke of the approaching train was already visible. Richard looked at his companion and as their eyes met Roger grinned and winked. His look said, 'We've made it!'

Behind him, Richard sensed movement. He turned. Two men in grubby uniforms were advancing towards them, un-slinging their rifles as they came. Neither he nor Roger understood what was being said to them, but the vicious prod with the muzzle of a rifle that accompanied the words left the meaning in no doubt.

Chapter Seventeen

On his return to London after his leave Merry was informed that he had been booked to give a series of concerts in Manchester and Liverpool, to help restore civilian morale in the two battered cities. He telephoned Felix at the Belleview to check that there was no immediate prospect of his having to leave and, reassured, headed north.

One of his assignments in the Manchester area was a concert given under the auspices of the Didsbury Music Society. At the end, as he left the platform, he was accosted by a middle-aged woman with a slender, erect figure and handsome but severe features.

'Lieutenant Merryweather, I'm Ada Stevens, president of the society.' The voice was precise, with only the faintest hint of a Lancashire accent – the voice of a woman used to getting her own way. 'I just want to thank you so much for such a lovely programme. I particularly enjoyed the Mendelssohn.'

'Thank you,' Merry responded automatically. Something was stirring in his memory. 'Mrs Stevens? I don't suppose there's any connection, but I once knew a singer called Richard Stevens. He came from Didsbury, I seem to remember. Is he a relation, by any chance?' A second later, looking at the unrelieved black of her dress, he could have bitten off his tongue.

The woman's face lost some of its stiffness. 'He's my son. You're a friend of his?'

'We worked together before the war, in Fairbourne.'

'Merryweather! Of course! I remember he mentioned you in his letters. He spoke very highly of you – but I had no idea you were a concert pianist.'

'Well, I wasn't then,' Merry said, and pressed on hastily. 'Have you had any news of him? We . . . I haven't heard anything since Dunkirk.'

'He's a prisoner of war,' Ada Stevens told him. 'Apparently he was injured on the retreat to Dunkirk and captured before he could get away. It took a long time for the Red Cross to find him and let us know. We heard nothing until nearly the end of August. He was still in hospital at that time but I understand his wounds were almost healed.'

'Oh, that is wonderful news!' Merry said. 'Of course, it's sad to think of him as a prisoner, but at least he's alive.'

'And out of danger until the war is over,' Ada Stevens pointed out.

'Have you actually heard from him personally?' Merry asked.

'We had one letter. It had been a long time getting here, but he wrote that he was being well treated. We've replied, of course, but so far we haven't heard anything more. I imagine the Red Cross have their work cut out trying to keep in touch with so many prisoners.'

Merry fished in his pocket for a notebook. 'Do you have an address for him? I'd like to write.'

Richard's mother delved into a capacious handbag and produced a piece of paper with the Red Cross symbol on the top of it. 'Here you are. I'm not sure if he's allowed to receive letters other than from his family but I suppose there's no harm in your writing.'

Merry copied the address and then took the plunge into what he suspected were dangerous waters. 'Mrs Stevens, I wonder if I could ask you a favour. There's a young lady. Her name is Rose Taylor. She and Richard were . . . friends – in the Follies. I know she's worried about him. When you next write to him, could you give him this address?' He was scribbling as he spoke. 'She's living down in Dorset at the moment, to get away from the Blitz. I'm sure he would want to let her know he's all right.' He smiled his most beguiling smile. 'Perhaps you'd like to drop her a line yourself, to let her know he's safe.'

Mrs Stevens took the piece of paper from him as if doubtful about its cleanliness.

'A young lady? Oh yes, come to think of it he did mention someone. I'll pass the address on. It'll be up to him then.'

But not with any encouragement from you! Merry thought. He murmured something about being glad to have met her and took the opportunity to turn away to someone else.

When his concerts in Manchester finished, Merry found himself with a day to spare before his next engagement in Liverpool. It was not hard to locate the whereabouts of the Malpas estate in Cheshire, and a short diversion brought him to a handsome, half-timbered manor house set in gently undulating pastureland. As he drove round the sweep of gravel that led to the front door he noticed that the area in front of the house, which had obviously once been an expanse of lawn, had been dug over and planted with potatoes. Coming to a standstill, he saw that his arrival was being observed by a gaggle of children between the ages of five and fifteen who had appeared round the corner of the building. The refugees, presumably.

His ring at the bell was answered, not by a butler as he had expected, but by a homely-looking woman with flour on her hands.

'My name is Merryweather,' he announced, 'Guy Merryweather. I wonder if I could see Lady Malpas. I'm a friend of her son's.'

'Her Ladyship's down at the farm office,' the woman replied. 'Come in a minute. I'll telephone.'

Merry waited in the wide, wood-panelled hall while she relayed his message.

'You're to go down,' the woman said. She went to the front door and shouted, 'Peter!'

A gangling youth in trousers several sizes too big detached himself from the group and wandered over.

'Take this gentleman down to the farm office to see her Ladyship.'

The boy led him round the corner of the house, followed at a discreet distance by the rest of the gang.

'Refugee?' Merry asked.

'Yeah.'

'Where from, London?'

'Yeah.'

'How do you like it here in the country?'

'Not much. Too quiet.' The boy was studying his cap badge and other insignia. 'What outfit you with, then?'

'SIB,' Merry said. Someone had suggested that Stars in Battledress might be a catchier title than the Central Pool of Artistes.

'What's that when it's at home?'

Merry tapped the side of his nose. 'That's classified information.'

The boy gasped. 'Secret Intelligence Bureau!'

Merry laid his finger warningly on his lips.

The boy nodded sagely. 'Right. Careless talk costs lives, eh?'

'Quite,' Merry agreed.

They had rounded the far corner of the house and come into a big yard where chickens scratched and a tabby cat prowled warily. On the far side a large pig stood on its hind legs to peer curiously over the gate of its sty, and two or three horses looked out of a range of loose boxes. Merry paused for a moment to take in the scene. It gave him an odd feeling to think that this was where Felix had grown up, the place from which he had been so summarily and mercilessly expelled.

At the end of the nearest range of buildings a half-open door gave on to what was obviously the farm office. Peter jerked his head and confirmed, 'In there.'

Merry thanked him and tapped lightly on the door. A woman's voice, low, cultured but authoritative, bade him enter. Lady Malpas was unmistakably Felix's mother: the same colouring, though the rich gold of Felix's hair had faded to something closer to straw; the same classic bone structure. Only the mouth was different. In place of the almost too generous curve of the son's, the mother's lips were thin and set in a hard, straight line. Now, however, they parted in a smile as she came forward and offered her hand.

'Lieutenant Merryweather? I'm sorry, I was expecting a naval officer. How nice of you to call. It's always a pleasure to meet a friend of Anthony's. How is he?'

Merry took her hand briefly. 'I'm sorry. I don't know. I'm a friend of Edward's, not Anthony's.'

He watched the colour come and go rapidly under her fair skin. Then her mouth hardened.

'Did he tell you to come here?'

'No. He doesn't know I'm in the area. It was my idea to call.'

She took a deep breath. 'I'm very sorry but I'm afraid you've had a wasted journey. Edward obviously hasn't explained to you that our ways parted several years ago. I no longer wish to see or hear from him.'

Merry gazed at her in disbelief. 'You know, of course, that he is a hero.'

'I heard he had been given a medal, yes.'

'And you know that he was shot down and badly burned?'

'His commanding officer telephoned me.'

Merry said softly, 'Lady Malpas, he's suffered greatly. He's been badly disfigured and faces a long period of plastic surgery. I really think he would like to see you.'

The woman opposite him drew herself up. 'I have no wish to see him,' she repeated.

'Surely,' Merry persisted, 'whatever he may have done to displease you, his current conduct, the debt we all owe to him and people like him, wipes that out.'

She stared back at him, her eyes like blue stone. 'What Edward did is none of your business. We are a God-fearing Christian family. He chose to go against the laws of God and the Church and he is no longer welcome here.'

For a moment Merry was bereft of words. Then he said, 'I was under the impression that Christ told us to forgive those who trespassed against us.'

Her face flushed. 'How dare you come here and preach to me! Please leave!'

'Very well.' Merry turned to the door, then paused and looked back. 'I assume you don't regard the parable of the Prodigal Son as an essential part of the Church's teaching.' With that, he turned on his heel and marched back to his car.

Once beyond the gates of the estate he stopped the car and turned off the engine. Clasping his hands on the wheel, he rested his brow on them and closed his eyes, thinking of the two women he had recently encountered. Both were mothers, yet they stood at opposite poles: the first so possessive of her son that she would not, Merry was quite certain, contact the girl who was waiting so anxiously for news of him; the second so hardened in her blinkered disapproval that all maternal feeling had been banished. He remembered his own mother, so dearly loved and so early lost, and raged, not for the first time, at the mad inequity of fate.

That evening he wrote to Rose.

Dear Rose,

I have some wonderful news for you. Richard is alive
and a POW. By pure chance I happened to run into his
mother, who is president of a music society I played for
the other day. Apparently they were informed that he
was safe by the Red Cross back in the summer, but they
have only had one letter from him since then. I imagine
communications must be pretty disrupted so we can't
draw any conclusions from that.

Of course, it means there is no chance of seeing him
again until the war is over, whenever that may be. But at
least we know he's all right.

I enclose the address of the place where he is being
held. It's a hospital, so presumably he was still being
treated for his wounds at the time, but don't worry about
that. His mother says that they are not serious. I suppose
he will have been moved by now, but perhaps letters will
be forwarded. I shall write, of course, but I'm sure a
letter from you will mean much more to him.

No time to write more.

Love,

Merry

By the time he got back to London it was the second week in
December and he found that Colonel Brown had arranged a
full schedule of performances for him over the Christmas
period. He scrutinised the list bleakly. There was not even half
a day when he might be able to get away to spend time with
Felix.

'I was hoping to get a bit of leave over Christmas,' he said,
looking at his commanding officer.

'So were we all, old boy,' Brown said cheerfully. 'But it also
happens to be a time when entertainment of any sort is
particularly welcome, perhaps even necessary. So I've had

to restrict leave to men with young families. You're a single chap, aren't you, and I had the impression that you have no close relatives since your father died. You seem the obvious candidate for helping to hold the fort over Christmas.'

'Oh, no doubt,' Merry said bitterly. 'Season of comfort and joy and all that, except for single men with no family. One does have friends, you know.'

It was the nearest he had ever come to hinting at any kind of personal commitment, and Brown regarded him shrewdly for a moment.

'Tell you what. I might be able to wangle forty-eight hours over New Year for you. That any good?'

Merry smiled gratefully. 'Thanks, I'd appreciate it.'

Returning to the office he shared with several others, he found a note asking him to telephone Felix at the Belleview. It was half an hour before he could get a call through and by the time he was connected he was in a state of heightened anxiety. To make matters worse it took some time to find Felix and the operator kept threatening to cut him off. Finally Felix's voice came over the receiver.

'Merry? Thanks for calling back. Sorry to bother you.'

'Felix, are you all right?'

'Yes, fine! Fit as a fiddle. Actually, that's part of the trouble.'

'Trouble?'

'I wanted to ask you a favour.'

'Then ask.'

'Do you think I could use your place at Seaford over Christmas?'

'Seaford?' Merry groaned. 'Felix, there's no way I can get away over Christmas, even for a few hours. Brown's got me playing to half the hospitals and officers' messes in the country.'

'Damn!' said Felix.

'He's going to give me forty-eight hours at New Year.'

'Well, that's something, I suppose.' Felix hesitated. 'Thing is, Merry, they want me out of here. I'm not ill any more and they need the bed. Do you think I could go to Seaford on my own?'

'On your own? Felix, you can't cope all by yourself. You can't even light a match.'

'I can use a lighter. And I'm learning to do a lot of things I couldn't manage before.'

'But you couldn't cook. It wouldn't be safe.'

'I'll go out to the pub.'

'For every meal? It's just not practical, Felix.'

'Problem is, I don't have an alternative.' Felix's voice sounded so desolate that Merry felt a lump in his throat. 'They keep talking about sending me home, but you know I can't do that. I suppose I'll have to get a room in a hotel somewhere.'

Merry's mind raced through possible solutions and came up with nothing better. 'I hate to think of you stuck in a hotel room on your own all over Christmas,' he said.

'Well, let me go to Seaford, then. I'd much rather be there.'

Merry sighed. 'Look, give me twenty-four hours to see if I can come up with something better. If I can't think of anything I'll post you a key to the house and see if I can get someone from the village to come in and cook for you. OK?'

'OK. Thanks, Merry. I'm sorry to be a nuisance but you do see the problem.'

'I do, and you're not a nuisance. Don't be an idiot.'

'You'll give me a ring tomorrow, then?'

'Yes, tomorrow. 'Bye till then.'

Merry sat for some time turning over various plans and wondering whether there was some way he could pressure Colonel Brown into giving him at least one day off over Christmas. It was not until he had given up and gone to practise some new items for his repertoire that inspiration came to him. He went back to the telephone and put through a call to Wimbourne.

The following morning he rang Felix again. 'Felix, I've cracked it.'

'You've got time off after all?'

'No, not as good as that, I'm afraid. But the next best thing. You remember that Rose and her family went down to stay with the Willises at Wimbourne?'

'Yes.'

'I've spoken to Rose and the Willises would be delighted to have you to stay over Christmas.'

There was a silence at the other end of the line. Then Felix said, 'Oh, I don't think so, Merry. I mean, it's a nice idea but it wouldn't be fair.'

'Why not, for heaven's sake?'

'Well, for one thing they must be horribly overcrowded as it is.'

'No, I asked about that. They had a family pow-wow and called me back. Babe can't get leave, so she won't be there, and they reckon they can juggle the existing arrangements to fit you in. They say they can manage it perfectly well and they'd really like to have you.'

'How can I, Merry?' Felix sounded exasperated. 'Rose's sister's there, isn't she, with her two boys? I'd give the poor little buggers nightmares.'

'Look,' Merry said patiently, 'Rose has been to see you, hasn't she? She knows what you look like. If she thought it would upset the kids she wouldn't ask you to come. Kids are a lot tougher than we give them credit for, you know.' He wasn't sure where that piece of wisdom came from but he was convinced of the truth of it.

'No!' Felix said obstinately. 'I won't go and be a skeleton at the feast.'

'OK, right!' Merry snapped. 'You go and hide your head in

some seedy hotel and feel sorry for yourself. And I'll tell the
Willises that their offer's not good enough for you.'

'It's not that, you know it isn't!' Felix cried.

'That's the way it's going to look to them,' Merry said
mercilessly.

There was a silence. Then, 'Look, do you know if Rose has
talked to the others – about me, I mean? Do they know what
they're letting themselves in for?'

'That's what the family conference was about,' Merry
assured him. 'They all understand and they are all quite
prepared. They *want* you to go, Felix. Believe me!'

Another long pause. Then Felix said, 'OK, if you're sure.'

'I'm sure. Now look, I've got to do a concert in Portsmouth
on December the twentieth. I could pick you up the previous
day and drive you down to the Willises. Will that be all right?'

'Wonderful! Then you can stay the night.'

Merry sighed. 'I don't think so, Felix. That really would be
straining the capacity of the house beyond its limits – and
anyway, there wouldn't be much point, would there? Me
dossing down on the sofa or something . . .'

'No, I see your argument,' Felix said regretfully. 'Oh well,
I'll see you on the nineteenth, then. What time?'

'Soon after lunch, hopefully.'

'OK. See you then.'

On the morning of the nineteenth Merry set off in a steady
drizzle, driving Felix's Lagonda. He had reached the crest of
the Hog's Back, just beyond Guildford, when a series of jolts
and a marked tendency to swerve to the left warned him that
he had a puncture. Swearing to himself, he got out and began
the process of changing the wheel. He had never been of a
mechanical turn of mind and the Lagonda was unfamiliar
territory, so it was a long, wet half-hour before he got the spare
wheel on and was able to resume his journey. South of

Winchester, to his utter despair, the same thing happened again. By now it was early afternoon and he had not stopped for lunch, and to add to his misery the rain was coming down even harder. He jacked up the car and removed the offending wheel, but he now had no spare. It was twenty minutes before an army lorry stopped and gave him a lift into Otterbourne, where the only mechanic mended the puncture but explained apologetically that he did not have enough petrol to drive Merry back to his car. In desperation he went to the local police station and told them he was on official business – which was nearly true. After some negotiation a police constable was dispatched to drive him back to the Lagonda and help him to replace the wheel. By then it was nearly five and the winter darkness had fallen.

By the time Merry drove up to the front door of the Belleview, Felix was white faced with anxiety.

'Where the hell have you been?' he demanded. 'I thought you said lunchtime.'

'Sorry,' Merry replied tersely. 'I had two punctures on the way down.'

'*Two* punctures! What are you driving, a perambulator?'

'Your bloody Lagonda!' Merry snapped. He was chilled to the bone, hungry and dog tired and this was not the reunion he had been planning for the last week. 'Shall we go?'

They went out to the car in silence. Merry slammed the gear lever into reverse and, to his immense chagrin, reversed smartly into a flower bed and stalled the engine.

Felix said nothing until they were moving again. Then he muttered, 'Look, I'm sorry. You've had a bloody day. It's just that I was convinced you'd crashed and killed yourself, or something.'

Merry did not respond for a minute, then he dropped a hand from the steering wheel and found Felix's. It was the burned right hand and Felix gave a sharp gasp of pain.

'Sorry! *Sorry!*' Merry exclaimed. Then he laughed. 'God, I don't seem to be able to get anything right today, do I?'

After that things were easier. Merry related the full story of his day and Felix tried to insist that they stop and get him something to eat. Merry, however, was determined to get to the Willises's as soon as possible.

'Oh, by the way,' he said, 'I've got some news.'

'Good news?'

'Very good. Richard's alive.'

'Richard! How do you know?'

Merry told him about his encounter with Mrs Stevens. He did not mention that he had also visited Lady Malpas.

Felix said, 'Does Rose know?'

'Yes, I wrote to her and we spoke about it on the phone last week.'

'She must be overjoyed.'

Merry frowned ahead into the rain. 'She's delighted, of course. But somehow not as pleased as I thought she'd be.'

'Bit of a shock, I suppose,' Felix suggested.

As the winter evening drew on and the rain continued to lash the windows Rose began to grow anxious. Her mother and Mrs Willis had prepared a special meal and both families were gathered in the large kitchen to wait for their guests. The two boys had been told that they could stay up to meet them but they were beginning to grow tired and fractious and everyone was hungry, so in the end it was decided that they would have to begin without them. Rose's anxiety was double edged. On the one hand, she was becoming more and more convinced that there must have been an accident of some kind, or that Merry or Felix, or both, had been caught in a bombing raid. On the other, she was uncomfortably aware that it had been her suggestion that they should take Felix in for the Christmas period and she was unsure of the effect he would have on the others. So when she heard the car draw up outside her relief was tempered with a tremor of nervousness.

She went quickly into the hall, closing the kitchen door behind her so that the light would not infringe the blackout regulations. Merry and Felix were huddled in the porch, both faces visible only as pale ovals in the darkness.

'Here you are at last! We've been worried about you. Come in quickly, both of you.'

They stepped inside and Rose closed the door behind them and switched on the hall light. Felix was closer to her and she reached up impulsively and gave him a hug.

'Felix, I'm so glad you came. How are you?'

'Fine. How are you?'

'Oh, I'm well – tired but well.' She turned to kiss Merry on the cheek, then stepped back with a little shriek of dismay. 'Merry, you're soaked! Whatever have you been doing?'

'Mending punctures,' he told her. 'But it doesn't matter. We're here now.'

'Well, come on in,' Rose said. 'We've had tea, I'm afraid. It got so late and we were all starving.'

She opened the door and, in a moment of intuitive sympathy, saw how the scene framed in the doorway must look to the two cold, hungry men behind her. It might have been posed for a photograph or a painting – the archetypal image of the cosy family kitchen. After the dimness of the hall the room was bathed in golden light. The coals behind the bars of the kitchen range sent a warm amber glow across the red tiles of the floor. The table was still laid for the meal and round it expectant faces turned towards them: Bet and her mother, plump and rosy; Mrs Willis with Babe's smooth schoolgirl face and Jack, her husband, in his shirtsleeves. Then, at the far end of the table, their faces alight with curiosity, the two small boys.

As Merry stepped into the light, apologising for his late arrival, the two boys launched themselves round the table with joyous cries of 'Uncle Merry! Uncle Merry!' Billy was shouting something about camping out in the loft and Sam was babbling on about a cat that had had kittens. Meanwhile Felix had followed him into the lighted kitchen and Rose heard herself saying, 'Everybody, this is Felix – I mean Flight Lieutenant Mountjoy – Edward – the Honourable . . .' She floundered into silence. 'Oh, Felix, I don't know what to call you!'

'Felix,' he said. 'Please, just Felix.'

To Rose's relief, her mother stepped forward and held out her hand. 'We're very pleased you could come, Felix. We've heard so much about you and we're so proud of you. It's like you were one of the family.'

Felix took her hand awkwardly with his left and murmured his thanks, then the Willises crowded in, followed by Bet.

'You're very welcome! We're so glad you could come.'

'It's a privilege to have one of the Few under our roof.'

'Hello, Felix, remember me? Rose introduced us in Fairbourne.'

Rose felt her throat constrict as they pressed round him, shaking his hand.

By the time the greetings were over the two small boys had turned their attention from Merry to the stranger in air force uniform. Turning from Bet, Felix came face to face with them. Rose held her breath.

Billy put out his left hand. 'I'm in the Cubs. We always shake hands like this. How do you do, sir?'

Felix extended his own left hand. 'How do you do – Billy, isn't it?'

'Do you fly Spitfires?'

'Yes. Well, I did.'

'Can I have your autograph to show my mates at school?' Billy's face glowed. 'They'll be mad jealous when I tell them I know a real Spitfire pilot.'

Sam moved closer to Felix, his eyes wide. 'Aunty Rose says you can make things disappear. Can you?'

'Er, sometimes.'

'Will you show me how?'

'Well, perhaps. I'm a bit out of practice.'

Bet cut in, 'Now, boys, give the flight lieutenant a chance. He's hardly got his coat off yet.'

Over the heads of the two boys Rose saw Merry catch Felix's eye and wink, and saw Felix respond with a shaky half-smile. Then the general hubbub resumed. Merry was divested of his damp coat and fresh places were laid at the table and set with two steaming bowls of leek-and-potato soup. Merry remembered that he had gifts in his suitcase and produced a bottle of gin and a tin of biscuits, both rare luxuries in the current circumstances. Felix added a bottle of Scotch and then, after ferreting about for a moment in his bag, called the two boys to him. With a flourish he produced, from under an apparently empty handkerchief, a large bar of Cadbury's Dairy Milk.

'Gosh, chocolate! Thanks!' gloated Billy, while Sam's eyes grew rounder than ever.

Bet said, 'Oh, you shouldn't use up all your sweet ration on them,' and Felix looked at Merry and winked in his turn.

'Oh, don't worry about that. It's amazing what you can scrounge from the NAAFI if you know the right people.'

Glasses were produced and drinks mixed and the now empty soup bowls were replaced by plates of boiled ham and potatoes. Then everyone settled down to exchange gossip.

'How's it going at the farm, Rose?' Felix asked. 'I bet you've got those cows doing a tap routine by now.'

'You don't want to worry about any old cows,' Bet cut in slyly. 'She's got the farmer dancing attendance.'

'Oh, leave it out, Bet, for goodness' sake!' Rose replied. She knew she had spoken sharply and felt herself blush, but really there were times when she could have smacked her sister.

As they talked, Rose watched Merry and Felix. There was something different about their behaviour together. When they were all in the Follies she had often winced at what seemed like casual cruelty on Felix's part. He had been the young god, dispensing the occasional favour or the more frequent rebuff, and Merry had been the humble worshipper. Now she caught the frequent exchange of glances, the winks and smiles, and saw Merry lean across with the ease of established custom and cut up Felix's meat for him. Was it simply Felix's new dependency which had wrought the change, Rose wondered, or was it something much more fundamental? There was something about the way he looked at Merry – was it just her imagination? Surely the effects of his crash could not have brought about such a radical transformation?

Her thoughts were interrupted as Merry sat back and caught her eye. For a moment he looked embarrassed, then he turned away and remarked, 'What were you saying, Billy, about sleeping in the loft?'

Billy's eyes brightened. 'Uncle Jack's made us a proper den up there, with camp beds to sleep on an' all. In the summer he says we can go in a tent in the garden, but it's too cold for that now.'

Felix said anxiously, 'I hope this isn't all for my benefit. I didn't want to cause you any trouble.'

Jack Willis chuckled. 'You don't want to worry about that, boy. Just look at their faces. They're thrilled to bits. So that room's yours for as long as you want it.'

Sam materialised beside Felix with a black-and-white kitten in his arms.

'His name's Patch,' he said, laying the small creature carefully in Felix's lap. 'Aunty Enid says he can be mine, but he has to stay with his mum until he's bigger.'

'He's a splendid little chap, isn't he,' Felix said, stroking the kitten with his good hand. 'But you'll have to keep him away from Uncle Merry because they make him sneeze.'

Sam leaned confidingly against Felix's knee and looked up into his face. 'Does it hurt?' he asked.

There was a frisson of concern around the table, but Felix replied gravely, 'It did, to begin with. But it's much better now.'

Sam nodded sagely. 'I fell off Johnny Tyler's bike and scraped my face like that. It hurt a lot when I did it, but it's better now. I expect yours will get quite better soon.'

Bet said softly, 'Come on, you two. Time for bed.'

Billy jumped out of his chair with surprising alacrity. 'Come on, Sam. Bags I first up the ladder!'

In the general exchange of 'goodnights' Rose saw that both Felix and Merry were moved and glad to have the opportunity to collect themselves. When the boys had gone all conversation stopped for the nine o'clock news. There was the usual account of bombs dropped on English cities, retaliatory raids on Germany, enemy aircraft shot down, a convoy torpedoed in the Atlantic, and when the wireless was switched off again the convivial mood of earlier had evaporated. The women began to clear the table, Rose being excused on the grounds that she had already done a day's work.

Under cover of the general bustle Merry said quietly, 'It's good news about Richard, isn't it?'

She looked at him and drew a deep breath. 'I'm so glad he's safe! Thank you for finding out for me.'

'Have you written?'

'Oh yes. I wrote as soon as I got your letter, but of course it's too soon to get a reply.' She hesitated. She had not put the next thought into words, except in the privacy of her own heart. 'But don't you think, Merry, that if he really wanted to he could have written to me, in all this time?'

'I don't know,' Merry answered consolingly. 'It may be that he's not allowed to write to anyone except his family, or perhaps he has written but the letter has been delayed. After all, he doesn't know where you are yet.'

'But our neighbour's been sending on letters,' Rose replied. 'If one had come for me I would have had it by now.'

'Well, don't give up hope,' Merry told her. 'There could be any number of reasons why you haven't heard.'

She sighed. 'Yes, I suppose so.'

Since receiving Merry's letter she had struggled to contain the violent swings of her emotions. There was relief, of course, at the knowledge that Richard had survived, but with it came a bitterness that she could not stifle. He must guess what she was suffering without news of him. Even if he had decided not to continue the relationship, surely he might have had enough consideration to write to her. She tried to believe that, as Merry suggested, the letter might have gone astray. But if he had written to his mother could he not have included a message for her? She tried to take refuge in anger, telling herself that she had known all along it would be like this and he was not worth her tears, but she could never quite conceal from herself the gnawing regret at the centre of her being.

Merry looked at his watch and eased his shoulders wearily. 'I'm sorry, ladies and gents,' he said, raising his voice, 'but I'm going to have to be on my way. I've got to be in Portsmouth for tomorrow.'

'Oh, but you can't go out again at this time of night,' Mrs Willis exclaimed. 'Listen to it out there.'

It was true that the weather seemed to have worsened. The wind was rattling the window panes and throwing the rain against them with a sound like handfuls of gravel hitting the glass. Merry looked as though the very last thing he wanted was to venture out into the darkness again.

'Do you have to be in Portsmouth first thing?' Jack Willis asked.

'No, not till mid-morning,' Merry admitted. 'I'll probably find a pub on the way that will put me up for the night.'

'Well, can't you stay here, then?' Jack asked. 'We could fit him in somewhere, couldn't we, Mother?'

'I suppose I could stretch out on the settle there, if you wouldn't mind,' Merry suggested.

'Why, there's no need for that,' Mrs Willis exclaimed. 'That's a double bed in the boys' room. I'm sure you two gentlemen could manage in that for one night. That is if the flight lieutenant doesn't mind.'

Rose caught her breath and opened her mouth to speak, then closed it again. Across the room she caught Merry's eye and he looked away quickly.

'You wouldn't mind, would you, Felix?' Mrs Taylor asked. 'Just for the one night?'

Rose looked at Felix and saw that his eyes were gleaming with suppressed mirth.

'Oh, I expect I could put up with him,' he said lightly. 'That is, if he doesn't snore. You don't snore, do you, Merry?'

Merry kept his eyes on the tablecloth. 'No,' he replied, carefully. 'Not as far as I'm aware.'

Chapter Eighteen

'I've been thinking,' Mrs Willis said the next morning. 'We should invite Matthew Armitage to spend Christmas Day here with us. We can't let him be all on his own, poor man.'

'But there are so many of us already!' Rose said. 'It's too much for you to cope with.'

'Oh, nonsense,' her hostess replied. 'What's one more mouth to feed? Anyway, I don't mind betting Matt'll bring something along to help out the rations.'

'But then there's the farm,' Rose went on. 'The cows still need milking and the hens need feeding . . .' She trailed into silence. She was not sure in her own mind why she was objecting. It was obviously the only charitable option and, after all, she enjoyed being with Matthew. It was Mrs Willis's idea, she reminded herself, so there was no reason for anyone to read any special significance into it.

'You'll be there to help out, won't you?' Mrs Willis said. 'Then, when the chores are done, you can both come on down here for your dinner.'

Rose was aware that, even with the addition of Matthew, the party would be far from complete. Bet's husband, Reg, had been unable to get Christmas leave. He was still stationed up in Catterick and there was no possibility of him being able to make the long journey to Wimbourne.

'Just as well, really,' Bet commented, in a tone that struck

Rose as being surprisingly offhand. 'If he did come, God knows where we'd put him.'

On Christmas morning, after Rose returned from the farm, they all went to matins in the village church, though everyone said it didn't seem like Christmas without the church bells ringing.

'You want to be glad they're not ringing,' Jack pointed out. 'If they were it would mean the Germans had invaded.'

Back at the house the women bustled around preparing dinner. Matthew had earned his place at the table with the gift of two brace of pheasants. They had all pooled their ration 'points' to buy dried fruit for the Christmas pudding, while Felix had produced from the depths of what Sam had christened his 'magic suitcase' two bottles of good burgundy, relics of the excellent cellar of the one-time Hotel Belleview. There were no oranges or tangerines, but plenty of fresh vegetables and Cox's Orange Pippins from the Willises' orchard, and everyone declared that it was as good a Christmas dinner as any pre-war feast.

All too soon after the meal Matthew had to return to the farm to do the afternoon milking. 'You stay here in the warm, Rose,' he said. 'I can manage.'

'I know you can,' she replied, 'but it takes twice as long on your own. I'll come.'

'Look here,' Felix put in, 'why don't I go? I've never milked a cow but I'm sure it can be done with one hand.'

Rose looked at him and then at Matt and giggled helplessly.

'It's nice of you to offer, Felix,' Matt said, 'but it's not that easy. You'd best leave it to me and Rose.'

'OK, then,' Felix said. 'I'll come along and watch. I could do with a breath of air.'

Rose looked at Matt and caught him frowning at Felix with visible irritation. Felix saw the look too and changed his tone.

'On the other hand, I shan't be much help, shall I? Perhaps I'll just stay here by the fire.'

Obeying an impulse she did not quite understand, Rose tucked her hand under his arm and said, 'Come on. The walk will do you good.'

So they all went and returned glowing from the frosty air to a tea of hot soup and cold ham and Christmas cake made with grated carrot instead of raisins.

On Boxing Day they were all invited up to Wimbourne Manor, the Big House, where the squire and his lady had laid on a party for all the refugee children in the village. Felix held back, as usual, until Billy looked so crestfallen at the notion that he would not, after all, be able to show off his hero to the other kids that he had to give in. In the event, the afternoon children's party merged seamlessly into an evening party for the adults. The carpet was rolled back in the hall, a gramophone was produced and they all found themselves learning to dance the Sir Roger de Coverley. After that they danced waltzes and foxtrots and quicksteps until one of the young men home on leave from the army and his girlfriend decided to demonstrate the latest craze, the jitterbug.

Their moment of glory was eclipsed, however, when Felix found a record of 'Jealousy' and called out, 'Come on, Rose! Let's show them how to tango!'

For Rose the music brought a poignant memory of dancing with Richard, but she had to admit that Felix danced the tango with a grace and lack of inhibition that none of the others could match. For a short time everyone present forgot his disfigurement, as it seemed he had done himself. They sat down to loud applause.

The intervening days returned to something like normal routine. Rose got up at five and worked through the day, and tried not to look for post when she got back to the house in the

evening. Felix started to relearn his conjuring tricks to entertain the two boys, practising in secret to find ways of coping
with only his left hand. He went up to the farm sometimes, but
was careful not to stay too long. Matthew whistled as he went
about his daily tasks.

Merry, comforted by the memory of one night of passion
made more intense by the necessity for absolute silence, and
the assurance that Felix would be well looked after, struggled
on icy, unmarked roads from one venue to another, arriving
chilled and weary to give yet another concert. But here, too, he
found things to cheer him – hospital wards decorated with
home-made paper chains, the determination of nurses to give
the 'boys' in their care the best possible Christmas, men
coming to terms with the loss of sight or limbs lustily singing
Christmas carols. Then, perhaps later the same day, there was
the camaraderie of the officers' mess, where the starchiness of
pre-war tradition had relaxed in the melting-pot of Dunkirk,
or the raucous voices in the NAAFI belting out 'Roll Out the
Barrel'.

His final concert of the year, on the evening of the thirtieth,
was at a Royal Artillery base on the Essex coast. Realising that
he would have a long drive the following day, probably in poor
conditions, he telephoned Wimbourne and warned them that
he might be late. He did not want to put Felix through a repeat
of their last delayed rendezvous.

That night, after the performance, he was invited to what
turned out to be an extremely drunken party in the officers'
mess and woke the next morning with a pounding head and a
tight chest. Both of these cleared as he drove towards London
and, on more or less empty roads, he made good time. He had
not reckoned, however, with the effects of the massive fire-
bomb raid that the city had suffered on the night of the twenty-
ninth. As the car threaded its way through streets of charred

and ruined buildings, from which smoke was still rising to join the black pall that hung over the whole area, Merry marvelled that any kind of normal life could still go on, but people were clearing the rubble, while city gents in black jackets and pinstripe trousers skirted the ruins on their way to lunch.

After many diversions Merry finally found his way out to the southern suburbs and breathed a sigh of relief as he joined the main road heading for Guildford. His hopes of a rapid journey from here on were quickly dashed, however, when he found himself sandwiched in the middle of a convoy of army vehicles. In the Surrey countryside the road was often reduced to two lanes and there was no hope of overtaking the long line of trucks and armoured cars, so he had to school himself to patience and hope that the convoy's destination was not the same as his. Before long he was diverted on to an even narrower lane and then, to his intense annoyance, the whole convoy came to a halt. He sat for a while, waiting for it to move again, and then turned off the engine and got out. The line of vehicles stretched ahead of him and disappeared round a bend in the road. He walked along the line until he eventually came to the leading car, which was stopped at a police barrier. A captain wearing the insignia of the Signals Corps was talking to a police constable. Merry approached, came to attention and saluted.

'Can you tell me what the hold-up is, sir?'

'Unexploded bomb, I'm afraid,' the officer replied. 'On a railway bridge just down in the dip there. The bomb disposal chappies are on their way but there's nothing we can do until they get here.'

Merry stood talking in a desultory fashion for a few minutes and then returned to his car. He was closely wedged between two lorries and behind him was a line of seven or eight other vehicles. The lane was too narrow to turn round in so he gave up any hope of finding another way round, got back into the

Lagonda, pulled his coat collar up around his ears and settled down to wait.

'Hello, Rose, love! You're back early.' Mrs Taylor looked round from the sink where she was peeling potatoes as her daughter came in through the back door.

Rose gave her a brief, slightly abstracted smile. 'Matt let me off early so I could come and get ready for this evening.'

'Oh, that was nice of him. He's very thoughtful like that, isn't he?'

'Yes. Yes, he is.'

'Do you want a cup of tea, love?' Mrs Taylor started to dry her hands.

Rose shook her head. 'No thanks, Mum. I think I'll go straight upstairs and have my bath.'

Bet looked up from preparing sprouts at the kitchen table. 'Is there something wrong with you?'

'Wrong?' Rose replied. 'No, what makes you think that?'

'I dunno. I just thought you sounded a bit off.'

Mrs Taylor looked at her. 'I hope you're not coming down with something.'

Rose turned away impatiently. The last thing she wanted at that moment was a heart-to-heart with her mother and sister. 'I'm just tired and cold, that's all. I'll be fine when I've had a hot bath.'

'It's too hard, that work, for a girl,' her mother grumbled, 'even though Matt does try to take as much of the load off you as he can.'

'Oh, do leave off, Mum!' Rose exclaimed, and ran upstairs.

It took two hours for the bomb disposal squad to make the bomb on the railway bridge safe. The long wait was made just about bearable by a group of local residents, who noticed the plight of the stranded soldiers and organised themselves to provide relays of hot tea and sandwiches. Even so, by the time they eventually moved off Merry was feeling as though he would never be warm again. It was one of those drear winter days that never seem to get fully light, and as they started off dusk was falling and with it a light sprinkling of snow. To his great relief the convoy kept on down the road towards Portsmouth, enabling him to strike off in the direction of Southampton and Bournemouth on a more or less open road, but even so it was impossible to make up for all the time he had lost.

At Winchester he realised that he would have to stop and get something warm to eat and drink, much as he begrudged the time. The manager of the hotel he chose informed him in supercilious tones that they were fully booked for dinner but after some persuasion produced a pot of tea and some sandwiches, and at least there was a fire in the lounge and he was able to thaw out his icy feet. It was an effort to drag himself away and get on the road again. The snow was falling faster now, and he began to wonder whether he would manage to reach Wimbourne in time to see in the New Year. In the treacherous conditions and with his headlights masked except for narrow slits it was impossible to hurry.

Even so, he nearly failed to see the solitary figure huddled under a soldier's cape, raising a dispirited thumb at the side of the road. With a sigh, Merry braked and pulled in. The last thing he needed now was to go out of his way to drop off some hitch-hiker, but he could not leave anyone stranded on a night like this. Heavy boots clattered on the tarmac as the man ran up and Merry leaned over and opened the passenger door.

'Where are you trying to get to, soldier?'

There was a sound rather like a gasp, followed by a brief pause. Then a familiar voice said, 'Good God! Merry? What on earth are you doing driving Felix's car?'

★   ★   ★

At the Willises' house the feast was prepared. Jack had killed two capons that he had originally been fattening up for Christmas and Matthew arrived promptly, looking, as Mrs Willis remarked, 'extremely chipper' and bearing two bottles of claret that he had obtained from the local publican in exchange for another brace of pheasants.

When Rose came down to the kitchen, after spending longer than usual in the bath, her mother looked up. 'Oh, Rose, love, don't you look nice! It's lovely to see you in a skirt for a change and that Fair Isle jumper I knitted for you really suits you.'

By nine o'clock the table was laid and the two boys were getting irritable from over excitement. They were given their supper and eventually persuaded to go to bed, in spite of their protests that they had been promised they could stay up to see Uncle Merry. By ten Felix was prowling the house and glancing at his watch every five minutes. Rose found him standing in the darkened front room, watching from the window for the first glimmer of headlights. She went over and slipped her hand into his.

'Don't worry. He'll be here.'

Felix looked sideways at her, seemed about to shrug the remark off, and then simply squeezed her hand and replied, 'Yes, of course he will.'

By eleven Mrs Willis declared that the food would be ruined if they kept it hot any longer and they sat down to eat. The meal was almost over when Matthew tapped on his glass and raised his voice. His face was flushed and his deep-set eyes were unusually bright.

'Ladies and gentlemen, I should like to make an announcement.'

Rose, seated next to him, tugged at his sleeve. 'Matt! Not now!'

'Oh Lord! Look at the time!' Mrs Willis's voice cut across

both of them. 'It's almost midnight. Quick, Jack, fill up the glasses. Someone turn the wireless on.'

'Just before we see the New Year in . . .' Matthew persisted.

'Not now, Matt,' Jack said, 'we don't want to miss Big Ben striking.'

'We need a tall, dark man to come in with a lump of coal,' Mrs Willis went on. She looked from Felix to Matthew. 'Oh, you're no good, either of you! Jack, you'll have to go outside. You're the darkest one.'

'Hang on,' her husband objected. 'I haven't finished topping up the glasses.'

In the background the voice of the radio announcer was counting down to midnight. Matthew was still trying to speak above the general hubbub but Felix rose abruptly to his feet.

'Wait! Listen! I'm sure I heard a car.'

In the lull that followed they all heard the sound of someone stamping his feet and shaking off a wet overcoat in the little lobby outside the kitchen door. Big Ben began to chime the hour.

'He's made it!' Felix cried triumphantly.

The door opened and Merry stood in the doorway, brandishing two bottles of champagne. 'Sorry I'm late, everyone, but I have brought a little something to drink the toast in. And I have a surprise. I think the first person across the threshold is supposed to be a tall, dark stranger. Am I right? Well, behold!'

He stood aside with a theatrical gesture and a mock fanfare. From the wireless came the first stroke of midnight. A dishevelled figure appeared, blushing in the light from the kitchen and carrying a lump of coal.

'Happy New Year, everyone!' said Richard.

There was a moment of stunned silence, then a babble of voices – questions, exclamations of surprise, greetings. Only Rose was silent, first flushing scarlet, then deadly pale.

As if there were no one else in the room, Richard moved up the table until he stood beside her, and held out both his hands. 'Rose, I'm so sorry it's been such a long time. I know what you must have been thinking. I asked my mother to get in touch with you, but it seems she didn't, and since I wrote that letter I've been on the run and there was no chance to write. But I'm here now. Eighteen months ago, when I asked you to marry me, you said it was too soon and that you thought my feelings for you wouldn't last. And I asked you, if I came back in a year's time and repeated my offer, would you reconsider – and you said you would. Well, it's been longer than that and my feelings for you haven't changed. So now I'm asking you to keep your promise. Darling Rose, I've never stopped loving you. Will you marry me?'

If you enjoyed Now is the Hour
then don't miss the second book in the series.
They Also Serve *will be published by*
Hodder & Stoughton in hardback
in August 2007. Read on for the first chapter . . .

HODDER

Chapter One

'I don't know who the hell you are, but you're too late. Rose is going to marry me.' Matthew's voice combined surprise and indignation in equal measures.

For a moment Rose Taylor felt as if she had left her body and was observing the scene in the crowded kitchen as if it were a still from a film. There was the long table, covered with the debris of a festive meal, the wineglasses still full, ready for the New Year toast that would now never be proposed. There were her mother and her sister Bet, wide eyed and open mouthed with shock; and Jack and Enid Willis, whose home this was and who had taken them in as refugees from the Blitz, gazing at her in puzzled embarrassment. By the door, Merry and Felix were frozen in the act of shaking hands, the snowflakes still melting on the shoulders of Merry's overcoat, Felix's handsome, ravaged face further distorted by surprise. And on either side of her, Matthew and Richard; Matt with his weather-beaten farmer's face creased with anger and confusion, and Richard, so thin and gaunt, with his dark hair plastered to his head by the snow and a terrible realisation slowly dawning in his brown eyes.

It was that look which undid her. Suddenly she was no longer an observer. She felt something rising and swelling within her, like a balloon that must either burst or suffocate her. For a moment she thought she might vomit or faint, then the balloon burst in an inarticulate howl of despair. She thrust her hand into her mouth to stifle it and ran out of the kitchen.

*   *   *

As the door slammed behind Rose, Merry felt the mood of happy triumph in which he had entered the kitchen turn to one of anguished disappointment. He had brought Richard with him, expecting his arrival to add the crowning surprise to the celebrations, and the result had been disaster. At the same moment, the people in the kitchen seemed to come to life. Both Matthew and Richard started after Rose, both calling her name, but Jack Willis interposed his burly frame between them and the door.

'Now then, gents, hold your horses. Happen she needs a few minutes to collect herself.' He looked at Richard. 'I don't know who you are, son, but you've certainly given some of us a shock.'

Merry stepped forward and laid an arm across Richard's shoulders. 'This is Richard Stevens, Jack. He was with us all in the Follies in the summer before the war. For a long time we thought he'd bought it at Dunkirk, then we found out he was a POW. I still haven't discovered how he came to be thumbing a lift a couple of miles outside the village.'

'Well . . .' Jack extended his hand. 'I'm sure we're all glad to see you back, Richard. I'm sorry things aren't quite what you anticipated but I expect Rose'll be down in a minute to explain.'

'I'll go up and speak to her – get her to come down,' Bet said.

'Good idea, love,' Jack agreed, and went on as Bet left the room, 'Now, why don't we all sit down so Richard can tell us what's been happening to him? Mother, these two chaps are starved, I'm sure. Can we find enough for both of them?'

'Of course we can.' Enid moved to the kitchen range. 'I was keeping a plate hot for Merry, anyway, and there's still some meat on that capon and plenty more veg. Sit down, both of you.'

Merry propelled Richard gently to the table. He could feel that he was shivering, but whether from shock or from the effects of a long wait in the blizzard that had been raging all day he could not be sure. He had not spoken since he blurted out his proposal, except to call Rose's name, but as Mrs Willis set a steaming plate in front of him he stirred as if awakening from a nightmare.

'I'm terribly sorry. I seem to have ruined your evening. I had no idea . . . It was stupid of me to assume that nothing would have changed . . . stupid . . .'

'You weren't to know,' Merry said. 'None of us had any idea, until tonight.'

'Well, what did you expect?' Rose's mother spoke for the first time. 'All these months and never a letter. You gave her nothing to hope for. Was she supposed to wait indefinitely?'

'I couldn't write.' Richard looked at her, his face haggard. 'I've been on the run since August. How could I have written?'

'Tell us about it.' Felix sat opposite them. 'How did you get away? When did you get back to this country?'

Merry watched as Richard picked up a forkful of chicken and crammed it into his mouth. He recognised the impulse. He had learned on the retreat to Dunkirk what it was like to be starving, and how, even after weeks, the sight of food could produce an almost Pavlovian response.

'I was wounded at Dunkirk,' Richard said, through a mouthful. 'Both legs shot up. I couldn't walk so they had to leave me on the beach. For months I was in a prison hospital. I can't fault the Huns. I had several operations and I was well looked after. But I never let them know I could walk properly again. One day, when we were being transferred by ambulance from the hospital to a prison camp, I managed to escape. I hid out in the forest with a wonderful family of woodcutters for a while. Then they passed me on to one of the escape lines that are springing up. It's amazing. There are people in France, men and women, who are risking their lives to get escaped POWs back to England. They got me into the unoccupied zone and down to the south coast, and then to the

Pyrenees. Then a guide took us through the mountains to the Spanish border.'

'What a fantastic story,' Felix said. 'So when did you get home?'

'That wasn't the end of it,' Richard said. He laid down his fork and took a gulp of the wine Jack had set in front of him. 'The Spanish police caught us and we were interned in a hellhole called Miranda. I can't tell you . . .' He stumbled into silence, but as Merry was about to speak he seemed to revive and went on. 'The conditions were appalling. We were all covered in lice and nearly starving and the guards were sadistic brutes . . .'

'Oh, you poor man,' Enid Willis murmured.

'In the end,' he said, 'the British consul managed to get me out and smuggle me into Gibraltar. And from there I got a ship back to Liverpool. I got there just before Christmas but the army kept me cooped up in a hotel in London for several days, asking a lot of bloody silly questions.' He raised his eyes and sought out Mrs Taylor. 'As soon as they let me go, I came to look for Rose. I had the address in Lambeth but the place was all boarded up. There was an air raid on and I couldn't find anyone who knew where you'd gone. The army had given me a travel pass for Didsbury, so in the end I just had to get the train north. I got home on Christmas Eve.'

'Your family must have been so delighted to see you – at that time of all times,' Enid said.

'So how did you find out where we were?' Mrs Taylor asked.

He looked at her and the bitterness in his face made Merry wince inwardly. 'I found out yesterday that my mother had known all along. You told her, didn't you, Merry?'

'It's true,' Merry said unwillingly. 'I happened to run into her when I was giving a concert in Didsbury. She's the president of the local music society. That was when I found out that Richard wasn't dead but a POW. I gave her this address and asked her to get in touch with Rose.'

'A fact that she only let slip by accident,' Richard confirmed. 'So I got the first train this morning and managed to get as far as Winchester. From there I hitched, but if Merry hadn't happened along I'd be out there still.' He sat back, his shoulders drooping. 'Anyway, it doesn't matter. Like you said, I'm too late.' He looked across at Matthew, who had listened in silence. 'I've ruined your big moment. I'm truly sorry. I'll push off now and get out of your way.'

'Good Lord!' Jack Willis exclaimed. 'You can't go anywhere at this time of night, and in this weather. Surely we can find him a bed somewhere, Enid?'

'I don't know,' his wife said doubtfully. 'Of course he can't go out in this, but we're bursting at the seams already. We managed to squeeze Felix in, while he's waiting to go into hospital, by putting Bet's boys up in the loft, but as it is poor Merry has to share a bed with him when he comes to stay . . .'

Merry caught Felix's eye and looked away quickly. As far as he could tell, both the Willises and Mrs Taylor were too innocent to guess how well that arrangement suited both of them.

'I don't understand,' Richard said. 'Why are you all here like this?'

'Oh, that's easily explained,' Mrs Taylor responded. 'We came to get away from the Blitz. Bet and her boys were bombed out, and Rose and I didn't fancy spending another night in a shelter with the bombs coming down all round us, so Rose telephoned Enid and Jack here and they offered to put us up.'

'Well, it was the least we could do, in the circumstances,' Enid Willis put in. 'With Barbara away in the Wrens we had the space. You remember Barbara, Richard? She was one of the dancers with you in the Follies, that last summer season before the war.'

'Oh, Babe?' Richard's confused expression cleared slightly. 'That's what we called her, because she was the youngest.'

'Yes, that's right. Rose was always a good friend to her, so when she telephoned and we heard she's had to give up dancing . . .'

'Give up dancing? Why?' Richard looked from Enid to Rose's mother.

'She had an accident,' Mrs Taylor explained. 'She was in a show in France, entertaining the troops before Dunkirk. The building where they were performing was strafed by an enemy plane in the middle of a performance. All the lights went out and in the confusion Rose fell off the edge of the stage. She broke her ankle and tore the ligaments and the surgeon told her she'd never be able to dance again.'

Merry saw the look of shock deepen on Richard's face. 'Oh, that's terrible! Poor Rose!'

'Well, she's over it now,' her mother said. 'We all moved down here and then she felt she wanted to make herself useful so she joined the Land Army and went to work for Matthew here.'

'But then,' Enid Willis added, 'Merry phoned to say that Felix had got to leave the convalescent home and had nowhere to go. We couldn't let him spend Christmas all on his own, so we moved Bet's boys up into the loft and put him in Barbara's room.'

Richard turned to Felix and Merry saw him swallow hard. He guessed it was the first time he had taken in the scarring on his face.

'Felix, Merry told me in the car about you being shot down and the Spit catching fire. Rotten luck!'

Felix smiled. 'Not to worry. Some chaps have had much worse to put up with. I'm waiting for plastic surgery and everyone tells me that the surgeon is an absolute wizard. I'll be good as new in no time.'

It was Merry's turn to swallow. Both he and Felix knew that that was a vain hope.

Richard's attention switched to Merry. 'So where do you come in? How did you know Rose and her family were here?'

'Because I've been using their flat in Lambeth as a base,'

Merry explained. 'When I was seconded to the Central Pool of Artistes, which is what the army calls its entertainments unit, I had to find somewhere to live in London and the Taylors kindly took me in. I still stay there when I'm not touring.'

'I'm beginning to get the picture,' Richard said slowly. 'It's just really odd to find all you old Follies people together in one place, after everything that's happened.'

'Well,' Felix said with a smile, 'you know what Monty Prince used to say. Once you've done a season with the Follies, you're family.'

'This is all very well,' Jack Willis remarked, 'but it doesn't get us any nearer finding Richard a bed for the night.'

'Perhaps I could just stretch out on the floor,' Richard murmured. 'It wouldn't be the first time.'

'To hell with that!' Matthew cut in. 'There's plenty of spare room in my farmhouse. You come up with me.'

Richard began to protest but Jack overrode him. 'Good idea, Matt. Now, it's very late and some of us have to be up early, so I suggest we call it a night. It doesn't look as if Rose is coming down. Let's all get some sleep and sort things out in the morning.'

There was a general scraping of chairs and clatter of dishes as the women began to clear the table. Matthew got up. 'Come on, if you're coming. Like Jack says, some of us have an early start.' He turned to Mrs Willis. 'Thanks for inviting me, Enid. Sorry the evening turned out like this.'

Merry accompanied Richard to the door. As they reached it Felix intercepted them. 'It's good to see you, Richard. I'm sorry the circumstances haven't been happier, but don't give up hope. I'm sure things will sort themselves out.'

Richard held out his hand. 'Thanks, Felix. And good luck with the plastic surgery.'

Felix shook his head. 'Sorry. This hand's us at present.' He held up the claw-like fingers of his right hand. 'Another job for McIndoe.'

'You coming, Richard?' Matthew called from the porch, and Richard ducked his head, muttered 'Goodnight' and disappeared into the darkness.

Upstairs in the bedroom she shared with her sister, Rose sat huddled in the eiderdown, her hand still pressed to her lips to stifle her sobs. She was shaking all over and the only thought she could frame was 'What am I going to do? *What am I going to do?*' It went round and round in her brain, like a rat in a wheel.

'Rose? *Rose!*' Bet's voice broke through the tumult in her head, sharp with anxiety. The handle of the door rattled. 'Rose, open this door! You can't hide in there all night.' She began to pound on the door. 'Let me in – or do I have to fetch Matt to break the door down?'

Rose got up and stumbled across the room. As soon as she had turned the key Bet pushed past her.

'Rose, for God's sake pull yourself together! You can't leave everyone dangling like this.'

'What am I supposed to do?' Rose cried. 'What can I say?'

Her sister looked at her. Her face was flushed with an expression that could have been exasperation, or perhaps embarrassment, but the sympathy Rose craved was missing. 'Well, Matt's proposed and you've accepted, haven't you? Just come down and explain to Richard that you'd given up hope of ever hearing from him and now it's too late. Who does he think he is, turning up out of the blue and just taking it for granted that you're still free? He'd hardly got through the door before he was proposing to you.'

'But I can't just turn him down,' Rose wept. 'He's waited for me all this time. I promised him that if a year passed and he still loved me I'd marry him. What can I tell him now?'

'You've promised Matt now,' her sister said mercilessly. 'What are you going to say to him?'

'I don't know. I don't know.'

Bet's face softened. She took hold of Rose's arm and pulled her down to sit on the edge of the bed. 'Look, you always said that that fling with Richard was just a summer romance. You never expected it to last.'

'But it has!' Rose protested. 'I didn't realise until it was too late how much I loved him. But then the months went by and he didn't write and he didn't write . . . I thought he must be dead. Then, when we heard he was a POW and he still didn't write I decided he'd forgotten all about me, just like I thought he would. That's why I said yes to Matt this afternoon.'

'But you love Matt, don't you?'

'I thought I did. Now I don't know any more.'

Bet got up. 'Your trouble is, you never know when you're well off. There's Matt, a good man, solid, reliable, owns his own farm – and he adores you, any fool can see that. Richard's not right for you. I've always said that. Too stuck up, with his fancy ideas about being an opera singer. And it's obvious he's never mentioned you to his family, or they'd have been in touch. If he thinks you're not good enough for his posh folks, what sort of a future is there for you? You come down and tell him it's all off and you're going to marry Matt. That's my advice.'

Rose gazed up at her. She felt chilled to the marrow and utterly alone. 'Go away, Bet. For God's sake, let me be! You don't understand. You've never understood. Please, *please*, just shut up, will you?'

She twisted round and stretched herself out on the bed, burying her face in the pillow. After a moment she heard the door slam and her sister's departing footsteps.

The first hours of 1941 were the worst Rose had ever spent in her life. She cried for a while, silently so as not to wake Bet, feeling the tears well up in her eyes and run down the sides of her face to soak into her hair. After her tears were exhausted she lay staring up into the darkness, going over

and over the events of the previous evening, until the alarm
clock beside the bed showed 5 a.m. Then she got up quietly
and gathered up her clothes in the icy, pre-dawn gloom of
the winter morning. She crept out of the room and splashed
her face with cold water in the bathroom, then tiptoed
downstairs to the kitchen. It was a relief to find the room
empty. She had half expected to discover Richard asleep on
the wooden settle against the wall. The big iron kettle was
sitting on the side of the range. She pulled it on to the hob
and began to put on the heavy sweater and the bib-front
dungarees that were the working uniform of the Women's
Land Army.

She had just finished dressing when a sound at the door
made her swing round. Merry and Felix stood in the doorway,
tousled and unshaven, woollen dressing gowns over their
pyjamas. They were old friends, from the summer of 1939
when she had been a dancer with the Fairbourne Follies
concert party, and now both their faces were creased with
concern. Her throat tightened on a fresh sob. The last thing
she wanted at this moment was to have to talk through her
dilemma, even with these two.

'I'm sorry,' she croaked. 'I didn't mean to wake you. I tried
to be quiet.'

'We weren't asleep,' Felix said. He came into the kitchen.
'Rose, what are you doing? You're not planning to go up to the
farm today, are you?'

'The cows need milking, New Year's Day or not, war or no
war,' Rose replied.

'But surely, after last night . . . you can't just carry on as if
nothing has happened.'

Rose sank down on to a chair and rested her arms on the
table. 'I know,' she mumbled wretchedly. 'But what can I do?'

Merry moved behind her and poured boiling water into the
teapot. 'Stay here,' he said. 'You're in no fit state to make
decisions right now.'

Felix said, 'Is it true, Rose? Have you promised to marry Matt?'

Rose nodded miserably. 'He asked me at Christmas and I said I needed time to think. Then yesterday he wanted to know if I'd made up my mind and I said yes – yes, I would marry him. It seemed . . . I dunno, right. It seemed the only sensible thing to say.'

'You can't go up to the farm, Rose,' Felix said. 'They're both there, Richard and Matt.'

'Both?' she queried, startled. 'You mean Richard is staying with Matthew? How on earth did that happen?'

'We couldn't let him go off out into the night,' Merry pointed out, 'and there was no bed here for him, so Matt offered.'

'Which was big of him, under the circumstances,' Felix concluded.

'So they went off together?' Rose caught her breath. 'Oh, you don't think . . . ?'

'Fisticuffs in the farmyard? Pitchforks at dawn?' Felix queried. 'Not a chance! They're both far too civilised for that – and anyway, from the look of him, Richard wouldn't have had the energy.'

Merry sat beside her. 'What are you going to say to them, Rose?'

She shook her head miserably. 'I don't know! I just don't know!'

'But it's Richard you've been waiting for all these months, isn't it?' he prompted.

'Yes . . . no. That is . . . I don't think I ever really believed in it. It was just a sort of dream. I'm not the right wife for him. I've always known that, deep down.'

'What makes you say that?'

'You've heard him sing. You know what a wonderful voice he has. He was wasted on a little end-of-the-pier show like Follies. It was just a way of filling in a summer for him. One day he's going to be a great opera singer. I couldn't fit in to that sort of world. I'd just be a drag on him.'

'That's rubbish!' Merry said. 'You'd be perfect for him. You're a fellow performer. You know all about the stresses and strains of the profession. What better sort of wife could he want?'

'Oh, someone much cleverer, more sophisticated than me.'

'But he's proved that it's you he loves. It's not his fault that he's been out of touch for so long,' Felix said.

'I know. But now I've promised to marry Matt. Poor Matt! He's had enough misery, with his first wife being killed like that. What would people say if I went back on my promise?'

Felix leaned across and put his good hand over hers. 'Rose, listen to me. I want to give you a bit of advice from my own experience. For years I tried to ignore my real feelings, tried to pretend I was someone different from my real self, all because I was afraid of what "society" would do to me if I was honest. It was only when this happened . . .' He raised his claw-like right hand towards his damaged cheek. '. . . that I had to face up to who I really am. And I was lucky.' He glanced towards Merry. 'In my case, it wasn't too late.' He gripped her hand. 'You have to follow your heart, Rose! To hell with what people will say.'

Rose met his blue eyes. It was the first time she had ever heard him allude to his relationship with Merry and she was amazed by the intensity of feeling in his voice. This was Felix, the ladies' man, the conjuror whose most potent magic was his own charisma. Felix who, in the old days when they were all in the concert party, had always had girls queuing at the stage door for his autograph. Mysterious Felix, whose real name was the Hon. Edward Mountjoy, but who always refused to talk about his family. All through their summer seasons with the Follies she had watched Merry suffering in silence while Felix flaunted his latest lady friend. Yet it had been Merry who had telephoned to say that Felix had got to leave the convalescent home where he had been recovering from his injuries and had nowhere to go for Christmas, and to ask whether the Willises could fit him into their already overcrowded home. And now the roles seemed to be reversed, with Felix relying on Merry for comfort and support. She had assumed that it was the result of his disfigurement, but now he was suggesting something much more fundamental.

'Felix is right,' Merry said.

'But I don't know what my heart is telling me!' she said, her voice breaking. 'I thought I loved Richard, but then I met Matt and he's kind and gentle and . . . and solid. I can imagine living with him on the farm. I can't imagine what living with Richard might be like. Oh, I don't know. I don't know what to do.' She put her head down on her arms and wept again.

Merry put his arm round her shoulders. 'What you need is a good sleep. Why don't you go back to bed?'

'But I can't,' she wailed. 'There's the cows to milk.'

He gave a brief chuckle. 'Anybody would think you'd grown up on a farm. How long have you been a Land Girl? Two months? Three? Before that you didn't know one end of a cow from the other.'

'I've still got my job to do,' Rose said doggedly.

'Look,' he said, 'Felix and I will go up to the farm and give Matt a hand. And while we're there we can recce the situation from Matt and Richard's point of view. They may have come to some understanding. At least we should find out. You take a couple of aspirins and go back to bed. Everything will be clearer when you've slept on it.'

Rose lifted her head and looked from him to Felix. 'You're very kind. I'm lucky to have such good friends.'

Felix squeezed her hand. 'Nonsense. We're all old pros, after all, and show-business people look after one another. Remember the saying – "the show must go on".'

'Except there isn't a show,' Rose mumbled.

'Oh yes there is,' Merry said heavily. 'A bloody great, dangerous show. We may only have bit parts but we've still got to do the best we can with them. Come on, Felix. Let's get dressed and see what's going on up at the farm.'

When they let themselves out of the front door Merry saw that the snow must have gone on falling all night. It had stopped now but the ground was covered in a thick, unblemished carpet, and theirs were the first footprints to sully it as they trudged up the lane towards the farm. Felix yawned and pulled his greatcoat closer round him.

'You OK?' Merry asked.

'More or less,' was the gruff reply.

Neither of them had slept much that night. Merry tried to suppress a sense of injustice. He had forty-eight hours' leave, two precious nights to spend with Felix, and one of them had been wasted in uselessly going over and over the events of the evening. Still, he told himself, there were more important things to worry about now.

They found Matthew at work in the cowshed. He looked up from milking, his face bleak. 'Don't tell me. She's not coming to work this morning.'

'She's not feeling too good,' Merry said, 'so we volunteered to take her place. And before you say anything, I can milk a cow. I used to help out on a local farm during the school holidays. Just point me to one that doesn't kick.'

Matthew got up. He moved like an automaton and Merry felt a stab of sympathy for his tightly controlled grief.

'I'll get you an overall and you can start on that old girl in the next stall,' he said.

'And I'll just pop in and see if Richard's awake, if that's OK,' Felix said.

Matthew shrugged. 'Please yourself. Door on the right at the end of the passage.'

Merry had just got into the rhythm of milking again and was

almost beginning to enjoy himself when Felix reappeared. He
hunkered down beside Merry and said softly, 'Richard's done
a bunk.'

'*What?*' Merry exclaimed, and the cow stamped irritably.

'Bed's not been slept in and I found this.' Felix held out a
folded piece of paper torn from a notebook and addressed to
Rose.

'Christ!' Merry said. 'You don't think he's . . . ?'

'No, surely not. Oh God, I hope not! What should we
do?'

Merry considered for a moment. 'I think we'd better read it,
just in case.'

'Are you sure? It's not intended for us.'

'I know, but we need to know that he hasn't done anything
bloody stupid. Rose will understand.'

'Here goes, then.'

Felix unfolded the paper and held the letter so that they
could both read it.

Dear Rose,
    *I can't begin to tell you how sorry I am about last night. I
obviously blundered in and upset everyone. It was stupid of
me to imagine that everything had stayed the same while I've
been away. I have to report for duty by six o'clock tonight so
I'm going to make an early start. Please thank Matthew for
his hospitality. I hope you and he will be very happy.*
    Yours,
    Richard

'Sod!' said Merry, in an undertone. 'The silly bugger! Now
what do we do?'

'God knows,' sighed Felix. 'Better explain this to Matt for a
start, I suppose.'

'He's gone, then?' Matthew said when they told him about
the note. 'Left her in the lurch again? Might have had the

decency to hang around until we found out what she's decided.'

'I think he probably thought he was doing the right thing, for both of you,' Merry said defensively.

'He won't have got far,' Matthew said. 'I don't suppose there'll be any trains today – or not till later, anyway.'

'He's probably hitching,' Merry said.

Matthew grunted. 'He won't get far that way, either. There won't be many people about, not this early.'

Felix said, 'You don't think he might still be standing down on the main road, waiting for a lift, do you?'

Merry looked at Matthew. 'Matt, can you cope on your own? I'm sorry, but I'm a bit worried about Richard. I think we ought to go and see if we can find him.'

'I've managed on my own for years,' Matthew responded. 'Don't see why today's any different. You get off. Silly bugger'll be half frozen by now, I shouldn't wonder.'

They hurried back to where Merry had parked Felix's Lagonda the night before and drove down the icy lanes. The recent snow had covered any tracks but there were only three routes Richard could have taken. They followed them all, without seeing any sign of him. In Wimborne Minster there were a few people about, heading for work or opening shops, but no Richard.

When they reached the main London road Merry stopped the car.

'He may have walked on,' Felix pointed out. 'He could have covered quite a few miles by now.'

'That's just the point,' Merry replied. 'Look at the petrol gauge. If we go much farther I shan't have enough to get back to town myself and I've no more coupons.'

'I guess that's it, then,' Felix said. 'We'd better go back and break the news to Rose.'